VOYAGE IN, VOYAGE OUT

ALSO BY JEAN RIKHOFF

DEAR ONES ALL

Voyage In,

JEAN RIKHOFF

Voyage Out

JONATHAN CAPE
THIRTY BEDFORD SQUARE LONDON

F 14244

The poem quoted in part on page 78 is Copyright 1923, 1951 by E. E. Cummings,
from his volume *Poems 1923-1954*,
by permission of Harcourt, Brace and World, Inc.

Printed in Great Britain by Lowe & Brydone (Printers) Ltd., London
Bound by A. W. Bain & Co. Ltd., London

To Helen K. Taylor
whose assistance, belief, and suggestions
sustained an original idea
I gratefully give this book

CONTENTS

But never have I had so firm a conviction that our lives can live upon only a few things, that we must find them, and begin to build our fences. All creation is the building of a fence.

Chapter One

"MONEY's everything—the one universal," Stu said bitterly. "It's the only thing I know that everyone agrees on—you have to have money. It keeps the world away from you and it lets you buy your way out of the messes. There isn't one of us that wouldn't want her money," he said to Lois. "Esther's money." He waited for a denial, sipping his gin and tonic, staring across the cluttered living room, over the books and newspapers scattered about, but she was still, sitting in her chair, gazing absently out the window at the brick building across the street that cut off the New York sky.

"Maybe," she said at last, talking really, he thought, to herself. "I wonder—" And then she let it go at that, she shook her head. "Not that it matters. Esther isn't going to leave the money to us anyway, Stu, not to you or me."

"We're traitors," he said. "We ran out on Springfield."

Lois leaned forward. "Anyway, I've never been sure she is rich, I've never been sure that the whole story of how she supposedly took all Aunt Clara's money wasn't just another of the family exaggerations."

Stu had to laugh. "You know goddam well she did, you—"

"No, I don't," Lois said to him, and he saw she was serious. "I only know what everyone says, but that doesn't make it true." Her voice had got stubborn on the word *true*.

"Well, I haven't got any *proof,* but I'd be willing to stake my life on it, and that's knowing enough for me."

Esther took the money all right, Stu thought, walking from the Twenty-third Street subway station, reviewing the conversation. He wondered how Lois could have any doubts. God, everyone in the family knew she'd taken the money. When the old woman was dying, Esther was the only one with her. No one ever found a will. That trunk where they found the stocks and bonds, some loose cash, anyone could have got in that. And what was left, there in that old chest, well, it wasn't anything like what everyone knew the old woman was supposed to be worth. How much proof did you need?

Let Esther have it, he thought angrily. Okay, so I could use the money; okay, so part of it should be mine, or at least Mother's; okay, it would—it *might*—make a lot of difference; but it's gone, it's been gone years and years, what's the point of harping on the same subject, the way the rest of the family has all these years?

Money, the eternal master, he thought. Money, the root of all evil, he thought, remembering something he'd said earlier to Lois, and then her answer, Not money, the Bible doesn't say money, Stu, it says *love* of money.

Okay, he thought, *love* of money. It's the same thing in the end, isn't it? But he wasn't so sure. Something about the way Lois had looked at him when she said *love,* as if he were talking a lot of nonsense and they both knew it.

Money, he thought, god, what I could do with some money.

Forget it, he told himself.

The wind was hot and the air coming from the subway vents stinking; he was sticky with sweat, but it was to be expected. These New York summers. Anyway the weather was always lousy the one Saturday a month he got off.

He passed the familiar paper kiosk on Twenty-seventh Street, the Greek and Armenian delicatessens, the liquor store, the Chinese laundry, the Italian vegetable hole-in-the-wall where the baskets with their bright fruits were set out on the sidewalk no matter how many times the cops told old Maggio he couldn't keep his things on the public thoroughfare. He walked past the two bars he always frequented, the modern neon joint where the old Greeks sometimes came and occasionally danced, and the old family place, where they always showed up and never failed to dance. The young toughs went to the new place because they considered it tonier, but Stu liked the old one better. Still, he never felt at home in either. Standing in his shoddy suit and run-down shoes at the bar, with his *ouzo,* trying to look inconspicuous, he felt they all recognized him for the outsider he was.

He felt lightheaded and slightly off-center. He knew better than to drink in the middle of the day, but Lois had called up and said she was going home, back to Illinois, could he come up after lunch and have a farewell drink with her, she was going to catch the six o'clock train. I only called your mother last night, she said, I just made up my mind.

God, he was tired. Tired and, though he didn't want to admit it, troubled. Knowing Lois was going back had brought on a feeling of depression. She had surprised the hell out of him. She had said, cool as a cucumber, that she had been thinking it over and she had decided to go back, for part of her vacation at least; she might even stay longer if things—well—worked out. You know your mother, she said. And of course she didn't have to say any more.

After a pause she had said very slowly, I want to see the house—Grandmother Timble's house.

You what? he had asked, more surprised by this than by the fact that she was going back at all.

I've got it in my head to see the old house, she explained in her apartment after he had gone over. I don't know why, I just want to.

It's been sold years and years, he said. *It's probably all changed.*
Probably.

And I mean, he went on, a little annoyed at the way she was so readily agreeing with him, as if she didn't care one way or the other what he thought, which was probably true, *you can't just go up and say your grandmother used to live here and you want to walk in and have a look around.*

I can call up first and ask, she said.

Yeah, I suppose so.

There had been a silence in which she lighted a cigarette and picked up their glasses to refill them. She had the gin and tonic in the little kitchenette off her big room. She always gave him gin, never whisky. In the winter she served martinis, very cold, very dry, and very, very good; in the summer gin and tonic, also cold, also astringent, and not quite so good. He watched her go, feeling uneasy, as if he were supposed to say something, to give her a kind of commission, but she must know he couldn't, he was through with Springfield, finished with the family, his mother, and that house, that big old painted brick monstrosity his mother thought was so special—Sans Souci, she always called it, giving one of her pretentious little smiles; hell, it was the Green Lawn Boarding House, and she knew it, no matter how she carried on it was a famous landmark—it signified for him nothing but misery and loud voices, slamming doors in the night and strange faces and feet on the stairs during the day. But it wasn't just his mother, it was the whole goddam mixed-up family—aunts nobody ever called Aunt, just by their first names: that goddam Esther who had stolen the family money; Ada who hated her for it; screwed-up Frances; and last his mother, his crying, nagging, overworked, under-appreciated mother.

Lois's mother, the fifth one, of course—only she was dead, she didn't count.

Let Lois go back if she wanted, that was none of his business. He'd held out all these years, hadn't he? I'm *never* going back, he had told himself. He wasn't even going to let on he still thought about them at all. Still—

"You've been gone a long time yourself," he had said.

"Almost two years."

"How's come you never took it in your head to go back until now?"

"I don't know—money, for one thing," she said, and had to laugh. "Always money. But you know, I didn't like to ask your mother to pay for the trip and—I don't know." She looked away. "I guess I wasn't ready. I feel kind of sorry for her," she said, "your mother"—and then she picked up his glass and disappeared into the kitchenette.

He was left alone in her crazily slanted front room. As long as he had known his cousin here in New York, she had lived off Riverside, but the place still looked as if she had just moved in and were in the midst of getting settled. There were books piled in the corner, books she never got around to getting bookcases for, they had been there two years, waiting; there was still no rug, and the lamp cord was frayed and shorted constantly, and in the bathroom she still hadn't hung up a shower curtain, although she had finally got around to painting the walls. But the apartment was hers and what right had he to judge, living as he did in that dirty one room on Twenty-ninth Street that smelled of sleeping, eating, loafing, and moral turpitude, and had that miserable air of ten-bucks-a-week all those places had, no matter how hard you tried to fix them up, and he hadn't tried very hard.

He paused for a moment, debating whether or not to buy a paper. Hell, it was too hot to read and anyway what was there in the paper he was so all-fired anxious to know—just more troubles, more strikes, more people being burned out of their homes, some crazy bastard run berserk and shooting up people.

As he stood on the hot sidewalk, looking down on the black head-lines, watching hands dart out from behind him, snatch up a paper, fling down a coin, he thought for a moment of Lois's hands as she handed him his drink, the strong, blunt fingers with their unvarnished clipped nails, the prominent blue veins in her wrist. Strong hands, she was a strong girl.

A girl like that, you'd think she'd want to fix her place up, settle down, but it was more like she was camping.

Still, he liked it she hardly ever had lipstick on when he went up to see her; it made her more real. When she got dressed up, she didn't seem like the same person. When he looked into her painted and pretty face, he felt she was someone in camouflage, someone he had to be wary of.

Her mouth, greased in bright red, and the long, trembling, too-black lashes frightened him; it was like looking at someone you couldn't quite place who knew things about you no one was supposed to know. Only the hands, firmly holding a cigarette to the lipsticked mouth, remained the same. Lois smoked as if the whole messed-up world became for an instant, as she inhaled, a stable and permanent place, pivoted and pinpointed into something recognizable, definable, capable of being borne.

She had been damn decent to him—having him up for dinner every once in a while and asking him out to the theater, saying she had an extra ticket, she still felt funny being out alone at night, she was so Midwestern; and all the time he knew she was really making excuses so that he would come because they both knew he didn't have any money and wouldn't ever have any, was one of those people with no future at all, just lucky to be making it day by day, so that he could never repay her kindnesses, they were kindnesses without any motive save good will—but more important, she never criticized him.

Again he wondered what in the name of god had ever prompted her to phone him the first time and how she had ever found out where he was working. There he had been, two years before, down in Blooming-dale's stockroom, he was strong, he could usually turn up something in the way of shoving or lifting, and that pimply guy who had finally got on his nerves so he quit before he got in a fight with him had said, Hey, Ashwell, you're wanted on the phone, Stu thinking there was some mistake because he didn't know anyone in New York who would phone him at work, even Ethel had better sense than to pester him on a new job, she waited until he settled in; and he went out and stood in the middle of all those crates and picked up the phone, saying, *Yeah*, and this voice from the other end had begun, *This is Lois, Lois Greer, your cousin. I wonder if you remember* . . . That's how it had all started. Later she said she got the name of the store where he was working from home, and he had been sufficiently upset not to press the matter. Who at home kept tabs on him that well? Whoever it was, he didn't want to know. He didn't want any ties in Springfield, and just knowing someone kept that close account of you—he had only been at Blooming-dale's three weeks or so—was frightening; it meant the ties were there, whether you wanted them or not.

"You don't want me to—to say anything?" she had asked just before he left her apartment.

There was no answer really. He just shook his head *no*, then turned at the landing, shaking her hand formally and absurdly before he left, she standing there smiling up at him with that wonderful smile that always moved him. He felt, stupidly, as if she were granting him some kind of honor, smiling at him like that. Sometimes he thought it must be the contrast between her ordinary sad, puzzled expression and the instantaneous change that came over her when something pleased or amused her.

Walking down the steps, he had been ashamed suddenly of the knowledge that what had made her smile was his shaking hands with her; she must have sensed that it was a special act he performed only—and infrequently—for "ladies." In his world the women either clutched you lasciviously, making a show of their vacant lust, reeking of heliotrope and fried onions; or they spied out some new find and forgot you completely so that you snuck away in a few moments, unnoticed, utterly humiliated. Lois's smile, he knew, blushing, had come because she knew he liked her enough to make that silly gesture.

That smile exasperated him just as her cool voice, just as the omnipresent bottle of Gordon's, exasperated him. He had the feeling she was going to make it. In another ten years she would be one of those sleek, highly paid women whose careers, while unknown to the public, were sufficiently important to net them good salaries. She might be working on that chic magazine for peanuts now (or what, it suddenly occurred to him, would be peanuts for her but would be a damn good wage for him) but she was on her way up.

Stu turned into Twenty-ninth Street, deciding to take a shower (if he could get in), maybe hit an air-conditioned movie, stop by a bar for a couple of beers, get a bite to eat. No more than two beers, he warned himself. In the hot weather he got worked up too fast; before he knew what was happening, he was in a fight. What the hell, why shouldn't he get in a fight if he felt like it? What was there ahead except drying out on Sunday and then Monday morning shoving furs around Thirty-fourth Street?

With money— Cut it out, he told himself, forget it.

Christ, what a street this was. The filth, the poverty, the overcrowding struck him more forcibly after the quiet containment of Lois's neighborhood. But what disgusted him most was the sham pretense at genteel respectability that still went on here, in spite of the milk cartons on window ledges and four, five, maybe ten people living together in one room. There was a dry-cleaning establishment on the corner, a dry-cleaning establishment when people couldn't even afford a little refrigerator, and a big bright modern drug store that displayed expensive lipsticks and perfumes, the kind that were on sale uptown, and these stupid people went and bought them. To keep up appearances, so nobody would know the miserable lives spent in those overcrowded, under-equipped rooms.

Why couldn't they admit what they were—dumb jerk Puerto Ricans, spics, spics goddam it, he wanted to yell at them, Polacks and Hunkies who were nothing but cheap labor and not even good at that. Failures, all of them. We're all alike, he wanted to shout at them. We can't go back and we can't go ahead. We'll spend the rest of our lives in holes like this.

"Hello, Mrs. Polaski," he said, coming up the stoop. "Hot enough for you?"

Mrs. Polaski was the janitress. Her husband was supposed to keep the halls clean and put out the garbage and make whatever repairs were necessary (that was a hot one, the whole place was falling apart), but all he ever did was check the racing forms, buy the Eighth Avenue broads beer, and in summer sleep out on an old army cot in back where the trash barrels were. Mrs. Polaski was the worker.

Now she looked up as Stu came abreast of her and said, through broken teeth, in broken English, "A telephone call you got, earlier, that woman." She fanned herself with the *Post*. "Ninety-five tomorrer, the paper says. What I wouldn't give for a bottle of beer."

It was persuasive advertising. Stu felt sorry for her anyway and he knew she never asked the tenants for anything outright; she had a kind of gentle blackmail he had come to admire. A second later she said, softly, "I looked at that leak in your faucet this morning. A plumber we gotta have. But you know how much they charge and Mr. Spitztoni, he don't want to put no more money in the place. He wants to sell. He says the neighborhood's going down. He's losing money every day. So he don't want to make no investments." When Stu said nothing, she continued, "It ain't my fault, Mr. Ashwell, you know I'd fix it if I could. You know that, don't you?" she insisted.

"Sure, Mrs. Polaski," he assured her, thinking nothing of the kind. What she was really doing was waiting for him to say why didn't she go down to the A&P and get them a couple of cold beers and she would ask some friend or other of hers to take a look at it on the sly. But he was too hot and tired for sharing beer, the way he sometimes did, sitting with Mrs. Polaski, hearing about the way Mr. Polaski threw his money away on horses and whores, and her without even a cold can of beer.

He rose, nodding for no reason except that he felt some gesture was necessary since he wasn't going to make the one she wanted. "Mr. Ashwell," she said urgently, looking at him with hurt eyes. "Mr. Ashwell." He paused on the top step. "That woman, she said you should call her *right* back. She said it was *important*."

"Thank you, Mrs. Polaski," he said, going in. Ethel, he thought, as the rank breath of the downstairs hall enveloped him, it's Ethel again, after I told her not to call, after I told her it was hopeless, that all I wanted from her was to be left alone. Even as he was saying that to himself he knew two things: that she would never leave him alone and that more than likely he did not want her to. Neither pleasure nor compatibility joined them, but he knew that they were nevertheless in possession of one another, something like the union of the devil and god, unwanted but indissoluble.

Was it, he asked himself, putting his hand on a railing that felt to the touch like cold cabbage, because neither had anyone else? Was it the terrible tie of loneliness that inevitably reunited them in spite of all their quarrels and differences, of his own determination not to have anything to do with her and her equally determined protestations that she was *through* with him?

Twelve years of fight fight fight, he thought, with time off for the war. Like time off for good behavior, he thought, the war had been his little respite from Ethel. Not just Ethel, he thought; from the hideous sameness of everything, from the boredom, the monotony, the drag of day after day.

Christ, how could anyone show any interest in just going to work, eating, sleeping, and screwing? He tried once in a while—not very hard, he had to admit, but he made a little effort to get with it. His energy never lasted more than a couple of months; no matter what resolutions he made to settle down, to stay with a job, he always ended up with the violence working itself out, like the old pieces of shrapnel from his wounds, the anger working its way out through his flesh just the way the bits of metal did.

The war, he thought as he started up the stairs, was the only time I could legitimately get mad and stay mad and use that anger for something. Killing, he thought, and for a moment closed his eyes, seeing inside the vast battlefields about Saint-Vith, remembering that even in the end the sense of power the gun gave him, and the feeling of release the firing of it imparted, could never make up for the lumps of dead like question marks all over the landscape—as if these lifeless bodies were asking, Why? Why?

It was a good question.

A torpor, so fierce that it seemed to him more burning than the heat, pressed down on his mind, and he stood in the murky light of the first-floor hall wishing himself, for the first time, someone else.

Who?

Someone capable of change, he thought. My life is summed up in this: I will either call Ethel and—reluctantly—agree to meet her or I'll go down to the RKO, have a few beers, and get in trouble.

He knew he couldn't stay here; boredom, reflection, analysis were harrowing, but self-recriminations in Mr. Spitztoni's ten-dollar-a-week room he knew from past experience to be unbearable. He had to get out, if only to a movie. He couldn't lie on a bed and think. Because when you thought, you saw the uselessness of everything, people came and went without meaning, like that man he had come home from the war to find Ethel shacked up with—where had he gone and who, even Ethel, cared? Certainly he, Stu, hadn't. The guy was just gone, gone like all those other things Ethel had picked up when she was working as a welder, gone like the stuff he himself accumulated and kept for a while and then left or lost, gone without anyone knowing where or how or why it had all disappeared, whether there was even any loss involved.

If something was gone, let it go, forget it: that was his philosophy. She was crazy, that's what Lois was, going back to look for what was lost, plain crazy. It was a family of nuts.

He thought of his sister standing in the kitchen that night, the night he walked out, screaming at their mother, "You know you steam open Stu's letters, you know it, admit it." Then she had turned, his sister, and looked at him as if he should be upset, as if he should care. With an effort, he tried. He was sick and tired of the whole family, they had worn him out, now they expected a scene out of him. You couldn't very well say, Go ahead, Mother, steam Ethel's letters open, read them, I don't really care. It's all right, Carolyn, let her steam them open. It really doesn't make any difference. But his mother and sister were looking at him as if it should. He got up and tried to act enraged.

So there he was, suitcase in hand, out on the sidewalk in front of the Green Lawn Boarding House, and what was he going to do? Go all the way, he kept telling himself. If you start a scene, give it all you got. So he had gone over and got Ethel and they had left for New York and she was smart enough to get him to make it legal.

Well, whatever had made him do it—whether he was really angry or only playing at it, as he had done for so long that he didn't really remember any more if he had ever behaved the way other people had, had ever just got mad because he was mad, had ever done anything on impulse, instead of having to work himself up to the responses everyone had—all he knew was, as far back as he could remember, the world was crowding in on him, he always seemed to be shoving, just trying to get a little room for himself, and people wouldn't give it to him.

That night had taught him something, though: every time he got to the point where he couldn't stand it any more, he knew what to do: pack a suitcase and move out. He had been moving out on Ethel for years, and then she was back on the telephone, and he finally said okay, he would come up and see her; he went and one thing led to another, she was always smart enough to put in a bottle of booze when he was coming, he started to drink, and then he got to feeling sorry for her, he kept thinking that if he hadn't dragged her off to New York, maybe —just maybe—she would have had a better life.

In and out, moving and packing, getting out his damn suitcase and shoving his stuff in and going out on the street, usually in the middle of the night, and generally half plastered, feeling that awful sensation of outrage and indignation and fury rising up inside him; then he was at a bar and before long involved in a fight and then back, bloody and disheveled, around dawn, pounding on Ethel's door. Once he lost his suitcase and another time he managed to make it to a rooming house and keep away from her for a while, but it wasn't really until the war that he was able to get away. And that was because he put distance between them, a whole body of water which she couldn't walk upon, which she couldn't telephone across, which she couldn't do anything about at all.

Well, he thought, I had sense enough not to move back in when I came back. *Move back in?* he asked himself. Who do you think you're kidding? That other joker was there, she didn't seem exactly overjoyed to see you, that other guy was a "swell provider," something you could hardly say for yourself. By the time the other guy had scooted out, Stu had established a pattern, and even Ethel with her everlasting telephoning and pleading and her interminable scenes couldn't make him come back.

The telephone was ringing now and he knew, the way he knew so many things so clearly this afternoon, that it was Ethel, beefed up on beer, weeping on the other end of the line, sitting in the soggy heat, clutching her soggy handkerchief, waiting to pour out her soggy grief. For a moment he poised, ready for flight. Nothing would be easier than to turn back, hastily hand Mrs. Polaski the money for the beer, send her off, and then let the phone ring until Ethel finally gave up.

In a second he saw his escape: he could move and not leave a forwarding address; he could go to another city, take another name. But just as surely, he knew, she would never give up. If it was not tonight, it would be tomorrow night, next week, next month, next year, until she cried out the final accusation over his coffin.

Oh god, he mumbled, stumbling toward the shrilling phone, I'll have to ask her to the movies. And then take her to bed to make up for the fight last night. And for such a small gesture you don't get any points Up There at all.

Chapter Two

THERE was still packing to do. Lois stood for a moment in the middle of the living room, holding her drink, reviewing what had been done, what there remained to do: she had called Iris yesterday—Aunt Iris, she reminded herself, knowing she would never be able to think of any of the "girls" as Aunt.

"The girls"—Lois took a drink, seeing in her mind a succession of figures, as if the door had opened to admit them one by one: Ada, the oldest; Esther, the queerest; Frances, the frivolous; Iris, the worker; and the last, the baby, her mother, the beautiful one.

She bent over the nearest table and took a cigarette from the package lying there. It was strange how the past sometimes seemed more real than the present. She was going back, home to Springfield, back to Erwin, Frances's son, that cousin she cared about most in the world, the one everyone in the family said was the best-looking, the most well rounded, the one, Lois thought, they would have voted most likely to inherit Esther's money; back to the rest of her cousins—Eileen, who had kept a thin strand of communication with her these past two years, who had been the one who had told her where Stu was working; back to Carolyn, with whom she had played tennis while Carolyn's husband was away at war; back, too, to Pete and his wife, whom she had never come to know, they were voices to her, not faces; and back, of course, to "the girls," the four living sisters who were left and the fifth, the dead sister, her mother, all alone out in the Protestant cemetery that had been, because of her mother's sin, the only place where she could be buried.

It was past three o'clock, she had to finish packing, take a bath, get dressed, grab a sandwich, get down to the station. Still, there was time for one more drink. There is always time for one more, she thought, if you really need it.

Ella, she had forgotten Ella, Ella who of all the family was most like herself—the outsider. There had been no place else for old, half-blind, black Ella to go after Grandmother Timble's death except Iris's, just as there had been no place else for Lois to go; they had clung together, an old woman and a little girl, in Iris's big, strange house.

You can go a long way shut up inside on your own, Lois thought, and then you must stop, go back, see where you left the things that keep you from going any farther. To voyage out and then to voyage back again; how much distance did you make like that? Anyway, it wasn't how far you went that mattered but what you saw on the way, how you handled the difficult passage of the frail vessel that was the self. *I perceive this voyage will be with hurt and much damage, not only of the lading of the ship, but also of our lives. . . .*

She would go back and see the house, her grandmother's house, would stand at the front path and look up at the big windows, remember how years before the whole family would gather there, her grandmother and Ella spending the weeks before getting ready, all the children and grandchildren crammed into the living room; the good front parlor not big enough to take them all, it remained closed, a sealed-up smell of camphor and furniture polish and floor wax escaping under the door, her grandmother bustling through the house, keeping everything—the dinner, the girls, the girls' husbands and children—under control, a stern, confident, small woman with a will of untemperable iron. She had known where she was going and had gone, the whole long voyage made on her own terms.

Lois stood in the middle of her living room, holding on to her drink, a small voice inside her head saying, as it had so many times the past weeks, *All is lost but a tiny core of stillness in the heart like the eye of the violet. . . .*

It had been a long winter, the winter with Neal; spring had come and passed, the spring when she had lost Neal, sent him out of her life; soon summer would be gone, and she felt that fall and winter would come and go and there would still be that dead still sadness at the center, the heart of the violet down there where the heart of the heart had once been, the still eye of the violet.

And some there be which have no memorial; who are perished as though they had never been; and are become as though they had never been born. . . .

Mama, her heart cried, why did you do it?

She stared out at the dirt and soot that filtered, like small dark dewdrops, through the bright summer day. There was an ailanthus tree thrusting itself skyward toward air and light and freedom, the only tree that could take root in the cement city. Oaks and elms could not live here, only the ailanthus, the tree of heaven on which the silkworm would no longer feast, and who even remembered that, far away in China, this plain tree had once been venerated and worshiped for its strange and exotic leaves? Here people only complained that those same crushed leaves gave off a queer smell, that the tree itself was a nuisance.

Lois turned away quickly from the window and went into the bedroom. On the dresser was a picture of her mother, taken the year before she died. Her mother's face, severe, unsmiling, stared back at her, the black hair emphasizing the white skin, the streak of gray near the temple cutting through the dark hair like light through darkness. The big dark eyes were full of the whole mystery on which her mother had brooded and whose secrets she had never shared. When her mother walked, people turned to look at her, not at her face, but at the whole of her body moving down the street, slowly, surely, beautifully, head held high, arms swinging lightly at her sides, the long, lovely legs brushing gently against each other as they trod the dark black earth.

Her mother loved that dark rich earth. She was always going out to her garden to bring up color, big clumps of hyacinths in the spring, big clusters of dahlias and beds of nasturtiums—bent over the earth, she stroked it, loving the dark kernels in her hand. When she put a plant in the ground, it was as if she were giving back to God what was meant to be given back.

The flowers and her deep sense of God, that was what Lois remembered most about her. Her mother would get up every morning and go to six-o'clock mass, and if you came home at an odd hour of the afternoon you often surprised her kneeling in deep and solemn prayer, the act of contrition. *O my God I am most heartily sorry for having offended Thee . . . I detest all my sins because I dread the loss of heaven . . . I firmly resolve . . . to confess my sins, to do penance, and to amend my life. . . .*

Her mother never prayed out of doors; all the kneeling she did there was to put color into the earth, to press the small green shoots into place so that they might spring up to the sky.

How would it feel to fall, Lois asked herself, falling down, plunging through space to the hard earth below, that earth her mother had loved so much that she put her hands into it to make life, falling through space, the still hot rush of silence before the great tearing shock of despair and death? My mother, my beautiful, beautiful mother, hands pressed down in dirt, lips parted in prayer, the final vision of her grasping the window sill and raising herself up, standing for one long last moment in the world she knew, and then falling down to the one she did not, looking and believing even as the illusion eluded her, hanging on to the deception, as we all hold on to it, holding fast to the image in her heart, running, seeking, searching, run away from Springfield, run back to Springfield, seeking and searching, clinging to her faith, looking for love, believing in love, sure of it as those madmen of old were said to stand up and shout of the fire of moonlight to warn against the burning wounds of the sun, who heard with their own ears the terrible sound of the snowflake falling and echoed with their own heartbeats the dying turns of the universe.

Chapter Three

"A PARTY? Oh no, Mother, please," Carolyn said. "Let Lois come home in peace; you don't have to give one of those parties."

"But Carolyn," her mother protested from the receiver at the other end, "what else can I do? Lois hasn't been home in two years and everyone will expect me to give a party, we always give a party—"

"No, *we* don't always give parties. You always have to have a party. 'Let Iris give the party, she likes to,' that's what they all say and you just eat it up. You're not even thinking about bringing up that stuff from the basement, are you, Mother?" Carolyn did not wait for an answer. "I know you are. You're going to make us all drag up that stuff and—

oh god, Mother," she pleaded, "if you must have a party, can't you at least keep it simple?"

"But we haven't had a get-together, a real family get-together, not for years, not since Erwin come home, from—from—" Iris hesitated.

"From Biarritz," Carolyn supplied.

"Yes, from Biarritz," Iris continued, sounding relieved. "And that was years ago, we didn't have the good things up then, just some of the china, and to tell you the truth, I don't think it went too well. I mean," her mother said hesitantly, "Erwin drank that way and Esther—well, she sang, you remember?"

"Well, that's Esther. A miser doesn't change her money."

"What?"

"A leopard doesn't change its—you can't expect—"

"Oh, yes, I see," her mother said as if she didn't. "But the thing is, Lois is family even if we don't see much of her, and now she's coming home it's only right we show her we care."

"Can't you show her you care in a reasonable way? After all," Carolyn continued, quoting one of her mother's favorite maxims, "it's not how much you spend, it's the thought behind it."

"Oh, I'm not going to spend a lot," Iris assured her hastily. "I'm just going to see that what we do is done properly."

"And Peggy and I will get stuck with the job of digging around that dirty old cellar," Carolyn said.

"I'm not *asking* you or Peggy to do anything," Iris said with dignity. "It's my party, I'll do the work. I've done the work all my life, why should I shirk now? I have two perfectly good hands, I know how to use them. I wouldn't think of asking you, now that I know how you feel."

"Now, Mother—"

"You ought to be glad to see your cousin, you ought to—"

"I am glad to see her. I just don't like the idea of having to go down that grisly basement and start—"

"If that's the attitude you're going to take, I'm not even going to discuss it. Good-by, Carolyn, you ought to be ashamed of yourself, that's all I have to say"—and she hung up before Carolyn could answer.

I am, Carolyn thought, but not for any of the things you accuse me of. Unloving, ungiving, ungrateful, her mind ticked off.

She got up and took a cigarette from the ceramic box on the table and sat down, remembering that for a brief period, during the war, she and Lois had been close. It was because neither of them had anyone else. Lois and she had been like two stranded survivors of a family disaster—Ralph gone off to war and Carolyn living alone in the apartment that was too big but wonderfully free of noise and confusion after the Green Lawn Boarding House; Lois out there in the boarding house with Iris and the boarders, cut off from her father in California, cut off from her mother forever.

For those few summer months before Lois went to college they had seen a good deal of each other, in spite of the age difference. It had all started with the tennis. Ralph's mother knew some old lady who had courts no one used; somehow it had worked out Carolyn ought to go out and play. The woman was lonely, or the courts needed to be kept up, something. Carolyn had asked Lois to come and play with her; she didn't know anyone else she could ask. She didn't really have any friends of her own in Springfield, not anyone she really cared about, and Eileen, the cousin who was closest in age, Eileen never did things like play tennis. She stayed home with her mother. Poor Eileen, Carolyn thought, as she had thought so many times. It seemed to her then that there had never been anyone to whom she had felt truly close—not her mother or father, not either of her brothers, none of the cousins. She had tried with Ralph when they were first married, but it just hadn't worked out. She had begun to think she was one of those people who would never have known what was meant by the word *love* if she hadn't read about it, hadn't heard other people talking about it.

The old woman who owned the courts would come down with her big hat, her handbag full of knitting and pills and magazines, to watch. Whenever they did something wrong she would shout at them. "Turn, for your backhand, *turn*." Click went her knitting needles. "Carolyn, throw your ball up for the serve, *way up*." Then, when the really hot weather started, she had stopped coming and they had begun to enjoy themselves.

Carolyn saw in her mind's eye a picture of Lois and herself, tanned, sweating, laughing, running after difficult shots which they never managed to get back and calling to one another, "Wonderful, you really put that one in." Lois had been the better of the two. She had had those lessons when she was young. But of course they never talked about that, those tennis lessons years before that had been the start of all the trouble for Lois and her mother.

She thought of Lois—tall, thin, intense—running in the bright sun; then a picture of the birds leaped into her mind. She had forgotten them, the blue-green birds on the lawns up near the big house, the open cages behind them shining in the sun.

On the tennis court those late summer afternoons she and Lois matched balls against the flashing birds; on the near hill the big gray house of the old woman in white and her husband whom they had never seen, those people who had no children, only birds—we used to say that to one another, Carolyn thought, They don't have children, they have peacocks, and we would laugh.

Inside Carolyn's mind there was a vivid picture of those hot late afternoons: the birds flashed in the sun, the balls flashed in the sun, she and Lois ran the courts, panting and sweating, while the sun glanced against the bright blue, the bright green necks of the birds. The balls splashed on the colorless courts, the sun spun against the trees, the sky glittered like a bright blue gem, the voices of the peacocks rose fierce against their laughter; they hit the ball, *twang,* and it rang against the clay courts, while on the near hill the birds' throats reverberated the sound of the strings, the cries in their own throats; they ran and sweated and laughed, and were, hot and dripping, close, laughing against that cobalt sky, while the ball hung, for one long breathtaking, precarious moment, on the edge of the net, and fell, languishing, on Carolyn's side of the court. They were both laughing, the birds sang out, the sky seemed to cry, and she had lost the point, lost it, and didn't care.

It was a long time ago, Carolyn thought, and only a game we used to play to get out of ourselves for a little while. I have two children now and this house. I'm different, Lois is different. . . .

Ralph came back. Ralph came home. Ralph *lived.*

She stamped out her cigarette and looked around for something to distract her. But the room was bare of diversion. The architect had impressed on her the need for severe elegance, that clean-swept look in an age of informal formality, he had called it, and, faithful to his admonitions, she went through the house every morning and picked up anything that remotely suggested occupation. All the magazines were in their proper iron holders, the cigarettes and matches cleverly hidden in deceptive receptacles, the books tidily alphabetized on the built-in bookshelves, the children's toys in their rooms where they should be. At that moment there wasn't anything to pick up except the butt of her still smoldering cigarette.

I could listen to a record, she thought and immediately dismissed the idea. The records were in a special cabinet in the wall, low down where they were out of sight, but it was hard, stooping, to find one you wanted, and, even if you did, harder still to get the machine out of the wall and the mechanism running. The automatic buttons stuck—

something about their having been installed when the varnish was not quite dry.

The house had cost forty thousand dollars and it was worth a lot more now, Ralph continually assured her, but even so at four o'clock in the afternoon it was apt to be, like so many other things in her life, an accusation. All that sun pouring through the picture window, for instance: it made the room terribly hot, but if you pulled the dark green drapes there was no light, and there was something disquieting about having to have a lamp on in your living room in the middle of the afternoon.

Ralph's house, which he had paid for; Ralph's wife, whom he had bought with his money. She stared down, asking the beige rug if she had gone away to New York, like Lois, might she have one day succeeded in shaping what she should like to be with what she actually was, demanding of the dark green drapes whether Lois had gone out and found something to be grateful for, something that needed to be done, that only she could do, not even a big thing, but something, no matter how small, in which she could believe.

If Ralph hadn't come back, if something had happened overseas, if she had money—Esther's money, the money Esther had taken—might she have gone to New York, like Lois, might she have turned out different?

But he came back. There were the house, the two children, the country club and Junior League—Ralph's mother's pull, nothing else. Carolyn knew the women didn't like her, and they were right not to, she didn't like them, it was pure hypocrisy, those little luncheons at which they all planned good works and where the others, daringly, drank Alexanders while she stared at them remorselessly over the rim of her own martini, blaming them in some obscure way for the loss of all the expectancy she had felt when she was alone during the war, seeing them as symbols, like their uplifted Alexanders, of the rich, wasted cream of life.

Ralph kept saying she ought to have another baby. Why was it men always thought the best antidote for restlessness was pregnancy? Because it tied you down for a year, she supposed, and in a year presumably you changed enough or took on enough new responsibilities to forget what was tormenting you. You didn't have time to think.

That was the remedy: not to think.

If the second one, Bobbie, had been a girl, she would have been obligated to go on. Ralph had had his heart set on a boy; he had been so disappointed that Sally had come first, and even naming her after his mother—that fashionable cold woman who had never, in all this time, really accepted her—hadn't assuaged his disappointment. Men were mad to reincarnate themselves in a son. It was simply beyond Carolyn, that concept. Flesh was flesh, wasn't it? But no, Ralph wanted a son, he had nearly driven her out of her mind with his constant chatter about a "boy to carry on the name."

The child is a girl.

Where is the monument to my flesh?

I have tried to make it another way.

She jerked the ceramic box up and took another cigarette. Had someone said that or had the thought come into her mind of its own accord? And what made her think of it now? It was the discontent bubbling up, throwing up random remembrances—the courts, the laughter, the flashing birds in the summer sun, the telegram that never came. If she didn't hold on to herself firmly, she'd find a cocktail in her hand and the clock just striking the hour. On the bad days . . .

Her mother's salvation was in having parties—no, not in having them, in the planning; the execution never equaled the anticipation. Nothing that was real ever satisfied her mother; she lived in a world of her own making, where the truth receded in proportion to its unappropriateness. Carolyn was sure her mother didn't ever think of why Stu had left—that it was she who had steamed open his letters—but only that he had left without so much as a good-by. In her mother's version of anything she cast herself in her favorite role: the martyr; whereas the truth—

—the truth was something even Carolyn herself was unsure of, only filtered through a scene that she had carried in her mind all these years: the kitchen, the family at the table, the smell of cabbage, a door banging upstairs, one of the boarders on his way to the bathroom. Her father was lowered over his plate, eating with steady concentration, just as her mother was talking with the same steady concentration, and then the quarrel. How it had started, Carolyn no longer remembered. All she knew was that something had made her tell what she had promised herself she would never tell, that she had caught her mother steaming open Stu's letters.

God, Carolyn thought, I need a drink.

Stu, she thought, it was my fault you went away. I know that, but it was Mama's too. You see that, don't you?

Her mother exposed all their flaws, destroying everyone else's faith while she rebuilt her own. It was a diversion for her. Though the boys throw stones at frogs in sport, the frogs die not in sport, they die in earnest.

I've got to have a drink, Carolyn thought, getting up and going out to the kitchen for ice. One day she and Ralph were planning to have a little wall refrigerator next to the bar in the living room, but he felt they couldn't afford it now. It was a nuisance to run to the kitchen every time you wanted ice, but Ralph economized on the extras. He went to no end of expense on what was absolutely essential, insisted on the best, but the things that would have made life truly pleasant he resented as a man will resent paying a just tip after an expensive meal.

She thought of the quarrels, the angry, abusive words, and then the silences, how nothing ever seemed to penetrate through to him, he was like a man half alive, taking the good with the bad, like cloaks that all came from the same closet, because he no longer cared what he was wearing so long as his skin was thick enough to protect him from feeling what he did not want to feel. He lived with his world of graphs and facts, the bare, basic essentials outlined in bold black and white, which showed nothing of the blurred center which was the truth.

"Over half the people of the leading Western industrial countries are seriously neurotic, another one-third to one-quarter ill"—staring at her to see if she had been drinking before he got home.

"What do you mean 'leading Western industrial countries'?" she had challenged him.

He chewed on, oblivious. "It's a serious situation," he said solemnly.

When they had their silent sessions, when both of them went without speaking, it didn't seem to bother him a bit; he simply wandered through their room, picking up his clothes, getting his things together, looking through the drawers as if he were utterly oblivious to the fact that for four solid days they had not said one word to each other and that she was sleeping on the couch downstairs in the den.

"You feel too much," Ralph constantly accused her. It was more than an indictment, the way he said it, closer to a final summation of everything in life that was repellent to him.

"No," she wanted to shout back, "the rest of you don't feel enough. Can you imagine what it's like trying—all the time trying—to move people to react, to feel something?" But of course he couldn't. That was exactly the trouble between them.

They were at opposite ends of the emotional pole, as if one were to try to put flame and frost together and neutralize both into cozy warmth instead of destroying each. She could never shake Ralph from his everlasting complacency and his belief that the best way to preserve the self was to immure it in rationality. It was like trying to quicken the dead—first the decision, then the determination, and finally the despair.

She thought about the nights her restlessness sent her prowling about the house looking for relief, when the relief always seemed to come from the liquor closet, how she would sit up drinking, her mind funneling into a kind of tipsy concentration, an idiotic and passionate hope that maybe something would happen, that she could change her life, violently uproot herself, "begin again," and then she would see Esther dying and leaving her money, she would see someone she didn't even know coming to save her, and all the time she knew there were no more white knights, there was no reason on earth why Esther should leave her any money, and to "begin again" at thirty-two, how ridiculous!

The boredom, oh, the terrible boredom, and the desperation—and she would pour another drink and another, until in the midst of the wide uncluttered living room she found herself weaving about, glass in hand, and escape seemed not only possible but imminent. It was merely a matter, she thought in those unreal hours, of concentration; she had to will her way out. Then she would stumble up to bed and lie in paralyzed and insomniac thirst as the alcohol began to fade. Her tongue crowded her mouth, her throat closed up so that she could scarcely swallow; she tossed and turned, parched, wanting to cry out for water, until at last she got up, desperate, to search for a drink, and discovered that her head was spinning, she couldn't control her legs. Around and round the room she groped, looking for something to moisten her mouth.

"What are you doing? Looking for a drink at this time of night?" It was Ralph, awake.

At that moment she had seen the luminous dial on the clock between their beds. It was five-fifteen. Ashamed, she had said, "I'm looking for a glass of water." But he knew, Carolyn thought, he knew.

Carolyn lifted the shaker and poured herself a double martini. It was cold and clean to the taste, made her think that in this house it was the only drink that ever ought to be served, reminded her of the wind-swept look of her living room, the clean, antiseptic halls, the sterile kitchen and bathrooms.

For a moment she hung, suspended, looking blankly at the bottles on the shelves, clinging to the chrome of the red bar, blank inside and out, the small voice of conscience echoing and re-echoing inside. He came back, he's come home, Ralph's alive.

They don't have children, they have peacocks.

He's not dead, he's alive.

Carolyn got up, carrying her cocktail with her, and went to the French doors. The children were playing in the sandpile. She could see Sally's fat little posterior, upside down, looking like a mushroom, trembling with activity. She must be digging very hard. Bobbie, quiet like his father, was watching his sister, standing back, silent and absorbed, in consideration of her furious activity. Sally was so much like herself, furious activity without any direction, and Bobbie was so much like his father, happier to watch than to participate. It was something Carolyn disliked in him; she did not want to, but she couldn't help it. He was so much the son the father had wanted.

He had an odd habit, Ralph, of sitting in a chair, staring off into space, his son on his lap, the two of them sitting very still, silent and withdrawn that way for hours. Maybe Ralph had marked Bobbie, sitting there with the child, staring off into space, looking at god knew what. He had seen enough people killed, Carolyn supposed, to be troubled—at close range, that is. She wouldn't have known if she hadn't come across his citation when she was unpacking his foot locker.

When she asked him about it, he said he didn't want to talk about it; then one night, about a month later, when they drank a lot of martinis before dinner and he got into a talkative mood, he told her some of it. He had a friend, a good friend, whose name was Wesley, and Wesley had been one of those people that got on with everyone, and, for some reason Ralph didn't understand, Wesley had singled him out as his special friend.

They had gone around together, taken a leave in Paris together, and once in the country near the lines they had stolen a chicken and roasted it in secret and eaten it all by themselves, though they felt ashamed later. That chicken, the way Ralph described it, seemed to Carolyn one of the few things that had ever touched her husband. Ralph described the little fire he and Wesley made and how they hunched over, protecting the embers against the wind, and watched the chicken cook. The feathers weren't all off—they had done a haphazard job of cleaning—and there was the smell of singed hair in the air. Wesley told him, kneeling and watching the chicken avidly, about his home in Indianapolis and the private school he'd gone to, about Jody, the girl he wanted to marry; he talked about his sister and his mother and father and the big house they had, and how he wanted to be an engineer, and when the chicken was nearly done he told Ralph that one day they would be back home, and they would meet each other's families and forget there was ever such a thing as this plain, with the stolen chicken and the resinous bottle of wine they'd paid a fortune for and knew wasn't any good when they were buying it, but, god, you stole a chicken, you had to have a bottle of wine to go with it, didn't you?

Ralph said he told Wes he would never forget that afternoon, and he said to Carolyn he was sure he never would. Wesley was everything, Carolyn suddenly understood, that Ralph wished he were: tall and clean-cut (he didn't wear glasses, the way Ralph did) and eager. He had that glow of life that attracted people; standing next to him, Ralph said, men felt safer, stronger, even there in France in the middle of a war.

It was Ralph's platoon that found Wesley. He was in a ditch with twenty or so other men. Their hands had been tied behind them with wire and they had been shot and then dumped in the ditch. There wasn't time to mess around with prisoners, Ralph said, everyone knew that. But I just can't get over the idea of Wesley being shot with his hands wired behind him. I think I could stand it better to know he had just been shot —you know—without being tied. It was the tying his hands that got me. They didn't have to do that.

It must have degraded a man like Wesley, he said.

Later he said an even more curious thing. I loved Wesley, he said. If he hadn't died—and then he said the really incomprehensible thing— you would have loved Wesley too. I can never get over that either.

Ralph would never let her buy anything German. He said it was a small protest. He didn't care about the Japanese, but he was dead set against the Germans. He said that if he ever found anything German in his house he would throw it out, and Carolyn knew by the tone of his voice that this was one of the few things he still felt strongly about. There were so few that she always made a special effort to look at the label on things. She wanted him to feel for something, no matter how absurd.

His hatred of the Germans, his love for his son: those seemed to be the only things to which he reacted.

Was he thinking about Wesley when he held his little boy in his arms, looking out far in the past and seeing the two men hunched over the fire, cooking the stolen chicken, and then later seeing himself looking down in the ditch, seeing the tied hands behind the back of his friend?

He never said. There was no way of knowing.

Just as there was no way of knowing so much about Ralph. People said war could make or break a man, but Carolyn wasn't so sure. With some men she thought it possible that it simply emptied them. They had been called on to give the little they had, and when that was exhausted there was simply nothing left over for the life that came after—the walking human deposits, empty, with nowhere to be returned for future use.

Why couldn't he want things the way other people did, and fight for them and be jealous of keeping them? Why couldn't he just once break through his shell and shout at her that he loved her and knew he had lost her and wanted her back?

What was the point of his having been saved if he had been saved for nothing?

She had wanted him dead and when she knew he was coming back she had told herself that maybe they could make a life together, but the bald, taut, withdrawn man who had come home was not someone you could believe in, not someone you could give your life up to.

The image Ralph brought home and carried inside his head was of a dark ditch and death. Now that image was with her. She never thought of him without thinking of death, of a dark grave, and a dead man.

She finished her martini, seeing Sally suddenly rise up and hurl a pail of sand at Bobbie. The maid, rightly, was horrified, and Carolyn watched, unmoved, while her daughter got the spanking she deserved. Bobbie did not cry; he simply looked at his sister, puzzled and hurt. Like his father, he did not betray his emotions.

Well, Carolyn thought, I don't understand my own children any more than my mother understood any of us. She thought of Stu, gone all these years, and how his clothes were still in the closet upstairs and how, no matter how parsimonious her mother was, she had never rented his room. Wasn't that a sign?

And the other brother—it broke your heart, going into Pete's house, seeing the laundry board up in the front room and all those damp things piled on chairs. In the kitchen there was a line across the room with drying clothes, and the family ate everything out of tins, the radio going full blast, and Peggy standing in the middle of the room saying, "Oh, I wish you'd let me know you were coming, Carolyn, I'd have done something about my hair."

Peggy dressed the boys and girls alike, everything was handed down, nothing ever fit. Five children, and Pete working as a clerk in a department store, in the basement, selling seconds and buying a ticket to the Irish Sweepstakes hopefully every year. All because when he was seventeen he got a girl in trouble.

How long did you have to go on paying for your mistakes?

The children were sitting, sulking, on opposite sides of the sandpile.

The maid was attempting to pacify them. Carolyn could see her mouth moving slowly and insistently, the put-upon look on that paid face. If they were the maid's own children, Carolyn wondered, would she just give them a good whacking and forget about them? But Miss Miller was paid a salary to be long-suffering.

Carolyn disliked the maid but depended on her. The woman was uppity, she ate like a horse, she got a ridiculous amount of money—it was the postwar prices. All the girls had found out what money was when they went into the factories, and the money had made them independent. This woman, for instance, insisted on leaving at eight and getting overtime if she had to stay in and baby-sit, but she was all there was at thirty a week, two *good* meals a day, and carfare; Carolyn had to put up with her gluttony, her insolence, and her independence because she herself didn't have the patience to tend a fretful child more than ten minutes.

Going to the bar, lifting up the bottle of gin, she considered a second drink, then pushed the cocktail shaker away impatiently. It was absurd, this drinking in the middle of the afternoon, just as her drinking far into the night was absurd.

She would read. Her Baedekers to experience those free years during the war had been books: she looked up alien experiences, running a finger hastily down the page, looking for a clue to her own emotional location.

With such guidebooks it was not easy to call out, I am lost.

She picked up an anthology; idly her hand rippled the pages until the book fell open at random and she glanced down, reading:

The Trojans have that glory which is loveliest: they died for their own country. So the bodies of all who took the spears were carried home in loving hands, brought, in the land of their fathers, to the embrace of earth. . . .

It was something she did not know, and she leafed back until she came to the beginning. Euripides. *The Trojan Women* . . . that glory which is loveliest: they died for their own country . . . it made her think of Ralph's friend.

Then it seemed to her Wesley, that strange man who had died so far away but had been born and raised in the next state, might almost be here in this room, not of course in body, but the spirit of him, watching, waiting, looking at her with pale recognition, the eyes of his dead head cloudy with comprehension. Might the dead not better understand than the living because they saw more? Because they could see inside.

If he had lived, she would no doubt know him well, a tall, cheerful man with big hands and feet—Ralph had remarked on those—he would bring his wife and children over to Illinois to visit. But supposing he hadn't married—supposing he were to come alone, were at this moment to walk through that door and stand, smiling, looking at her?

She saw the picture very clearly. Wesley would sit in the brown chair, he would be big even for that, the largest chair in the room, the "man's chair" that she had bought for Ralph and which he never used, saying he felt lost in it.

She leaned forward. I've been wanting to talk to you for such a long time, she would say. But not here, not in this house. I want to go out to the country, to where it's green and quiet and safe. I know a place, she would say.

Carolyn, he said, leaning forward, *Carolyn*.

"Mama, Mama," a shrill voice protested. "She hit me."

Carolyn opened her eyes. Sally was standing in front of her, angry and bent on justice. "Beatrice hit me," she insisted. "She shouldn't do that. Tell her she shouldn't do that. She's only the maid."

"Miss Miller, Sally. Say Miss Miller," Carolyn said, shaking her head, brushing away the vision of a moment before. "You threw sand, didn't you?"

The child shook her head.

"If *Miss Miller* spanked you," Carolyn said, "I know she had a good reason. Besides," she ended, wanting to finish the matter, "I saw you throw sand at Bobbie myself."

"Oh." Sally was twisting around on one foot, looking at the floor. "Oh," she repeated.

"I don't like tattling and I don't like lies."

Abruptly her daughter changed the subject. "Can I have ice cream for supper?"

Automatically Carolyn said no, wondered why, and then thought, I'm tired, I ought to try to be more patient with her. "We'll see," she amended and watched as Sally sat down and started pushing her fingers into the thick nap of the rug. "You're not supposed to play in here," Carolyn said sharply. "How many times do I have to tell you that? These colors soil easily. You have your own room."

"All right, all right," Sally said sullenly. She got up and went out with dignity, not looking back, while Carolyn felt a twinge of regret. She loved Sally, she loved Bobbie, but—

But they were in part a payment for her guilt, for Ralph's having come home.

Lois was coming, it was summer. They might borrow some rackets and go out into the country. They might talk, they might rest under the trees, they might even be close again—but the house was sold, the birds gone, the old lady dead.

What that summer had once promised could never come again. The present, Carolyn told herself, does not hold on to the possibilities of the past, only the remorse and regrets of what has gone before, of what should have happened and hasn't, of all the long nights you lay awake regretting the way life is, but unable to change it, unable to go back, unwilling to go forward, caught in the fantasy of false deceptions and the dream of lost chances, paralyzed by the power of God, that greater glory in which you no longer believed—nor perhaps had ever believed—but only held on to, as a child holds to its mother's hand before it walks by itself out into a narrow, cruel corner it calls the wide, wondrous world.

Chapter Four

IN TWELVE years Peggy had never gotten over the uneasiness she felt at the sound of her mother-in-law's voice. It wasn't really uneasiness, it was plain humiliation. The misery behind Iris's every word seemed to intensify when she spoke to Peggy, as if she were crying out, *It's your fault, all your fault Pete's the way he is and you don't even care, you've* NEVER *cared.* All the while Iris went on talking brokenheartedly—and everything broke her heart—Peggy cringed. The boarders, the babies, the price of food and gas, the Korean War, anything and everything were Peggy's fault; because twelve years before she had gone and got pregnant and Pete had had to marry her.

The only time Iris had begun to forgive her was during the war when, what with the babies and his asthma, Pete hadn't been called up. "The country shouldn't call up fathers," Iris always said, and then added, "and of course he has that terrible asthma. Stewart's family all had weak respiratory systems." Peggy couldn't help feeling that to Iris a weak respiratory system was preferable to defending your country. Then Peggy had come to realize that Iris was terrified Pete might go to war and come home wounded—turn into an invalid, the way his father was. Of course Father Ashwell wasn't a real invalid, he was just lazy.

The war, Peggy thought, was awful for everyone else, but it was the only time I ever had any relaxation. We had steak then, she thought in wonderment.

". . . Carolyn didn't even seem interested in the party," her mother-in-law was saying, and Peggy knew, looking up and staring into that fat, flushed face across from her, that it was her fault Lois was coming back at a bad time, her fault it was so hot that Iris just couldn't get everything done that had to be done, her fault no one was enthusiastic about the party.

". . . said she wouldn't go down and help me bring up the things from the basement. You know how hard I have to work, it's not asking much for her to bring a few boxes up to the kitchen, but she doesn't want to, she . . ."

Peggy, trying for the thousandth time to please, shook her head as if dismayed, as if it were inconceivable to her how Carolyn would not want to help.

"I guess," Iris resumed, fanning herself, "I have no right to expect anything. She doesn't have any feeling for family. Nobody does any more. Why, my mother used to . . ."

It was after five and she still had a million things to do and the last thing in the world she had expected or wanted was the arrival of this intolerable talker, but, a quarter of an hour before, Iris had come panting up the walk, excited and outraged, saying she was going to give a party, a party for Lois, she had been trying to get Peggy on the phone for over an hour, who was she talking to all that time, and before Peggy could answer she had plunged through the living room, talking, threaded her way through the mess in the kitchen, talking, rummaged around for a glass, talking, turned on the water, still talking, and she had only stopped when her mouth was full of water.

Every time Iris came in she looked Peggy up and down suspiciously, even though it had been five years since the last baby, looking sharply at Peggy's figure to see if she were just letting herself go or if there were another grandchild on the way. God, Peggy thought to herself, what if I am pregnant again?

She shook her head. No, it was only two or three days more until she got her period, she always felt depressed around that time; she mustn't get excited. Quickly counting back in her mind, she remembered with relief that she and Pete had taken no chances this month. In the beginning they had tried the rhythm system and that was what had got them in trouble—well, got them in trouble after the first time. Because you had to allow at least a whole week; otherwise, as she knew too well, you weren't safe. Nowadays she counted very carefully; as soon as the first nine days of her post-period were up, she wouldn't let Pete put a hand on her, no matter what, for the next twelve days. She had to be absolutely sure. Five mistakes were enough.

Not that she didn't love the children; of course she did. She might resent Frank, but she couldn't really hold it against him that he had been —well—the reason she and Pete had to get married. I mean, she thought, I've always *tried* to be fair to him. I don't know, I've made a mess of so many things, she thought, feeling her heart drop, and pretty soon Pete would be home (but she gave a silent prayer of thanks he had to work Saturdays, she just couldn't have stood having him around the house two days in a row), and the kids would come in starved, and right up until this moment she hadn't planned a single thing for dinner. Were there a couple of tins of spaghetti or macaroni she could maybe heat up? And of course the whole point of her mother-in-law's visit was that she wanted her to come over and get down in that awful basement and bring up the things. And Peggy knew she would do it, as part of her penance.

". . . Carolyn has a maid and everything," Iris was saying, fanning herself. "If she doesn't want to come herself, she could certainly send the maid, you know that, Peggy, but she wouldn't think of that. Not Carolyn, she's too selfish. She's always been that way. She wouldn't even be married in her own home, our lovely lovely house, and it was the only *real* wedding we were ever going to have a chance to have," she went on as Peggy winced. "And she wouldn't do it because she was ashamed, that's what, ashamed of her own house. Because we take in boarders. It makes you want to cry, thinking how selfish and thoughtless your own children can be, and now I'll have to do everything myself because of course I couldn't ask *you* to help, I know how busy you are with the children and all . . ." She stopped, staring at Peggy a moment. "You have to work so hard and Carolyn doesn't have to do anything and she begrudges me one afternoon of helping me with a party for Lois, and you know the doctor told me I had to be careful, with my heart and all, I could go any minute, he said, Carolyn knows that too, but does that bother her? No, she probably wouldn't think twice about it if I dropped dead on the steps. She only cares about herself. Honey," she said, leaning forward, "you're not—not that way again, are you?"

The unexpectedness of the question threw Peggy for a loss for a moment. And in the second of hesitation Iris took her reticence as an affirmation. "Oh no, that's positively the last straw," she cried. "I just can't take any more. Not another thing. Oh my god, where will I get the money for the hospital, and then it's diapers all over again, and I thought we were through with all that at last now that Blake's finally toilet-trained, and you've gone and got yourself in a family way again." Then the tears came.

Peggy stared at her, unmoved. She had seen her mother-in-law cry about a bad piece of meat, about Ada's saying Esther had taken the family money, about the disappearance of her son, about the roomers' burning holes in the bedclothes, about a broken cup and a torn sheet, about each and every disaster, major or minor, that touched on her life. "No," she said at last, "I'm not. You're getting yourself all excited about nothing. I'm just not wearing a girdle, it's so hot."

The tears stopped. "Thank god," Iris said. "Thank god for small favors."

Peggy looked at her, then leaned forward deliberately and picked up a cigarette, while Iris watched, her eyes widening. "Well, if you must," she said in a disgusted voice, "you must. Personally, I'd hate to be that much of a slave to any habit."

Peggy struck a match, thinking, I wish I had a beer. She could just imagine Iris's face if she went to the kitchen and came back with a can of beer, but there was only one in the refrigerator and Pete would raise the roof if he came in and found it gone. He hated having to work Saturdays, and when he came home he always went straight to the ice-box for a beer; he could do without it on weekdays, but on Saturday he wanted a reward. Well, one beer wasn't much of a reward. What good was *one* beer?

Pete's brother was the only one in the family with any sense, Peggy thought. He walked out. Peggy admired Stu for that; she thought there was something wonderful about his taking off, not even giving Iris a chance to put on one of her scenes.

She bet Stu smoked and drank and did all kinds of awful things, and she hoped he did, just to spite Iris. More power to you, Stu, she thought silently, looking at her mother-in-law's pursed lips and disapproving eyes.

It would make this whole day, Peggy thought, if I could just drink one can of beer in front of her.

You mustn't think that way, she tried to remonstrate with herself, but her rebellion was growing. She wanted to stand up and scream in Iris's face, "Shut up, shut up, I can't stand another word."

"It seems to me people sometimes just try to plague me deliberately," Iris said, sighing. "I'm not naming names, mind you. No, let the blame fall where it will, I won't point a finger. They say ours is not to reason why, ours is but to do or die, and I try to *do*. You can't say I haven't tried, but I just want to say one thing: when your own children won't help you, when your own children don't care how hard you work, then what's the world coming to, that's what I want to know?"

"I don't know," Peggy said evenly, trying to keep sarcasm out of her voice. She was experiencing a terrible, piercing sense of bitterness. In another moment she thought all her control would leave her and she would jump up and tell Iris what an old windbag she was.

"I want to tell you something, Peggy," Iris said, leaning forward. "Peggy, are you listening? I don't believe you've been listening at all, I think you've—"

"I'm listening, Mother Ashwell, it's just that it's after five and Pete will be home soon and the kids come in about this time and—"

Iris stood up. "I'm sorry I've taken up your valuable time with my poor pitiful complaints," she said. "Of course I should have realized you couldn't care about Lois or the party or Carolyn helping. Why should you?" She headed for the door, her back quivering with indignation. "I wish I had just one child who cared about me," she said bitterly.

Peggy's first reaction was raw anger. She bit her tongue. "Please, Mother Ashwell," she began patiently. "You know I didn't mean it like that, you know—"

"I know very well what you meant," Iris said with great finality. "You don't have to try to gloss it over. You can't hurt my feelings, no one can any more. Everything that could happen to me has already happened. I've been hurt past the point of caring. I just thank God for that."

"Oh, bat shit," Peggy said, losing complete control.

Iris stopped dead. She turned around. "What did you say?" she asked, her eyes round as half-dollars.

All the endless irritations of the day came flooding back on Peggy— the terrible necessity of getting up every morning at six and never getting to bed before twelve or one, the terrible tired feeling she carried around with her all the time, that made her cross and sick and snappy; she thought of all the breakfasts and lunches she had to fix separately every day, the dinner waiting to be prepared now, the laundry that was piled over on the chair and just had to be done; she pictured the pile of socks to be darned, the shirts with collars to be turned, and there was the worry if she would really, in spite of all the planning and keeping Pete away from her, get the curse this month; but most of all she was thinking of the unending bills, the things they absolutely needed and couldn't afford, the mortgage and the car payments, and the bank account which was down below twenty-five, and Pete's measly salary and no hope for a raise, all they could wait for was the Christmas bonus, and it was only July. They couldn't even take a vacation. He would just hang around the house—and be at her.

Peggy looked at Iris, hating her, hating the son who had got her in trouble, but hating more his mother, this awful lying old blowhard who would go on and on if she let her. "Go suffer someplace else," Peggy said into that astonished face. "Go tell someone else your troubles, I've got enough of my own. What do I care," she asked, breaking down, "about whether you have a party or not? What do I care whether Lois comes or not? What's she to me?" she demanded. "It's all I can do— *all I can do, I tell you*—to make ends meet for my own family." And then she burst into tears.

Instantly Iris was all consolation. "Honey," she murmured, embracing her, "oh, honey, don't cry like that. It just breaks my heart to see you so unhappy. You know you're like my own daughter to me. Honey, you mustn't. Don't. You'll spoil your pretty face."

"Spoil my pretty face! It's been gone for years, just like my figure. How can you expect me to care how I look when it's nothing but run, run, run, morning, noon, and night? I'm only thirty years old," she said, sobbing, "and I look and feel like a hundred. And you talk to me about troubles. Listen," she said, brushing Iris's hand off her, "I want to tell you something. I haven't had a new dress in three years. *Three years*. The only 'new' things I get are the hand-me-downs Carolyn gives me. I've come," she declared, the passion making her voice rise until Iris protested, "You don't have to shout, I'm standing right beside you," and Peggy went right on, paying no attention to her, repeating, "I've come to hate every one of you."

"Honey—" her mother-in-law pleaded urgently, but Peggy paid no attention. Peggy didn't care if she ever heard another word from Iris. Iris put her arm around her shaking shoulders, but Peggy pulled away, lay crumpled in the chair, sobbing.

"Honey," Iris repeated. "Honey, listen. I've got a little something put aside, something I've been saving, something even Dad doesn't know about." She waited, but Peggy let her wait. "Honey, you can have it," Iris said triumphantly. "You go get yourself a dress, a brand-new dress. For the party." She was waiting, Peggy knew, for her to say thank you, to show how grateful she was, how eternally grateful she would go on being the rest of her life, and Peggy let her wait. She wasn't going to say a single thing to make her mother-in-law feel better.

"Peggy," Iris said. "Peggy, honey—" Peggy waited. "You know I give you what I can. But money—we never got the money from—"

Peggy rose up, her eyes blazing. "If anyone ever says another word to me about how Esther stole the money we were all going to get," she shouted, "I'm going to walk out. Do you hear—walk right out and keep walking and *never* come back!"

Chapter Five

PETE stepped inside the drug store, walking toward the counter marked

T O Y S
B I G   S A L E !

He had seen the sign in the window and, even though he knew he ought to watch every penny, he had felt that old rebellious sense of, Why not? Why can't the kids have a little something extra once in a while?

The truth was that he and Peg lived on the edge of want so much of the time that almost the only pleasure they had was in spending money foolishly once in a while. The sense of recklessness, of heady adventure, that overcame him when he slapped a dollar bill down for something that wasn't essential was better than going to bed with his wife.

To be honest, he thought, that pleasure had been spoiled a long time ago. She made so many bones about it— *Be careful, Pete, oh we've got to be careful, I don't think we should now, not for at least another day—* that he finally just got fed up.

He felt a twinge of uneasiness. Whenever he thought of Peggy his next thought was of the little girl who wrapped packages on the first floor. She gave him the same sense of reckless pleasure, that spending money he shouldn't did—with her wet lips, coated with a thick layer of lavender, those heavy breasts pressing out against her tight bodice, the hard, bright glint in her brown eyes. What was really irresistible, though, was that she had told one of the salesgirls that she thought he was cute.

People pitied him—or scorned him—but it had been a long time since anyone had thought him "cute."

A hand darted out in front of him and removed a large stuffed panda. Five bucks at least, he thought. The synthetic slates were only fifty-nine cents. He could buy one, all the kids could share. Then he paused, looking down at an array of miniature two-way radio sets.

CLOSE OUT   PRICE CUT
$2.98 $2.98

Frank, he thought, thinking of his oldest boy, would really get a kick out of one of those.

Two ninety-eight was out of the question, of course. God, that was practically a week's lunches.

He picked up the slate and handed it to a bored salesgirl, gave her a dollar, and was disappointed that he felt no elation at all, only a gnawing dissatisfaction that he could not make a real gesture, pull out a five, and carry home the panda or the radio set.

His package wrapped, his change in hand, he started for the door, thinking that people didn't recognize how hard he tried. People had no realization whatsoever of what it was like to be poor, to be worried *all* the time about money. Morning, noon and night: money money where am I going to get the money to pay for the rent the lights the car the kids clothes the phone the new medicine Blake needs schoolbooks taxes car license. He was thirty years old, could expect to live to be, say, seventy: that meant he had FORTY more years of worrying about money.

Forty years, he thought in despair. That was forever, an infinity.

The word reminded him of his mother. *Tell me,* she had said the week before, gripping his arm in a frenzy of fear, staring up at him with her little button eyes embedded in all that fat, *what do you think of infinity?*

Pete had stared at her uncomprehendingly. What the hell did she mean, asking him an unanswerable question like that? Then the next minute she had gone on, *I want you to tell me the truth, son. You do believe in the hereafter, don't you?* And Pete had been afraid she was going to start one of her religious sermons, so he had said, Yeah, said it curtly and angrily, trying to pull away from her, but she wouldn't let him go. *Then, tell me, what do you think of infinity?* she had insisted.

Well, he said, trying to make a joke and get away from her at the same time, I think it goes on an awfully long time.

But what I want to know, Iris said, her face a study of puzzlement, *is this. I mean, if there's an end to space, what comes after space? If space . . .*

Infinity means there's no end, Pete said shortly. He hated the times she got like this more than he detested the times she went on and on about how she got down on her knees and prayed for them every day of her life. The only time I had her off my back, he thought, was during the war. He thought about the small-parts plant where he had worked the crash hours, he thought of the pay checks, he thought of the black-market steaks and the taste of good Scotch.

He opened the door of the drug store and was met with a blast of heat. Thinking that no one—not even God or his mother—would begrudge him a Coke, he turned back toward the soda fountain.

"With cherry in it, please," he said to the girl behind the counter, feeling a surge of guilt for even this small expenditure. A nickel here, a nickel there, over forty years, added up to a small fortune. Isn't there anything, he thought to himself, that's just mine? Isn't there one single bit of money I can do with as I want? No, there wasn't.

Work, go home, mess around with the kids, fix something that had gone wrong, listen to Peggy bellyaching, go to bed, get up, and start all over again. There was no money to hang around with the fellows bowling or playing poker, there was no money to take up golf or drop in a couple of times a week at the neighborhood bar. There was just no money, period.

He drank the Coke begrudgingly. His wife was a nag, he worked six goddam days a week, and all he could look forward to were debts, hard work, and worry—and his mother dying, he thought suddenly. That would shut her up once and for all. And give him a little money.

God, what a pretty pass he'd come to when he sat around thinking about how he would spend his mother's money after she was dead. He was getting just like the rest of the family; money, money, money, that was all they ever talked or cared about. The fool's gold that they had planned their hopes on, old Aunt Clara's iron pyrites.

My own children, he thought, are growing up in shoes that pinch and pants that are patched. It broke his heart to see how ragged they were. And then there was that business with Frank, the eldest. Peggy was after him all the time. The other four could get away with murder, but it was like she was just waiting for Frank to get the least bit out of line. He had a house he hated to come home to.

Pete thought of Sans Souci, that big house his father was always trying to get away from, too; how his father had taken him out to Lake Springfield. They were going to hunt frogs. His father carried the flashlight, he had the sack in which they would put the frogs.

They left the house around dusk and took the car out to a particular spot his father favored. His father's eagerness always made them early; they had to wait in the car until it was thoroughly dark. Then they went silently through the rushes, the deep-throated songs of the bullfrogs hurrumping on either side of them, his father not even smoking, concentrating all his energy on the contest in front of him.

As they neared the water, the noise increased until Pete's ears rang with it, but he knew better than to comment. His father was using his ears to track down his victims. Creeping up soundlessly, his father suddenly flashed on the light. In that second the frog was blinded, lost. His father's deft hand snatched up the trophy.

Those strong fingers and talented hands were linked forever in Pete's mind with his childhood. He remembered how his father's hands had closed over his so many times when he was a boy, the fingers imparting a sympathy and understanding his tongue could never tell. His father's mouth rarely moved in approbation or defamation, but the hands themselves were strong in their declarations of love.

Pete thought of those hands turning out pastries, parting kidneys, slicing evenly the heart of a calf. Now the hands were freckled with yellow, feeble facsimiles of what they had once been. Trembling around the coffee cup, hesitating over a line of print, clumsy in cutting and untrustworthy in measuring, they fumbled and groped where once they had been swift and sure.

Those drives out to Lake Springfield for the frogs had turned into nightmares of unwanted revelations as his father sought some way to make Pete see why he was the way he was. Excuse after excuse, justification on top of justification, rationalization after rationalization poured from his lips, a steady chant of self-pity. All the years had not dimmed the agony Pete had felt in the face of those unwanted confidences. The familiar landmarks of their drives became markers of past agonies; his father's voice droned on and on in its terrible quest for a moment of illumination when the explanation for his wasted life would burst upon them both.

"Your mother's a good woman, you mustn't blame her if we all . . .

think about me years ago trying to figure out a way . . . we thought we'd get a new start with the money from that old woman's estate . . . then there wasn't any will . . . no money at all really . . . not what we'd been counting on . . . see how things happen when you're older . . . forgive . . ." the words dropping slowly, inevitably, into the sharp twilight, like honey from a dipper.

His father would stop at last, near their destination. Pete, his head bowed in shame, saw from the corner of his eye the familiar hand turn the key in the ignition. The motor died and in the next instant his ears were filled with the thick grunting of the frogs. Quietly his father leaned forward and looked into the night. "I never wanted things to turn out like this," his father said. "But there wasn't anything I could do about it." His father had lived in a house he hated too.

I'll never behave like that, Pete told himself, thinking of his own children. I'll have better sense than to run after them trying to excuse my failures. Okay, so I'm broke and not much of a success, I'll probably never amount to a hill of beans, still, I'm not counting on anyone else's money. Oh, you're not? a voice inside asked. What about the money from your mother? What about your wanting your own mother dead so you could get her money?

Standing up, he put a nickel on the counter. Get a girl in trouble, have to marry her, can't support her decently, have to live off your mother half the time, want your own mother dead, no, you're not counting on anyone else's money; no, you'll never act like that. . . .

He was in front of the toy counter; the salesgirl gave him a peculiar look, as if she thought he might be someone to be watched, a thief or a queer. Pete glared back at her, trying to stare her down, and she, flushed and determined, stared right back at him. If he could only buy that radio set, that would show her.

Then he thought how mad Peggy would be, out in the kitchen, opening up cans furiously, her face set in rigid indignation. They would eat in silence, the children strung out between them, messily spilling milk and dropping food, the radio blaring from the kitchen. Whenever she was angry she turned the radio up full volume, knowing that after a day of noise and confusion all he wanted was a little quiet. They ate those terrible tinned dinners to the news of the disasters that had erupted round the world the past hours. It often occurred to him that someone ought to do a fifteen-minute newscast on the personal hell a man went through during one small day.

Up at seven-fifteen, temperature eighty-two degrees and rising, humidity high, wind seven miles per hour—forecast, hot and humid with no relief in sight.

Seven-twenty, into the bathroom and the cries of hungry children echoing to some account of Congress. Shave, shower, dress, one cut and a missing button. Second shirt has slight tear. Third scorched. Fourth striped and doesn't go with the suit. Change to another suit.

Breakfast: two children won't eat and a third has a crying spell. Blake has a tantrum because Emory took his toast. His wife in tears over the absence of eggs. He had forgotten to pick them up on his way home even though she had telephoned him the day before at four to be sure and remember.

Cold coffee.

The car nearly out of gas, another delay. Late now he drives in the heat and runs into a traffic jam at Jackson. Five minutes at one light. Just set to get across when it switches. Another hold-up. No parking space. Circles three times. Finally takes the cheap lot down the street because he can't be later than he already is. This substantially ruins an already overstrained budget.

Punches in at nine-fourteen. Frowns all around. His counter is a mess, and no one has gone to the trouble to try to help. A woman customer first. One of the fat kind with a big pocketbook and no taste. She looks at everything and doesn't buy anything. Merchandise all over the counter. As he is trying to put things away, Morris, the floor manager, comes up and says, "Ashwell, that's the sixth time this month you've come in late. We can't—" He is saved by a man who wants a size shirt they don't have. Pete knows they haven't got it but he pretends to look anyway so that Morris will get off his back.

Eleven o'clock: someone collecting for charity. Another dollar down the drain. How can you turn down widows and orphans or the Red Cross and still look the people you work with in the eye? Decides to do with a small lunch. Eleven-thirty the air-conditioner goes on the fritz. Peggy calls and says will you please pick up some Kleenex on the way home.

Fighting hunger and nausea, wishing he had remembered the eggs the day before and had something solid on his stomach, because it turns out this is his late day for lunch: one to two. A rush at the noon hour. All the secretaries are shopping and the section is short-handed. He waits on three people at once and succeeds in annoying all of them. One of them protests in a loud voice. Morris is menacingly near.

Just before he goes to lunch he discovers that in the confusion an expensive tie-pin display has been copped. Morris is now in a lather. Says that if anything else is missing from his counter this month it will be deducted from his salary.

No seats at the corner drug store and a big line in back of the eaters. Goes down the street to a hamburger joint and has the fifty-cent special: a greasy hamburger on a moldy roll, cup of coffee, and some pie. The pie is terrible, all crust and no apples. Picks up the Kleenex and goes back early, hoping to curry favor. Morris is on his lunch hour and misses the gesture.

New stock in and the afternoon is a nightmare of women who can't make up their minds; Miss Crimm, on gloves, has the monthlies and has to go home. She is crying and carrying on before Morris gives in and the look on her face reminds him of Peggy and how she will act when he says he had to park the car in the lot.

Goes to the can and discovers his piles are starting to act up again. Borrows an aspirin from Taylor on the ground floor. Taylor tells him her son has been held back in school and that her husband is drinking again. "What should I do, do you think?" she asks, and he has to tell her he doesn't know. She asks him where he is going on vacation and this brings back the realization he can't afford to go anywhere. Tells Taylor he hasn't made up his mind yet and goes back downstairs.

A terrible row going on. The boxes of new shirts have been upset and the tie rack is knocked over, ties all over the floor. Morris has sacked the summer stockhand and is standing, in the middle of a muddle of ties, threatening to fire him. *Why weren't you where you were supposed to be?* Morris shouts in the heat, mopping his forehead and breathing garlic into the small space behind Counter Eleven.

At three-thirty the ties are back, the shirts are where they should be, and the air-conditioner is functioning off and on. He is looking forward to the dull hour between three and four when it's Peggy again. "Your mother's just been on the phone, Pete. It's about Lois. She says Lois is . . ."

Morris tells him this is positively the last personal call he can have. He tells Morris it's the last one he *wants*. He and Morris stare at each other. Then Morris says, "Your wife, huh?" For a moment there is a feeling of affinity with Morris, whose wife is the kind who dyes her hair and wears big flowery hats. Then he remembers Morris's wife can't have any children. What does Morris do with all his money?

Punches out at five-fourteen, trying to recoup his honor. Walks by drugstore and sees sign:

TOYS
BIG SALE!

Walks in and buys slate, sees two-way radio set. Can't even afford a two-way radio set for his son, his oldest son that his wife resents and that he too is beginning, at the end of this long hot day, to resent. Then home and dinner and the radio, "Today the Russians . . ."

Aw, to hell with it, Pete said to himself suddenly. "Miss, oh miss, would you wrap up this radio set?"

Pete walked out into the heat, into the humidity, clutching his packages to him, unmindful of the people streaming up and down the street. He had spent every last cent he had except the money for the garage and maybe twenty or thirty cents over. Something for the ten-o'clock newscaster? he asked himself. MAN SHOOTS WIFE OVER LUNCH MONEY, he read in black headlines inside his head.

Where could you go when you were washed up? Someone—someone on the radio, he thought bitterly—was always telling you to see such-and-such an agency, borrow money with practically no interest, start all over again, your bills paid, your worries behind you. If you were in trouble . . . Well, he was in trouble. Where was the agency for the man who had got himself in up to his neck?

Where did you go to redeem your whole hopeless life?

He had started to cut across a lot on Ninth when he saw the sign. KEEP OFF THE GRASS, it warned, VIOLATORS WILL BE PROSECUTED.

Pete stopped. For a moment he felt like running out into the middle of all that wide expanse of lawn and jumping up and down. He would hang the slate around his neck. On it would be printed, I WON'T KEEP OFF THE GRASS, and he would be shouting into the little radio set as he jumped up and down, I WON'T KEEP OFF THE GRASS, I WON'T WORK SIX DAYS A WEEK, I WON'T PAY MY BILLS, I WON'T DO ANYTHING I'M SUPPOSED TO ANY MORE.

Chapter Six

"What's the matter with you anyway? You sit there looking so—"
Ethel was obviously searching for the right word and Stu saw the triumphant flush spread over her face as she came on precisely the right one—"so distracted" was what she said with a flourish.

Such a singular accomplishment, Stu decided, deserved the truth, no matter how absurd it would sound to her. "I was thinking about going skiing," he said.

"Skiing!" She glanced at him contemptuously, her mouth curling up in scorn. "You nuts or something? What do you mean, skiing? You never been on skis in your whole life. Skiing, that's work, exercise, you wouldn't even walk around the block you could maybe catch a bus." Suspicion clouded her gross, plump features. "You pulling my leg or something? It's the end of July, what do you mean, skiing?"

"Now I know why we couldn't make a go of it. No imagination, all the way down the line, Ethel. Can't you see that's just why I would think of snow and mountains, some place cold, because it *is* the end of July?"

Her small plump white hand made a motion, brushing aside his indictment. "You just like to be different. You always did. No matter what a person says, you take the opposite position. You do it on purpose just to be contrary. Don't think I don't know you backwards and forwards after all these years. I know you like a book."

"What book?" He was being deliberately, happily vindictive. She never read anything except scandal, advice to the lovelorn, the write-ups on disasters and medical cures, the scoops on sex crimes. The news she left strictly for whoever had the stamina to fight through all those intellectual intricacies. She thought the time he spent in the library was to get out of work; to her books were the excuse of failures.

"Very funny. I thought you said we was going to the movies. I should have knowed better. This is the way it always ends up, just sitting around doing nothing."

Of course—as usual—she was wrong. They were not doing nothing; they were hard at work at their favorite recreation, the one and only thing that could keep both of them deeply engrossed, more alert than the prospect of making love or the pleasures of eating and drinking, the one thing they really cared about: arguing.

Endless wrangling, about nothing, about everything; grinding out misery after misery, justifying themselves by blaming each other; scrabbling around in the ugly, dirty past to scratch up all the discontent—that was what made an evening's entertainment for them. The pattern sickened him, but he was caught in it. He didn't know any other way to behave with her any more.

In the silence she scratched her head, carefully examining her fingernails—an old habit. She was looking for dandruff. A phrase floated up in his mind: the fingernail test. Your best friends won't tell you, he thought. Was that B.O. or halitosis? B.O., he decided. What was that jingle about bad breath? He couldn't remember. If only one of those things were the matter with him—B.O., bad breath, dandruff. But his trouble went deeper, much deeper.

A clean, cold mountain somewhere, away from everyone, lots and lots of pure white snow, a bright sun, lots of sun on the snow, maybe a cold clear stream tumbling down the mountain, cutting through the white snow, green water next to white snow. When you looked deep inside the drifts, if they were dense enough, there was always a queer green glow, the pale green glint of what? Some facet of light, no doubt. Refraction? Maybe. It was the color that counted, not how it got there. The color of those deep holes in the snow in France when he lay hurt waiting for some medic—or Kraut—to find him. It was a fifty-fifty chance, he tried to tell himself, knowing all the time most of the company had pulled out and he had been left behind.

"Well, as long as we're not going to the show, we might as well have another beer." Heaving her flesh about her like a woman struggling with wet laundry, Ethel battled her way to her feet. "You'd just sit there and do nothing, not even get a beer, if you had your way. And me on my feet all day."

What was it she did now? Wait tables? Sell ladies' hose? Clean up in Schrafft's? He couldn't remember. She was always changing jobs, getting fired or leaving of her own accord because she thought she wasn't being appreciated. Change, that was it, she made change at the Automat. "I thought you sat down," he said to her back. "Everyone I've ever seen was sitting."

She turned around. "What are you talking about?"

"They let you sit down in those booths."

"What booths?"

"Those booths in the Automat."

"I don't work there no more. That was last month. I'm down at Klein's now. It just shows how much attention you pay to what I say. A whole month I've been at Klein's and you don't even remember."

"You can't expect me to have the picture perfectly clear in all this heat."

"I don't expect nothing. Never mind the weather. Skiing!"

Just her saying the word took some of the hope away from his picture —dirtied it up, as if she went around deliberately tracking up that fine clean white snow. It was the kind of trick she would pull, too, anything to spoil his pleasure. She had never been able, after the swell provider took off, to stand seeing him have any chance of getting away too.

"They got a comedy on at the RKO," she said, standing in the doorway. "Myrna Loy. It's supposed to be very funny. All the girls say I shouldn't oughta miss it. *Father of the Bride,* it's called."

"Some other time," he said. "I don't feel like the movies tonight."

"You never feel like doing nothing you start out to do. If you ever once in your life did something you said you was going to do, I'd drop dead of shock."

"Is that a fact?" Little whirls of white were exploding in his head: a blizzard.

"Yeah, that's a fact. You *can't* do anything you set out to do because that'd mean you'd get somewhere. Even if only to a movie. And do you want to know why you can't? I'll tell you—because you're afraid. That's why. You don't have no responsibilities so long as you don't never make anything of yourself, but—"

"What kind of responsibilities?" he asked sharply, blinded by a shower of snow and anger.

"Like maybe doing something about me."

He looked up at her, surprised. There had been real pain in her voice. "What is it you want me to do?"

She looked down at her fat hands, twisting them in embarrassment— it was real embarrassment, he could hardly believe his eyes. "I want," she said, after a pause that seemed to him hopelessly sad and full of the slow ugly truth that she had seen at last, "I want you should show a little affection maybe—sometimes. You know," she finished helplessly, "like other husbands."

"I haven't got any left," he said quickly and bitterly. "Maybe I never had any to begin with. What about that beer?"

"Yes, you did. Stu, in the beginning—you must have felt something," she said. It was a question not a statement, her voice dying out at the end. Then, as if she were terribly tired, she sat down on the hard chair by the door, her dress pulled tight across her stomach, that little mound of flesh where sometimes, sighing, she rested her hands, like a woman hanging onto the flesh to ease the spirit, and he saw the thick white thighs. She sat with her thighs exposed when she was trying to win him over. He supposed she thought it would excite him. But now he realized she didn't want to arouse him, she was trying to get him to see something else. She had fallen into that pose only because it was the one that sooner or later she adopted with him. Could you love a body like that, fat all over, bulbous breasts with big brown nipples like stars, swelling buttocks, all that white flesh that he knew too well?

He lighted a cigarette, waiting. It was impossible for her to keep anything to herself for any length of time. Sooner or later she would tell him, if he just kept his patience.

Finally she said, looking down, "I think I'm preg."

"More like change of life," he said cruelly, getting up to get the beer himself. And if it were true, if it were true, he thought, how do I even know it's me. No, it couldn't be me. I couldn't create anything.

"It's been over a month," she said stubbornly, watching him at the refrigerator. "Over four whole weeks."

"It's not me if you are," he said. "That would be a good one, getting knocked up after all these years, wouldn't it?"

Unbelievable as it was, she actually looked down demurely, spreading the rolls of her cotton dress evenly over her stomach with those pudgy little hands. Then she was moving her big body around. No, he was wrong. She wasn't fat, just solid, big, big limbs and all that terribly white flesh making her seem bigger than she was, one of those pale, dead-white Germans with golden blond hair which was going gray, ruined because she had touched it up with cheap tints. At nineteen a plump, pretty girl, now a heavy, fleshy, faded woman, not old, not yet, but give her a few more years, she'd be completely finished.

"Cat got your tongue?" she asked.

A big fat woman full of slang and clichés, and on her feet all day at Klein's.

"I said, 'Cat got your tongue?' "

He didn't want to spar, was far too tired, his visits to Lois and all that heat and thinking all week, something was draining out of him. She was right, he wouldn't be going skiing. Ever. Skiing was a rich man's sport. A young man's.

"No, I'm just surprised," he said, trying to sound interested, trying not to let his voice show how little he really cared.

"You can't know for sure, the man at the drug store told me, until the test comes back. Monday. They make a test. On rabbits. With my—my wee-wee, and they'll see."

"Oh, for god's sake," he said, impatient now and sick of the whole farce, "stop it. You can telephone whenever you want. Call me up day and night, I don't care. But don't start something stupid like this."

"I tell you I'm preggy, it's been over a month." She got up, looking at him with determination.

"I don't care if it's over a year, you're not pregnant and you know it."

"How can you tell? How can you be so sure?"

"Because I don't want you to be, that's why," he said, his voice rising. "And if you are you'll only have to pay someone to get rid of it. I haven't got the money and—"

"I won't," she said furiously, standing up, two splotches of red on her white cheeks. "I'm not going to get rid of it. I knew that's what you'd say, I knew—"

"What do you mean you're not going to get rid of it? We can't have a kid. What would we do with a kid? Who'd take care of it? Who'd—"

"I'd take care of it, that's who."

"You?" He started to laugh. She must be crazy. "And who'd pay you to sit home taking care of a—"

"You would, that's who!" she answered angrily. "I'd make you. If I have to, I'd write your mother—"

He crossed the room quickly, took hold of her arm. "Stop that kind of talk right now. You're not going to write anyone, and you know it."

"Yes I would too," she insisted, but her voice was full of doubt.

"You go back to that damn druggist and tell him to give you something and cut out all this nonsense. I've got enough on my mind without your starting something like this."

She was crying. Big, oozy tears were working their way out of her eyes. It was horrible, grotesque. He shook her. "Stop it," he said. "What's the matter with you, anyway?"

"I never wanted it to be like this," she said, sinking down in the hard chair, so that he was hanging on to her limp arm, her arm swinging crazily above her head. "I want to be like everyone else. I want a husband who lives with me and comes home—I want a husband who loves me. Like everyone else." She sobbed. "It isn't fair, you ought to love me. Husbands—"

"Listen, Ethel," he said more gently, releasing her arm, kneeling before her. "You remember what it was like? Always quarreling, never having a moment's peace? Don't you remember all the fights and how we—"

"But it doesn't have to be that way," she said pleadingly, raising her tear-stained face to his. "We could try." She wiped her eyes with those fat little hands that were so like his mother's. "I want a baby," she said, biting her lip. "Why can't I have a baby like other women?"

"Because," he said, completely exasperated, "we aren't like other people. People like us have no business bringing kids into the world."

"Why not? Why don't we have a right to kids like everybody else?" she demanded. "Is it because you don't want to pay for one? Because you don't want the responsibility, is that why?"

He could not commit his flesh and blood to a world in which he did not believe. He could not ask his poor frail flesh to be carried on yet another generation. She would never understand that he had lost his belief in living, in life itself.

"I can't have a child," he said, standing up and finding it a shock that he was actually trembling. "I'm not fit to be a parent. That's why."

"And what about me? Don't I have no rights? Isn't it mine too?"

"It's yours all right, but how do I know it's mine?"

"You know it's yours."

He shook his head. "No, Ethel, I don't. That's why I'm asking. How do you know it's mine?"

"Because—because you're the only one I been with, for a couple of months."

"Well, at least you're honest," he said, trying to get a grip on himself. He knew why he was trembling. He had admitted the possibility. A child. His flesh and blood. A reason, he thought, to do something. Make money. Come home. Go on day after day.

You fool, he told himself, you damn fool, you complete and utter fool. You know damn well there's no reason for anything.

"All right," he said more calmly. "Stop crying. Drink your beer. There's no sense getting all upset over nothing. You don't really know whether you're really—really that way or not."

"I feel that way," she insisted. "I never felt like this before. Funny, in the morning. Quivery, kinda. And I'm tired all the time. It's not just being on my feet all day. It's not that kind of tiredness. I know that. I've worked hard, you know that. I know what it's like to be tired, real tired, all right. Well, this is different. This is—is inside."

"You're probably just imagining it—" he began.

"And I threw up, this morning I threw up everything. Right after I got to work. So I said to one of the women on my shift, one of the married ones who has a couple of kids, 'What's it like—you know, when you get hung up?' and she said I had all the symptoms. She said I should test my breasts, that was the sure way. Was they real swollen and hot. And they are."

He imagined those big brown stars swollen and hot and he tried to blot the thought out of his mind.

"And something else," she was insisting. "I feel like doing it. Making love," she added, seeing his face. "I do. Real bad, Stu. I really do. You don't know. I got these kind of hot flashes all the time, making me want to."

"Stop talking like that, I tell you it's all in your mind."

"You want it there, that's why you say that, but I tell you it isn't," she insisted. "It's here." And she put those hands over her fat stomach and clung to it, looking at him with mascara-streaked eyes, her fat lips trembling in a smile.

Preggy, she had said: having a child to her was getting preggy. It was getting hung up. What did she really know about being hung up? She didn't have the imagination to know what a noose was unless you showed her a piece of rope.

He looked out the window, trying to think of something to say. It was dark now, that strange darkness that came down over the city, never complete and full as it would have been out in Illinois, but a murky darkness diminished by the lights of the city. They glowed up from the concrete, a sheen against the sky. The heat would lie on the city all night, like a sickness; then in the morning, in the very early morning, a mist would rise, a promise of coolness, just as quickly taken back; the sun would start in again, it would get hotter and hotter, the sickness would be back worse than ever.

"Listen, Ethel," he began, while she looked at him with great, pleading eyes. "I'm—I don't feel so hot. My stomach—" Her face was going all to pieces. "I'm—gotta get some air," he said thickly, bolting for the door, catching a last look at her crumbling face, and then he was in the hall, racing down the stairs, and out in the street and into the first bar. He ordered and drank swiftly a beer, then asked for a whisky and drank that a little more slowly. He had to get hold of himself.

Supposing they bring up the tanks, supposing they bring up the tanks, supposing . . . Over and over his mind was pounding it out, and he gripped the bar and tried to fight back that one terrible phrase.

But he was started, he knew all the signs. First he started to think about the tanks and then he thought about the first attack; then he got thirsty, the way he was thirsty now, had already signaled for another drink, remembering the men huddled, freezing, worried, asking one another, Supposing they bring up the tanks?

He made one final and determined attempt to take hold of himself. He got up from the bar stool and started to walk out.

"Hey, mac, you ordered this, you gotta pay for it."

Angrily, belligerently, he paid and tossed off the shot. If you paid for something, you had to use it, that was some kind of maxim of life, wasn't it?

What the hell, he thought, motioning for another drink, why try to make it more complicated than it is? You're just one of those guys who started off on the wrong foot and never got off it. Ethel was just the inevitable.

She hadn't been bad-looking in the beginning. He thought of the pale face and the white silky arm she raised as she put the coin in the miniature paddlewheel machine of the bus they rode together every morning to work. He remembered them sitting next to each other, her warm flesh pressed up to his, he remembered how she looked up at him, her eyes soft and radiant with anticipation and expectation.

He thought, leaning over the bar and staring into his empty glass, of how he had asked her out and how they had gone on the same bus but in the opposite direction, not into Springfield but out into the country, and she had made a picnic lunch, those big frankfurters the Germans ate and a funny kind of potato salad. She had carried a bag of red, juicy cherries. They had eaten under a big elm; then they lay down, careful not to touch each other, lying still and taut, a current passing between them so that they kept shifting their bodies, then lying rigid again; in the twisting and turning, their flesh would touch, they would both draw back quickly; and then after a time they began to relax, he felt her arm press up lightly against his, and a little while later their thighs touched, brushed against each other gently; then they lay still and close, intimate, flesh to flesh; he was like one in a dream, staring up into a dome of leaves, the sky speckling through; they had been still that way for over an hour, wordless messages flowing between them, still, close, communicating; when he glanced over at her, he saw that her eyes were open like his, she was staring up at the sky through the bright green vault of leaves. He looked away quickly and tried to compose himself. He knew that if he looked at her closely, if he propped himself up and stared down at her, he wouldn't be able to control himself, not with this current moving back and forth between them.

Suddenly she sat up and said, "Let's eat some more cherries. I'm thirsty."

She had big strong legs, smooth, hairless, and there under the pants he had glimpsed the light blond hair. When she bent down to hand him the cherries, he felt his whole body register a shock.

"Another whisky."

She had been so soft and warm. It was hard to think of Ethel now as she had been that day. He thought of how they lay together on the grass, pressed up against each other; he had kissed her all around her lips, letting his mouth make little small caresses of endearment above her lips, at the side of her lips, all around her beautiful mouth, while he looked down at her, they both had their eyes open, and their eyes were speaking while their mouths were kissing, and then he had kissed her, really kissed her, his tongue meeting hers; he remembered how, later, the sun lay in small patches all over her body, and how scared she had been that he might have forgotten some kind of protection until he leaned over and left her, lying naked and wide-eyed on the grass, and searched through his pants pockets, and she had said in a soft, faint voice, "You did want to. Oh Stu, you did want to, you bought those because you wanted to."

He remembered, though it seemed to him impossible he had ever felt it, how he had loved to fall down on that flesh, how he had been transformed for those first couple of months, could hardly wait to get off work so that he could be with her. Even when they couldn't be alone, couldn't go anywhere to do it, it didn't matter. What mattered was that he could be with her. She made him feel safe, safe and special.

"I think I'll switch back to beer," he told the bartender, spreading a circle of coins on the counter.

He had brought her to New York. He had married her. He had escaped her with the war. He had killed and almost been killed himself. It was only a piece of luck some of the stragglers had found him, and a greater piece of luck that they had the decency (the courage, he thought, the cowards all ran) to pick him up and lug him along with them. Krauts were on all sides, and they weren't taking prisoners. He owed his life to luck—luck? he asked himself.

Who the hell knew?

After the war he came back to New York, not even writing to Springfield; he doubted anyone out there knew he had even been in the war, how lucky he was to get out of it in half a piece, and there was the disability money, that was a help—not much, but enough to tide him over —because he wouldn't go back to work.

For a while, after the war, his occupation had been that of The Walker. An explorer of the city streets. A tramper of the parks and back streets. A discoverer of the rivers and docks.

Then he had just started to sit. It was a city hard to sit in. That's how he had first come on the library, not the big one, not at first, but one of those little antiquated branch ones. Looking in, he had seen straight off that was where the people who were sitters went: filled with old croupy men, highly sensitized adolescents, women with no place else to go, hiding behind frayed fur pieces and historical romances.

Dreaming, he thought, of other homes.

Of other places.

Places where there was still green, some trees, a place of privacy where you could lie down and make love. Like Springfield.

Better to stay in New York, better to fend off Ethel with her eternal supplications "to give it another try." He had looked around a bit, at other women, and sometimes he gave one a try, but most of the time he didn't bother.

Lois is going back to Springfield, he thought. She's on the train right now.

Let her go, he thought. What's that to you?

"Whatcha looking at?" he demanded, feeling the rage run through him. "What's the matter? Who you staring at, anyhow?"

The man at the other end of the bar started and looked away self-consciously. "You," Stu said. "I'm talking to you. Who the hell do you think you're staring at anyway?"

The man mumbled something, and Stu got off his stool and started toward the back of the bar.

"Hold it, mac," the bartender said.

Stu stopped. He lifted himself on the balls of his feet, feeling a little warning signal at the back of his head, the tightening of the muscles there, a sure warning that danger was near. The guy behind the bar must have a weapon back there. Take it easy, he said to himself.

You can't get in a fight now, you've got more important things on your mind, a small voice inside said to him.

The hell I have, he answered it savagely.

He stood for a moment poised on his insteps; then he dropped back, turned with a shrug, and said, "What the hell, if that bastard wants to stare, let him stare."

The man gulped his drink, threw some money on the bar, and left a moment later. He didn't look at Stu as he went out.

Look at the world, what's wrong with you anyway, Stu asked himself, you want to bring a kid into a world like this, a world where they *always* bring up the tanks?

For a moment his mind seemed to blank out on him. He saw only an endless stretch of snow and the big terrifying tanks coming across it. A man against a tank: what chance did a man have against a tank? None, he thought, shaking his head. But it was never just one man against the tanks. There were always lines and lines of men waiting for the tanks, waiting for the tanks to come and overrun them. The whole freezing night they lay awake asking themselves, asking one another, Supposing they bring up the tanks, supposing they bring up the tanks, supposing . . .

He was standing in a bar, a drink in his hand. The war was over, France a long way away. And anyway, he had learned one thing: There are never as many tanks as you think there are going to be.

C

SATURDAY

BOOK II   **SUNDAY**

MONDAY

TUESDAY

WEDNESDAY

THURSDAY

FRIDAY

SATURDAY

Chapter One

LOIS came out, carrying her suitcase, not expecting to have anyone meet her, and there they stood: small, stubby Iris; thin, overdressed Frances; morose, ugly Esther—fat Timble, lean Timble, eccentric Timble, but there was no mistaking they were all Timbles.

Five, you know, Lois could hear the voices of her aunts' friends reciting . . . their mother died just before the war . . . shock . . . it's a close-mouthed family but that sort of thing always gets out . . . I always say what they needed then was a detective, not a lawyer . . . one of the girls accused another of stealing . . . killed her mother . . . dropped dead on her daughter's living-room rug; no, not the one that took the money, the one with the big house . . . a family of troubles . . . one that took money, one that divorced, and one that ran away with another man and killed herself . . . the youngest . . . Organdy, funny name, wasn't it?

The Dead One, Lois thought. The One Nobody Talks About.

The rest of the family was buried in the family plot out at the Catholic cemetery. There was a big red oak at one end of the enclosure and near her grandmother's headstone a wrought-iron bench, painted white, where Lois sat when she was a young girl while Iris went around distributing peonies on Memorial Day, bending over, crying as she stuck the blooms in old rusted containers sunk in the ground. Every Memorial Day and every Labor Day, Iris made her pilgrimage, stopping at the gate and getting chrysanthemums in the fall, carrying her own peonies in the spring, big red and white flowers with ants crawling all over them. Iris always cried at the graves first and then went back and had an argument with the man who was in charge of keeping the lots up. She said he was neglecting the Timble plot. Was she still going out there to weep and wrangle?

But her own mother was interred by herself, away from family or friends, on a single plot of land, where neither the husband she had fled nor the daughter she had left would be buried next to her, all alone, in the Protestant place.

Iris sprang from between Esther and Frances, started to run toward her, then stopped, looking at her in alarm. "Oh, honey, you didn't go and cut that lovely hair, did you?"

How else would she have got rid of it? Lois wondered. Putting down her suitcase and bending over to distribute hasty kisses, she said, "It's not fashionable to have a lot of hair, and anyway in an office . . ."

Her lips on Esther's scaly cheek, her eyes so close to Esther's big flecked gray ones that she could see the amber and green specks embedded there, she remembered disbelievingly that her own mother had once said Esther had been a beauty, the prettiest girl in her class, maybe in the whole school. How, her mother had said, could she have taken the money? She couldn't, she just couldn't.

"Your hair, your lovely hair, your best feature, you went and ruined it. Look at it," Iris cried dramatically. "You can't fool me. You *had* to cut it. You've been putting it up with water. After all I told you, you went and put water on it. Oh honey, I told you water would rot the roots."

"I like her hair," Frances said. "It looks real Frenchy. Chic," she said, pronouncing it *chick*.

"It makes you look too old," Iris insisted. "Let it grow back," she urged, grabbing Lois by the arm. "Your hair grows fast, it won't take long."

"This all the luggage you got?" Esther asked.

Lois nodded and they fell into line, a miniature squadron to march the length of the station. Downstairs it was worse than Lois remembered, dirtier and more disorderly, but the real shock came when they got outdoors. "What's happened to the trees?" she asked, staring past the traffic toward the center of town.

"Trees? What trees?" Esther asked, looking around.

Iris, busy trying to unlock the car, did not answer.

"The maples and elms."

"Put your suitcase in back with us, there'll be room," Esther advised.

"That's a good idea," Iris agreed in a muffled tone, bent over, struggling with the lock. "Then we won't have to fuss with the trunk."

"It's civic improvement," Frances answered, taking the key from Iris. "Here, let me have a go at that." The little knob inside the window flew up. "There," Frances said triumphantly, handing the key back to Iris. She turned, looking down the street at the trees. "Horrible, isn't it?" She opened the door to the back seat and got in. "I don't know why you insist on locking a car that has nothing in it, Iris, really I—"

"They take cigarette lighters and—"

"Well, you don't smoke."

"I should say not. But supposing we wanted to sell the car—or trade it in—and the cigarette lighter was missing."

Lois slid her suitcases into the back seat, careful not to snag Frances's stockings. Frances's legs were crossed, the crossed one swinging impatiently. Inside the calf were tiny broken veins, small arteries like roads of a map, that ran down toward her ankles, while from the ankles up ran other roads, bluish, and along one inner leg was an enlarged vein, a major highway. Birth had done that, Frances explained bitterly. The strain, she always finished, looking down, as if her life had been completely altered by that moment of creation, that from that moment on she had been sunk in regret.

Lois remembered all those long summer afternoons spent over a card table inside Frances's house—Frances setting up the bridge hands, looking first at her son, then at her niece, pointing with one long, exquisitely polished nail, saying, "If you have length and strength and not too much honor count, open three."

She loved Frances, but more she loved Erwin, that cousin whose shadow she would have liked, in the fashion of the books she read as a child, to sew onto her own image, so that he might never leave her—worshiping him as the brother she would never have, as the father who would never have her.

Frances made the two of them learn duplicate and she took them with her whenever she went on her salt-dip searches, packing them into the old Dodge, hitting the highways in search of out-of-the-way antique shops, "those dinky little houses no one else knows about," Frances would say, revving the motor to top power and letting the car out for a good run. "None of those places where they plant a good Sèvres cup out on the kitchen floor for the cat's milk and you're supposed to think it's an *accident*."

Up and down the Illinois countryside the car bounced, in and out of unmarked lanes the Dodge sped, until Frances, spying a tumbledown old house with a half-legible sign, would slam on the brakes, light up a cigarette, and begin her instructions. "Now you two go in there and start making them nervous. Bump against the bric-a-brac, pick up the china, handle it real rough. Only don't break anything. I want a bargain, not breakage."

Frances had cupboards and cupboards of salt dips—bright azure ones in the shapes of fruits and flowers, blunt amber birds and small rose-colored cups, row after row of clear crystal, a whole case of milk glass, salt dips of every conceivable size and shape, and it was Frances's boast that she had never gone beyond two-fifty. "When they say three dollars," Frances said, "I give them a look and stalk out. You can bet your boots they come running after."

Sometimes Lois and Erwin were spared their performances. Frances had certain reliables where she made the assault alone, Erwin and Lois staying behind in the Dodge. They would scrunch down on the back seat, staring at the worn seat covers, picking out threads, talking about *hit*.

Hit was Erwin's euphemism for sex. As soon as he had come on the forbidden fundamentals, he had hastened to halve the secret with her. His having singled her out to be the first to share his knowledge was the highest accolade he could ever give her. Erwin liked to tell her everything he knew; what he didn't know, he guessed at—a conversation of infinite possibilities.

"You think they do it every night?" Lois would ask. "Those married people?"

Erwin shook his head. "Couldn't take the chance, they'd end up with nothing but a houseful of kids. Must be some system so they can do it okay sometimes and lay off the others. Still," he conceded a moment later, "there are those things."

Lois nodded eagerly. He had been promising her he would buy one and show her what it was like, but thus far he hadn't gotten around to it—not that she blamed him. It would be terribly embarrassing to go into a drugstore and ask for *that*.

God, how she had loved him. Any question she was afraid to ask a grown-up she went to him with. He had always given her answers and if, later, she found the majority of them inaccurate, that hadn't mattered in the least. The thing was, she had wanted some answer—any answer—and he had understood that and done his best never to disappoint her.

He had given her the pass keys to adulthood—the only person to teach her how to inhale, that you never drank Scotch with ginger ale, and that boys expected a certain amount of petting but they didn't want you to go overboard. He had given her her first copy of *The Prophet*, her first Lawrence, her first Miller.

Gone away to war and come back all changed, older and better-looking, but changed—now they scarcely knew each other; at the end, just before she left for New York, they had assiduously avoided one another. But it was not this she held on to, but the memory of those afternoons in the back seat of the Dodge, the summer plains spread out before them in rich sunlight; the sound of Frances's high, determined voice drifting out to them from behind the screen door; a gray, paintless place with a lopsided sign and piles of dusty, useless objects in the window. At those antique shops there were always old furniture piled up on the porch and copper pots hanging haphazardly around the frame of the door.

"You sit next to me, honey," Iris said from the front seat.

Obediently Lois climbed in front without answering. For the first time she could understand completely why Stu didn't want to come back. Two years was a long time, but twelve years might be forever.

Iris was sitting in perplexity, looking at the dashboard vaguely, as if she weren't quite certain how all the gadgets worked. "They're pruning them," she said, lifting her head and nodding toward the trees. "Cutting them back so they'll be thicker, easier to manage, it's part of a plan." She looked down, paused, considered, then slipped a key into the ignition, turned it, gripped the wheel, bit her lip, and brought her foot into position over the accelerator. "Have you got all your knobs up?" she demanded, as her foot made the decision, fell on the gas pedal, and the car shot forward, scraped the curb, ran up on the sidewalk, swerved, and flung itself into traffic, while Iris strained forward, anxiously glancing down at the speedometer. She liked to keep at an even eighteen.

"Your knobs up?" she repeated sternly.

Years before Iris always used to insist that the knobs be down. She was afraid of robbers, it was true, but her real fear was molesters. She insisted she knew someone who knew someone who had a friend who slowed down at a railway crossing, and "it was dark and she was all alone," Lois could hear her saying, "but she wanted to be safe. She didn't want to be hit by a train. So she stopped, to check, and this man jumped out from behind the bushes and grabbed the door and it wasn't locked, and he had a knife on him. He took her purse and—and her you-know-what-else. So always keep your knobs down." For years she had driven everyone crazy asking if the knobs were down.

Then Iris heard another story. Somebody told her about a woman and her four children who were in an accident. All the knobs were down on the car, the car caught fire, nobody could get to them, they were all burned alive. Now the cry was, "Keep your knobs up. Remember the woman and her four children who were burned to death because the knobs were down. Always keep your knobs up!"

Faithful to the speed at which she felt safe, Iris aimed the car east, while Lois stared at those terrible trees. The maples had been especially beautiful, full and green, an avenue of shadowy coolness in summer, proud patricians pointing as far as the eye could see down the wide avenue that led at last to the open fields of countryside beyond the city. Fall stripped them of strength; in winter they had been gaunt and flesh-less, old men with weak limbs protesting their disfigurement. Now all the branches had been hacked off. They were bare and broken. She was looking on mutilation.

"It was awfully nice of you to come and get me, Auntie," she began. In the beginning you always made a real effort, you thought it would make a difference. "I really didn't expect it. I know how much work you have with the house and all." Iris sighed, and Lois decided this was the time for the supreme tribute. "It's good to be back," she said, try-ing to sound enthusiastic. It all looked so small, so much smaller than she remembered. Springfield looked as if it had been laid out by an Oriental architect.

"You're smoking, Frances," Iris accused the back seat. "I can smell smoke," she went on in that aggrieved tone she used every time she spoke to her divorced sister.

"King-size," Frances remarked cheerfully.

A Walgreen's, the big department store, the bargain linen and lingerie flashed by; there was a sale on at Lerner's. Everything was the same and yet different, as if this were a city she had first seen in a dream and later come on in actual life. The people, hurrying by, didn't look quite real either, something about the way they walked and the angle of their bodies, bent as if in a wind in the midst of a still summer day.

Faltering, she held on to the image of Erwin and herself in the back of the Dodge examining ruthlessly the anatomy of love. Now he was married, to a woman she had never seen. He belonged to somebody else. Everyone in the family her age did—except Eileen. Just the two of us left, alone, Lois thought. Everyone else has found someone, has a house and things to fill it. The unmarried ones: is that what they call Eileen and me? Lois wondered. She turned to face the back seat and Frances fiddling with her cigarette. Frances was knocking ashes off, out the window. "Erwin," Lois began as her aunt looked up, smiled mechanically, then looked down quickly to see if she'd spilled any ashes. "How's Erwin?"

"Honey, he's married into one of the best families," Frances said happily. "Helen's father is a very high-placed person. You mention his name anywhere, people know it right off. I know you're going to like Helen. She's a Smith girl," Frances said proudly. "That's one of the best women's colleges," she explained, looking across the back of the front seat at Lois, her face suspended over smoke, as if fog were moving in to obscure her permanently from the critical view of her sisters. "You know Smith?" Frances asked anxiously. "Smith College for girls—it's somewhere in Massachusetts."

"You'll be pretty," Erwin had told her once. "You wait and see. You've got a real—a real interesting face." He had been embarrassed. "Nice eyes," he said and let it go at that.

It was almost the last truly free gift he had made her; the rest were all presents he had had to pay for, conscience offerings. He couldn't, she figured, counting back, have been more than fifteen or sixteen at the time he had made her that happy. He was twenty-seven or -eight now. A long time back. A lot had happened. They were no longer the same people. Even, Lois thought, my eyes are probably changed, they have seen a lot since then, and not always the right things.

A girl from Smith College for women, somewhere in Massachusetts.

"I want you to come visit me," Esther declared, moving over a little, away from Frances. Like Iris, she had a thing about tobacco. "I'll tell you the day. I'm a very busy woman," Esther said, as if someone had denied it. "I can't have people popping in and out."

"Who can pop in and out of a place that's got more locks than the county jail?" Frances asked.

"I have to protect myself. You read the papers, you know what's going on." One of Esther's fingers went up, stabbed at her ear, then began to bore in. She extracted it, looked at it, pried some wax from under the nail. "You can't trust anybody these days, and that's a known fact."

Frances threw her half-finished cigarette out the open window, leaned over the front seat as Iris made a left turn, and said, "You're Virgo, aren't you?"

"What?" Lois asked, startled, looking into her aunt's suddenly serious face.

"You were born in September, weren't you? Virgo, aren't you?"

"September, oh yes."

"Well," Frances said, smiling, "I looked you up this morning. The stars are very favorable. Here," she said, leaning back and rummaging through her purse, pulling out a tattered, gaily colored book and thumbing through it. " 'Your sixth house is activated considerably this month,' " she read. " 'The time is ripe for new occupational starts. You may even find romance where you work.' " She looked up, pursing her lips, nodding approvingly. "That's the kind of forecast I like to see.

'Your well-being is favored by these transits, and the affairs of uncles and aunts are under cosmic sanction.' See, I told you this stuff was straight from the horse's mouth," she said to Iris. " 'Buy a pet for your-self,' " she finished. " 'Also a favorable cycle of office furniture. Uranus is adverse to your twelfth house all month so—"

"Twelfth house?" Esther inquired, looking up. "What twelfth house?"

"Astrology," Frances replied in a disgusted voice. "*Not* real estate. The twelfth house is—wait a minute," she said, looking in the back of the book. "Oh, here it is. 'Twelfth House: hospitals, public institutions, sorrows, limitations, defeat, undercover activities, confinement, occult study, labor unions. Large animals. Feet weaknesses.' That's a funny one," she said, puzzled. "What do they mean—fallen arches, things like that? The stars have influence over things like that, who'd ever think it?"

Clubs, Erwin loved organizing them, declared himself president and treasurer at the same time—collecting dues, holding a meeting or two, then going into bankruptcy, organizing a new one. He had an old card table down in the basement and a blanket draped over that; after he had initiated and dissolved enough organizations he accumulated quite a fund, enough to buy himself a bright red lantern which worked on a battery. He liked to cover the card table completely with the blanket, hang the lantern from an improvised fixture made of milk-bottle wires, string, and a curtain loop. Sometimes he let her hold office, sometimes not, but he was always willing for her to come into his "office" and discuss *hit*. He must have organized a hundred clubs before he was fifteen and quit forever.

Just before he went overseas he came, unexpectedly, out to the campus. It was the last day of his leave and he told his mother he had to be back at camp earlier than he did; he used the extra time to spend his last hours with her. She was just coming out of the dormitory on her way to Lit 101 when he stopped her. All around girls were looking at her enviously; he had been not quite believable in uniform. "I came to give you this," he said and held out, right there and then, in the middle of the campus, a hundred-dollar bill. It was the first one Lois had ever seen, and all she could do was stare at it. "I know you never have any money," he said, forcing the bill between her fingers, "and I thought you ought to have a big wad just once to blow the way you want."

"Books," she had begun, "and some clothes—"

"I don't care what you do with it," he said shortly, as if he didn't want to talk about it any more. "Just so long as you enjoy it."

They had drunk beer and eaten pizza together and he had agreed, after an argument, to let her pay for it out of the hundred dollars. When she tried to give the bill to the waitress, the waitress had been mad, but the manager had taken it as a joke. He and Erwin had laughed together, and of course Erwin had ended up paying. She remembered that hundred dollars as one of the most important moments in her life.

"Here's our turn," Iris said with a moan. "I tell you I offer up a prayer of thanksgiving—and a real one," she shot over her shoulder significantly to Frances, who had never been strong on religion when she was younger and had since given evidence of just how a weak a link in the chain of salvation she was—"every time I get the car back in the yard. One more mishap and the company's going to cancel the policy. The man made a special trip out to tell me that when I dented the fender on that parking meter. All the money I've paid in over the years, and they complain about a couple of little scratches. They have their nerve. Everybody knows what goes on in those big insurance companies."

Iris swung the car left at the big sign: REASONABLE RATES *Hot and Cold Running Water in All Rooms.* "Does it look the same?" she inquired anxiously.

"Just the same," Lois reassured her. And, for a fact, it did. The letters of the word ROOMS were still crowded together; the big pots of ivy and the urns of wandering Jew were in their ordained places; the grass needed cutting, but in her memory it always needed cutting. She knew already that her Uncle Stewart would be in the dingy kitchen, hidden behind a magazine, and that the cows, in that dreadful picture painted in Decatur, Illinois, would still hang over the mantel in the dining room; the springs and stuffing in the chairs and sofa would be coming through, and Iris proudly pointing to the teak floors and waiting for commiseration because all the silver was tarnishing in the basement, all the boarders were marking up the stairs, the plumbing was always stopped up, and she, Iris Timble Ashwell, was working herself into her grave and not one single, solitary person in the whole wide world appreciated what she was doing or had done or would have to do.

When the children are young they tread upon their mother's breast,
When they are older they tread upon her heart.

Oh, the times Iris, moisture gathering at the corners of her eyes, lifted her heavy, martyred head, pursed her little mouth, and began, *When the children* . . . Whenever Lois thought of her, her picture of Iris was always annotated with a curious little note in the margin of her mind: *When the children . . . tread upon their mother's breast. . . .*

Still, Lois thought, it was she who took care of me, she who cared, she and Ella. Daddy never cared, I was just a duty, a duty and a burden and—of course—an extra expense. He was glad to get rid of me, marry and get away from that responsibility, the way he was glad to get rid of mother.

Was that fair? To accuse her father of something for which she had no proof?

For a time he had written to her, after his move out to California and his remarriage, three, four times a year, and always, in the beginning, at her birthday and Christmas. There was a ten-dollar check enclosed at Christmas and then a five-dollar one at her birthday. Then, gradually, those letters had gotten fewer, farther apart, until there was only the annual birthday check and finally not even that. She didn't know really what he was doing any more, or whether there might be any half-brothers and -sisters, out there in Califorina, and she didn't want to know.

Iris slowed down at the entrance to the garage and peered out of her window nervously. "Just look on your side, will you, Lois?" she asked. "And tell me if I'm going to scrape the fender. I don't know, I can't seem to judge distance any more, I always—"

"You're all right," Lois reassured her, holding her breath as Iris closed her eyes; the car shot forward and hit the back wall with a jolt. The motor raced; Iris opened her eyes and smiled. "We made it," she said gratefully. "Just go right on up to the house and—oh," she wailed, "oh dear god, I hope she's not planning to stay for dinner, I haven't got enough." It was Carolyn she was talking about, Carolyn crossing the lawn toward the garage, an older, more sophisticated Carolyn, but her face and figure were better than ever. She still looked, Lois thought, the way she had at the tennis courts—young and intense and excited.

"Get that look off your face, Mother," Carolyn said as she came up to the car. "I only stopped by to ask Lois if she wanted to come over to the house—"

"Her first night home," Iris interrupted, "I'm sure she wants to spend it here, where she grew up. Dad and Ella and I have planned such a nice—"

Carolyn leaned down; she was smiling. "Hello, Lois, back to the old homestead and the shenanigans are still the same. But it's good to see you, it really is."

"Ask me," Frances said, opening the car door on her side. "I'd love to stop by and get a free drink."

"You haven't started drinking, Lois, have you?" Esther demanded. "You haven't got the habit, have you, the way all those people in New York . . ." She looked at Lois critically. "I can tell you're not well, you're all sallow. Oh, I want to tell you . . ." Esther stood clutching the top of the car door with one hand, the hand of a woman who did her own work, all of it, even the hardest manual labor, the kind hired men and janitors did. Lois could picture her saying, The way to get rich is to work, to work hard, the way I did.

And the way to love, she wanted to ask, what way is that?

"Your elimination, how's your elimination?" Esther asked her in a worried voice, looking at her with that long, sad face of longing, the long, sad face you see on those looking for love. "You look terribly sallow to me."

Living in sin, *in sin,* Lois has been living in sin, she could imagine Esther shouting, and that's not the worst of it.

Tell me, she would ask, which do you think is worse—living in sin or stealing?

We could look them up, Lois decided. Run right down the rules: there it is, rule number six, Thou shalt not commit adultery; and right after it, Thou shalt not steal. Does the order of precedence have anything to do with the degree of seriousness? Because if it does, adultery comes before theft, and that must mean it's worse. Is there a degree to the sins, the big mortal ones? Tell me, she would ask, do you think murder is the worst of all?

She looked at her aunts, at Esther, Iris, at Frances hanging on to her side of the car, half swinging on the door, and the faces seemed to her devoid of any desire to be loved; they were the faces of women who had denied love, subordinated it to their hunger for power; long ago love had hurt them and they had made up their minds never to be hurt again; all the softness had gone from their bodies, all the radiance had fled their faces; they were hard, determined, ruthless women who would battle those who still wanted to love them in order to show how strong they were; they would talk of love and cry out for it, but they would never take it, never, never give up anything for it, because they had learned, they thought, how to be stronger than love; it was pride they had now, not love, and if their faces were jubilant, their voices gave them away, voices of women who had had to wrench out lives alone and in their pride pretend that was the way courage, not necessity, had sent them. Their voices, as they never talked of anything important, terrified of talking of anything that might actually touch them, passed their lips with a reluctant harshness, out of faces like silver masks over secret and disappointed lives.

I know those faces, Lois thought. You saw them in the pictures of those Frenchwomen who packed picnic lunches to go to the guillotinings, frozen in stiff curiosity while the head leaped from the still-pulsating body; those faces were in the friezes of Roman villas, mosaics of the warrior queens who poisoned their emperor husbands and lay down on soft beds with the chosen successors; in the Persian tapestries, the faces of those Oriental empresses who had their unwanted sons strangled by deaf mutes who told no tales, and whose legitimate ones were taught all the useless virtues—to ride, to shoot, and to tell the truth—of all those lost queens who lived by lust instead of love.

Lois looked at Iris, she looked at Frances, she could not bring herself to look at Esther. God grant me, she thought, that I can change what makes my face like theirs.

Where, she thought, looking around at them, would the face of my mother fit now?

What, she wanted to cry out, was the face of my child, whose flesh is forever dead, extracted before it was scarcely begun, and flushed down that old-fashioned sink in the Eighties?

Chapter Two

THE Lois Carolyn remembered was an awkward girl; the Lois who got out of the car and held out her hand was a woman, tense and tired, but full of authority. When Carolyn took that hand she felt the strong, firm fingers press hers; then Lois released her grasp, and—with the brief flicker of a smile—started up the path. She had said nothing, but in the intense heat of three o'clock Carolyn felt cold to the bone.

All morning Carolyn had been imagining Lois's homecoming. She saw Lois at the country club, the two of them on their way to play tennis. They would be out of practice and clumsy, hitting balls for the sheer joy of moving their bodies about, not because they cared about winning. But the Lois going up the path ahead of her was impossible to picture in shorts, running after a little white ball.

Walking with slow, measured steps, Lois reached the back door, paused, as if getting together her strength; then she opened the door quickly, and the last Carolyn saw of her was a flash of hand as she closed the door behind her. "Hello, Uncle Stewart," Carolyn heard her say, and then "Ella!" When Carolyn opened the door Lois was in Ella's arms.

For a moment Carolyn had the impression they were both crying, but it was just the way Ella held Lois; Ella had her arms around Lois as if she were holding someone in great grief.

"You got any ice tea, Iris?" Frances asked, opening the back door and going, without waiting for an answer, straight to the refrigerator. "I'm parched."

"There's some coffee from breakfast," Iris said doubtfully. "We could pour that over ice."

"Is it coffee coffee or Sanka?" Frances asked. "I can't drink real coffee, it makes my eyes puff."

"I've missed you," Lois was saying, standing back and holding Ella out, smiling, and it cut Carolyn to the heart that blind old Ella could not see the look on Lois's face.

"Is there any lemonade?" Esther said. "I like lemonade."

"Dad, are there any lemons? I thought we had some lemons. . . ."

"Never mind, Iris," Frances said. "I'll just have a glass of water."

"I'm just sick about her hair, Ella," Iris said. "She's gone and had it all cut off."

Ella raised her hand as if she were going to reach out and touch Lois's hair; then abruptly the hand dropped. She had not said a word since Lois had come in; now she opened her lips and for a moment Carolyn thought she was about to say something, but it was only a funny little gasp Ella gave.

"You want a glass of water, Lois?" Frances asked over her shoulder.

"She doesn't look like herself at all," Iris insisted.

"No, no water right now, thank you. It isn't that bad," Lois said, smiling. "It's not *terribly* short. It just doesn't hang down to my shoulders any more."

"It's too bad it can't grow back by Friday."

Mother's going to bring up the party now, Carolyn thought.

For a second Lois looked startled; then she said, "You're going to give a party. I should have known. You always give a party, Auntie. But I don't want to put you to any trouble."

"Iris adores trouble," Frances said. "Don't deprive her of her pleasure. Anyway she can't help herself. All Aries are like that. Nervous, jittery—thrive on disaster. Of course they try to gloss it over, horoscopically speaking, but I wouldn't have been born from the middle of March to the middle of April for anything in the world. I know," she said consolingly, trying to placate Iris, *"you* couldn't help it. Nowadays parents with any sense plan better than Mama did."

"Mama never planned," Iris objected heatedly. "Mama was a good Catholic. She wouldn't dream of such a thing."

"I guess you're right," Frances agreed. "Five girls. Whoever heard of such a thing? Thank god there wasn't a dowry system in this country or we'd all have been out in the cold. As it was, Mama was pretty lucky—nobody was left on her hands. I wonder what happens with that dowry business the second time round."

"You've still got a husband," Esther said.

"Other than being tactless, that remark is untrue. He has another wife, so presumably that leaves me—"

"He will answer to his Maker," Iris said. "Divorce," she began, forgetting the forbidden subject, "is worse than intermarriage."

Now we're in for it, Carolyn thought, watching Lois's face. But Lois wasn't listening. She wasn't, Carolyn thought, even in the room.

"Tell me, Iris," Frances asked, "do you happen off chance to know what year this is?"

"Know what year this is? Of course I do. Why?"

"Go ahead, tell me, just so I can make sure. I have the impression you think it's—"

"It's nineteen fifty and you know it," Iris said indignantly. "And I think you're trying to make fun of me. Nervous, jittery—I want you to know—"

Carolyn watched her father, standing next to Lois, suddenly come to life. His head snapped up; from two watery sockets his eyes peered out of deep wells of gloom, "Lois," he demanded, "how did you come?"

It took Lois a moment to answer. She has to come back here, Carolyn thought, to this town, to Springfield and all of us. "On the train, the New York Central," she said finally.

"Why?"

"Well, I suppose it was because the man in that station sold me that ticket." Lois was looking at him helplessly, as if she were trying to think of some other reasonable explanation.

"It's a rotten railroad," Carolyn heard her father say, his voice rising in anger and conviction. "Any fool knows you get better service on the Pennsy, *much* better service."

"Oh, the service was very good, Uncle Stewart, we—"

"Have you taken the Pennsy? I took the Central back in—" His voice stopped. "When was that, Iris, I made the trip to New York about those stocks that turned out—not to be worth much?" he said sadly.

"Forty-two."

"It was a disgrace," he said. "The toilet didn't even work."

"But that was during the war," Lois began. "All the railroads—"

"Why didn't you fly?" Frances inquired.

"Well, it's more expensive and anyway you know how I am about flying, I—"

"It's not really more expensive," Frances insisted. "You know, not when you consider paying for your meals and tips and all. Actually it's cheaper. Everyone says it's cheaper. And faster. You'd have done *much* better to fly."

And now, Carolyn thought, they have her just where they want her. She hasn't been in the house five minutes and they've got her on the defensive. I know just how she feels, she thought, looking at the bewilderment on Lois's face. She doesn't give a damn about either one of those railroads, they can both go bankrupt tomorrow for all she cares, but now she has to justify the fact that she took the wrong one. Next time, Carolyn thought, tell them you walked.

This house is just like purgatory. In purgatory, you don't suffer—not in any nice dramatic way; you're just caught in a permanent paralysis. In purgatory you are forever trying to explain why you took the New York Central.

"I've got to run," Carolyn said, unable to bear the scene any longer. "Let Lois come with me, Mom," she said, "just for a little while." Just, she thought, for a couple of drinks. She'll need them. "She can get a cab back in time for dinner."

"It's not up to me," Iris said, looking upset. "I want her to do what she wants. You know I try never to stand in anyone's way. I want you to feel this is your home, Lois. Do what you want, but you know Dad and Ella and I have been looking forward to your coming home. I made a special prayer in church this morning. I know you had to miss mass,

Lois, being on the train and all, but—Carolyn," she said, turning, alarmed, "Carolyn, did you go to church this morning?"

Carolyn turned away, hesitating.

"Don't tell me if you didn't, I don't want to know. But drinking, I know that's what you're going to do. I don't want Green Lawn to get the reputation for—I don't want people to say—"

"Come on," Frances said, taking Lois by the arm. "Let Lois off the hook, Iris. I'll take the blame. Blame me," she said to her sister. "Say it's all Frances's fault, she made her go. Frances is the one who gets them into trouble, but what can you expect, a *divorced* woman!"

"If you want to ruin your lives," Esther said, "I won't stand by and watch. I'm not going with you; I'm taking the tram."

"If you'd just use your car like anybody else—" Frances began.

"I'm not wasting my car, I'm not wearing it out on trips that aren't necessary."

"Well, then, take a cab," Frances said. "Live it up a little."

"I don't waste my money, that's why I've got it. You pour all that money into liquor, and what do you get? Nothing—nothing but brain deterioration. Alcohol destroys the brain tissues, everyone knows that. It *eats* them away. The streetcar goes right by my door; I don't mind changing."

"Good grief," Frances said disgustedly, "I'll bet you will take the streetcar. Well, suit yourself, you're old enough to know your own mind."

Esther was hunting around in her big handbag. "I know I have a token here somewhere," she said. "You have to *tip* cabs."

If she took Aunt Clara's money, Carolyn thought, why can't she get a little enjoyment out of it? It's not the taking it that bothers me so much as the way she hoards it. Carolyn could picture Esther climbing onto the trolley, thinking to herself, *Frances is going to end up in the poor-house, mark my words.* (It was what she always said about Frances when Frances wasn't around to defend herself.) *She's just like Organdy, the two of them were cut from the same cloth. You ask Ella, she had a time with them when they were little. Frances and Organdy were the ones who gave Mama trouble right from the start, and they turned out just the way you would have expected. Imagine Organdy going out to Denver, Colorado, the way she did and . . .*

Carolyn could picture Esther fighting her way to the center of the streetcar, pushing and shoving, knocking anyone aside who was in her way—she had a phobia about sitting in the back; she was afraid there would be an accident and she might get hurt. *In the middle you're safest,* she always said, *people in the middle in an accident don't have as many broken bones as those sitting in front and back. Let the young sit in front and back. Their bones mend easily. I can't afford to be in bed a long time, not with all the work I have to do. There isn't one of the janitors who wouldn't steal me blind behind my back.*

And Carolyn imagined her, out at her barred and bolted house, going triumphantly to a ledger and writing under the entry for the day's expenses: $0.10 for the bus in the SPENT column, and in the SAVED column $1.10 (est.) for not taking a cab.

Frances was holding the back door open. "Oh my god," she said in despair, "you've got a crow on your grass, Iris."

"Lots of people have crows. Can I help it if birds—"

"It's bad luck," Frances said decisively. " 'One crow sorrow, Two crows joy; Three crows a wedding, And four a boy.' Oh, look, we're in luck, there goes another. Two, make a wish. Come on, baby," she said, rubbing her hands together, "go for three."

Carolyn stood hesitantly at the doorway. "You win, Mom," she said at last. "When do you want me to come over and get down in that grisly cellar?"

Her mother's whole face lit up. Appeasement, Carolyn told herself. Give in and give in, one Munich of the soul after another. The harder I try to pull away, the harder she tries to hold on. A regular tug of war for our independence—no, not independence, for our right to say No.

I thought when I married Ralph I would get away from this house, but I'll never get away from it. Living with Ralph in his forty-thousand-dollar house was no more an escape than drinking in the afternoon.

What was an escape? she asked herself.

She stopped, staring down, as if Ralph were gazing up at her from the matted grass at her feet, a kind of grave of green from which Ralph sprang, Ralph waiting at home, she thought, waiting and waiting for something to happen. Does he still wonder if there's anything left to hang on to, anything left to hope for?

We cannot go a week without a fight, a big one, not just words, but the violence, she thought. There ought to be statistics on the number of times a year husbands ask their wives for forgiveness, get it, and then commit the same transgressions all over again before the week is out. That would make an interesting set of facts for Ralph. Give him some justification. You can find justification in anything if you look hard enough.

Gone, she wanted to cry out to the stunted houses all around, to Lois walking ahead of her; to Frances still and silent, making her wish, asking for another husband, a nice rich pliable husband, staring at the sky with such intensity that she must be mesmerizing god; to her mother helping Esther search through that terrible brown bag for her token. Gone, don't you see? There's nothing left. The beginning was all wrong. I married for the wrong reason.

Still, she told herself sharply, at the beginning there must have been something.

She paused and stood still, letting Lois go on ahead. A clatter of heels on the pavement: it was Frances gone back to the house. She had left her purse, she said. But the sound reminded Carolyn of the noise her own heels had made on the sidewalk one rainy night; years before inside her head she could feel Ralph's arm go round her, the way it had as they started running down the street, the rain hitting them like a barrage, thunder like cannon fire all around them; inside her head she remembered the way he laughed as he flung open the door to the car and they threw themselves into shelter. The rain was streaming down his face, he was laughing; he had looked so vulnerable at that moment and because of that so full of life.

He hadn't laughed like that since Carolyn didn't know when—at least not since the war. Sat in that chair, staring into space, Bobbie on his knee, silent, absorbed, abstracted, poring, she supposed, over his statistics. If you knew enough facts about the world, perhaps you controlled it in some way, perhaps you could make sense out of it.

But that night he had turned and put his arms around her, they had clutched each other, laughing, their mouths thrown back in laughter, loving each other the way children sometimes do.

Yes, in the beginning there had been something. A lot. A long time ago.

And now?

Carolyn saw suddenly an image of that first night of their vacation the month before, when she and Ralph found themselves face to face across the dining-room table in the Lake Champlain hotel. There was no one to lean on, neither the friends and family back in Springfield, nor the children left in care of the maid, so that Carolyn, spreading her napkin over her lap, had looked around desperately at the other tables, shocked to find that at most of them other couples were staring at each other wordlessly, the same silent look of hostility on their faces.

Picking up the menu, she had asked herself, How will I get through these two weeks?

At that moment she had looked across at Ralph, who was staring sightlessly at his own menu, and she was certain that there was nothing on earth that could prevent them from speaking that final sentence of disillusionment between lovers: You've done nothing but fail me, nothing but disappoint me.

Whenever she thought of that vacation—those terrible silent meals and that quiet, desperate moment when they went up to their room together, closed the door that shut them in together until morning, and had to face each other for all those dark long hours—she remembered one thing. It was about his making love to her. He had made love the first night; he had started to make love the second and stopped; he had not made love the rest of the two weeks.

Yes, he understood.

Carolyn walked on, watching Frances come up beside her. Frances was carrying her handbag like a retrieved battle standard, proudly and happily hoisting it over her head. It lay against the blue sky in full honor.

Lois was already sitting quietly in the car, staring out at the disfigured lawn. Was she thinking too, that cousin come home to see them all again, come back to see the same old past in all its rigid, tight regimentation, was she thinking that what she had come back to look for was that precise same thing, what she had lost here, or before, when her mother—when her mother had done that terrible thing; or was she all right, was she intact, inside?

Have you been able to break all the images and still persevere? Carolyn thought, looking at Lois. Are you whole, Lois?

Carolyn Ashwell, she said to herself, that girl who grew up in the boarding house and couldn't forget; who drove her brother from his home and couldn't forget; who wished her husband dead and had to live with him ever after, not forgetting.

"Hot," Frances said, climbing into the back of the car. "I hate heat. It wilts you, it ages you."

Lois turned and faced her. "Well, you got to wish, anyway."

"You're right. I should be grateful. You don't get a chance like that every day. But three—"

"Did you?" Lois was asking. "Did you make one too?"

Carolyn tried to decide. She supposed, without even being conscious of it, she had. A phrase rose in her mind: the peace that passeth understanding. From catechism, she thought, or the Bible, it's been so long I don't remember. Someone to respect and admire, she thought, the love that would come with that, the peace they say you find; and there came a sudden vision of what *permanent* signified, what people meant when they said "the permanent life": children of the flesh (but I have these, she thought), material things that meant more than their function (that awful house), desire and love, and the long warm words after love (had she ever had those, even in the beginning, the beginning you never lose?), a part of the world, she realized, that was marked off as her own: I am a part of this, the man and the house and the children and the love; I am this: this piece of sod held immutable for itself, but in itself something more, undying; a man put down his seeds and brought up many things, not the least of which was a beginning, but a woman only put out the tender tentacles of desire, half formed, knowing all the time that without the man nothing took hold, nothing could come into being. Without the man there was no beginning, and one of the first laws of life was that everything had to have a beginning.

Aloud she said, "A beautiful motor car, low, sleek, white, the kind people turn around to look at."

Lois was looking at her with the face she remembered from years before. Whenever she had pictured Lois, Carolyn always thought, She just missed being beautiful—and it was this face she saw now, even though the clipped hair made it seem so much older. Then Carolyn realized it wasn't the hair, it was the slant of the mouth, as if the words that came from that mouth presupposed an attitude of faith in which the person no longer had belief. Lois is afraid too, she thought, Lois isn't intact either.

"A symbol, that's what I'd ask for," Lois was saying. "Something like that tree that was at Grandmother's house, maybe the house itself. The streetcar, the stables, the chickens Grandma and Ella were always talking about. A bed upstairs where you had all your children and where the people you loved were born and died. A symbol that stands for your life. If you want a car, I want a sword," she said.

"What are you talking about?" Frances demanded. "What good would a sword do you?"

"Not just any sword, but one I read about some place. It belonged to Godfrey somebody or other, and it had this wonderful quality about it, it always warned when there was danger near."

"That sounds practical enough," Frances admitted.

"Godfrey would carry the sword in his shield and whenever there was any danger near, the sword would start clanging. In battle, when he took the sword out, it always pointed straight at the enemy, even the traitors in his own line. It made Godfrey charmed."

"Well, what happened?" Frances demanded. "If he had this great sword, what happened to him? How come I never heard of him? You'd think he would have been famous, with a thing like that."

"He took it out one day and there was blood all over it. He knew he was going to die, that this was the end of his crusade."

"Creepy," Frances said. "I'd just as soon do without a thing like that if it—I tell you, this is going to be the day of *my* death if I don't get a drink pretty soon. Listen," she went on. "I have a marvelous idea. Let's stop by Erwin's and show Lois the new house. Erwin'll be home from the golf club by the time we get there, and Helen—we can cheer old Helen up. She's going through that fifth-month feeling of being unwanted. Didn't you know Erwin's wife was having a baby, Lois? Didn't he write you? I can't understand that," she said in disgust. "You two used to be so close."

"I don't know," Lois began, thinking it was odd that, close as they had been, she didn't know something as fundamental about him as his going to be a father. Well, there were similar fundamentals like that, she thought a second later, that he didn't know about her. "Is there time? I mean, we told Iris—"

"Oh," Frances said offhandedly, "we can always call Iris up with some excuse or other. She doesn't really care whether you get back to dinner or not. God knows, she's got enough people to feed as it is. If I had to feed all those people every day, I'd be dead by now. I don't know how she does it."

Dead, Carolyn thought.

She had lied.

The wish she would have made she knew well enough. But she had not wanted to say it, even to herself.

Bring Wesley back from the dead.

A strong man to take me in his arms . . . we would go away and start all over again. A man I could love . . . a strong man I could love. . . . *By night on my bed I sought him whom my soul loveth: I sought him, but I found him not. . . . I sought him, but I could not find him; I called him, but he gave no answer. . . .*

"What's holding us up?" Frances demanded, and Carolyn began to back up, but not before her mind had time to recall an entire little set of different lines in front of her, so that she saw quite clearly, not the stripped elegance of Iris's lawn or the disemboweled bank in back of her, or the dream of deliverance of a moment before, but

> *Buffalo Bill's*
> *defunct . . .*
>> *and what i want to know is*
> *how do you like your blueeyed boy*
> *Mister Death*

Chapter Three

ERWIN's house was in one of the new developments. There were several postwar annexes, strange, broken bits of the city scattered at the outskirts, as if they were still trying to cling to Springfield, hanging back from the silent spaces beyond where the isolated farmhouses were strung out, dilapidated houses that seemed, in the never-ending wind, to be tugging at their roots and trying to flee farther west, away from the disorder and chaos of the city, in an endless battle to breathe in open air amid the wide plowed plains. Lois would never have identified the place if it hadn't been for Carolyn. As Carolyn swung the car into the first grouping of houses, she said, "You'd hardly recognize it, would you? It's where we used to play tennis. They went to work on the hills with bulldozers. It took less than a week to level all of it."

A HARMONIOUS COMMUNITY, the sign to Twin Acres said as they turned in, IS A HAPPY AND INTEGRATED ONE. Lois stared at the sign. Integrated? Not the way you mean, she thought; their kind of integrated means sticking together, holding off outsiders, that's what their kind of integrated means.

Don't be so quick to jump to conclusions, she rebuked herself. You're always ready to take offense. Not for myself, she thought, for Neal; Neal, whose parents wanted to hide him behind an ordinary name, an everyday Anglo-Saxon name, but whose eyes gave away the deception, those lovely, lovely eyes.

Twin Acres, Frances let them know, was the deluxe development.

They start at thirty thousand, she said. It wasn't like those little Cape Cods down the road where they let just *any*body in.

There was no denying the proportions of the houses, but size itself could not overcome the razed look all around. The bulldozers had plowed the earth down to uniform compactness: there was not a hill, not a tree, not even a bristling bush or oversized weed in the whole area; the houses hugged the flat earth like a camouflaged communications center. Waiting for an enemy attack, Lois thought: the enemy, the unknown; the enemy, the outsider.

The car swung down Hollyhock Lane, made a left turn at Dahlia Drive, forked into Myrtle Mile. Erwin and Helen were at the end, facing Lilac Lane, Frances said.

The house, set on a quarter-acre, was squat, held together by oversized toothpicks, thin stilts of black wood that marked off the breezeway, the carport, an ell that Frances identified as the "utility room." There was a big back yard, strung about with high wire, like a stockade, the majority of it covered in concrete, at one side an enormous German shepherd bounding against the fence. Carolyn swung the Buick into the driveway, and the dog seemed to take leave of his senses; he was frothing at the mouth and barking hysterically.

"The Captain," Frances said. "He cost a hundred and fifty dollars, that little dog"—and she had an awed tone to her voice, as if any animal who could command such a price deserved her uncritical respect. "But he's a little temperamental," she said after a pause. "I wouldn't go too close to him if I were you."

Carolyn pulled up; the car stopped with a shudder. I've got to make more of an effort, Lois told herself, staring out at the spindly tufts and wizened clumps of grass. That dog, that grass, those terrible stilts . . .

"They're encouraging it," Frances said, stepping out onto a dying patch of green that was lawn. "There's some new theory. You have to love things to get them to grow. You sit around loving your grass and it gains confidence and starts growing. This man who sold Erwin the grass told me about it. According to him, Erwin's grass came with an inferiority complex. So it's up to Erwin to rehabilitate it—at least that's what he said *after* he'd put it in and been paid." She looked up at them. "I wish people felt the same about me. I could use a little rehabilitation."

They were all out of the car now, staring at the lawn, self-consciously standing together at the bottom of the front path. No sidewalks here, Lois thought, looking around; that would spoil the effect. What's the matter with you? she asked herself angrily.

She thought of all the girls Erwin had gone around with, all those beautiful, self-assured girls who had made her so jealous. They were always tall and dark and always, always laughing. She thought of an evening when she and Erwin were still young, she had been staying with Frances, it was right after she had come to Springfield, Erwin couldn't have been more than fifteen or sixteen, and the two of them had gone down the street where a bunch of Erwin's friends were congregated— or rather he had gone and she had tagged after—it was late spring, the evenings held the light, and six or seven boys and girls stood around talking and laughing, while she stayed on the edge, knowing she was too young for them, but refusing to go away, happy just to be able to listen. Erwin had only recently started smoking; he took out a cigarette majestically and anchored it against his teeth, struggling to get a light. The girls had watched him in fascination.

When he brought the cigarette and match together, he had some trouble getting the cigarette going, and in his nervousness he threw the match away without blowing it out. It had landed in one of the girls' hair—Nancy, that had been the one—and she had laughed. While they were all frantically beating at her head with their hands, she kept right on laughing, looking at Erwin all the time as if he had done it just to single her out from the others.

She knew just what Helen was going to be like: tall and dark and dramatic, full of the splendid sense of her own infallibility. A small New England accent, exquisite manners, pale pink nail polish and lipstick; and in the background the radio-phonograph on with something classical and slightly obscure. A nice rich Smith girl.

She probably won't even be Catholic, Lois told herself. No, Erwin would marry a Catholic. He wasn't religious but he was superstitious. Nobody discriminated much against the Catholics any more. Not here, at the deluxe-development level.

All right, she told herself, so they don't let Jews in. Is that any reason to— You don't even know they don't let them in, maybe they do. It was only at the country-club level people discriminated, wasn't it?

Why do they discriminate at the level of playing tennis and swimming? It isn't that, she answered herself, it's the dancing. People in such close contact are apt to want to get closer. They might even want to marry. Divorce is worse than intermarriage, that's what Iris had said. But Iris never thought about Jews at all; to Iris intermarriage meant with a Protestant. That was bad enough, but a Jew, a Jew . . .

Neal, Lois thought, all our effort ought to have turned some kind of wheel. Not *our,* she reminded herself. Not *we.* He never said *we,* he never said *our;* it was always *I* and *mine, you* and *yours.*

Inside her head he put his arms around her and held her close, his white, soft, sweet flesh pressing up against hers—whenever she thought of him, she thought of that beautifully white flesh and how its touch had the effect of miraculously moving her, that fine fabric of flesh she wanted to be a part of and never was.

He had seemed so strong at first, big and tall and so in possession of himself, a marvel of self-assurance. Only later had she divined the fragility that was there. The least thing wounded him; she always had to be careful. His Jewishness—that, yes, but that wasn't just it; more, something about his whole masculinity. It was always on trial. He had an obsession he wasn't big, like other men. He was ashamed—had, Lois had come to feel, connected it with his religion, the whole rite of circumcision: a punishment. Once he had told her a story about some girl who had let him go to bed with her, but then wouldn't let him make love to her. She took me in her hand, he said with a terrible ache in his voice. I couldn't go inside her, I was only good enough for teasing. *Neal,* Lois had begun, frightened at the cruelty that went, like a swift shadow, across his face and then disappeared, leaving his face blank and abandoned, a derelict in the emotional world of closeness, so that she had wanted to sit up and cry out to him, It's all right, it's all right, my love—and she got no farther than *Neal* when he said abruptly, angrily, "Don't give me that stuff about being afraid. Her *hand,"* he said after a moment and looked down at himself, measuring. It was true, too: he was small. Most of us fear the things we should.

Maybe you could be Jewish and live here, maybe you couldn't, but you couldn't be colored, of that there was no question. You could be colored and work here, you could live *in,* but you couldn't *live* here. The little lessons of life, Lois thought, as Frances lifted her head, her throat swelled, and a tremulous pitch of sound pierced the air. "Yoo-hoo," she was calling. "Yoohoooooo. Anybody home?"

The dog clawed the fence and set up a series of howlings that must have reached the ends of Twin Acres, but the door remained closed, the house sat, squat and determined, as if no one had ever penetrated its geometric defenses.

"She's probably lying down," Frances said uncertainly. "You know how tired you get when you—"

"I'll ring," Carolyn said and pressed the bell. Chimes sounded.

"That hundred-and-fifty-dollar dog is going to have a heart attack if he keeps that up."

"I'll try once more," Carolyn suggested. "And then we can run over to my place and—"

The door was opening and Frances was saying all in one breath, "Honey, this is Lois, we thought we'd just drop in and say hello, Lois has been dying to meet you, haven't you, Lois, is Erwin home, honey, we don't want to intrude, we just thought we'd drop in, I know Erwin always plays golf on Sunday, but he's usually home now and anyway I wanted to see how you were, how are you?"

"I'm expecting him any minute," Helen said in a low, formal voice, looking past Frances, staring straight into Lois's eyes, a thin, pale blonde in an expensive outfit, obviously pregnant, standing there with her hair neatly tucked behind her small ears, her hands clasped in front, her make-up on to just the right degree, quiet and contained and poised, carefully put together, utterly the opposite of what Lois had expected, looking so pale, almost transparent, as if only the shadow of the body were there, the substance was off some place else. Where? Lois asked herself. The mind, she thought. That girl's all mind; her body must bother her terribly.

Smith all over her. The blouse, so quietly expensive, cut in good, elegant, simple lines, and the earrings—little small seed pearls. The ears were pierced; that meant there was family jewelry, old-fashioned good earrings that you needed pierced ears to wear. Money, Lois thought, that's what Aunt Fran was trying to tell me. Not just money, lots of money. Oh god, she thought.

Stop it, she told herself.

Helen stood in the doorway, holding the screen door, not asking them in, but not stopping Frances as she pushed past, and Lois found herself following, on the edge of the living room. There was a Stamos, a big blunt black and green Stamos on one wall, over the pale green carpeting. The little piece of sculpture on a block atop the sideboard stopped her: a small David Smith puritan sitting on the sideboard surveying the world with hollow, unhappy eyes. Not a print in the place. She stared unbelievingly at the little drawing on the wall. A real honest-to-god Picasso. And a late one: '48, it said under the signature; that meant a trip to Europe and the rest, money to buy the things you wanted. She looked at Helen again. In the doorway she had seemed an elegant nonentity, one of those girls who went on the college's Junior Year Tour and never saw anything past the Impressionists.

"That's a beautiful Stamos."

"You like it?" Helen asked in her cool, cultivated voice. "It was a wedding present. From my father. He said if there was one thing he couldn't stand it was reproductions, even on somebody else's walls." She looked at the painting. "I think it goes very well with the rug. But of course the interesting thing is that." She waved her hand at the little line drawing. "That's my pet."

A German shepherd in back, Lois thought, and a little pet of a Picasso in front. And good gold earrings in your ears. No, she decided, they do not let Jews in here. Suddenly, unaccountably, in this big, beautiful room she wanted to sit down and weep.

"I'll get you a drink," Helen began. In the archway into the dining room she paused. "I meant to ask you, Frances. Did you get my reading?" The sarcasm was so thinly veiled that Lois started, turned instinctively to see the look on Frances's face. It was bland and happy.

"Estrella's doing it, but it'll take a day or two. It's her busy season. Everybody wants to know when it's favorable to go on vacation."

"I'd like to get away myself," Helen said. "But then you know how close we came—Paris," she said, her voice trailing off. "I had my heart set on Paris and now—well, maybe later, maybe—" The voice died, the hands went up and clasped each other. Helen stood in the middle of that doorway like a deserted Madonna, hands pressed together in supplication. Botticelli, Lois thought: no, not Botticelli, van Eyck: Giovanni Arnolfini and his wife, that pale, bloodless woman, the white cowl over her head, that heavy green dress pulling her down, the enormous stomach, distended, the little hand, hovering on it, as if feeling for life, reassuring the fetus within, those sleeves of ermine trailing shoulder to knee, and the little dog, with more life than his master or mistress, with so much more life than Giovanni Arnolfini or his wife would ever know, standing at the bottom of the picture, seemingly puzzled by what he was doing there.

Dog, Lois thought, a dog. Was that what had made the connection? No, the dog in the van Eyck picture was small; a spitz, she seemed to remember. It was something else about the comparison: the skin, the pale skin, that skin that never shone from the wondrousness of touch, that never took on the assurance that radiates from a woman who knows what it is to love.

Neal's beautiful, radiant skin. His Jewish skin. Stop it, Lois told herself, just stop it.

"I've heard so much about you from Erwin," Helen said to her from the doorway.

Lois watched as the hands raised themselves, parted, one stole up to the hair, smoothing. There is life inside, Lois thought, a child, inside.

"He tells me"—a smile, small, satisfied, slightly superior—"you're the smart one in the family, the intellectual."

"It was the only label left," Lois said. "The others had all been passed out— The Pretty One, The One with the Big House, The Rich One, The Difficult One—" She paused, and then she said slowly and deliberately, "The Thief. The Dead One."

For a moment there was absolute silence; not one of them moved, though Lois thought she heard Frances catch her breath, there was the sharp sucking noise of someone frightened and excited. Lois opened her purse and took out a cigarette, fighting not to look away. All right, go ahead, she thought, staring at Helen, say something now.

"Well, actually, you know, it wasn't," Helen said with a little cold laugh. "I think there's The Unmarried One, I think that's still left." Helen waited, letting the words sink in; then she added, as if she had meant to append the sentence all the time, were only working it out in her mind, "Or is that what they call Eileen?"

The voice, like the face, had been bloodless, the words had to sink in before Lois felt the sting. Oh, Lois thought, very Smith, and started to say, I don't know what they call Eileen, when Carolyn spoke up from the opposite side of the room. "Oh no, nobody ever calls Eileen that. They always call Eileen The Sweet One." So Carolyn doesn't like her either, Lois thought. Why not?

Instinct, she thought, the way it is with me.

It wasn't instinct with you at all. It was seeing her so big that way, so complacent, standing in the door, in the dark shadows looking at your slender waist and smiling that secret, pleased little smile. Why did pregnant women always have that damn superior secret smile?

You know damn well why, she told herself.

The sound of a car came clearly and distinctly from outside. The dog started to bark, but not so frantically. "That must be Erwin," Frances said quickly, with apparent relief.

Every time we get together it turns into a contest, she had said to Erwin the last time she had seen him, and I'm beginning to feel unequal to the fight. And he said? He said, It isn't a fight, Lois, it's— His voice had stopped. It's what? she had asked. I don't know, he said, looking down, something else, just not a fight.

He had been in France when the war finished and he had got some kind of scholarship and stayed over there, something the Army gave. She had understood it once, but it was complicated and now she couldn't remember the details. It was hard to think of Erwin studying economics at one of the most famous schools in Europe, but he had, stayed two years studying, and he had come back hard, lean, tanned, handsomer than ever, an anachronism in Springfield. He looked as if he ought to be on the West Coast going from casting office to casting office, with time off for swims and plenty of parties. In a white dinner jacket he would have been something to behold.

Iris had given a welcome-home party, and Esther had been so excited that she had sung the wrong song to welcome him back. "From the halls of Montezuma," she had shrieked off-tune as he came in the front door of Sans Souci, and no one could persuade her, not even Erwin, who certainly should have known, that he had been in the infantry. It had been a painful party all around.

Erwin was drunk on a bottle someone had outside, Iris crying and carrying on, she herself dully sober, seeing everyone with too clear eyes. Erwin had taken her aside and told her he had something he wanted to say to her. In private, he kept repeating with the drunken persistence which makes a phrase or a word the key to what is lost in repetitions, stammerings, hesitations.

They had gone at last to a little bar over on the west side of town, and he had done the most incredible thing of all. He had lost all his composure; it seemed to her that even his tan was fading as he hung on the edge of the booth, blurting out one painful sentence after another, unloosing them as fast as his stumbling tongue could force them through. "I didn't want to come back to this place," he said. "How'd you like to live in France and then come back here? Did you see her, did you?" And it took Lois a moment to realize he meant his mother, it was Frances he was talking about. "She had all that jewelry all over her. She was covered with baubles. She looked like a goddam dime store. And all she ever talks about is taking her to a movie. Let's go to a movie: that's all I ever hear. I'm not taking a whole dime store to the movies.

"I never wanted to come back, not here. But now that I'm here, I'm going to make good. I'm telling you that, I'm going to make good. You just watch and see. In ten years I'll be on top."

At the car they had had an argument over who was going to drive. He

D

kept insisting that it was his car and he would be goddamned if anyone else was going to drive it. She had pleaded and waited and, finally, out of patience, started to get out. "You're not getting out," he had said in an ugly voice. "You came with me, you're going home with me."

"Listen, Erwin, you know how Iris is—"

"I don't give a damn about Iris."

"Well, I do. I have to. I live there. And you're hurting my arm. Now let me go and—"

He yanked her around so that she had to face him. She saw that for this one instant he was quite himself. In spite of all the drinks, he knew what he was doing. It was that brief instant of illumination when the alcohol lifts and the mind clears itself, the truth is forced out before the alcoholic film descends again and everything is blotted out in self-pity. "I love you," he said, then an instant later was sobbing against her shoulder, "And I'm going to make it, I tell you, no matter what happens, I'm coming out on top. You just remember I told you that. You remember and watch. . . ." He had gone on and on, but she had managed to pry herself loose, to stumble out of the car. For over a year she had avoided seeing him alone. Then, just before she went to New York, they had gone out together—constrained, embarrassed, sensitive to what had happened that last night they had been alone together. At the end—it was at the end she had said that about the contest, about not wanting to turn their relationship into a battle.

Why, if they cared for each other, must they hurt each other?

Now he stood in the doorway, tall, blond, a little heavier, his golf jacket slung over his shoulder. He looked around at them for a moment in stupefaction, staring from one to the other, and they stared back at him. Like something in an oldtime movie, she thought. Under the screen the dialogue would be written out in those white letters on the black: *What a surprise!* Then the people would suddenly speed up, rushing around the screen in two-four time, hugging one another, their mouths moving a mile a minute, and there wouldn't be any dialogue at all, just exclamation points on the black.

Yes, it is like an exclamation point, she thought.

Suddenly he was smiling, coming across the room and smiling at her with an expression of satisfaction. He was remembering not the end of that terrible evening together but only his prophecy, that he was "going to make it." He had made it and he was looking at her for approval for the fine house, the fine wife, the fine dog, the fine pictures on the wall. The next moment he pounded her on the back so violently that she nearly cried out. "You're looking great, Lois, just great," he said. "God, it's good to see you. I feel golden," he said. "Let's have a party. Helen, get on the phone and let's get some people over and have a real celebration."

Helen smiled, as if she knew exactly what it was Lois felt, as if she could read right down into her mind and see everything that was there. Helen stood at the phone, dialing, turning her little waxen head from side to side, saying nothing, simply smiling.

"Let's have a drink right now," Erwin said.

"Erwin's cousin is here," Helen was saying into the phone. "I know you'll want to meet her. Come on over and—" She looked up, smiling into Lois's face. "Just a minute," Helen said as she took the phone away from her ear. Looking straight at Lois, she said, "Frances, would you mind doing me a favor? Would you mind showing Lois around the house while I'm on the telephone?" Without waiting for an answer, she put the phone back and said, "So come on over right away, Erwin's getting the ice out now."

First there was the tour of the house, and then drinks, all of them toasting her return, and then Helen said, smiling—always smiling— would Lois mind helping her out in the kitchen, with the glasses and the cocktail things, she was just dying to talk to her; when Lois came back, Frances was asking for another drink, and when she tried to go out to get a chance to talk with Erwin alone, Helen said she had to see the dog. After that people started arriving, more drinks had to be made, introductions seemed interminable, she found herself crowded into a corner with Frances, the rest of the guests holding up an assortment of never-ending glasses which Erwin went back and forth to fill.

All Erwin's friends wanted something special to drink—vodka and orange juice, just a little gin on the rocks and a dash of bitters, a dry Manhattan or a whisky sour or a Singapore sling—no one drank plain old martinis except Frances and herself. There didn't seem to be any prospect of getting Erwin alone for even a moment.

"If I don't find a husband this year," Frances confided over her cocktail, the fourth that Lois had counted, "I'm really going to get discouraged. Just a nice reasonably rich husband. One who travels a lot and is over the menopause," she specified. "I don't want to be bothered with too much of *that*. Tell me," she said, fixing Lois with a sincere, puzzled look, "where do you think my best chance of finding one is? It's more expensive than you'd think. There's a whole organized thievery in this country and it's called the beauty business. That's straight from the horse's mouth," she said, tapping her glass.

"I don't know," Lois answered, trying to work up some interest. She was worried about Iris. She had phoned a few minutes before and Iris hadn't been easy to deal with.

"Don't worry about me," Iris had said in that cold put-upon voice that meant just the opposite. "Just enjoy yourself, have a good time"—and there had been that little grief-stricken catch at the end, which meant that she never had a good time, she never had a chance to enjoy herself.

Well, Iris would have to wait; the pressing problem was Frances. Lois had been surprised that Frances wanted a martini—she had assumed Frances would want something exotic and impossible—but then Frances leaned over and said, "I owe it to myself; gin gets into your bloodstream quicker," and flashed her such a winning smile that Lois had found herself clutching the arm of her chair and hanging on.

If only I could get some food down her, Lois thought helplessly. Half an hour before, someone had called up a delicatessen for chicken and assorted sandwiches, but there was no knowing how long it would take for the order to get out into this wilderness. In the meantime—

Lois stood up abruptly, saying, "Listen, Aunt Fran, I'll be right back. You sit right there." Seeing the determined look on Frances's face, she gave the only excuse she thought would make sense. "I want to get another drink. You wait right there."

Pushing her way through a crowd of people, she caught sight of Carolyn sitting on the end of the couch. In all that noise and confusion Carolyn was quietly reading a book, one hand slowly turning the pages, the other holding a highball.

"Carolyn," Lois said urgently, "we've got to do something about Frances, she's—"

"Frances always gets that way," Carolyn said calmly, putting the book face down on the davenport, open at her place.

"But she's going to make a spectacle of herself. You don't want her to do that in front of all these people, do you?" She debated for an instant whether or not to say "in front of Helen," then decided that there was no reason for her to hold back with Carolyn. "Not in front of Helen."

"I suppose I could run her home. If she'd go. Frankly, I don't think wild horses could drag her away at this point. She'd be too afraid of missing something." Carolyn took a puff from a cigarette. "Look, there she goes now."

Across the room Frances stood up with a bright, fluttering smile, clutching at the nearest man to her. She said something to him, and Lois caught the look of disbelief as he turned around and stared down at her.

She started to get to her feet, but Carolyn put out a hand and caught her. "Leave her alone," she said. "She's not at the bad stage yet. Wait until later when the games start."

"Games? What games?"

"On top of old Smoky," someone sang ebulliently, *"all covered with snow . . ."*

All around voices joined in. *"I lost my true lover . . . acourtin' too slow . . ."*

Frances was standing on a chair, shouting something unintelligible. A group of singers gathered round, chorusing up at her. *"For courtin's a sorrow and . . ."*

"First they drink and then they sing and last they play games. It's a kind of ritual. You start drinking and then you start singing and finally you finish by playing games."

"Are you joking? I'm—"

"Turn the phonograph on, drown them out. . . ."

"Put on something South American. . . ."

"Who knows how to rumba anyway? Let's have something slow and . . ."

"On top of old Smoky . . ."

"Hey, Erwin, how do you turn this thing on anyway? The go button doesn't make anything go."

"Erwin, hey, Er, over here, you're all out of vermouth. And your mother wants another martini."

"Coming, coming," her cousin answered, threading his way through the crowd.

"He isn't going to give it to her?" Lois asked incredulously.

"You want them to like you, you play their games. It's a party; nobody wants to be a wet blanket at a party."

"I don't know any of these people. I'll probably never see them again in my life. The only person I care about is—"

"—is Erwin, and he plays games. He *loves* games. Monopoly, parchesi, chess, bridge, canasta, golf, tennis, poker, the lot of them. They always start their parties upstairs, but sooner or later we all wind up downstairs where there is less light and more dark corners and where they have that cute little bar they put in last spring." Carolyn smashed her cigarette out in the ashtray. "I loved that remark about The Thief and—" She didn't say "—and the Dead One," just as Lois knew she wouldn't.

Lois put her glass down on the table and looked across at Carolyn. She was aware that her three martinis had caught up with her. She was angry and outraged, and there was nowhere to focus her emotion. "What's the matter with you, Carolyn? Frances has lots of faults, but she's always been good to us, you know she has. I think we ought to—"

"I have tried," Carolyn said, and Lois saw she meant it. "I even had her out to the house once when Ralph had a nice man coming over that I thought would—you know, be suitable for her. Well, it was a terrible mistake. The minute he said he was a widower she was practically all over him. Then she started calling him 'that darling man.' At dinner she leaned over and speared his asparagus right off his plate and said, 'He doesn't mind if we share, I know he doesn't, he's such a darling man,' and I never heard anybody put such a load of meaning in any word in my life as she put in *share*. The long and short of it was that we never saw that darling man again and Ralph lost a good account."

"Two drinks and the Whites are at it," someone said, laughing, near her.

Lois turned. The Whites had been one of the first couples to come, the man strangely like his name, his hair so light he looked almost like an albino, his small blue faded eyes shaded by white lashes, smiling to right and left, looking at no one. The wife was big and pregnant, as so many of the wives in the room were pregnant, and all the wife had said was, "Keep him away from the bourbon." She hadn't said it amusedly or resignedly, but with malevolence.

"If you would just keep your hands off me," his wife was saying now, almost in tears. "Every time you put your hands on me—look at me, just look at me. I told you three was enough and now—"

"What do you expect me to do with it," he said, trying for a laugh, shrinking back as she advanced on him, "put it in the freezer?"

"The Catholic crowd," Carolyn said, as the Whites suddenly disappeared from sight, their voices still audible after their faces had disappeared. "But the doctor told you . . ." "I can't help it if I love you. . . ." "The doctor *told* you . . ."

Carolyn had picked up her book again. It lay in her lap tenderly, the pages softly fanning the summer night, light wings of small suspended birds. She seals herself off in a walled world of words, Lois thought, the way I try to sometimes.

A feeling of sadness and longing,
That is not akin to pain,

And resembles sorrow only
As the mist resembles the rain.

Come, read to me some poem,
Some simple and heartfelt lay,
That shall soothe this restless feeling,
And banish the thoughts of day.

Whittier? No, Longfellow. They always taught children Longfellow. Longfellow was safe. It must be Longfellow.

". . . rings the cash register, it registers with me," she heard, and someone laughing, laughing in a forced way, the way people do who have heard a joke time and again and are only laughing out of politeness.

It was Erwin who had used that phrase. She knew without looking. He had said it to her, he had said it to Carolyn, he had even said it to his mother. Slapping someone on the back: "If it rings the cash register, it registers with me"—his voice came to her now from across the room and she winced, just as she had winced at his other favorite expression, "I'll buy that." Could you go through life buying what you wanted? Or stealing? she thought a moment later. Wasn't there another kind of payment which had to do with a different medium of exchange?

But he understood more than money—giving her the hundred-dollar bill had been giving more than money. Then how could he talk like that? How could he say the things she had heard him say this evening?

That business about the franchise, for instance. Awful, just awful. He had the Springfield franchise for one of the lower-priced cars. (Everything was a euphemism, it seemed. Nothing was cheap, the laundry was the utility room, it was the deluxe development.) There was a contest, "to beef up sales," he had explained. The company had offered a trip to Paris for two, all expenses paid for ten days. You had to sell the most cars in the Midwest territory. "It was in the bag," Erwin had said, laughing. "Helen had even started buying clothes. And then you know what?" he demanded. "I lost by two cars."

I lost by two cars: it was the sort of statement which stopped her, like, "If it rings the cash register, it registers with me."

I came in second, or I was a close second, or I almost made it—any number of ways of putting it came to her, but "I lost by two cars" was irretrievably Springfield. It went back to the days when you computed in hogs and cows, when you weighed your wealth in produce and poultry, livestock and grain.

She had looked at Erwin closely at that moment. He stood grinning ruefully at the man to whom he had told the story, laughing a little at his own disappointment. The man was worrying the loss over in his mind. From the expression on his face, Lois could tell he was plainly searching for some expression of condolence. "Hell, if you'd known," he said at last, "you could have ordered a couple yourself. You'd have made it up on the trip."

I loved him best of everyone in the family. I used to follow him around, begging him to love me. No matter what he did, it was never wrong. He could do no wrong because I believed in him.

Everybody liked him. Everybody still does, she thought, looking around. No, these people liked him. But Carolyn? "He *loves* games." No, Carolyn did not like him.

I never really believed in Neal, not the way I believed in Erwin. Erwin was the only person I ever felt that way about. Was it because I was so young then, I couldn't really see? Can we only worship what we can't see? When we get older, don't we have heroes?

"You having a good time? You getting along all right?"

It was Helen. Helen, she wanted to ask her, do you believe in him? Believe in him, Helen, she wanted to cry out.

A phrase came across her mind as she watched the smile on Helen's face, *She married beneath her,* as she herself said aloud, "It's fabulous," and knew her words had the same faked joviality all the other voices in the room seemed to carry.

"I'm so glad. I want you to feel at home here. Erwin was always so fond of you."

Was?

"You want another drink. Let me get you another drink."

"No, I'm fine, thanks. Really."

I've had too much to drink already, she told herself, or not near enough, watching Frances emerge from the center of the room and screech above all the noise, "The cards, someone get the cards, I'm going to read the cards."

A great cry went up. "The games, it's time for the games," people were shouting on all sides of her. "Let's go down cellar and start the games."

In the pandemonium someone jarred the table, and what was left of Carolyn's drink upset. Carolyn looked up, put down the book she had been reading, took a crumpled napkin from near the cheese, and wiped it up. The man who had nearly ruined Helen's table paid no attention; using his elbows like bayonets, he was cutting his way to the front of the line to the basement. But he met, Lois saw, his match in Frances.

Frances took one short look at him as he shoved her aside. Without hesitating, she brought her spiked heel down on his instep. He let out a pained yelp, and Frances surged past him, waving her cocktail aloft victoriously.

"Coming?" Carolyn asked.

"Is there a choice?"

"Is there ever?"

"Well, you know what your mother always used to say. Better suffer a great evil than do a little one."

"She always says something."

They were pushed to the top of the stairs. The passageway down was painted red and black, in wide stripes, and there were little signs all over the wall.

GRAPE JUICE KILLS MORE THAN GRAPE SHOT

ABANDON HOPE, ALL YE WHO ENTER HERE

THE MORE ACQUAINTANCES THE MORE DANGER

WHO KEEPS COMPANY WITH A WOLF WILL LEARN TO HOWL

THOUGH YOU GET THE BEST OF WHISKY,

IT WILL GET THE BEST OF YOU

YOU KNOW WHAT THEY CALL THOSE WHO GET CARELESS: PARENTS

"I'm giving them one next Christmas: MALT DOES MORE THAN MILTON CAN TO JUSTIFY GOD'S WAYS TO MAN," Carolyn said.

"Hey, Lois," Erwin shouted from the bottom of the stairs. "Mom wants to do you first. She says you're the guest of honor, you should be first."

Holding her glass very carefully, Lois went down. Frances was already at the bar. In back there was a big wine keg; where the wine normally went in there was a colored electric light bulb. Someone was fiddling with the knobs, trying to make it work. "You turn it the other way, the *other* way," Erwin kept insisting.

The bar was well stocked with glasses; marching along the top, a row of enormous beer steins. With music boxes? Lois wondered. There was row after row of liquor and liqueurs, a refrigerator at one side from which Whitey was helping himself to beer. He's going to drink beer on top of all that bourbon, Lois thought, and then wondered what difference it made to *her*. It is his wife who ought to be worried. *Was,* she corrected herself.

Frances was silhouetted in the dim lights, two converted running lamps, the kind you used on a sailboat when you were in passage at night, red for port, green for starboard. "Where did you put the cards?" she was shouting over her shoulder to Erwin. "I thought you always left them by the sink."

"They're right there, next to the ice pick," Erwin shouted back. "Get Whitey to light a match. You'll see them. Look in back, maybe behind the dish towels."

"Here they are, I've got them. Where's Lois? I want Lois!"

"I'm right here, Aunt Fran."

"You sit down here, next to me, on this stool. Watch out for the runners," she warned. "That dog has chewed them all and you'll catch your hose if you're not careful."

"I'm not wearing any," Lois said.

"You're not? I could have sworn—say, is that some kind of new leg make-up?" Frances handed the cards to Lois. "I have a little trouble keeping the system straight," she confessed. "But I always say it's the general impression that counts, not just those finicky little particulars." She took a puff of her cigarette, laid it down in the ashtray that had a slogan running around the edge to the effect that wine, women, and song do this life prolong, and then took a gulp of her drink.

"The Seven Packs, that's the one I use. You make a wish—only don't tell. If you tell, it's no good. It upsets the cards." She looked at Lois. "Dark hair, dark eyes—the queen of spades is your court card, I guess." She drank a part of her drink, truculent. "Have you made your wish?"

"I'm trying to think how to frame it," Lois said, trying not to smile. Frances was *so* serious.

She watched Frances ruffle through the pack, discarding the twos, threes, fours, fives, and sixes. Frances counted, half aloud, until she was finished. "I have thirty-two the way I'm supposed to," she said. "At least I think I do. Just to be sure, you count." She handed the cards to Lois.

Lois counted. "Thirty-two," she agreed.

"Now, shuffle and cut once." Frances finished her drink, leaned across the dimly lighted bar, and shouted to Whitey, who was standing next to Erwin talking over his problems. Lois heard the end of a phrase; she wasn't certain but she thought he said "conception complex." Were even the Catholics in analysis these days?

"Light on the vermouth, Whitey," Frances called. "Just wave the cork over the gin."

When her newly filled glass was in front of her, Frances picked up the pack with professional adroitness and dealt it out, six cards in a semicircle turned down, the seventh in the center turned up. She distributed the cards evenly in each pile, with four left over, which she discarded. Then she gave her attention to the first pack, turning it over and spreading it out like a fan.

"The first pack here represents yourself," she explained, picking up the cards and turning them over. A frown rippled the make-up of her forehead. "H'm," she said, staring off into space. "Well, I don't know," she said, pointing down to the cards, "it says here a man is going to follow you to Springfield, a man you don't expect at all."

Lois gasped. She stared down. There were only four ordinary cards staring back up at her.

"A man you know real well," Frances said. She scratched her head. "Of course I get things all balled up once in a while."

Don't say anything, Lois cautioned herself.

Without waiting for an answer, Frances took a swig of her martini and turned over the next stack of cards. "Oh-oh," she said, seeing the ace of spades on top, the spade symbol inverted. "That's the death card. This comes In Your House. Death, with the jack of hearts—death in connection with family. I don't like *that*"—and Frances sounded genuinely moved. "But I don't get it," she went on. "Why would the eight of clubs turn up *here*? I mean, that's supposed to signify pleasure in society, but I can't imagine whooping it up at parties when there's a death in the family, can you? And it's plain as day, a death in your house, parties, social gatherings. But nobody's died in our family. I just don't get it."

The death card in connection with family . . . the jack of hearts, someone you care about . . . the death card, someone you care about . . . the death card, In Your House. And Frances saying, But nobody's died in our family.

Frances was bent over the cards, beads of perspiration jeweling her forehead. "And now," Frances went on, turning over the third pile of cards, "What You Expect. A trip, a trip—the ten of spades means a trip by land. It's here again, someone coming to you, someone you don't expect. Have you got a secret beau, Lois, one you've been hiding from us? Someone who's coming to meet the family?"

The death card, Lois thought. Someone you care about. The death card in your house . . . someone coming to see you . . . Lois stared at Frances. No, it wasn't Neal who would be coming. Neal would never come. He wouldn't even *think* about coming. Who?

Stu, she thought suddenly, Stu's coming home. That feeling you had on the stairs, when he took your hand.

Don't be foolish, she told herself. It's only a game. Even when Frances is sober, she isn't accurate, and after all that gin—

"And now," Frances went on, "What You Didn't Expect." The cards were all black. Even to Lois that looked ominous. Frances was looking at her with a strange, puzzled expression, as if she were genuinely worried. "A dark man has failed you. You've had a great disappointment, a terrible loss, one you'll never get over. A man, a dark man, has made you terribly unhappy, has been the cause of a great loss."

The death card in your house . . . a dark man has failed you. A great loss . . . one you'll never get over . . . failed you . . . death . . . in your house . . . Lois stood up. "Maybe we should finish some other time," she said quickly, pushing the bar stool between Frances and herself. She didn't want to hear any more. I won't faint, she thought, I won't. *Stop it,* she said to herself.

"I'll hurry," Frances promised. "Don't you want to know about your wish, about what you wished?"

No, Lois wanted to shout, no, I don't, but already Frances had finished off her martini, was turning over the next pack. "A Great Surprise," she said. "Your wish is across water."

She held up the eight of hearts and the ten of clubs. "Across water is a dark man," she went on, pulling out the king of clubs. "That man will play an important part in your life. This is getting interesting. Here." She turned over the last unexposed pack. "This Is What Is Sure to Come True. Lois," Frances said in astonishment, looking up at her, "you're going to marry a man across the water and live in a huge house, a man with a title. Look here," she went on excitedly, throwing the four "wish" cards across the table, "here's the nine of hearts, the wish card, and it's in your wish house. Oh, Lois, you're going to have everything you ever wanted or dreamed," Frances said breathlessly, while Lois thought, You're crazy, we're all crazy, it's only a card game, you don't know what you're talking about.

"But, honey," Frances was saying, "just look, it's the ace of diamonds —a wedding, honey, and if he doesn't marry you at least he'll give you lots of jewelry. Oh, it's too good to be true. I wish this were *my* fortune. You're young, you've got plenty of time, but I—"

"What's this queen of hearts?" Lois asked, looking at the last card.

"Oh, that, some other woman, only I don't think it's very important. You'll have lots of money and live in a big house, be rolling in diamonds, you'll be a countess or something—oh, Lois," Frances said, throwing her arms around her, "I'm so happy for you. I can't think of anyone I'd rather see have it. This calls for another drink. Landlord," she shouted at Erwin, half laughing, half crying, "fill the loving cups. Lois is going to marry royalty."

Chapter Four

IN A ditch, his hands tied behind his back, the wire around the wrists. Half his head blown away. And the body almost black.

Ralph shifted his little boy's weight farther back on his thighs; his legs were going to sleep. He wondered if one day he would be able to tell the boy these things instead of thinking of them. Did thoughts ever go directly from one person to another, doing away with the need for speech?

Probably you would have to be gifted with a really sensitive system to communicate that way, one of those people that college somewhere down South was interested in, people who could control the dice and who knew a high percentage of the cards that were coming up and who had seen ghosts or gotten mixed up with something supernatural—he seemed to remember that there had been a lot of strange stories those people had researched and a lot of them had turned out to be true, but the figures escaped him. He would have to look them up again.

Had they researched that story Wesley had told him, about the man in Alabama or Georgia—he couldn't remember which, some place in the South, anyway—who was coming home from a college dance with his girl, a foggy night, it had been raining all evening, and it was late, one or two in the morning, they were driving back through the rain in a two-door car. That was important: the car only had two doors, and there was no way to open the back to get in or out. They had been driving along slowly, the streets were slippery and the fog made it hard to see, when they came upon a girl sitting on the curb, crying.

She had on a white dress, one of those things that never go out of style, a simply cut filmy white dress, and she was sitting on the curb, crying her eyes out. Something, the couple in the car had thought, with the boy friend. He had been fresh.

They stopped and asked if she wanted a ride home, and she said yes, and the girl in the front right seat of the car leaned forward and the other girl climbed in back. She didn't seem to want to talk and it was a long way to where she wanted to go. They drove in silence, going on and on, nobody talking, and then they saw the street and there was a little old run-down house at the end with a light on and they turned around to ask the girl if that was it and she wasn't there.

They parked the car and sat for a while, not saying anything, both of them trying to think what to do. Finally they both agreed they ought to go up to the house. The woman who answered the door was fully dressed and looked almost as if she expected them. Come in, she said before they had a chance to explain. The house was small and poorly furnished, but there was a little upright piano at one end of the living room, one of the kind popular in the thirties. The couple told the woman they had found a girl on the corner of—

The woman went over to the piano and picked up a photograph; then she came back and handed the boy the picture. "Is this the girl?"

It had been the same girl.

Then the woman asked them the name of the street where they had first seen her, and after they told her she said, "Seven years ago tonight my daughter was killed at that corner, and you're the fourth couple this evening who's tried to bring her home."

Carolyn, he asked himself, if something happened to you, would you try to come back?

Does Wesley try to come back? All the way back across the water?

Since 1945 I have never bought anything German, but it's a small protest. I know it doesn't hurt the German economy or the German people—and, I suppose, to be honest, the government takes my taxes and sends part of them back to Germany, so I am supporting the Germans—but there are some things you can never forgive: it's a necessity, like feeling loved even if you aren't.

So when things go wrong, like today, I sit around hating the Germans. It's easier to blame a nation than to blame yourself.

Carolyn isn't home again and when she is she's usually been drinking and I don't know which is worse, to come in and find her happy and half drunk or sober and sullen. A choice like that is impossible to make.

Awful, what women could drive a man to, Ralph thought. The only times he seemed to move from his passivity was when she looked at him a certain way, the mouth curled down in disdain. Then all his indifference dissolved; he felt he could kill her—because he knew he was responsible for that look. It was a look of deep and desperate disappointment, the kind only a man could put on a woman's face.

How many men beat their wives? Must be figures on that somewhere. Kinsey, probably. A high percentage, Ralph decided, a very high percentage.

Why should he expect her to be home? Why should he expect anything? Half a man shouldn't expect a whole wife. The difference was, she still held the possibility, he felt, of being whole again. He didn't.

Carolyn's vitality—how he envied and hated it. But at the same time he couldn't keep back the thought that what he would really like to be doing at this moment was making love to her. When she let him make love to her, he had the brief sensation that some of her energy went into him, that inside her he absorbed some of her strength, some of her beautiful, beautiful will to live and experience everything she could.

In the white, hot light of the afternoon, he thought; the curtain partially drawn, Carolyn smoking a cigarette lazily, he would take his time. He always started with that idea in mind, but something always got out from under control and he couldn't hold himself back. Most men didn't last long. What was it that book had said, not more than two or three minutes, most of them, but some—a lesser percentage—made it maybe five. Only a few could really hold on. Still, he wished he were one of the ones that could control himself. Mink and sable, that book had said, cohabited for as long as eight hours.

Ralph stirred restlessly, shifting Bobbie's weight. The pressure on his thighs wasn't helping any. Carolyn had such a white body—so smooth except for those two little dark moles near her stomach, the belly button a curl of dark brown stamen, folded petals of skin: three little dark roses on her stomach. She would lie still and quiet, her eyes getting wider and wider, until he felt he would drown in their depths. His lovely, lovely wife that he would never understand.

Twelve years now, and she was still a mystery to him. She was different and yet the same, willful, stubborn, rebellious, beautiful—as determined to have her own way as she had been the first night he met her. It was a prom, and her date was fumbling in his pocket for the tickets. Carolyn had on a pale dress and her hair was plaited with bright ribbons. That dark hair, which had been twisted around her ears, was woven with ribbons. It shone under the light, a tangle of dark brown hair and brilliant satin ribbons. All around her girls were swinging their hair as if it were a scarf thrown over their shoulders; but Carolyn's hair had been braided close to her head, as if she had helmeted her hair against touch.

He had stopped and stared at her, and she had looked back as calmly as if she were measuring him. She probably was, he thought, measuring me for the wedding band. Then she had turned, with a lift of her eyebrows, and started searching around in her purse for a cigarette. When she came up with it, her date had found the tickets, and the two of them went through the door, Carolyn carrying the unlighted cigarette in her gloved hand. Her white gloves had reached to her elbow.

He knew now that the gloves were borrowed and the dress remade, but it was not the clothes she wore, it was the way she carried herself.

He had wangled an introduction and seen that they had a dance together, but she had stayed detached and slightly antagonistic, as if she suspected him of some ulterior motive. Well, he had had it. In the beginning he hadn't had marriage in mind; then, later—it happens to us all sooner or later, Ralph thought—he would have done anything to have her as his own.

That first year with Carolyn he had been sure that they would have the life together that he had imagined. She was like an exasperating and intricate puzzle that kept you excitedly seeking the solution. Then after a time he had begun to feel that there was no answer, that she was a problem that could be worked on for the rest of his life and at the end he would have a mass of data, nothing more. It was the hard central fact of her that he could never grasp.

He sighed, shifted the boy's weight again, and said, "You all right, Bobbie?" and his little boy looked up, unsmiling, and said, "Yes, Daddy."

He was too weary for insoluble puzzles and too empty inside from looking for impossible answers; all he wanted in the world, he thought, was something to hold on to. Well, he had it. His son.

He thought of how he got up and went to work and came home and went to bed, and sometimes she was there to be loved and sometimes she wasn't, but that didn't change the world, did it? He would still have to get up in the morning, go back to work, come home again; on and on until he died. It was a little like death, he sometimes thought, because it was so endless and enduring.

But he never lost sight of his son. You had to have one thing, Ralph thought, to care about, that gave the world meaning.

My son is the best-looking boy in the family, Ralph said to himself proudly, not just the best-looking, but the best-behaved, too. Quiet, he thought, thinking of how Pete's children bumped into furniture, wrestled, raised a racket. I wouldn't stand for that kind of behavior, he told himself. Not that there was any need to. Look at Bobbie, a quiet, really well-mannered child.

Maybe, he considered, it had something to do with the way we were so close at the beginning, used to sit in a chair, I would just hold him for hours, not saying a thing, and he would sit there, cradled close to me. I miss that, Ralph thought. I haven't really had much time with my children in so long. A survey somewhere had determined the average father spent exactly seven minutes of his whole week in direct communication with his children. There was a nice chilling statistic for you.

How much time a week do I spend with my children? he asked himself.

He tried to think when he had last done anything directly with either Sally or Bobbie, not just the run-of-the-mill, Hi, and Get your pajamas on, and Don't you think it's time for your bath, but taken them some place alone, without Carolyn, without that battleax of a maid. A horror, he thought, picturing Miss Miller. In the infantry they would have made her a scout. She'd sneak up on the enemy, they'd get one look at her face, just throw down their guns and run.

Efficient, though, he considered—if you like that Germanic kind of efficiency, all curtness and carnivorous teeth, the everlasting efficiency of the humorless.

Carolyn defended her, said she was good with the children, but in his heart Ralph didn't believe that. Miss Miller was a convenience. She had never cared for anyone, he was sure, in her whole life. As for love—she wouldn't even comprehend his kind of love for Bobbie.

And his love for his son, he thought, was something to be understood. It was more than just love of your own flesh and blood. But it had something to do with that. Loving Bobbie, loving—he thought an instant later —Carolyn the way he did, it was difficult to understand what it was Carolyn felt for her own family—not just himself and the children, but her mother and father, brothers and aunts. Not that you could say she loved or didn't love them—who was he to draw the thin division between love and hate? Perhaps in Carolyn exasperation was some kind of love.

The boy climbed down, and Ralph looked at his son. Don't grow up like me, he thought. Be better. Be happier.

How many people in the world looked at their children and thought that? Looked at their families, the way Carolyn did, and thought, Be better, don't be what you are?

God, what a commentary on human existence that was— Don't be like me, don't be like you are, be happier, be better.

His son walked slowly and silently across the thick rug of the living room. Carolyn wouldn't let either of the children play in this room when she was home, and when she was away he always brought them in. He knew that, despicable as it was, he wanted his children to love him more than they loved her. Because she was easier to love, he supposed, in spite of all her rules and regulations, her complexities; she had the mother instinct and, even though she tried to suppress it, it was she who cuddled them when they cried, she who had given them their bottles at all hours of the day and night when they were infants, she who really knew what went on in their childish heads. He only placated them or tried to please them by allowing them to do the things they weren't supposed to do.

I was never afraid in France the way I was afraid when one of them was sick, really sick. You can't be afraid for yourself the way you're afraid for your child. That time Bobbie had the croup and they kept the room full of steam, changing that special contrivance every two hours, making sure there was enough moisture in the air so that he could breathe, and all the time he got worse and worse, coughed and hacked, unable to get his breath, until he turned blue, Ralph had been paralyzed with fear. Nothing like active combat or seeing a friend lying in a ditch with his hands wired behind his back, no fear like the fear of watching a child sick and unable to do anything to help.

Every day you read in the paper about some accident—drowning, being run over, falling out an upstairs window, swallowing poison, smothering—and your heart stopped, you thought, What if that happened to mine? How could I face the death of one of my own children? How can any man?

Divine justice took the weak, the innocent, the untried, without hesitation. God had to be terrible to do that.

No God, he reminded himself. You began to believe, if you believed anything, that if there were gods they had created man in a moment of absent-mindedness. Nothing but chance, he thought.

Can I control chance? Statistics about it somewhere. Even in the end, chance was supposed to have a certain predictability.

He rose and ran after his son, bent down and clasped the boy to him wordlessly, feeling an overwhelming surge of love for that flesh that was part of his own. Never go to war, he cried out silently in his heart, never lose what you hold dearest. Find someone to love who loves you, he prayed wordlessly over the boy's puzzled face. "Let's go out to the icebox and see if there's some ice cream," he said aloud, wanting to give the child everything he could now, before it was too late.

Chapter Five

"Lois should have come back," Iris said sorrowfully, "her first night home. It wasn't fair of Carolyn to go and take her off like that—it wasn't fair, but it's what I expected, Carolyn never thinks of anyone except herself. More potatoes?"—and Ella waited, the plate went by her. It must be to Stewart Iris was speaking.

"Here, give me your plate, Ella, and I'll cut the meat for you. We should have left it in longer, it's tough. I told that butcher he had been sending me tough meat, but he wouldn't listen. They never do. Well, I'm not going back there again!"

Silently Ella raised her hand and held the plate out in the direction from which Iris's voice came. In the past years, since her increasing blindness, she had learned that people saw how helpless she was and tried to help. There was something painful about the dependency, but she had tried to accept it as a partial payment for her pride. She had always felt, secretly, that without her the family wouldn't have—

A hand brushed hers, the plate was gone.

It was their mother made them do right, Ella reminded herself, not me.

I tried, though, I still try, even old and helpless as I am, I try.

What you going to do, old woman? she demanded of herself. You don't even see no more, you don't even know what Lois looks like, never mind she cut her hair, it the face you care about, but that face you want so much to see, it just a shadow, a shape between your hands, if you have the courage to put your hands up and touch it, those hands you got to trust because you can't trust your eyes, a life led with touch and sound instead of sight, what kind of a life is that, how you help anybody with a life like that?

I don't know, she thought, I try, though, and that all you can ask.

You suppose, she asked herself, that girl look like her mama now? Her voice like her mama's. "Ella, oh Ella, it's been such a long time. Seeing you, I know I'm really home." Her baby, Organdy, say that the last Thanksgiving she come home, the last party in the old house. Sold. Somebody else living in hers and Lydia's house. Organdy dead. Lydia dead. Lois come home.

How could you have a family, a real family, when the thing that held it together, their mother, dead? When the house where they all born and grow up gone? When the whole world seem to change and instead of a help you a hindrance?

Old and blind and black and not able to see her baby's baby.

I used to love Frances best, Ella thought, and she like a stranger now, a woman who comes and goes with a loud laugh and bad manners. Lois and me, we close, though.

Was, she told herself. How you know what she like now? She like her mama, Ella answered herself, the same voice. The same feeling.

Like her mama, Ella thought and was frightened.

If only I'd said something, Ella thought, but I didn't understand about her mama. I didn't know then that when you feel something you don't have to wait to know, you can trust the feeling.

Maybe, she thought, if I'd done something that Thanksgiving, everything would have been different—Organdy still alive, her mama still here. Maybe it was all my fault.

Nothing I could do about Esther, about the money, she told herself. No way to stop that quarrel with Ada that kill their mother, she consoled herself, as almost daily she consoled herself.

March, Lydia's birthday, she was sixty years old. Iris was giving a party. Insisted; say her mama wore out from Thanksgiving, and just before Frances come to get us, the tree, *her* tree, go down. The sky white, the whole world white for a minute, and right on top of that a big clap of thunder, she and Lydia look at one another and at the same instant that grinding sound in their ears. The tree.

Lydia ran. While she was trying to get the door to the parlor open, she already knew. "My tree," she call out. "Something's happened to my tree."

Split right down the middle; on either side the white flesh of the trunk seared with the burn. Lydia wept as if her heart would break.

Organdy dead, the tree destroyed, and then Ada at Esther about the money: in the kitchen at Iris's, washing up, Ella had heard the bitter voices. *"Somebody took that money."* . . . "Prove it, just prove it." . . . "I'm on to you, Esther. I know you cheated us. . . . I know, I know. . . . You took the money. Took your own sisters'—your own mother's—money."

It kill their mama, that quarrel, just kill her.

Same as if they murder her.

Silent, Ella sat at Iris's table, trying to push out the thought. I could have run in from the kitchen, she thought—but no, *maids* don't do that. I'm not just a maid, she said to herself indignantly.

She heard the scrape-scrape of a fork rasping against a plate, Iris cutting up her meat, the meat she didn't want, she had explained and explained meat didn't set well on her stomach, but no one paid any attention, they kept pushing it at her; now she ate what was put in front of her, no matter how sick she got later. Silence was the best state of the old, the blind, the black, that was what she told herself—*servants* stay silent.

"Lois should be back here with us," Iris insisted.

"She's young, Mother," Stewart said in a conciliatory way.

The plate was put, with a bang, down in front of Ella. "Maybe so," Iris said angrily, "but there are things you do and things you don't. And it seems to me that one of things you do is stay in the house you've come to visit the first night you're home."

There was no point in saying anything, Ella knew. She moved her fork around on the plate, hunting out a scrap of meat.

"Isn't that so, isn't that what Mama would have said?" Iris demanded.

"I 'spect so"—while Ella was thinking, Lois come home, Lois come back. She put her arms around me and I felt like it was her mama come home again. Like, she thought, those weren't the arms I expecting, Ella thought. Why was that? When I love that girl so much? When I loved her mama so much—but not enough, Ella thought, none of us love her enough or she wouldn't have done that terrible thing.

". . . eat eat eat, that's all the boarders do, even in this hot weather, how can they . . ."

I was waiting all day for her to come in and then when she come in, something not right, it didn't seem like it was her I waiting for.

". . . no sense in just trying to pawn a salad off on them, you know what they say . . ."

I been in this house all these years and I been waiting, and I didn't know what for. Sometimes you think it death, sometimes you think it some kind of sign. I seen the girls grow and go away. I seen their children born and grow and go away, but that wasn't what I was waiting for. What was I waiting for, all this time?

A sign, Ella thought, some kind of sign.

". . . you can't give them stews and hamburger every night and the price of meat—real meat—oh, Dad, I don't know what we're going to do."

Ella felt the meat she was chewing ball in her mouth; she knew she couldn't chew any more if her life depended on it. Her stomach was throbbing, a kind of electricity ran through her, as if her whole body were vibrating. Her heart seemed to stand still inside her. There was this terrible feeling, for an instant, that she was going to burst out crying; then she felt as if she might faint. She clutched the table and tried to hold on, feeling the whole center of her burst into light, a whole hot white light like the night the tree went. Gripping the table, she cried out, "Miss Iris."

"What is it? What's the matter? Oh, Ella, you're not—"

"He coming back."

Iris's voice came to her, sharp and impatient. "He? What do you mean, he? It's Lois who's come back. Lois came right in here this afternoon and you know it, Ella; you know good and well she came home, can't you keep these things straight? I get so upset when you—"

"No, young Mister Stu, *he* coming back."

"What's the matter with all of you, you want to torment me like this? First Carolyn being so cruel, saying she won't help with the party—oh, I know she said she would, but she'll change her mind again, you wait and see—Peggy breaking down that way, scaring the daylights out of me, Lois going off on her first night home, going out to *drink,* and now you, Ella, of all people, saying something like that when you know—"

"I seen it plain as day," Ella insisted. "Here," she said, tapping her head.

"We won't discuss it," Iris said firmly. "The heat always affects you, you know it does, and you were at that hot stove all day, I suppose that upset you. I know I should have done the meat, but—but I can't do everything."

She afraid, Ella told herself, she wait too long. Once she give her whole life to hear those words, he coming back. Now nothing but the dead dream, the dead buried dream.

I got my own graves, she thought: the husband never bedded me, the children never suckled, the days gone without reason, gone without knowing where or why, all graves. But not untended, she told herself proudly.

She sat still for a moment, listening to Iris breathing hard across from her. "He is coming back," Ella said in a low voice. "I seen it. Inside. Young Stu coming home."

"I've had all I can stand today," Iris said, and Ella knew Iris had started crying. There was that sound Iris always made when she was upset, a choking sound of sobbing and that little small sniffle between the real sobs. "I tell you I can't take any more. Stu isn't coming, you know he isn't. He's never coming back, you all know it. We've just been fooling ourselves all these years."

"Now, Mother—" Stewart began.

Old and blind—listening for voices inside, seeing sights inside, old and black and blind, groping with ears and hands through a strange house and saying things she had no right to say.

"I sorry," Ella said.

"Sorry," Iris brought out with bitterness. "Sorry? We're all sorry, but that doesn't do any good. He'll never come back and I know it and I've waited all these years, kept his room ready and all, but—I'm sorry too, Ella, I don't know what's the matter with me, I'm just so worn out I can't think straight. I don't even want to eat," she said, and Ella heard her rising and knew Iris was really upset this time, not just carrying on the way she usually did, but really and truly upset. Nothing ever stopped Iris from eating.

"I think I'll just go lie down a little," she said. "Leave the dishes," she said after a moment. "I don't care whether they get done or not."

"I'll help," Stewart said, and Ella heard Iris give a little laugh, as if Iris knew better than to count on him.

"No," Stewart insisted, while Iris went right on with that mocking laughter. "No, it's all right, Mother, you go lie down."

"I don't want anyone to mention his name again, you hear? I don't want to hear his name again. If he's gone, he's gone and there's nothing we can do about it and I don't want to be reminded."

But he coming back, no matter what she says, Ella thought. I seen it. Plain as day, deep down here, inside, in the darkness.

Chapter Six

ALL over Illinois the sun lay low against the land, day was dying, the last light no more than a tincture in the sky. It was after eight, the summer hour between day and dusk.

From the porch Lois watched the light seeping back into the earth, the earth almost seeming, in that magic hour, to reach up and grasp at the sky, hold on so tightly that as the earth fell back the light went with it.

It was a summer night even as she remembered it, full of the summer noises of insects and the small rustling of birds bedding down until dawn; the sky, too, was as she remembered, a vast and cold dome that stretched out over the plain like a cup enclosing it. In New York the sky was close and intimate, a part of the city; here earth and heaven were forever pulled apart.

Neal liked the dark, she thought, the way I liked twilight, and winter, while I cared about fall and spring. He could only believe in the extremes —like Origen, who, in order to be pure, emasculated himself.

I used to try to find out what he did believe in, and he never could say. There were the scraps of paper I used to come on, with the jottings, but they were never anything that made up a belief. Why was his world so cruel it refused to let him impose any order over it?

And your world? she asked herself. What's so wonderful about your world?

A series of doors, Lois thought, some big, some small, most the same size, the same shape, the same contour. One door led to childhood and another to adolescence, the third to adulthood and the last to old age; and when you opened the final door there were no more rooms, only a blank wall. The problem was to find the keys that would get you from room to room, for the thing was, you always thought the next room might be better. If you could get the key to open the door from the room you were in, you might at last even get outside the series of rooms altogether, into a garden. So all your life you struggled to find a key to open the next door, and all your life you went on looking for the garden, until you came to the end, to the blind wall.

She thought of that night she and Neal had first made love, of how that had seemed a door that might open out into a garden; she thought of coming down the stairs with him later, holding the key to the front door in her hand, hoping it might be opening more than her own front door; she remembered how she had wanted to hold on to him, how she had got up and dressed, walking with him down the stairs, the key in her hand. They stood on the front stoop and the night was so clear that you could see over the tops of the houses clear down to Riverside, the air so still that she imagined she could even hear the tiny slap-slap of the waves on the Hudson River.

There were twinkling lights way down there, by the river, and a stream of lights, like smoke, swift and vague, car lights, going fast along the drive. A beautiful night. He put his arm around her waist and they stood and looked out toward the Hudson, the only two people on that still, dark street, and he said *Lois.*

That one word, her name, almost crushed her, it sounded so harsh in his mouth, and she turned to him, her eyes bright with tears, everything in that clear, sweet night blurred, and said, *Oh, don't.*

What is it? What's the matter? Tell me.

I can't, she said.

She began to walk down the street, wanting to feel the cool, clean air of the river, and he was behind her, talking on and on, something about taking a ferry and going over to Jersey and getting some clams, he would pick her up after work and they would have a drink in the park on the way, and she thought, well, at least he's not just going to walk off and never come back.

Some of them could. Tell you they loved you and you never heard from them again.

You ever been to the Tavern on the Green? he asked.

No, I never have.

She thought of Neal on the stoop looking for his cigarettes, and at the same time there came the image of Stu on her stairs, shaking hands with her. In some way she did not understand Stu and Neal were alike. What way?

In the way, she thought, that she could never get through to either of them.

That first night Stu came up to her apartment he said, "The way to beat New York is to find at least one person who cares enough about you to keep you from being lonely, from eating yourself up." After a moment he had added, "Without making too many demands on you."

She had picked up a book from the table and read to him: " 'Those who serve England must expect nothing from her; we debase ourselves if we regard our country as merely a place in which to eat and sleep. . . . The universe is so vast and so ageless that the life of one man can only be justified by the measure of his sacrifice.' "

"Who wrote that?" Stu asked sharply.

"I don't know. It's a letter, from an unknown sailor," she replied. "Someone in Britain writing to his mother during the war."

"Well, did he make the sacrifice?"—taking a sip from his drink. "Did he die?"

"Yes, he did. I guess that's why it's reprinted, because he did. It wouldn't be much good to have the words if they hadn't been put to the test, would it?"

"I suppose not. You know," he went on slowly, "that's a word—
sacrifice—I always associate with the family. War or no war. Giving up
what you really want. To have what you want was a sin. That's what they
always made me think. Is that the way you think too?" he asked, twisting
his lips into a sarcastic smile. "Like the rest of the family? Like all the
Timbles?"

"I want to find a place, Stu, where I feel needed, where, because I'm
needed, I can do some good. There aren't any *little* places any more."

"Then maybe you should try for a big one."

"I wouldn't make it."

He got up, went to the window, and stood looking out at the winking
lights from the big apartment house across the way. They could see the
silhouettes of people in various rooms moving about, getting dinner,
pulling down blinds.

"Some of us rebelled," he said, "like me. And what good did that do?
We got caught in a worse way. We wanted to live and we thought the
only way to do it was to escape, to get away from them. That's where
all the trouble started."

"No," Lois said, "I don't think so. I think the trouble started in not
accepting them for what they were. We thought they should be so much
better. Maybe we had to, because we had come from them, because we
were their flesh and blood, and we didn't want to see them as they really
were. We had an image," she said finally, "and when we grew up and
that shattered, we were maybe the ones who wanted revenge. It's true
with anyone, I think, but harder with the people who make us—we
always want revenge on the people who disappoint us, who are less than
we thought. Sometimes I think we all reach out, and no one ever sees
the hand until it is too late."

"Are you holding out a hand?" he had asked.

"I don't know."

"Well, I'm not any more, not to anyone. I'm through being involved
with other people. And if you think I'm going to tell you about Ethel,
you're crazy."

"I'll make a pact with you. Don't talk about my mother, and I won't
ask about Ethel."

"I'll make an even better one. Let's never talk seriously again."

And they hadn't. Perhaps it was better that way.

She had never, because of that treaty, been able to ask him how Eileen
had known where he was. She wanted to know, but she was afraid to
ask either of them. How could you ask Eileen anything, Lois wondered,

after you got one of her letters? The letters were long and incoherent, and there were clippings enclosed from all the tabloids, with the lurid passages underlined in red, torn pictures of murders and disfigurements and rapes from all the cheap pulps and penny dreadfuls. Eileen had begged Lois to cut out the gossip columns from the New York papers and save them to send to her; in New York, she had written, people really knew, they were informed, and she wanted to keep up.

Keep up with what? had been Lois's first reaction. Now she thought she knew: keep up with a world where people seemed glamorous and safe and enviable and, above all, rich and protected.

Carolyn was standing in the doorway. "They're just about ready for you," she announced. "Are you just about ready for them?"

"What goes on down there, anyway?"

"It's the blanket game. Everyone new is initiated. Even," Carolyn said with a smile, "the intellectuals."

"I try to play my part."

"Not in that simple little number you just happened to find on the racks of Bergdorf."

"Lord and Taylor."

"Same difference, different label. But I must say it does my heart good to see Helen, in *her* simple little Marshall Field number, take a second look." Carolyn paused, lighting a cigarette. "She's the kind who's amazed other people have eyes, ears, a nose, and mouth—to say nothing of taste. She sees herself as so damn unique." She took a puff of her cigarette. "Let me just give you a little advice, though. Don't take off all your clothes."

"What?"

"Don't take off all your clothes."

"I haven't any intention of telling the whole truth, if that's what you mean," Lois said.

"Well, that wasn't what I meant, but I guess that's a good idea too—though don't put anything past Frances and her pack of cards. Someone close coming back, her hands rummaging around the cards, *someone's coming back you haven't seen in a long time.* She gave me an awful scare," Carolyn said, and she puffed nervously on her cigarette. "Sometimes—" She broke off. "Madame Sosostris with a slight jag on. Here, she says, is your card, The Lost—Brother"—and Carolyn brought the last word out with a twist, almost with a forced malice, as if she had been about to say something else. "Do you suppose she has any idea at all of what she's saying?" Carolyn asked, finally looking at Lois fully.

"Did you think—did that hit you too? Do you think he's really coming back, Carolyn?"

"Of course not—well, not rationally. He's been gone for years. Nobody even knows where he is."

After a pause Lois said, "I do."

"*You* know where—where Stu is?"

"I saw him just before I came. In New York."

For a moment Carolyn struggled; then her face looked blank and composed. "What's he like?" she asked at last.

"Sad," Lois said slowly. "And—I don't know—crushed, if you know what I mean."

"And Ethel?" Carolyn asked quickly.

"I've never seen her. They've been separated for years, not divorced, just living apart. He never talks about her."

"But how did you ever find him? I thought he had disappeared, you know, really disappeared, years ago, that he was one of those people you would always wonder about and never know. Sometimes I've even been sure he was dead." Carolyn stared out the screens at the flickering lights of the night—a narrow moon, small stars, fireflies circling over the cement. "To tell the truth, I suppose what I really thought had happened to him was that he had gone down, you know, disappeared with the drunks and the bums, the outcasts—there wasn't any reason to think that, I just did. I *felt* it. Do you suppose it was because—because I wanted that to happen, to get rid of him, because he was something in my life I didn't want there? The brother," she said softly, almost to herself, "who ran off, the brother who would never amount to anything." She turned and faced Lois. "Listen," she said urgently, "have you ever felt that way, that you wanted someone to go away, never to come back, maybe even—even to die?"

"I've wanted people punished, I've wanted people hurt, the way I've been hurt."

Carolyn was fiddling with a tassel on one of the pillows. "You play tennis any more?" she asked at last, looking up, deliberately changing the subject.

"A couple of times, but nothing like that summer."

"It seems funny to think we played around here, doesn't it . . . that the old woman's dead . . . and the birds . . . no, I don't go any more."

Lois thought of that woman sitting under the big black oak tree at the far end of the court, watching them play tennis, her eyes following the

ball back and forth across the net, her head turning rhythmically. . . .
Lois thought of that other court, in Winnetka, that other woman, her
mother, a slim black-haired woman with a natural ribbon of white at the
side of her hair, a blade of grass between her fingers, her eyes on the
figure of a man raising his racket to explain a shot, her eyes intent on
that man. . . . I didn't even suspect, it never occurred to me, she could
be in love. I never even thought about love in those days, I took it for
granted.

It was only later, when I realized where the lack was, what was the
matter with me, that I cared so much, that I could never think of anything else. I always tried to bring the conversation around so that Neal
would have to use the word *love,* and he was always just as determined
to avoid it. . . .

Once, though, Lois thought, he almost did say it. Just once.

"But there are some public courts," Carolyn was saying. "We might
borrow some rackets and—"

"I think mine's still up in Iris's attic somewhere. I'll bet we could find
dozens of old rackets up there if we looked."

Carolyn laughed. "Well, how about it? You want to—"

"I don't know," Lois said carefully. "I guess—"

"Yes, I guess there isn't a whole lot of time. Not to play games."

The last time I ever saw him, before I went down to the Eighties, that
night we were going to borrow a car and go out to Long Island and drive
to the sea, have a lobster dinner, find some place to dance, and then it
rained and there was no point in going to all that trouble to sit in fog
and just hear the sea. We stayed in and I made the steak on a hibachi I
had bought especially *for an occasion,* there was that terrible mess in
the kitchen, and nothing went right, Neal was cross and I was so nervous,
wanting the evening to be as special in its own way as driving out on
Long Island would have been special, a memorable evening, Lois thought
now, all those memorable little evenings we like to store up for the future
when love is gone, only I didn't know that then, I just wanted things to
be right. At the end, with everything absolutely wrong, even the wine
tasted off, I cried and he held me in his arms and said, *Oh don't, lo—* He
almost said it that night, that forbidden word *love*—but what he ended
up saying was *Lois.*

Maybe Neal was right never to use the word *love;* maybe he understood he didn't know enough about it to use it. Or maybe he knew too
much about it.

Always running away from the final fact, all of us, using one excuse or another not to have to face final facts. Where's your mother? people would ask, and I would say, She—she died when I was little. Always running away, never able to say, My mother committed suicide.

"Carolyn," Lois said, rising, turning toward the darkness, "there's something I want to ask you. I'd probably normally never have the nerve, but with the help of a few martinis—" She turned. "Has Auntie—has your mother—ever said anything about—about why my mother jumped?"

"She never talks about it. Nobody does. It's a closed subject. I don't think she knows herself, Lois."

There was something unguarded in Carolyn's voice. Lois picked up the pack of cigarettes on the table and took one. "But you have an idea, is that it?" she asked.

"I guess we all have an idea about things like that. Don't you?"

"No, it wasn't just because—I don't know how to say it—just because she ran away with that man and something happened. There wasn't that much time for something to happen that would make her—for her to realize that she was going to fail. You need time to understand that, to see the blank walls. She wasn't even in Denver twenty-four hours."

Carolyn bent over to take a cigarette from the pack Lois had put on the table, lit it from the half-finished one she held in her hand. "Why don't you ask Ella? If anyone knows, she might. She knew them all from the time they were little; she really knows what happened all along the way. If she can remember now—you know, her mind's, well, pretty dim these days. She's just kind of putting in time, out there with Mother. But she and Grandmother Timble were the ones who raised them. If anyone would know, Ella would."

"Yes, she was the first one I thought of."

"She's the only one in the family I think has ever cared, all the way."

"I've thought about it and thought about it. I try to remember everything I can about her, but—but it was so long ago. I thought you might remember. You went out there to get her. Did you talk to that—that man?"

"Yes, we saw him, Mama and I."

"What was he like?"

"Oh, he was good-looking enough—"

"No, I mean really like?"

"We only saw him a little while. I don't know. I just think of him as —well—confused."

"So you don't think he knew, either?"

"I think he thought she was—well—maybe crazy."

"At the time, you mean? Or always?"

"He just said this strange thing. He said, 'She was always suffering. She *liked* to suffer.' "

"But that wasn't like my mother," Lois protested. "Not the way I remember her. Is that the way you remember her, Carolyn?"

"I always think of her as The Beautiful One."

"The labels, always the labels."

Outside, a car started, Erwin's dog began to bark again. Someone must have opened the cellar door; the noise from below funneled up to them, Erwin's excited voice over the rest. "Ready, we're all ready. Now don't tell her anything, Carolyn. You promised. Don't say anything, let her find out for herself. Don't spoil the fun. Come on, Lois, we're all waiting."

"Oh, I wouldn't spoil the fun for *any*thing," Carolyn said.

"Well, come on!"

"We're coming," Lois shouted back, trying to sound gay. In the beginning . . .

In the beginning you were sure that the doors opened onto something wonderful and worthwhile, and then later—but I forgot about the people, Lois thought. Never mind about the rooms, never mind the wall at the end: think about the people, all in their separate rooms, struggling to find their own keys, all those people who still believe that outside there are grass and trees and a still summer day, a place to rest in the shade. It is possible to care about the people, to want them to keep the dream; maybe that's more important than worrying about the rooms, especially about your own room. Maybe your own room was never important to begin with, you only thought it was.

"What's holding you guys up?" Erwin demanded, and they heard his feet on the stairs. "What's going on out here? Are you guys in the booze all by yourselves?"

"Now that you mention it," Carolyn said in a voice that struck Lois as patently false as all the others seemed, "I could use another."

"Well, get it down the basement. We're all waiting."

Obediently Carolyn and Lois fell into step behind him. They descended past the signs and stopped at the bottom of the stairs. People were standing in groups, chattering in the corners of the room. Frances, laughing, was swinging on her bar stool. Helen, silent and withdrawn, sat on one edge of the couch, Whitey's pregnant wife on the other. The center of the floor was vacant, in the middle a couple of pillows and a folded blanket.

Lois looked around at the faces. They were flushed with seriousness, deadly earnest in their concentration. Even their clutched drinks were held in a spasm of dedication. Staring, all eyes were focused on the floor where the blanket lay piled on the cushions.

Erwin started to laugh. "Now we'll see how smart you are," he said happily. "Lie down. On the pillows. That's the way. Now cover yourself with the blanket. Very good." He paused. "You *all* covered up?"

From across the room Frances's sparkling laughter struck sharp and triumphant. What have I got myself into? Lois thought.

"Now," Erwin said, hardly able to contain himself, "I want you to take off the thing you least need."

Don't take off all your clothes, Carolyn had said. *This* was what she had meant. A warning. They were going to make a fool of her, and Carolyn had warned her. If I only came home to find out I still like Carolyn, Lois thought, the trip has been worth it.

It's got to be a joke, Lois reasoned, something humorous, the thing you least need.

A wedding ring, was that what the wives were expected to discard—the thing they needed least and the thing they would, if they were sentimental, never take off? But I'm not married or engaged, she thought. What is it that I have on that is least needed?

She was aware that the party was shifting restlessly as she lay still, trying to concentrate. She felt as if she were compressed in a prison in which she could neither stand nor lie down, forced to squat, penitent, day in and day out, contemplating her crime. Of what treason was she accused? Not being like the rest of them? Despising their games and their social rooms (*rumpus rooms*), and they knew it. They have a right to want to get back at me, at Carolyn. For one of them this would be fun; for Carolyn and me it's a test.

"Come on," Erwin urged. "Take off what you least need. Don't be bashful. We've all done it. Why, Whitey's wife was down to her bra and pants the night we pulled it on her."

Make-up, Lois decided. She wiped her lipstick off with the back of her hand. There was a chorus of laughter. "Oh, that's good," she heard someone say. "That's the first time anyone thought of *that*."

Laughing, Frances shouted, "No, honey, that's not it. What is it you need least? Every woman needs make-up, you know that."

I'll be damned if I'm going to undress for these people, Lois thought, feeling the waves of anger start to rise. I'm not going to make an idiot of myself for them. Angry, she flung off the blanket.

"Oh." The party moaned in unison. "She got it right off."

"It isn't fair," someone said. "Nobody ever got it that fast. Nobody ever thought of the blanket that quick."

"Well, I guess they were right. You are smart," she heard Whitey remark.

"She may be smart," Whitey's wife chimed in, "but she's ruined the fun. She didn't take off anything. Not the way I did."

Standing up, Lois brushed off her skirt. She looked around. The faces turned toward her were filled not with admiration but with disappointment. She *had* spoiled the sport. And I'm too much of a fraud, she thought, to tell them it was an accident. Honesty comes high when self-esteem is at stake.

Sheepishly Erwin picked up the blanket. "I didn't think you'd get it that quick," he said in a contrite voice. "Well, I guess we can move on to charades. Anyone for The Game?" he called out.

"We're out of Scotch," Whitey announced from behind the bar.

"I've got some upstairs," Erwin said. "Hold on and I'll be right back."

The game had been a test. Maybe all games were. Instead of the strengths, more often it was the weaknesses that were revealed. Haven't you the courage, she asked herself, to tell a lot of people you didn't tell the truth about a silly game?

No, you haven't.

I could tell you all about a game, she thought, pausing halfway up the stairs and looking down on the party, one they used to play in Venice. A game you would have loved, she thought viciously. All you had to do was denounce someone. You wrote the name of the victim on a little slip of paper, she thought, watching Helen pass out pencils and pads for the next game, and then you went out at night and slipped that paper into the hollow throat of one of two lions they had made especially for the purpose. There were these lions in front of the Doge's palace and they had hollow throats, and that's where you put your little paper with the name of the person you wanted to be It.

There were three men, a secret body—you would have loved that—and no one knew them, not even the Doge, not even the senators of Venice. The secret Three met at night; they were masked and robed from head to foot so that nobody knew them, they didn't even know one another. They took the papers out of the lions' throats and decided

E

who was It. Then whoever was It got his name written on another piece of paper, and that piece of paper was passed to a henchman who went out and notified It he had been especially chosen. The victim crossed the Bridge of Sighs; it was covered so no one could see It go in. Then It was put into the dungeons below, and people got up the next morning and saw that someone else was missing, and they walked all over Venice talking about the new missing person, and all the time they were walking they were walking over the dungeon and no one knew It was down there. Isn't that a pretty game? she thought, taking one last glance at the party, seeing the teams begin to form. Isn't that the perfect game?

I have Neal hidden in a dungeon inside me, she thought. I know at every moment all that he is suffering, as if in some way, too, I were jailer and had passed judgment and sentence on him. That is my little game, she thought, the one I have been condemned to play in spite of myself. And my mother, she is in one of those little dark dungeons down in the keep of my mind, imprisoned there, suffering, while all the time I walk over her, but the difference is, I know she's there. She's down there and Neal's down there—and who else? she wondered.

Erwin was in the kitchen, reaching up into a cupboard for the Scotch. "It's great to have you home," he said, turning around, smiling.

Then that terrible moment that always comes in the midst of liquor plunged over her. She was at that ridiculous point of drunken demand— as he had once been—when she would have to shout out the truth. *The dark card in your house . . . failed you . . . a terrible loss, in your house . . . death in your house . . .* Like him, she was going to ruin everything.

"I haven't turned out *nice* at all," she found herself saying through clenched teeth. "If you must know the truth, I've just come out of an abortion and—and—" And now the real truth, the one even she hadn't known was going to come out, was forcing itself into words, into the open, where, precise and painful, it fell on the empty room. "And the truth is, it's just about broken my heart."

In the midst of his clean, sterile, modern kitchen she burst into tears; the next moment she was sobbing into his shirt.

SATURDAY

SUNDAY

MONDAY

BOOK III

TUESDAY

WEDNESDAY

THURSDAY

FRIDAY

SATURDAY

Chapter One

THE lights were burning—not just because Lois was late but because Iris was forced to leave them on all night. She hated the cost of keeping the electricity running, but if she turned it off the roomers complained and she herself spent a restless night imagining burglars at her windows, prowlers at her back door.

Solemn, stern, the thick brick columns rose to support the second-story porch that was almost never used and where, against the balustrade, Iris stored things impervious to the weather: the big outdoor Christmas lights, old wooden boards she wouldn't throw away (according to Iris, lumber got seasoned out there), army surplus tarpaulins, a rubber life raft, not inflated, which she had acquired god knew where or, as Carolyn had said succinctly, as mysteriously come by as kept.

By modern standards Lois supposed the house was ugly—and hopeless to heat of course—big, barnlike dust-catcher rooms, long drafty halls, outmoded fixtures, and faulty plumbing, but a lot of people could live in Sans Souci with a sense of privacy, and that counted for something. There were separate rooms for separate functions. You didn't eat in an ell of the living room. You sewed in the sewing room—or you had until Iris turned it into a bedroom to free the master bedroom upstairs for another paying guest. The high-ceilinged kitchen was cheerless as a cell, but it had possibilities. There were two living rooms, the parlor and the sitting room, and both had fireplaces, although to Lois's knowledge Iris had never used either, the one in the parlor filled with an enormous crock of preserved ferns that were shedding their lackluster heads all around the base, the one in the sitting room covered by a large screen showing a procession on the way up Fujiyama, most of the heads of the figures peeled away, many armless, others without legs, all seemingly ready to plunge over an abyss at the right of the mountain.

Carolyn had brought her home a moment before, leaned across the front seat to open the car door, and declared, "If you think I'm coming in for one of her scenes, you're crazy." Lois had laughed, turning her back on Carolyn after a final good night, and the whole image of the house had seemed, suddenly, to fall on her, as if the house had shied up against the black sky and then dropped back to earth again.

It was after two, and the dim glow from the slender hieroglyphic moon cast a pale silky light on the lawn. If Iris is up, Lois thought with a shudder, trying the front door, I'm really in for it.

Locked, and she had no key. Under the doormat? No doormat. In the mailbox? No mailbox, a brass slot in the door. A brass slot! She had forgotten they existed. It must have been a lovely place once, Lois thought, a big, wonderful, impractical, gorgeously kept showplace, servants on the stairs, a cook in the kitchen, a man out back looking after the horses, and someone on the porch polishing the metal slot of the mailbox.

In New York I always used to think of April and May in Springfield; I never thought of the wet, rainy winters or the hot, hideous summers. Spring—the great trees fleshy with leaves, the crocus and iris, the lovely yellow daffodils running around the corners of all the houses, that first hot sun, yellow paving all the streets, carpeting the sidewalks, striping the lawns, pouring in the windows, great wide swatches of sun in the woods. There were jack-in-the-pulpits everywhere in the woods. We used to go look for violets in the damp spots near the rocks, walking through trillium, buttercups, and patches of wild sweet grass coming up through the mulched leaves.

My mother would never let me pick the violets because she said they died out of soil. Your hand kills them, she said. After she was dead, that next spring, I went out and uprooted a fistful, but she was wrong. They did not die, enclosed in a palm.

When you are little, Lois thought, standing on Iris's front porch, gazing out at the pale lawn, you are so small that you can walk through fields of daisies almost over your head. Wherever you look, there are big black eyes nodding back at you.

Mama's eyes were like the centers of those daisies, big and black, full of the power of being alive.

It's just a picture you have, she told herself, an image. It isn't necessarily true.

But what's true is what's inside, in the mind.

The images.

In that case, she reminded herself, a lot of what you hold inside would only be true for you. Anybody else would see quite the opposite.

Neal?

Yes, Neal.

If Iris locked the door, she expected you to ring. It's direct collision

Iris is looking for. *Oh, Lois, Lois, it's after two, honey, how could you . . .*

She's playing her part, she's the mother. That's what the mother would say. Go ahead, be brave, knock, ring, do something sensible.

She rang. The sound was piercing in the stillness, a sharp, shrill stab at the stillness. *Lois, Lois, the boarders. It's after two. Oh, honey, how could you . . .* So I'll say to her, we were all in the bag and I lost track of time. *In the bag? What are you talking about, honey?* Our wheels were well oiled, we were on the sauce, the grape had got to us, we'd had too much of that good modern medicine. . . . *Oh honey, you've been drinking. . . .*

Auntie—bending over and planting a swift, alcoholic kiss on her forehead—I've loved you all my life, but there's no two ways about it, you're a trial.

So still, here in Springfield after two. In New York buses were always running, trucks grinding gears, old men in darkened coats feebly looting garbage cans, the lunatics and lovers prowling, all hours of the day and night the streets were a succession of noise. The dogs, she thought, don't forget the dogs. Rain, sleet, snow or hail, the dog-owners cannot fail. They have to get their animals on the street. *Curb* them. Don't gallop the horses in the park, don't let the dogs poo on the sidewalks. Make your grunty in the street, *dear*. The terrible, terrible indignity of those jewel-sweatered poodles squatting . . .

The sacred and the profane: my mother bent over violets, the poodles squatting over concrete; you must see life as it is, Neal said, not as you want to see it. And what did I say? I can't remember, but I could tell him now. It's the preposterously absurd in the midst of the intolerably tragic. And he would say, You make everything so intense. I'm tired of all this funny-funny stuff when the world is in peril.

Nonsense, Lois told herself, Neal would never say something like "the world is in peril." He'd say—she concentrated, trying to imagine what he would say in this situation—at this moment he'd say, Bang on the door, I'm tired, I want to go to bed.

Neal never had time for abstracts. Lucky Neal.

He could be pretty abstract about being Jewish, she reminded herself. That was because it was personal.

The quickest way to a man's heart is through his weakness.

Bang on the door, she admonished herself, make old Iris get up. She's the one who locked the door.

But what about the boarders?

To hell with the boarders, there are always plenty more where they came from.

Honey, have you been drinking?

Have I!

At that instant Iris opened the door, peering around the edge. Smelling, Lois thought. Doesn't have to sniff; all she has to do is look at her watch, that gives the whole show away. Say something, she told herself, make one of those famous proclamations heard round the world.

"There's something I've wanted to know for years," Lois said, leaning forward, bringing her eyes down to the level of Iris's, breathing in Iris's face. "Tell me," she said, "do you think Esther really stole Aunt Clara's money?"

Couldn't have been more effective, she thought, if I had pulled a gun. He took her money and her you-know-what-else. Knobs up!

"Lois!" Iris gasped. "Get yourself in the house this minute. I've never in my life—right this minute!"

Make an effort. Lois warned herself, try to be conciliatory . . . in the beginning . . . always make an effort in the beginning.

". . . worried half sick, waiting up for you. Do you know what time it is? Have you any idea how worried I've been, how upset . . . with my heart . . ."

Maybe I could tell her I'm slated to marry royalty, Lois thought. That ought to impress her. *Oh honey, we can have the wedding here, right in our own lovely house. You know how I've always had my heart set on having a bride come down those stairs.* Counts and dukes, their chests ablaze with ribbons and medals, their hands in white gloves, bringing back the glory that was Greece and the grandeur that was Rome, right here in little old Springfield, Illinois.

". . . wanted you to have things. I made a special trip down cellar just to get them and now . . ."

Lois brought her head up abruptly. Iris was standing next to the telephone table, holding two brown manila envelopes and a little box in her hands, her face all screwed up ready to cry.

"I'm sorry, I apologize, I—" For a moment she considered going down on her knees, her head hanging over, as if ready for the blade, saying in a hushed, theatrical voice, *Forgive me, forgive me, Auntie, for I know not what I do.* Better not, she thought, that *is* going too far.

Iris thrust the envelopes and box at her, and Lois fumbled as she took them. There was a brown tape running round the box, and someone had written *Lois's Baby Dress* on it. "We won't discuss it now," Iris said sternly. "Go to bed, be quiet, I don't want the boarders—we'll talk about it in the morning, but I just want you to know that I'm disappointed in you, Lois, that's what I am, disappointed. I thought you cared more for me than to . . ." She turned and went back through the hall, opened the door to the downstairs bedroom that had been the old sewing room, disappeared with a disapproving flip of her bathrobe.

Now I've done it, Lois decided, climbing the stairs as quietly as she could. Her heels rang on the bare wood and she stopped and took off her shoes. She made a little pile of the box, the envelopes, the shoes, with the shoes on top. If I'm out of cigarettes, she thought, I'll commit suicide.

The word had come without thought, a word she never used. Suicide. What would it be like to fall? Throw yourself out a window, falling through space, a concrete court at the bottom. Like going to the East Eighties, she thought. Scared to death . . . death . . . that other word she tried never to think of.

My mother killed herself, my father didn't want me, and Iris saved my baby clothes. Frances over the cards . . . *someone has failed you*. We all fail each other. Iris down in the basement digging around to find my baby clothes, and I come home half shot at two o'clock in the morning and say to her, *Tell me* . . .

Someone—Iris, of course—had turned down her bed. There was even a little lamp near the bed that had been left burning. She hates waste, Lois thought, and yet she left a lamp burning. I couldn't come home early enough so she could come up to me and I could say to her, "Oh, you turned down the bed, you left on the light, how sweet," and Iris could feel some appreciation, Iris could bask in the glow of her own good deeds.

Someone has failed you—well, Lois supposed every fortune-teller used that phrase; it must be right in the fortune-teller manual, three points that never fail:

1. Everyone is looking for appreciation.
2. Everyone thinks he had an unhappy childhood.
3. Everyone makes a mistake in love.

She sank down on the bed, letting the shoes, the envelopes, the box fall on the blanket. One of the envelopes spilled out its contents: baby pictures, certificates, a little lace hat and a pair of white and pink bootees, some telegrams.

She got up and closed the door, opened her purse and took out her cigarettes, looked around for an ashtray, and finally decided on the toothbrush glass. Lighting the cigarette, she reached down and picked up the first telegram. CONGRATULATIONS PROUD OF MY SIXTH GRAND-CHILD, MOTHER, it read.

CONGRATULATIONS FROM ERWIN AND FRANCES, DISAPPOINTED THERE ARENT TWO. Aunt Fran, she thought, feeling a little kind of horror building up as she turned over the next, yellow and frayed, ready to fall apart.

HURRAH A GIRL, ESTHER.

HEARTY CONGRATULATIONS BEST WISHES FOR HEALTH OF MOTHER AND BABY, IRIS AND STEWART.

Her mother's marriage license. Certificate of baptism, her own; footprints from the hospital on official paper, her baby prints; a little envelope, the back outlined in pink, the formal announcement of her birth; baby pictures, pictures of her as a little girl, on a tricycle, in a rocking chair, standing nude in a basin. She thrust the contents back and opened the next envelope: more pictures.

Her mother and father when they were first married, her mother's hair all combed over her forehead, wearing some terrible shoes with buttons at the side, her father looking incredibly young.

Her grandmother, Erwin on one side, she on the other. The picture was mostly grass, the top of her grandmother's head missing.

Another, almost identical, except that her grandmother was looking sideways instead of straight ahead, and there was less grass and almost all of her grandmother's head was intact.

More baby pictures: holding a Teddy bear, laughing, playing, serious, sitting with some children she didn't recognize.

Her father holding her, wearing a hat and a narrow overcoat.

A tinted picture when she must have been about six.

She opened the box and held up a tiny white dress, simple except for the neck and a border around the hem embroidered in tiny rosebuds. At the bottom of the box there was a hat to match. She refolded the dress and returned it to the box, put the lid back on.

Well, I've come home, she thought.

The past lay here on the bed, in scattered pictures, old telegrams, bootees and a dress; the people enshrined in faded photographs, her identity manifest in a small pair of prints, two little feet put in ink on paper. Was my mother unhappy then, Lois wondered, the day I was born, knowing in her heart she had put her life in the wrong trust, had given herself to a man she could not love? So that perhaps that hour when her mother lay on the clean sheets of the hospital bed was one not of joy but of sorrow. Still, she had had her child.

I exist because of her. Whereas my own child . . .

Neal had cared about her as much as he could, but it was not enough. Something was interred inside him, embedded down deep from those years in the Japanese prison camp, in the fact of his own birth, in that affair with the other girl, Dolores, who had had his child and given it away for adoption, and never told him until it was over. "She went away and didn't say a word—I had no idea—and then she came back a year or so later," he had said. "And once, at a party when she was drunk, she let it out. And then it was too late."

His voice was perfectly calm. He had never seen the child. A boy, he said. He had wondered, as if he were solving one of the practical, inconvenient problems of an off day, if he would have married Dolores if he had known. He didn't know whether he would have *wanted* to marry her or not. "Do you think she knew that, or thought that, and that was why . . ."

Neal hadn't known about the abortion either. Women were much stronger about facing the truth about love than men. They had to be.

The shots first, but she was too far along: nothing. Then that afternoon in the bright sun going down the pavement of the street scared to death and into the office and the instant when all her courage deserted her, standing in panic, clutching the fat handbag stuffed with all the bills.

The doctor wanted the money first. Perfectly understandable. If something went wrong he couldn't stand around arguing about payment, it was out in the street with you. That was the unspoken agreement between them.

Pleasant man with a big fat face and small talk, hands that looked competent. The place was clean. There was a nurse, a small scarecrowy woman about fifty who looked frightened. Shaking, Lois opened the purse and counted out the money. Five hundred dollars, three hundred of her own and two hundred she had borrowed here and there in tens and twenties, all the names written down in her little book so that she could repay the debts week by week. She kept trying, as she counted, to remind herself that courage was merely the control of the imagination.

Too scared even to smoke. That was true the whole time. She couldn't smoke. Her mouth was too dry. Strange. But everything was strange.

The brownstone had rooms with big high ceilings, like Sans Souci, she thought, looking around. There were two rooms that she saw on the first floor, a large waiting room and an office: on the second, a small operating room and a bathroom, one or two patients' rooms, empty, and stairs ascending somewhere. It was three-fifteen. She would remember all her life looking at her watch and saying to herself, It's just three-fifteen.

She went in and undressed in a little alcove, put on the smock they had given her. It was big and there was a huge gap in back where the strings didn't take in the slack enough. She lay down on the table and it was cold to the exposed flesh of her back. Her heart was pounding and for a moment she thought she was going to be sick. Then she said, "I'm ready," and they came in, the doctor and nurse, and he said, "Raise your legs, put them in these stirrups."

The nurse put a sheet over the lower part of her, as if trying to preserve all the decencies. Her own hand was gripping the side of the table so tightly that she could feel the circulation stopping. "About ten weeks," he said. "All right," he said to the nurse, and she had thought, There's no one in this house but the three of us, what if something goes wrong?

The nurse inserted a hypodermic in her arm. She was lucky. This doctor was one who gave you a shot. Some of the others, she had been told, just made you lie down and performed the whole thing without anything. Some had local anesthetics, but they didn't always take. One way or another, the child was cut right out of you, took less than twenty minutes.

One moment she had been lying on the table looking into the blinding light overhead, counting as she had been told to, one, two, three, four— all the way to nineteen and then that vivid vivid dream which she could not remember, only remembering that the nurse and doctor had been a part of it, knowing they were in the dream, but not remembering the dream itself.

She was lying on the table and the light hurt her eyes and there was a burning inside, as if she had been packed with dry ice, as if they had taken out the panic and put dry ice in. She looked at her watch: it was three-thirty-eight.

"Is it all over?" she asked.

"All over," he said cheerfully. "Eleven weeks."

The nurse started to help her up. Everything blurred. She hung on to the nurse's arm, feeling her fingers clutching, trying to get a grip. The nurse had cried out.

Then she was on her feet, her legs rubbery, the white light burning inside her skull, the doctor over at the sink letting the water run.

And some there be which have no memorial; who are perished as though they had never been; and are become as though they had never been born. . . .

She did not know how she got through the hall and into one of those rooms, but she remembered lying in bed, bleeding badly, while they kept telling her she had to get up and out. Only an hour, the doctor said, you can only rest an hour. What seemed only a moment later he came back and said, You've got to leave in half an hour. Then: fifteen minutes. But she couldn't move, bleeding that way. Finally the nurse came in, looking more frightened than before, and gave her some pills without touching her, just spread them out on the table, staring down at Lois while she pulled at her mouth with her teeth and seemed ready to cry. To stop the bleeding, she had said, and then added in a voice like Iris's, honey.

Lois had felt that this would never end, that this hour would be with her forever.

As she supposed it would.

She lay there listening to a voice inside crying out, You have killed your child. You had no right to kill the child. Your child.

They had got her into a cab at the end of the hour. She had no strength; motion came from an effort of will. She felt as if she were supporting herself, walking, going down steps, getting into the cab, through sheer will. There was what seemed an interminable ride back to the flat, when she lay on the back seat unable to move, bleeding, the blood coming steadily, she was afraid it would soak through the padding. Everytime she moved, she went weak, everything went black, a rush of blood left her.

How had she got into her flat? There had been two flights of stairs to climb. She must have paid the cab, gone in, put the key in the lock, and climbed *two* flights of stairs.

Lying on her bed upstairs, she had had her first instinct that she was going to get through. No one would ever know what that meant. It was a measure of what must be inside us all, she had thought, the ability sometimes to get through that which no one should ever have to go through—a citation from somewhere.

Neal had never used the words, *I love you,* never used the word *love* at all, even in a discussion. Love meant you had to cut part of yourself out and sacrifice it, for someone else.

But was it Neal she had really loved, or his need of being loved?

She was always trying to redeem herself by some small show of compassion, perhaps to make up for her mother, to rescue the unloved, she thought, looking down at the scattered pictures on the bed, picking up the little bootees, the way I wanted to rescue Neal and failed, seeing us all as sacred and suffering and deceived, profaned by something we do not understand, a pair of hands we have never seen, but that have been there, there are prints all around, the evidence; and wanting, determined with desperation, to abolish the impurities and return to the original innocence, but that which is once soiled can never be made pure again, no matter what we believe and hope and commit ourselves to.

In the beginning I thought an act of decency might be exchanged for one of evil, that the good of one moment might cancel out the evil of another. Now I know no such exchange is possible: the two live side by side, they are not interchangeable, and no act of the will or the imagination can make them so. We live in a world in which even our acts of decency do not cancel out the evils we leave behind us, may not even mitigate them. There are certain offenses of the flesh and spirit whose import we carry with us through death, and perhaps beyond—we, she thought, who have not learned to love correctly, we who have spent our lives in the unworthy search for happiness, bitter over our suffering, not understanding it is that which will purify us.

For it seemed to her only in her suffering had there been a kind of beauty, a price of purity. *Suffer,* she cried out to herself, *you haven't gone through anything. Neal, your mother, the child, they aren't* nearly *enough.*

Chapter Two

THE alarm sounded.

Eileen pulled the pillow over her head, struggling to retain her dream. A big house hanging over a cliff . . . a fur coat . . . flowers, roses in her arms . . . The alarm kept up a high clamor of outrage.

She always had to keep the clock out of reach; if she left it where she could get at it, she reached over, turned it off, and went back to sleep. It wasn't just that she hated getting up, it was the whole day down at the telephone company she dreaded—calling up people and dunning them about overdue bills, checking on summer service, seeing about changes of names, nothing but troubles to listen to and mistakes to straighten out all day long, sitting in that airless little office all by herself with people passing by and throwing her sympathetic smiles, as if she were sick, quarantined, and they had all been warned to be nice but to stay away.

Thirty-eight forty a week, how could that make up for all the terrible things she had to listen to day after day, week after week, year in and year out?

One of these days she would marry Stan and—

She got up, turned off the buzzer, sank down on the stool by the oversized vanity and stared into the smoldering eyes of Clark Gable. The picture was a half-portrait, beautifully done in real-life colors, almost like a painting; you could hardly tell it wasn't a real hand-done oil painting. She had taped the picture up on the mirror the week before. Clark Gable looked so sure of himself, as if he lived in a world where people never moved out and forgot to leave forwarding addresses; in that world wives weren't so frightened of their estranged husbands that they called up, hysterical, and demanded unlisted numbers; the poor weren't punished because they didn't have a twenty-five-dollar deposit to get service, and the rich didn't pay their bills until they felt like it, too busy having a good time to get around to a little thing like an overdue telephone bill, but nobody dunned them because of course they had money in back of them, those people who lived in the world of Clark Gable, the rich world of the unworried and the unharried.

The telephone company all day and then, at least twice a week, the shopping. So tired she could hardly lift her legs to get out of the bus, and there was still the shopping to get through. But of course her mother couldn't do it. She did the cooking and the mending, the cleaning and the tidying up, but she drew the line at the shopping. She didn't want to go out, she wouldn't go out, and that was that.

"Ada, Ada, how can you shut yourself up in the house that way?" one of her sisters was always demanding.

And her mother would say, "I just can't take people pushing and yelling and making scenes, and I do go out—I mean, I get to Iris's parties, at least most of them, but every day . . ." And her mother's voice trailed out into a kind of unspoken plea, the tic in her mother's cheek started again.

The funny thing was, Eileen did understand. She had watched her mother enough to know what "going out" cost her. Every time her mother got to the front door she froze. Eileen wasn't sure what it was out there; whatever it was, her mother panicked at the thought of "mingling."

That was the word she used. "I just don't like to mingle," she would say. "You understand, don't you, honey?"

Mama and I could get by on a little, I could get my big meal down-town in the middle of the day, we could eat lightly for supper, just something I picked up on the way home, but Daddy—

Her father gorged. "I have to keep myself up," he always said, leaning over the table and looking at them with greedy eyes. "If anything happened to me, where would you two be? Eileen doesn't know how to do anything really essential, and you—you"—turning to her mother, the lips curled back in contempt—"how would you get along? You couldn't help yourself if you had to. Why, you won't even go out of the house, like other *normal* people. So you see, it's an investment to see that I take good care of myself." Her mother sat dry-eyed, looking at him across the frayed oilcloth of the kitchen table, where they always ate. Her arms were raised to her head, she had let her head fall forward so that it was cradled between her blue-veined hands. Silent she looked at him, her food untouched in front of her.

"You don't want that meat? You're not going to finish that meat? Well, there's no point in letting it go to waste"—and her father leaned over and stabbed the cutlet; the next moment he was cutting it up, chewing with satisfaction.

He ranted and raved at her mother to do a little comparative shopping. "Get out, get around, see what the different stores have to offer, but no, you make Eileen go. You stay in here and what do you do? You complain, you get on the telephone to the doctor, more money wasted, you're on that telephone all day, calling up one or another of your sisters or the doctor, talking, talking, wasting good precious time."

But if her mother couldn't do anything right, neither could she. "What do you mean, you want to go to college? What do you want to go to college for? Your mother can teach you the things you need to know—sewing, cooking, things like that. You want to get a job, a nice steady job, something with a little pension attached to it. You can't do any better with a college education, not a girl. You work four years, you'll be ahead, you'll have experience, you'll make a lot more than those greenhorns coming out of college. You get yourself a good solid job and forget this college nonsense."

Well, that was a long time ago, over and done with. She would never go to college, just the way she was beginning to be afraid she would never marry. She knew her father would approve of her getting married because she would be off his hands, an expense he wouldn't have to reckon with. But her mother—

"You don't have any real affection for me, do you? If you did," her mother always argued, "you wouldn't go out—to see your *friends*—so often."

Friends, Eileen thought, looking at Clark Gable staring back at her. I haven't got any friends left, and she knows it. *Friends,* Eileen thought in despair; it's Stan she means, but she won't come out and say it.

Of course she saw Stan on the sly; what else could she do? Her mother wouldn't let him in the house. "Not in my house, he comes in over my dead body."

"Mama, please—"

"You want to leave me, you want to go away and leave me with *him.*"

Whenever her mother said *him,* Eileen had to see whether she lifted or lowered her eyes. If her mother lifted her eyes, *him* meant Stan; if she lowered them, *him* meant her father. Sometimes her mother hesitated, as if not quite certain herself which one she meant; then she let her eyelashes fall. It was easier for her mother to blame her father than to blame a boy she hadn't seen in years. Eileen doubted if her mother would have known Stan if she met him on the street—except, of course, her mother never went out on the street. It has something to do with Aunt Esther, Eileen thought, and the money, the way Mama thinks Aunt Esther took the money. "Esther and *him* ruined my life," her mother said, looking down.

Him would be up at noon, going the rounds of the real estate he had bought with the little money her mother got from Aunt Clara's estate. Her grandmother's savings had barely covered her funeral expenses, but the sale of her house had given each of the sisters a little legacy. With this her father had "invested." But his investments never occupied him much past noon; he was back by early afternoon, a brown paper bag under his arm, his hat set jauntily on his head, whistling or humming as he unlocked the back door and started down the cellar. Down cellar were his bottles and boxes. Her father stayed down there, drinking and raging against a world he said didn't appreciate him, breaking the bottles as he finished them, packing the shattered glass into carboard cartons. One whole corner was stacked to the ceiling with them.

No, Eileen thought, I can't go away. I can't leave her with *him.* Whatever I do, I can't do that. Well, she thought, shaking her head, trying to get up the energy to go down the hall to the bathroom, that's the excuse I use anyway.

But the real truth, Eileen thought, closing her eyes, trying to shut out an image of the pale distraught face of her mother as it came up close to hers and said, "Promise me you won't leave me, promise me, Eileen, it's the only thing I've ever asked of you"—the real truth is one excuse after another, year after year of excuses, and I don't know why myself. It's just the way things are.

She edged her way around the enormous bed and opened the door, feeling the hot air in the hall, hearing her mother downstairs getting breakfast together. No matter how many times Eileen protested it was silly for her mother to get up this early, her mother insisted. "I want to make sure you have a hot breakfast down you"—and then she added shyly, "You're so good about the shopping, it's the least I can do."

Eileen went into the small overcrowded bathroom, rinsed her face, spread some cream on it halfheartedly, brushed her teeth, and gargled. As she came back down the hall, her mother called up softly, so as not to waken her father, "You about ready?"

And Eileen answered, whispering, "I'll be down in a little while, I'm a little late this morning," trying to make herself hurry, but at the door to her room she stopped again, gazing at all that jumble of furniture. The bedroom was her despair; no matter how she or her mother tried, they couldn't do a thing with it; and oh, she wanted a pretty, feminine room so much, some place where she could be away from everyone, shut herself in, dream in a lovely glow of pink and tulle.

The room had been small to begin with, but with all that furniture her father had picked up jammed inside, there wasn't any room at all.

"Tell me, just tell me what's the matter with it? Go ahead, tell me, it's good solid wood, isn't it?" her father had demanded after he brought the furniture home.

"Well, it hasn't got much style," Eileen had said at last. Her mother had had enough sense to keep still.

"Style? What do you mean, style? Style costs money. This is a good serviceable set. You'll get lots of wear out of it."

In a way he was right; Eileen was sure the old heavy Germanic suite would never wear out. She looked around at the dark, depressing wood with its thick tacked-on scrolls, the enormous dissolute bed, big beyond necessity, ornate without reason, solid without comfort—but it had been cheap, and if there was one virtue her father esteemed it was knowing the value of a dollar.

When she turned over the twenty-five dollars a week to him for her room and board he always reminded her that it was a bargain to have a room all her own and all that good food for so little money. "The only way to learn what a dollar means," he always said, "is to see how far you can make it go. Some fathers, out of a mistaken idea that they're being goodhearted, might not ask for anything, but I want you to know the meaning of money. I'm taking this"—he held up the twenty-five dollars she had given him—"for your own good. If you don't have too much you'll learn to stretch what you have. That, Eileen, is the only way to learn in this world, through practical experience, through practical application."

Eileen stared at the huge bed, at the enormous vanity table, each shoved into an opposite corner of the room; she looked at the gigantic bureau, the two straight-backed chairs, like bishops, in the corners and, pressed at the side of the bed, the big table, upright as a Spanish count.

In the beginning her mother had tried to do something to soften the room. The vanity was crowded with glass bottles surrounding a big Swiss music box; powder containers and pin boxes jostled perfume bottles and porcelain figures; magazines of movie stars (her own addition) crowded one side of the top, and bobby pins were scattered, like a dark dew, over the white scarf with its bluebell border that her mother had found out at her grandmother's when the girls were dividing up the things in the house.

On the bed Eileen had tucked in a pink satin spread, bought at a sale after months of patient saving. But it was no use: nothing could change the fact that this was her father's house and in her father's house neither her mother's efforts nor her own hopes came to anything.

Mama tried, Eileen thought, even when she knew it wouldn't do any good. She tried for me. I do love her, if only she would understand. I love her so much that's why I've never run off all these years, why I've never—never done anything she wouldn't want me to, no matter how much sometimes . . .

I've tried to be a good daughter, Eileen called out to the silent walls, but I want a life of my own. I don't want to stay in this house with both of them, until I'm so old there's no hope of ever getting out. Why can't she understand? Why won't she let me out?

She heard her mother's footsteps on the stairs and knew that she must be late, real late. Eileen got up and went to the closet, opened the door, and looked at her pictures. Most of them were of the same man—there was a little legend over them, "The King Is Still Clark"—there were pictures showing him walking through rough country, carrying a shotgun; dreaming in front of a big fireplace in one of those houses out in Hollywood, big and modern and beautiful with everything in it new, not one single solitary thing picked up at a sale; a third showing him on the back of an enormous, muscled horse that was speeding over the countryside while he, Clark Gable, sat in the saddle as if there were nothing in the world to flying about the country on a big brute animal. There was a full-page portrait in color, smoke from a cigarette curling up and obliterating half his handsome face, masking it in mystery.

"Honey, you're awful late. Why, you're not even dressed," her mother said in surprise.

Eileen turned. Her mother was standing in the doorway, wringing her thin blue-veined hands together. She had on her old housecoat, and she hadn't combed her hair, there was a long loose strand hanging down one cheek, slipped free from the tight bun her mother squeezed into a little circle at the back of her head and pinned in with two big bone pins.

"Honey," her mother said more urgently, "you've just got to hurry. You're going to be late again and you know what they told you about being late again, you know—"

"I'll be right down, I'm just getting into my dress now."

"I'll put your egg on, then."

"Let it go, I don't want any this morning."

"Oh no, honey, you shouldn't skimp on breakfast. Like it says on the radio all the time, breakfast is the most important meal of the day, you should always eat a good breakfast."

"I'll have some coffee and toast, I just don't feel like an egg this morning."

"Well, let me make it. You might feel like it after you have your coffee."

"I don't want an egg. Just for once in my life can't I do something I want?"

The tic had started in her mother's cheek. Eileen thought of her mother talking about her own mother, Grandmother Timble. *She always had a wet nurse. That shows how much she cared for us. And I never weaned you until you were almost a year and a half;* she thought of her mother standing over the stove, stirring something and saying, her cheek working up and down, *The doctor says he can't do anything about it. Nerves, he said. What does he know about nerves;* she thought of her mother sitting on the edge of the pink tufted spread, saying, *I was so worried all during the war, you'll never know. Those soldiers, what did they care? I was so afraid you might—that one of them might take advantage of you, honey, you just don't know anything about life.* "I'm sorry, Mama," Eileen said, "I guess I'm just tired."

"That's when you need something to keep you going. You mind me, you eat your egg. I'll scramble it, the way you like."

"All right, Mama, I'll be right down."

Her mother stood in the doorway. "Today's Monday," she said. "Could you maybe get off a little early? I've got a big list."

"I don't know, Mama, if I'm late I'll stay late and make up the time. I'll see. Maybe I can do part of it on my lunch hour, the things that won't spoil, pick up the meat and vegetables on my way home."

"You'll only have to do it once this week if you get a little more than usual. Don't cut down on your lunch things, but go easy on the heavy stuff, the canned goods. We won't be in Friday, you know, because of Iris's party."

"I'll maybe take a cab."

"Well, don't let your father see. Get off a little down the block."

"You know I have to go out tonight and— Please, Mama, it's nothing to get upset about, don't look like that. I'll go tomorrow night if it makes it easier, with the shopping and all. I'm just—just going over to Carolyn's, to talk to her. Lois is coming over later."

"Oh, that's nice, honey. Carolyn and Lois—that's awfully nice for you, to see your cousins. But tomorrow would be better. Make it to-morrow."

"Mama—" Eileen began. She saw the relief on her mother's face. Her mother thought that her willingness to postpone meant that she was really going to Carolyn's. "Mama, do you think you could, maybe just this once, you could go—oh, never mind, I'll work it out. I'll do some on my lunch hour and some right after work and I'll take a cab. I'll manage some way."

"You know how much I appreciate it, but I just can't—"

"—mingle."

"No," her mother said seriously, "I just can't. If you knew . . ." Then she turned and disappeared down the stairs, and Eileen stood in the middle of the bedroom and thought, I don't blame her, I don't blame her a bit. I wish I could stay in all day and never have to go out and get on that crowded bus in the morning, listen to all those angry voices on the other end of the telephone, read all those terrible letters. I wish I didn't have to do the shopping and even more than that, that I didn't have to lie, that I could just tell her the truth for once in my life. "I'm going out with Stan and . . ."

I don't have one single solitary thing of my own, Eileen thought. I haven't got one thing that belongs just to me. Mama at least has me, she thought, but I don't have anything.

Mama, Eileen's heart cried out, why do you make me lie to you?

Why do you make me stay in this house? Mama, why won't you let me marry Stan? Why won't you let me get out?

Chapter Three

PEGGY settled down on a packing case with big letters in black stencil marked on its sides: SEARS ROEBUCK CO. There were tall, long boxes like this lying in odd places all over the cellar. At first it was a puzzle because all the boxes were the same and Peggy couldn't remember having seen any of them before. Finally she had asked Iris what they were. "Oh, showers," Iris said offhandedly.

"Showers?"

"Yes, honey. They had this terrific sale last month at Sears, and I knew I'd need them sooner or later—you know Dad and I have been talking for years about putting in more bathrooms and raising rents—so I bought some and put them down here."

Squirrels, Peggy told herself, they're all squirrels, lining their nests for winter. She thought of how the four girls had carried on out at their mother's house after it had been sold. They were all so afraid they wouldn't get their fair shares, fighting and crying and trading things back and forth and never satisfied with what they had, driving themselves crazy running back and forth between the house and the cars parked out in front. The whole livelong day Peggy had been helping Iris, lugging things up and down, in and out, she had heard the slamming of doors, the banging of trunks—one of them was out making sure everything was in the car it was supposed to be in.

Frances hadn't been too bad—at least she didn't want everything she could lay her hands on and make a big scene about it—but she wouldn't work, Peggy thought, and in the end that was what had started the big fight.

"I can't take any more," Frances had announced as they were all unwrapping the sandwiches they'd brought for lunch. "I'm just pooped. What do I want with any of this stuff anyway?"—waving her hand around the living room to encompass the stacked boxes, the jammed furniture, the china that was on every bit of free space of the floor. "My house is modern. I don't want any of these relics."

"But, Franny," Peggy heard her mother-in-law protest, "we all agreed we'd stick here until the job was done. I don't want you to say—"

"If I lift one more thing, I'm going to be down at the chiropractor's for weeks. I tell you, I don't *want* any of this stuff, Iris."

"That's what you say now, but—"

"I'll put it in writing. I promise I'll never make a fuss, no matter what you find—even Aunt Clara's money—if you'll just let me go free."

Peggy bit into her peanut-butter sandwich and prayed to God they wouldn't start another one of those maddening arguments about the missing money.

For a second there had been silence, but only for a second. Frances was good and fed up. She was still, Peggy thought, mad about Lois. Frances had thought Organdy deserved a share of the things, had kept insisting that Lois should get Organdy's share. But no one had been able to decide who should take the responsibility of selecting for Lois, and she was too young to choose herself, so the whole idea had been dropped. "Don't think," Frances said, "I haven't seen you all tapping on walls, looking around furniture for hidden compartments, peering in all the out-of-the-way closets when you think no one is looking."

Ada, her sandwich still unwrapped, looked up. "Esther hasn't been looking." The end of the sentence— *She doesn't have to*—lay unspoken but understood. "She took Mama's pearl earrings, when no one was looking. They're in her purse."

"I did not."

"I saw you."

"You couldn't have seen me because I didn't take them."

"Let's look in Mama's jewel case," Ada said calmly.

The earrings had not been there.

"You took them yourself," Esther screamed, "and tried to blame it on me."

"Search me," Ada said calmly. "Search my car." A little smile had come to her lips. "And then let's do the same with you."

"You've *put* them somewhere in my car," Esther said, standing stock still in the middle of the room and staring at her sister.

Frances had nearly been beside herself. "I'm not going to go through both of your cars and—" She had stopped, as if she wondered, for the first time, if Ada and Esther were supposed to be searched too. "Let's all go out of the room," she said in a pleading voice, "and one by one we can come back in and then go back all alone, and then whoever has the earrings can put them back and . . ." Her voice died in mid-sentence. She put her sandwich down and picked up her purse.

"Don't smoke in here," Iris pleaded. "Not with papers all over the floor this way."

Frances stood up. "I'll go out in the yard," she said in disgust. "It'll be just like old times when Organdy and I used to sneak behind the streetcar." For a moment, cigarette in hand, standing, she looked down on them. "That's what Lois should have had, the earrings. I think it's what Organdy would have wanted her to have." Frances bit her lip. Her face, for the only time Peggy could remember, was stern and serious. She looked like another person. "You know"—and she looked from Ada to Esther and back again—"I could almost hate you two—if I weren't so tired. But one thing I do know: I don't have the earrings and I'd be willing to make a good bet Iris doesn't, and it's funny, but I'd rather not have them than have stolen them." She turned to Iris. "Let whoever has them keep them, Iris. *We* don't want them."

"Well," Iris said doubtfully, and Peggy thought it wasn't the principle of the theft that was bothering Iris but the uneven division of the spoils.

"But I didn't take them," Esther said excitedly. "It isn't fair. *She*"—looking at Ada—"took them and now you think I—"

"I saw—"

"You can't see what didn't happen," Esther screamed.

"Oh, for god's sake," Frances shouted, "you're driving me absolutely batty with all this wrangling. I wish to god I'd never been born into this fruity family."

"Frances!"

"I mean it," Frances said guiltily and then, unbelievable as it was, it was Frances, not Iris, who started to cry. "Mama was difficult and she didn't—I don't know—understand us may be, but she— I really loved her, and now—*stealing Mama's earrings,*" she said, blowing her nose. "It's just not to be believed."

The earrings had never been found. Frances had stayed the rest of the afternoon until everything was disposed of, even though she hadn't taken anything for herself except some of her baby pictures.

How can they all face one another, Peggy wondered, after something like that? How can Iris even want Ada and Esther in her house, knowing one of them took her mother's earrings? But Iris was going to have a party, and a party for Iris meant the entire family, thief and all. *Tell me,* Iris had asked urgently the minute Peggy had come in the door, Iris looking at her watch as Peggy rushed in, breathless, late, half her housework undone, but Iris had wanted them all there by one— "After lunch," she had shrieked into the telephone; "I can't feed all of you, I'm sorry but I just can't, I've got my hands full without—" *Tell me, what do you think of ham, for the party, I mean?*

What the dickens does she think I know about ham? Peggy wondered. I haven't been able to afford a ham since the war. I haven't got, she thought desperately, any ideas on *anything.* I'm just coolie labor. Nobody ever accuses me of having a mind, and now, she thought sadly, no one will ever accuse me of having a body. It's broken down in service.

She looked around, over the tops of the crates and past the mounds of heaped-up furniture and old boxes. The whole of the basement was like a great underground fortification, some Midwestern bomb shelter hollowed out of the hard soil of Springfield. Let them blow the whole city up, Peggy thought, let them drop a bomb right smack on this house. I'd *like* to see it wiped out. Maybe we could start all over then.

Things change, she considered. Everything changes. I can change too. And, happily, remembering there was no longer any more reason to worry this month—all the other women she knew hated the days of their period, but those days she counted her best, she was free from worry, free from his hands at her, and she had bought a brand-new dress for the party, charged it to Iris, and—well, who knew.

The children had to grow up and then she might start all over. A little late—but better to make a beginning in the evening than not at all, Iris was always saying, and maybe, for once, something Iris said was true.

Supposing, she thought, I did walk out of the house? Just said I was going down to the corner for a pack of cigarettes and then never came back? She pictured Pete sitting in his chair in the front room looking at the paper as moment after moment passed, until finally he looked up and said to one of the children, "Your mother's been gone a long time, hasn't she? Where did she say she was going?"—and then, absent-minded, didn't listen to the answer but went back to his newspaper. After a couple of hours he would begin to worry, until pretty soon he went out to see for himself. No; the druggist would tell him, she hadn't stopped in at the drug store. No, the policeman on the corner would say, he hadn't seen her. No, the grocer would say, she hadn't come *this* way. So he would go back home to wait. Let him wait, let him sit there and wait until he drops dead waiting, Peggy thought passionately. It's all his fault, every single bit of it, and there's no way I can ever punish him for it, there's no way I can get even.

More than anything else, this bothered her. If only she had been able to make him pay—but how? She was married to him. She had to go on pretending that she loved him—and the children, she thought. I do love them, it's just that they all get on my nerves so much I can't stand that house another minute sometimes. And Frank, she was at her wit's end with the boy. The others, they misbehaved, but they weren't bad. Frank, he was bad. It's God's punishment for doing that with Pete, out in the barn, she thought. He's marked the boy.

She just wished, though, she had a chance sometimes to tell people how tired she was. In the pit, that was how the woman down the street described it when Peggy tried to tell her how she never felt like doing anything. "People," the woman down the street had said, "who don't have children will never understand. They get tired. They go out and drink and have hangovers and feel rotten, but it goes away. They just lie around in bed until they feel better. But when you have a couple of kids you feel hung over and exhausted all the time. In the pit." She had looked at Peggy half pityingly, half disgustedly. "I don't know how you stand it with five."

Rebelliously, knowing how horrified Iris would be if she could only see her, Peggy lighted a cigarette and moved over behind a big packing case. After all, she didn't want Iris to *catch* her. Carolyn, prowling about the packing cases like some underground spy, wouldn't care. For a fact, they had worked out a kind of password of expressions when they wanted to sneak away for a smoke or when they wanted to get away from Iris for a little while.

But weren't she and Carolyn down cellar, just as Iris wanted? The only person she hasn't bamboozled in this whole world is Stu, Peggy told herself.

She knew just how he looked—not like his father, not at all like Pete. He was tall and strong, with the kind of face people remembered, that was how she pictured him. He never talked much, but what he had to say was important. A man she could respect, that much she knew—someone who would make enough money to support his family, who would care about his wife and children.

Forget him, forget him, don't agitate yourself, an inner voice sounded, carry up some more boxes. The hell I will, Peggy thought indignantly, let Carolyn carry them, let Iris carry them, let Ella carry them, let Father Ashwell exert himself a little.

Fat chance, she told herself. He's up there *reading* while we're all down here working ourselves to death. Letting the women do the work, the way he always does. It makes me sick, she thought angrily, just good and sick.

"Peg?" she heard Carolyn call out. "Where are you?"

"Over here, behind this box, having a cigarette." Peggy threw her flashlight toward the ceiling and waved it. The one cellar light at the top of the landing was hopelessly inadequate. Peggy and Carolyn had been working with flashlights.

"Oh, all right, I'm going up for a little while." In the faint light of the stairwell Peggy saw Carolyn's silhouette move from box to box, her flashlight like a big full moon on the ceiling. Carolyn's heels made a brisk drumming as she started up the wooden steps, the shadow of her legs in the half-light looked like giant scissors opening and closing as they went up the steps.

Walk right out the door one morning, I will, cool as you please, saying, I'm just going down to the drug store for a pack of cigarettes. Dye my hair, go on a diet, get a boy friend to buy me some new clothes, nobody'd find me. He'd be stuck with the five kids, and then see how he likes it.

If I stay with him, Peggy thought with a sinking heart, there's bound to be another slip. I just can't take any more children, she thought in desperation, rising and throwing down the end of her cigarette, looking around at all the boxes, thinking, Go on, catch fire, go up in smoke, *I* won't care.

Then she remembered the new dress. But what good was a new dress if you didn't have someone you cared about to see it? Who in the family was there to care about?

Stu—but Stu wasn't going to be there. Stu was far away, and free. More than likely she would never see him, he was just someone she thought about, who seemed—even just thinking about him—to reassure.

Lois was standing at the top of the stairs. It was easy to make her out in the triangle of light that came from the open door. When she stepped forward and began to descend the stairs, she moved, as Peggy watched, from a bright clear outline, sharp as a well-focused negative, into the blurred outlines of overexposure. By the time Lois was halfway down the stairs she had practically faded into transparency.

Peggy stood still, watching as Lois struck a match and called out uncertainly, "Peggy?"

"Over here," she answered, standing up and waving her flashlight.

"Shine it straight up," Lois directed. "It's easier for me to find my way like that. Oh, ouch—" Peggy heard her trip, stumble, and catch hold of something. "It's a wonder I didn't break a leg. What is all this stuff anyway?"

"Name it and you have it. This," Peggy said, kicking the box in front of her, "is a shower. Everything from decks of forty-nine cards to bolts without nuts, bottles without tops, mattresses without springs. And of course old birthday cards and Christmas wrappings, everything that was left at the end out at the old house—Grandmother Timble's—that Esther or Mother Ashwell couldn't bear to leave behind. You'd have thought it was gold the way they carried on." Peggy gave a sigh. "How's the polishing coming?" That was one thing she was hoping to be spared.

"We haven't made a dent. I just came down to tell you to hold it up a little. I don't think there's room for any more boxes up there right now. You know how she feels about that china. She's got to unwrap, wash, and wipe every piece herself. She doesn't trust Carolyn or me. Oh good, you have some cigarettes. I can take time out for a smoke, I guess."

Peggy looked down at the crushed cigarette at her foot. "I suppose I oughtn't to leave that around," she said.

"Evidence."

"Yes, something else to be accused of." Peggy tried to think of something to say. Being alone with Lois made her uncomfortable. Lois lived in New York. She worked on that magazine. What did Lois care about things like keeping house or bringing up kids?

Finally Peggy directed her flashlight on the big pile of cartons opposite, pretended to be absorbed in reading the identifications on them— *Old Bath Towels,* she saw written in Iris's childish scrawl. *Second Silver. Extra Tools. Mama's Old Sheets. Harnesses. Saddles. Kerosene Equipment.*

It didn't seem to bother Lois they weren't talking. She just sat, smoking quietly.

"Lois? Peggy?" Iris's voice, shrill and martyred, came to them. Lois stood up and threw her cigarette to the floor, ground it out, saying in a low voice, "You stay here, I'll go on up."

"Well—"

"Don't worry, I'll call if we really need you. The way things are up there now you'd be more in the way than—I really can't blame this on anyone except myself. After all, I'm the one who decided to take my vacation back here. I ought to have known that would mean one of Iris's famous parties. A vacation in the basement," she said, starting for the stairs.

We won't get a vacation this year, Peggy thought as she watched Lois go back up the stairs. A vacation, that's a hot one. Last year it was that awful old crowded river in one of those cheap claptrap shacks and five times the work.

Something was always going wrong, the place leaked when it rained, Pete went off in the boat with Frank (he would, she thought) and left her to do all the cleaning up. All those fish to scale and gut. The thought made her wince even now. Pete called *that* a vacation.

She had been glad to get back home. The "cottages" were crammed so close together that you could practically hear the people on either side of you brushing their teeth; millions of kids running around and an argument somewhere every night, like as not in their own place; the garbage piling up (you had to drive it to a dump, where they charged you twenty-five cents a bag, and Pete protested and procrastinated, while the bags piled up and piled up); the toilet backed up, and the shower didn't work up enough pressure; the refrigerator never stopped running, and the noise it made was enough to drive you bats.

She didn't even like to go in swimming. The water was all brown but, worse, the bottom was slimy, mud and weeds. It made her flesh crawl to feel that slime oozing up between her toes. She was sure the place was infested with leeches.

Peter and Frank went out in that boat, she thought savagely, and there I was, with the rest of the kids, and what did they do out there all that time? I bet they talked about me, she thought. Not about, against. Pete always took Frank's part. Look at the way he had gone out and spent all that money, his lunch money, on a junky old radio set. Couldn't Pete see it was Frank's fault that their lives, his and hers, were the way they were? Couldn't Pete see that if it weren't for Frank everything would be different?

"You still down there, Peg?"

"I'm coming, Carolyn," she said, picking up a carton marked *After-Dinner Coffee Cups*. How many more boxes were left? Endless.

Carolyn met her halfway down the stairs. "Listen," she said breathlessly, "don't come up now. All hell is breaking loose—"

The door at the top of stairs opened, Lois appeared. "Carolyn—"

"Mama is carrying on like crazy, she—"

"Carolyn—"

"I'm coming, Lois."

"Carolyn, do you know where the smelling salts are?" Lois demanded.

"I'm coming." Carolyn turned and clattered back up the steps, leaving Peggy, her arms clasped about the box, standing at the bottom of the basement stairs looking up after her. At the top, in the doorway, Carolyn hesitated, turned, and said, "Maybe you'd better—" then turned and disappeared.

Iris is sick, Iris has had a heart attack, Peggy thought wildly. Iris is dying. Maybe, as with her own pregnancies, the thing Iris was afraid of, was always harping on, was going to happen.

Too good to be true, Peggy decided, reluctantly mounting the stairs. The confusion in the kitchen was terrible. Iris lay spread-eagled on a kitchen chair, her head thrown so far back that most of her extra chins had disappeared, her legs stuck out at grotesque angles, her shoes half off, the plump little insteps falling flabbily over the patent leather, Ella suspended over her, eyes wide with distress, hands massaging the back of Iris's neck, while Lois was attempting to pour water into Iris's mouth. Iris, her arms coming up with a great flapping motion, pushed her away; the water spilled, Iris jerked up abruptly, looked down with a pained expression, then fell back.

"It doesn't matter," she wailed. "Let it go. I'm going, I know it. What difference does a little water make?"

"Now, Aunt Iris—"

"No, Lois, I know, I know. Call Dad, call Pete, call Peggy, call— What does Carolyn care? Come in here and give me that telegram without a word, that shows how much she cares. She knows how I am about telegrams, but does she care; no, she doesn't, she—"

"Aunt Iris—"

"You were right, Ella. You saw it all. You said he was coming back. And I got mad at you."

"They're all dried up," Carolyn announced from the doorway, holding up the empty bottle of smelling salts. "They've been in the closet so long that—"

"It doesn't matter," Iris said. "Nothing matters."

"Just be calm, please, Mother," Carolyn begged. "Dad has called the doctor. He'll be here any minute."

"When did he say he was coming?" Iris demanded, sitting bolt upright in her chair, fixing Carolyn with a freezing look of authority. "When?"

"The doctor said he would rush right over—"

"No, no, not the doctor. I don't care about the doctor, it's too late, I can tell. The telegram, when does he say he's coming?" Iris's cherubic little hands clasped her heart, she leaned forward intently. "Read it, read it to me once more."

She won't die, you wait and see, Peggy told herself. There isn't a chance in the world.

"Ethel and I coming home Wednesday afternoon train," Carolyn read slowly, *"Stu."*

"He's come back," Iris said. "I knew he would. He's come back to ask my forgiveness. After all these years he realizes . . ."

But Peggy didn't bother listening. Peggy stood in the midst of Iris's drab kitchen, looking at the peeling mustard-colored walls, thinking, Stu is coming home.

She had been waiting all these years, maybe paying in advance for the happiness that was coming at last, going on year after year making her deposits in misery so that in the end she could have the rest of her lifetime free, in peace.

Right out the door and down the street, dye my hair and change my name, and he won't even know, she thought, that it was his own brother I ran away with.

Chapter Four

HE WAS no prude. Anybody who knew him would vouch for that, Erwin felt, but still he had been shocked. He had never known a decent girl who had got in trouble. Denise, she gave him a couple of scares, but he guessed the French took mistakes like that in their stride, because she went to the pharmacy and got some pills and was okay. I mean, Erwin thought, we generally were pretty careful, but you drink a lot of wine sometimes, you sort of get carried away, you don't want to use those things, you want to be real close. Or you forget, or something happens.

The three-martini babies here, he thought.

Nice girls, they fooled around, he knew that, but he had always tacitly assumed they were too smart to get caught. Knew the game, that was the way he put it to himself. Anyway Denise wasn't what you would have described as "nice." No nice girl lived with a man unless she married him. And why marry a girl you can live with? he asked himself. Those French girls, they didn't know how to play their cards right.

Lois might have had a baby, he thought to himself, shocked. God, think of the talk. A thing like that got back to Springfield—it wasn't like something happening in France. Who'd ever find out about that? But if Lois got drunk that way and went and blabbed, the way she had with him in the kitchen her first night home, who knew who might pick it up and start passing it around? God, he thought, I hope to hell Lois just keeps her mouth shut the rest of the time she's here. It isn't too long, he thought in relief. Today's Monday, the party's Friday, and she probably won't stay long after that. But she hadn't said. Maybe she was here on her vacation, maybe it was *two* weeks she was staying. In two weeks . . .

Helen would never have gotten in trouble, he thought. Of course not. What made Lois so hostile toward Helen? Jealous, he decided. Saw right off the kind of person Helen was, and women couldn't stand competition. It wasn't just Helen's money, he assured himself, it was more —brains, he thought, and knowing how to do the right thing at the right time, stuff like that. The Smith touch.

Lois didn't even look like herself any more, either. She wasn't at all like she was when she was at college and he went out to blow her to that big bill; he was living high then with all the money he'd won at poker in Basic. She had always been a nice quiet girl who thought he could do no wrong—sort of like Denise, he thought maybe that was why he had been attracted to Denise in the first place, because she had reminded him of Lois—and now, Lois just wasn't the same person at all, and since she wasn't the same person, she had no claim on him. Throwing herself on his good shirt and screeching she had had an abortion. Was that her idea of social know-how?

Well, he had managed to pass it off. "I won't buy that," he tried to interrupt, and then pretended he hadn't heard the rest, that final terrible bit about the abortion.

He threw the ball out and called, "Fetch." The big German shepherd, his tongue hanging out, his muzzle covered with spittle, ran toward him. "No, no goddam it," Erwin shouted, feeling rage run through him. "*Fetch*. The *other* way, you damn mutt."

The dog circled him, dancing up and down joyously. Erwin could have killed him. It was so hot back here; every nerve in his body burned with the heat; he ached all over with the painful exercise of running and retrieving what the dog wouldn't.

I'm about ready to pack up, he thought; the heat, I'm so damn tired, business bad, I don't want Helen starting in on me about how I'm not living up to my responsibility about the dog.

Loping like the dog, he crossed the cement and collected the ball. A hundred and fifty bucks for a dog that wouldn't even run after a ball. It was something he would never have admitted to anyone, but that kennel man had put one over on him.

He raised his arm and wiped the sweat from his forehead on the short sleeve of his T-shirt. He had enough troubles without worrying about Lois. He hadn't got his trip to Paris the way he planned, his wife was after him about the dog, business was lousy, his mother— His father had dumped the whole business of his mother on him. Of course his father sent her money, but that was only part of it. It was the way she *acted*. If only someone would marry her and she would move away, get off his back. If only Esther would die and leave him her money. If only Lois would stay out of circulation until she went back to New York. If only—

"Now fetch, goddam it," he shouted in desperation, throwing the ball with all his might.

The dog sat, fixed, stubborn, regarding him with sullen eyes. It was the same expression his father assumed when Erwin tried to talk to him about how he felt about his mother. Erwin kept thinking while he was growing up that he could force his father to take an interest in what was going to happen to her; those sessions with his father were his first lesson in learning you can't force people to do anything they're dead set against. When they're indifferent, maybe you can move them—but never, once they've made up their minds.

It wasn't fair I didn't get that trip to Paris, he told himself. Someone should have tipped me off. I could have put on the gas that last week and made it without too much of a haul. Probably, he thought, they were all glad I didn't win. Jealous, every one of them, because I married—

He cut the thought off. Formulating how and why he had married Helen was something he scrupulously avoided. Maybe he wasn't sure himself. Lots of motives behind everything, he told himself.

Even this damn dog.

Helen was so obstinate about Captain, as if using the dog to challenge

F

him. She was making him prove his mettle by mastering the dog. Erwin paused, looking down at the concrete, the dog near, watching, wary. How had she got him into a position like that?

Shaking his head, he said to himself, I don't know, it's just the way she is. She makes everything a test. No matter what I do, it's never quite enough. Something they teach them at Smith, he decided, how to get the upper hand and keep it. Without ever raising their voices.

"Let's give it one more try," Erwin said to the dog, hearing in his own voice all the counterfeit patience he was forcing on himself. He bent down and patted the dog, talking to him gently, trying (he told himself) to instill confidence, the way that damn book said.

The dog backed away from him, shrinking down, retreating backwards toward the fence. "Good boy, nice boy," Erwin entreated, finding himself shuffling after Captain, trying to retain the firm, friendly act he had started and knowing that if the dog didn't respond soon he would fly into a rage, pick up the ball, and throw it right at him.

It happened all the time. He tried and tried until something snapped and he lost his temper and screamed at the dog, ran after him shouting obscenities, or, worse, started hitting him; then he found himself, weak and shaking, face to face with his wife. She would have heard him shouting and come to find out what was the matter, catch him in the midst of his outrageous behavior.

Suddenly the dog darted around him and ran to the opposite end of the yard, stood there panting, one front leg lifted, nodding his head from left to right, agitated. How the hell could she expect him to train a dog in the odd off-hours he got a week? The whole thing was silly, and what were they training him for anyway?

"Damned if I know," he said aloud.

He would have to wait now until the dog was ready to cooperate. That was one of the things the training manual stressed—not to try to force an animal when it was actively balking.

You had to give everything your own confidence these days—your wife, your dog, even your goddam lawn. Pretty soon there wasn't going to be any left over for himself.

Erwin leaned against the fence, took out a cigarette, and prepared to wait. It had been a bad time, sales slumping in the hot weather. His stomach was bothering him, too much drinking lately, too many late hours, he was all tense and keyed-up, he wanted to call it quits, take a shower, eat, and get to bed early. But Helen expected him to spend at least an hour out here, no matter what.

On the concrete a tawny veil of late light spread; the square area of bright, white concrete was slowly turning yellow as the sunlight seeped forward. In another ten minutes I'll get it full face, he told himself wearily. "Look, Captain," he pleaded. "Let's just try it once more, what do you say?"

The dog stood still, almost challenging him to lose his temper. "Well, I'm not going to," Erwin said to the animal. "I'll quit before I start running around raving at you again."

He finished his cigarette and started to walk over toward the last of the shadows. He had made up his mind to try one more throw, and if that didn't work he was going to give it up. The whole day had been a waste. Everything he touched had gone wrong. If I'd had any sense, I wouldn't have tried anything important today, he thought. No wonder the Barlowe deal fell through, no wonder Captain is acting up. I'll bet Helen will say she's too tired to make love, or it's too hot, or the baby's moving around and we ought not to jiggle it up. Don't even try to make love to her, he advised himself, you'll just get into an argument. It's too hot to argue. Just go to bed and get some sleep.

Business falling off this way was scary. It kept him awake, wondering how he was going to keep up. The house ate up every bit of money he made, and even though Helen's father was generous there was never enough money for bills he didn't count on—the car needing repairs or a huge cleaning bill or the hot-water heater going on the fritz, the cleaning woman twice a week and the endless Scotch she sneaked; the washing machine was always running into snags and the house developing kinks nobody had foreseen (the windows were warped in their frames or the cellar inexplicably leaked); it was always money, money, money, people on the telephone asking for it or quoting prices on how much it would be to repair something (and it always turned out to be more), letters piled up with back bills stamped with red notices, men on the street stopping him and saying casually or not so casually, "Say, Erwin, you musta forgot about the oil, it's been due since last March," and he would laugh and pound the man on the back and say, "I sure did. Put a check in the mail for you tonight," and all the time the blood was beating up inside him, he was trying to figure out if there was enough in the checking account to cover that amount, if he *could* put a check in the mail without sinking into overdraft. Now this dog was eating them out of house and home—not that he wouldn't have been glad to be rid of the house and home and all the money it too was consuming, but . . .

But, he reminded himself, the Paris vacation. Now that Helen had the clothes, she wanted to go, and they had to go pretty soon. They couldn't go after the kid came. So it was now or never.

She never directly said she was disappointed, but he could tell: little things she let slip, the way she went on reading those French tourist books, sighing when she saw the clothes in the closet. Yeah, she had her heart set on going and—and the truth was that if she hadn't married him and she were living at home her father would have given her the money. Erwin couldn't get in the position, he felt, of not being able to match her father. One of those tests, he supposed. So, it was Paris.

He wanted to get back himself. Things wouldn't have changed much in five years. He was looking forward to taking her to all the places the other tourists wouldn't know, showing Paris off to her. Of course it was too bad they couldn't get south, where he really knew his way around, but then—he thought, reconsidering—maybe it was just as well. He might run into some people he had known, Denise herself; no, it would be better to stay in Paris, play it safe.

Biarritz: whenever he said it, even silently, a whole montage of scenes spilled over in his mind—the strong sea, it was never smooth and calm there, always high with big whitecaps pounding against the sand, and there was a funny quality about Biarritz, it wasn't sunny and happy the way you'd think of a resort, at least Erwin never thought of it like that, there were always, at least in his memory, storm clouds rolling in with the breakers, a heavy dark sky, low over the sea, a feeling of violence in the air; he remembered how cold it got there sometimes and how he and Denise would walk along, all bundled up but barefooted, how frozen their feet were when they got back to town, the sand was frigid under their feet, and they shivered now and then, but they had loved walking that beach in the dark days of November and December, when they were alone with the gulls and the surf and the big gray clouds coming in.

A dark-haired girl with big, trusting eyes. She thought he was going to marry her. She was always talking about how it would be for them in the United States, if she would "fit in," *s'adapter. Engagée,* that was another word she always used; she liked to be involved, with everything. He wondered what had happened to her. Probably helping out her father in the bakery. Or married to that boy who worked in the post office, the one she had grown up with and always expected to marry before he came along.

He had liked Biarritz as well as you could expect to like something so foreign, so dirty. It was a good town, better than most of the French towns, cleaner and all—probably the townspeople made an effort for the tourists. He had been lucky to be sent there, instead of going to some filthy backwoods place or—god—out to the Pacific.

Boy, he thought, mopping his brow again, I was sure lucky to pull that deal to get in school. But Chet got his cut, Erwin thought bitterly. His prices kept going up and going up. Every time there was a new list there was a new price. He hadn't minded giving Chet a couple of hundred to stay behind in personnel when they were first shipped in, but *five* hundred to get to Biarritz, just because the war was over in Europe and everyone was afraid of being sent out to the Pacific, he was crazy, that Chet. But what could you do if you didn't, like Erwin, have any decent points?

Erwin remembered how he had sweated out that two weeks of playing poker—and playing seriously—trying to get together the five hundred Chet wanted to get his name on the list. And his luck, his wonderful, wonderful luck in winning that big pot on three queens and a pair of tens, he had had a kind of feeling about that hand, but god, how he had sweated it out, knowing that it was all or nothing, and that other guy, from another company, going along bet by bet, both of them nervous but committed to going the limit of the three raises. There was a big stack of bills, over four hundred dollars, in the middle of the table by the time they laid down their hands. When he saw the three jacks and the kings, his heart had just stopped, and then, grinning, he had laid down his own hand. He owed Biarritz and Denise to three queens and a pair of tens.

But the thing was, he had had the guts to go along with his feeling that he *couldn't* lose. Other guys, they chickened out. Maybe they had the same feeling of being in the luck, but they didn't have the guts to go along with that feeling, they backed out, and so, he thought, they deserved to lose. Just the way I deserved to win.

I mean, he told himself, taking out a cigarette, in this life you have to be a *chancer*. The way I was with Helen. I knew she had lots of guys who had more to offer her than I did, but I played it odds on all the way.

That's the way to do it, keep raising and raising to the limit, scare the chickens out, and then go all the way if you think you have it. If you don't, get out early, don't waste yourself on in-betweens. I played it that way with Helen and it worked, he told himself in satisfaction.

We got along good from the beginning, he thought. And then, well, all those things Denise had sort of showed him—not taught him, mind you, he would have come on them for himself, but hell, she saved him time, learning from her that way cut out the experimenting he would have had to do otherwise—well, those little ways of lovemaking, they were a big help. He was sure Helen was impressed. Not that she ever went the limit, she wasn't like Lois, he thought, getting into *trouble*. But she went pretty far, he thought. For someone like her, he amended, so that showed you he must have been pretty good at the game. He was glad he could relax now. It was good now just to settle back and let it come naturally, straight off, the way a man really wanted it when he had other things on his mind. I got to worry about business now, he thought, she knows that.

I didn't marry her for her money, he said defensively to himself. Nobody's denying the money's a help, but that wasn't why I married her. We got along from the start. She was just what I wanted. And I've never given her any trouble. A couple of times, out of town, maybe I've played around a little, but not here, where she's got friends. Anyway on a convention everyone expects it, they'd think you were queer or something if you didn't.

Jesus Christ, she wasn't the prettiest girl he had ever known and her —well—body, it was just—well, okay, that wasn't it. It was the way she made him feel, that he was way ahead of all the other guys he knew, as if he were some kind of goddam exception in Springfield, the way he had felt when he was in Biarritz after the war with more money than anyone else and access to all those black-market things nobody else had, as if he were walking on top of the world.

It was tied up with the dog, too. The way Helen talked about breeding. He couldn't quite make the connection, but it was the way she talked about his family, especially his mother and Esther, in one tone of voice and the dog in another. He and Helen were both interested in good blood. She had been born with it, but he had had to prove it was there, taking long shots the way he did, showing he wasn't chicken, wasn't yellow, like so many other guys.

That dog, big and awkward, would run into the room, barking and sniffing, and Helen would smile, her whole face went soft, and she turned to him and said in her special voice, "Isn't he marvelous?" and Erwin felt she was talking about him, that she thought somehow the dog represented him, big and awkward and difficult to train. But he found himself nodding, smiling, sickish. "He's swell," he would say, and Captain ran around, pushing against tables, barking, disarranging chairs, nuzzling against the ashtrays and overturning them.

He shouldn't get mad at Captain. That dog brought a warmth between them. When they went to bed, squirming under him, suddenly in the middle of the whole love spasm, she would say, "Wasn't he cute, the way he barked when . . ." And Erwin would find himself laughing, clutching her more possessively, thinking, We've got something.

Now he stood in the full glare of the sunlight and thought, What? His wife's pores were large under the lamplight, she was a social snob under the Stamos; he knew in his heart that half the time she was feigning passion, but god, when she said, Isn't he cute? he suddenly felt that great swelling of pride, as if he were protecting her and the dog against the whole onslaught of an unseen enemy, the alien forces that raged against the house—the bills and the debts, the untold problems that weighed down on him and piled up and piled up and how was he going to fight what he only half understood? But that was precisely what he was supposed to undertake, wasn't it? That was the big test.

By Christ, he thought, there's no understanding love.

"Come on, Captain, let's take a last turn."

"You think he's making any improvement?"

Erwin turned. In the brilliant sunlight he could not see her. The light was in his eyes and she was standing in shadow behind the screen door. But she had her special voice. That he recognized at once. "He's doing fine," he lied. "You been watching long?"

"No," the voice answered. "I just came to see how he was doing."

He didn't want her to lose her confidence, not in either of them. "I tell you," he said. "I think I ought to call it quits now. It's hot and he's been working hard, I don't want to discourage him."

"No," she agreed, "you don't. Just throw the ball once more. Let *me* see."

It was exactly what he had been trying to avoid. He stood dumbly for a moment, trying to think of an out. "I tell you what," he said, trying to feign enthusiasm. "Why don't *you* try? He's so crazy about you and all—"

"Oh, but doesn't the book say he ought to stick with one trainer?" she asked doubtfully. "I thought it was bad to have a lot of people handling him."

"Naw. Try it. You're as much his master as I am."

Let her fail, he thought gleefully, let her see how it is to have him refuse to do anything you tell him. I'm sick of being the fall guy.

The door opened. She stepped out onto the back stoop. She was wearing a white jumper over a dark blue skirt and hardly looked pregnant at all. There were big gold hoops in her ears and a tangle of gold bracelets with bouncing charms around one slender wrist. In the bright sunlight she looked like a picture of what the well-dressed young mother-to-be should be wearing this year. She never looks dowdy or rumpled, he thought in wonderment. Even in the morning she has that crisp, put-together look. Her eyes are never clogged with sleep. She never has pillow wrinkles on her face. Her mouth was never swollen from the kisses that had been put there a few hours before. Even her nightgown held its press. How did she do it?

Maybe they teach that at Smith too. They certainly don't teach them anything about economics.

"Go ahead," he urged. Before she could change her mind, he darted over the concrete and pressed the ball into her hand. The bracelets gave a series of small giggles as she grasped it.

"Well—"

"Go on. I'll bet he'll—"

"You don't think you ought to check with the book first?"

"Go on, Helen. What's the matter? You chicken?"

She gave him a sharp, strange look, then grasped the ball firmly, descended the back steps quickly. She wasn't smiling. A little frown puckered the skin between her eyes. There were two determined creases at the sides of her mouth. "Well, in a way he is my dog," she said slowly.

"Sure, throw the ball. Look, Captain, look who's got the ball. Come on, boy, come fetch."

"No, don't you say anything. I want to do it all by myself."

The dog looked uneasy. He sat down, then changed his mind and stood up, looking at Helen guardedly. But he had closed his mouth. The jaws were locked tightly together.

For one wild, distraught moment Erwin had the notion that big German shepherd was going to charge across the yard and leap on his wife, paw her, cut her to ribbons with his strong teeth. My god, he thought, starting toward her, he *could* kill her, and the baby.

He never had a chance to express his fear, the obstinate periphery of his love. Helen held the ball up and in one piercing, shrieking sentence of command with all the words running together she shouted, *"Gofetch-captain."* The ball left her hand in a wide arch and flew to the other side of the yard.

Captain flung himself into the air, a silvery dart speeding through the lion-like light, his body silver and gray in the tawny mane of light, and Erwin watched in wonder and horror as the sharp teeth fastened around the bright red ball and clamped down, the dog turned, without lessening his pace, and leaped straight toward the still figure of the woman standing poised and sure, waiting for him to bring back the ball.

The next instant Captain dropped the ball at Helen's feet and stood looking up at her in tense anticipation. Still, flushed and triumphant, she let one hand smooth back a few hairs that had slipped loose in the excitement. And at that moment, looking first at Helen, then at the dog, Erwin was absolutely and positively sure she had been watching all along, that she had wanted him to fail, had been waiting to come out and prove her superiority, that she could always do the things he never could. He should have known that dog would fetch for her. She had always had better cards when she played for keeps.

Chapter Five

How sure was sure?

If Ethel hadn't shown him the paper, he would never have believed her. But there it was in black and white: *positive.* Just to check—he didn't put anything past her—Stu took the paper to the druggist himself. Well, that son of a bitch had confirmed it.

Christ, I'm too old to start this father guff, he thought, knowing all the same that he was putting on an act for himself, because deep down there was a flash of pride, the incredulous wonder of something important about to happen to him, maybe for the first time in his life.

It was like being given a medal when all the time you knew you had been a coward and only stayed in the lines because the sergeant had threatened to shoot you if you ran. It happened all over France, especially at Clervaux. But then what did they expect?—the goddam Germans swarming over the lines with those filthy big tanks, bigger than anything the Americans had, those damn Krauts coming at them like spooks. White capes, white sheets over their heads, and the snow, you couldn't even see them. What did the goddam generals expect? Two hundred and fifty thousand Germans against seventy-five thousand Americans, and most of those green troops just sent up to the front. Some odds, he thought sourly, looking out the window as a late afternoon landscape swept by in a flurry of summer scenes, the sinking six-o'clock sun giving the fields a burnished light.

No wonder I'm always thinking about snow, he told himself. Who the hell wouldn't after a couple of weeks up there?

Well, I came out alive, he reminded himself. I suppose that's something. Lots didn't. Lots of better men, he thought. That's always the way it works out: the good go first. It stands to reason. They're so goddam eager they stand up and rush right out into the lead. He had seen them cut down like green grass under a mower, their spattered uniforms so mockingly green in the midst of that winter white, while the Germans, the ghost patrols, marched over them, the winter marauders who had enough sense to take on the color of the landscape, while the green troops, complaining no one had seen to their mail getting to the front and asking one another who would attack so near Christmas, were sitting suckers.

Ethel was asleep, her head lolling back against the seat. How she could sleep in all this heat was beyond him, but he was glad she could. At least he didn't have to talk to her. She's got my kid inside her, he thought in wonder, gazing at her curiously, as if he might see inside her, watch the little embryo take life and form and grow moment by moment. He supposed she knew all the facts—when the thing got fingernails and eyes and hair and stuff like that—but to him it was just a big mystery, as much a matter of concealment as the whole horror of death.

No matter how many bodies he had seen—and some of them were dillies, the frozen, stiff corpses that were the crop that December of '44— he had never understood. Never got used to it. Only hardened. You could learn to walk on without being really sick, but inside, your stomach knotted every goddam time.

The only thing that stopped them, he considered, was that they ran out of gas.

It was stupid to think a thing like that, probably was something he had read somewhere and carried with him as the nice, precise explanation of the whole slaughter. He could imagine some journalist safe behind the lines composing that neat little phrase: The Germans lost the race to the Meuse because they ran out of gas. But there was a lot of truth in it too; anyone who had seen the graveyard of abandoned tanks huddled against that worn landscape could not forget that wars were won by more than the men whose rotting flesh lay everywhere. Machines in war were as important as—maybe more important than—men. What kind of world was it anyway where a machine could do what a man couldn't?

I don't know, he thought, and I suppose I don't much care. It's over now. The only place it still exists is inside my head, and then not too often. I've taught myself how to forget. And the shrapnel, he told himself—every once in a while a piece of metal works itself out as a reminder.

If the kid's a girl, he thought, she'd never have to go to war, never lie freezing in a foxhole with shells whistling over her head and her guts all cramped with the refuse she can't get out because she's too scared, saying to herself, What about the tanks? Supposing they bring the tanks up?

Your whole body gets jammed with all the filth and stink of war. You don't function right any more. At first you think it's only you; then you begin to realize that it's happening all up and down the lines. Men are always letting out that stinking gas, the whole lines stink with the crap within all the men, that crap they can't get rid of, except once in a while making wind. War is that special stink, outside in the dead, inside in the living.

Gas, he thought: there you have it again, not enough gas inside the tanks, too much inside the men. A play on words no damn jerk journalist would dare make. Too true. Nobody dares tell the real truth, it's too ugly. Oh, the goddam filth of the human race, he thought, wincing and looking down into Ethel's half-opened mouth from which the heavily accented breath escaped with a smell of onions. She had had them on that hamburger at the station, and she still smelled of them. Stink, we all stink, he thought, it makes you sick.

Ethel made a funny sound, a little moan, and shifted her weight. I'm taking my wife home, he thought, home to meet Mother. Isn't that nice? Taking my little wife home to meet my sweet little mother so we can tell her she's going to be a grandmother again. What a farce. And yet, to be honest, that was the first thing that had come into his head when he stared down at the word on the druggist's paper, *positive*. Well, I've got to go home now and face up to the whole mess. It's no good trying to get out of it this time. You don't get any points for that.

She's getting old, he had thought to himself of his mother, and I guess it's time to bury the past and start all over. I owe it to the kid. The kid deserves a break. If he made it up to his mother, she might leave the kid some money when she died. That would be giving his kid an even shake. It was the least he could do. The kid was never going to get much from him, that much was certain. And that damn Esther wasn't going to do anyone any favors.

He knew that, but sometimes he let himself forget, imagined what it would be like if Esther died and left him some of her money. A whole new beginning, he would think, before he was able to shake off the preposterous vision.

Esther's money—forget it, forget it, he told himself. Off your rocker like the rest of the family. Going home to Mama and dear old Dad.

At least Lois would be there. You can count on Lois to make an effort, he thought. The rest of them—I don't know, I can't really say. Maybe Carolyn's changed; maybe we'll get along. And Pete—I just don't know, we were never close, and I suppose it's too late now.

But Lois always talked about his brother and sister as if they had qualities that made them likeable. When Lois talked about Pete she was sad but sympathetic; when she talked about Carolyn she sounded as if she really respected her. Tennis, he thought, Carolyn and Lois played tennis together before Lois came to New York.

He supposed Lois was the only one in the family he trusted, and he wasn't sure how far he would trust her. He wasn't sure how far he would let himself trust anyone. He thought of Lois standing on the stairs. She even likes me, Stu thought. No discrimination at all.

He thought of the three men who had picked him up and carried him back behind his own lines. Why had they carried him back? What had made them bother? No one would have ever known if they had just left him. He would have bled to death or some Kraut would have come up and finished him off.

He didn't even know the names of the men who had saved him. He didn't even remember what their faces were like. They were just three men who came out of nowhere, stopped, looked down at him, turned to one another wordlessly, and began shifting their stuff around; then two of them bent over and lifted him up, supporting him as he stumbled along. Shifting him back and forth among the three of them, they could rest a little, but it had still been a hard haul. They had got him, after what seemed an eternity, back behind the lines, but not before the four of them had to spend a night in hiding, when it seemed they might not make it, any of them. He was only half conscious, but he knew, desperate as the position was, that not one of them had considered ditching him.

They were the most untalking men he had ever known. All that long, dark, cold night they had lain under the broken rubble of an old barn, silent, stiff with cold, and hostile to any sound that came from around. It was as if they were using their ears to fight their way out, as if they resented their own voices because they intruded on the main job of listening and identifying.

When they got him back to the medics, they left him. They didn't wait to find out if he was going to make it. They didn't ask his name, they didn't bother to tell him theirs. They just brought him in, dumped him, and went on their way, looking for their company, trying to get back to the regroupings. He supposed in the course of things one or two, maybe all three, had been killed.

What had made them do it? He knew that if he had been in their place he would have walked on, he wouldn't have thought about stopping.

If he knew what it was that made them, *without even thinking about it* (and this seemed to him the most pertinent point), stop to carry him along, a wounded, helpless man they had never seen before, he was sure that he would understand a lot of things, maybe even how in the end the points added up, what the final score was supposed to be.

He had trusted these men (I had to, he thought), but it was more than that, much more. He had known without question that they wouldn't desert him. It was the way they looked at him, the way each one went about shifting his pack, without anyone's saying anything about saving him.

Hell, he thought, I don't even trust my own wife. Had to go see the druggist myself.

But Lois,—

It was funny about her, but it was like he had a little hope for her. She should have been a loser—the things that had happened, her father going off and leaving her that way, her mother killing herself—but he didn't feel like that about her. He remembered how he had thought, coming down from her flat on Saturday, that she was "going to make it." Now he couldn't say that for sure; what he did feel was that she had a chance.

It was more than the rest of them had, anyway.

She's a carrier, he thought, that's why you like her. She'd stop and pick up someone who had been left behind, that's what makes you trust her.

Christ, what a boring landscape, so much of the same thing: sagging unpainted houses, unmended fences, pastures dotted with cow dung, the endless dust, green fields rusted by broken machinery, abandoned cars, and mounds of decaying debris. They ought to have a war run over them, he thought. Bet they wouldn't be so damn careless about their farms then. You value something you have to protect.

But this land was too good. It gave back wealth without trying. Those people near Bastogne knew what real work was, digging their places out, war after war, tidying up the measly little acre or so they called a farm, only to have another invasion rush across them and destroy everything. The Midwest makes me sick, he thought, watching the farms flash by.

Your day's coming, he told the vanishing landscape, and don't think it isn't. A big fat bomb is going to drop on you one of these days.

A long December, he thought, and cold . . . terribly cold . . . and a few men strung out across a front, nobody knowing anything that was happening on the other side because the goddam Krauts were so smart, putting down straw and moving their tanks at night so no one would hear them, sending in supplies bit by bit, building up, and not one goddam general or colonel or chickenshit lieutenant had an idea that all those white-robed men were waiting for the signal to come and get us.

The sixteenth of December, he thought, I'll never forget that date as long as I live. All night the guns going, barrage after barrage, the shells screaming and hollering, *We're coming to get you, coming to get you*—crouched against the earth knowing it was the truth, too scared even to say, *Come and get us,* only stop this firing; and then that terrible moment of silence, the suspension of all sound, and only the white earth, clawed by shells, blackened by blood and ripped with shrapnel, and then a moment of hush; I heard someone crying near me, *O mother of god, come on,* and suddenly the sky was lit with moonlight, a big giant moon seemed to have exploded and the whole landscape was flooded with moonlight; the crying stopped in that instant, and we stood looking at our blackened faces reflected in the eyes around us, those eyes that had seen so much and were going to see so much more, and suddenly we knew it wasn't moonlight but huge lights the Krauts had set up so that they could see when they came to get us.

O mother of god, they're coming.

And they had, he thought, shaking all over in the midsummer heat, they had. No wonder I never see colors inside my head, but only white, white lights bursting into the darkness of the corners of my mind.

It was as if the snow rose: all around the little banks of snow rose into the air and then it was an army of men, clothed in white, walking patiently and surely across that stripped expanse of no man's land, coming to get us.

We sat still and watched, too fascinated and frightened to fire, just watching them walking toward us, row after row of white men in the white light, seeing the big tanks on either side, more tanks than we had ever seen before.

Oh god, she was awake. He felt her stirring beside him, movements that signified she was surreptitiously trying to pull down her girdle—no, she had left off her girdle, he remembered, said that maybe it would be bad for the baby, so she must just be straightening her dress, a natural enough thing for a woman to do, why did it annoy him so? "What the hell are you doing?" he asked irritably.

"My dress hiked up."

"You sleep?"

"I guess so. Did you?"

"No, it's too hot."

"If we could have took a Pullman, maybe it wouldn't have been so bad."

"Ethel," he said, trying to be patient, "where do you think we'd get the money? When you just up and quit the way I did, the way you did, they don't give you a bonus, you know."

"What time is it? I'm hungry."

"Can't you hold off? You had that sandwich back at the station just before we left."

"I tell you I'm hungry. I should eat in my condition," she whined. "It ain't good to go a long time without food."

"All right, all right, we'll get something as soon as they come and say the dining car's open."

She let out a small whimper. He never understood Ethel's reactions. Laughing or crying was utterly arbitrary with her; she might just as well have substituted one for the other. It was beyond him. But one thing he did know: as soon as he got near her she put on a big sad face. She had it on now. And she always ended up making him feel that way, too—filled with one big sad ache.

"Here," he said, reaching into the bag in front of him. "Eat this." He held out a Hershey bar. Just before they had left New York he had garnered a supply of chocolate bars, movie magazines, peanuts, and gum. The all-night trip, sitting up, would be hard on her, but worse was the constant hunger she complained of. Well, he thought, I guess she has a right to gripe. It can't be much fun for her, coming back to Springfield with me like this. "We'll eat first call," he promised.

She had the candy in her hand, greedily ripping the paper off. Her big thick lips closed over the dark bar, tearing away a whole square. She chewed happily, stoking up, he thought, so she'll be ready to get me. Putting all that energy inside to build up her word machine. Pretty soon she'll start, talking, talking, carrying on, knowing she can go as far as she wants because there are people around and I won't dare make a scene. Even if you hit her, he considered, I don't suppose it would make much dent, there's so much flesh to absorb the blow. Sink down in that flesh at night and it smells like going into the five-and-dime: cheap talcum, cheap perfume, those gaudy earrings that always reek of plastic. My little dime-store dearie, he sang silently to himself, *I can't give you anything but love, baby. . . .*

Baby . . .

Yeah, he thought sourly, that's what you get from making love: babies. My brother ought to know. The whole damn family gets caught the same way. A hard-luck bunch.

Shove it, he told himself.

Ethel had peeled back the wrapper of a Tootsie Roll, and he saw the rich glow of chocolate underneath. It reminded him of that time with the chocolate milk in Paris. The R and R—to get patched up, to get rested and recuperated so they could send you back to the tanks, a little reward for your wounds. So what do they do? Ship you to some godforsaken place where there's nothing to do but look at stale movies and go over the whole thing in your mind. Men all around you and more of them coming in all the time. Some rest and recreation.

But he had fooled them. Took off, went AWOL and left that little covering card to the sergeant: *Got the itch to see something and will be back when my R and R is up. Don't worry.* He wondered what the first sergeant had thought when he saw that, but he hadn't worried too much. You can't shoot a man for trying to find a little real relaxation. Not after St. Vith, not after Clervaux.

He had picked up a little French girl in that town—what was its name? Unpronounceable, but the girl, Jacqueline, was great. Real R and R. Three full days of it. They stayed in the whole time, even ate some of their meals in bed, and then after the war when he was back in Paris and had a real leave he had been half crazy to see her.

He felt as if he were actually there, back in Paris, wandering through the city, five years before, when he had known every bar in Paris that sold chocolate milk.

Something of a feat, he told himself, the only unique thing I've done in my whole life. He would walk into a bar, looking casual and unconcerned, watching an irritable bartender slop wines down in rows of four and five, thinking that more than anything else in the world he would like a big tall glass of brandy at one of those expensive sidewalk cafés, that if he could sit down, drink his brandy, he would forget everything, the goddam war, those days at the front, the white humps of earth that had arisen into men and come across the frozen land, O mother of god, here they come, and most of all he would forget the cheap, stinking room where he was waiting for Jacqueline, the terrible wondering if she would come at all.

Pardonnez-moi, avez-vous du lait au chocolat? His great phrase in French.

Some of those bartenders' faces had been startled, others outraged, as they shook their heads, like an aroused enemy, in emphatic denial; still others had found nothing odd in his request—it was after all an odd world—had merely turned, wiping their dirty hands on their dirty aprons, to open an old-fashioned icebox, extract a bottle, uncap it, slam it down wordlessly, expressionlessly, in front of him. In those places—the cheap little bars that did have *du lait au chocolat*—the bottles had been stored in the moldy old refrigerators so long that the milk had all joined together in thick, mute protest and tasted sour and disgruntled.

It was a big city, Paris, and not the gay and charming Paris everyone talked about, not then, after what had happened. Hysteria there was plenty of, the kind of hysteria he understood: of being saved, of just being alive. It made people do absurd, terrible deadly things, gave them the feeling that, since they had been spared, all the rules went out the window. All over that mad city people were committing the most violent actions to prove that they were alive, that the war was over, that the whole thing was finished, washed up, kaput. He had walked in those wild crowds, exploring the wide main boulevards, losing himself in a tangle of alleys and passageways, *trottoirs,* confused back lanes.

He often found himself by the river. Whenever it leaped out at him, a coiled black snake in the midst of that insane release from the terrors of death and bombing, he would look down at the water and think, I got through. He always came back to the river, its refuse slapping against the quays—bottles and fruit skins, boards and dead bloated cats, limp contraceptives and broken shoes, all the flotsam of a human life that is essentially rootless and free of the old morality—and he would stand gazing out across the Seine, thinking absolutely nothing except that, god, he was thirsty. Then he would turn and hunt up another bar. *Excusez-moi, avez-vous du lait au chocolat?*

Monday and Tuesday, when the whole thing first started, he had been absolutely himself. He had come down from the front and he had seen Jacqueline on the way to Paris and she had agreed to come on Wednesday; then they would find a good, cheap place where there were good food and clean beds, beds with real honest-to-god sheets and blankets that had been washed and were not frozen in the form of bodies, blankets that didn't smell and didn't have holes in them, and for a whole week they were going to lie around and eat and make love and then, later, maybe, when it was quiet and cooler, go to see some of the things you were supposed to see in Paris.

It was going to be a fine week, a perfect week, he free of the front, she free of her family, just the two of them in that big, wild, hysterical city with all his back pay to throw away on a hotel with clean sheets, on food that was black market and expensive but worth it, and on all the wine they wanted. They were going to drink at all the expensive cafés on the Champs Elysées, and to hell with how much it cost.

Monday night, anticipating, he drank too much wine and then had two cognacs later at a sidewalk café, and he had come back to the cheap hotel very drunk. He thought he had been sick, but he couldn't quite remember. Tuesday he felt hung over and vaguely disturbed—there was something new about him, something he couldn't quite define, as if he had developed another arm or found a friend who wouldn't go away.

That was when he started the compulsive walking, and the walking made him thirsty, the walking and watching all those wild people. All over Paris he drank apéritifs until, lunchless, at four o'clock he realized he couldn't make it back to the hotel by himself and he had got, somehow, a taxi, and the hotel clerk and the taxi driver, he thought, had carried him, like a lumpy body that had left its life back at the front, up to his room. When he awoke, in his bed, he was in the midst of a twisted nightmare, hearing his own shouts, finding himself crouched in the middle of the bed as if he had been back in his foxhole trying to hide from the shells.

The only thought he had had was, Christ, I've got shell shock, I'm in a bad way. Supposing I can't make love any more? They say that happens to you. Had it been then or later, downstairs trying to get some supper at the little restaurant across the street that was closed, that he had made the vow to himself?

No more drinks until Jacqueline comes, nothing but chocolate milk until Jacqueline comes. It wasn't much: less than twenty-four hours of abstinence.

But, of course, like everything else, things hadn't worked out that way. Jacqueline hadn't been on the two-forty train and suddenly, frightened, he had rushed to the local telephone exchange. That goddam girl isn't going to come, he had thought. Here I go and save myself to come to Paris and—

Then, amazingly, he was through—the long cable of wire that connected their two voices screaming, protesting, carrying on a conversation of its own. She was sick. She was sorry, oh, she was terribly sorry, but she couldn't get down until— Where was he? All right, she would write it down, she would let him know—

You're not coming, goddam it, just say so, he had screamed into the receiver when something went off with a grinding jar and he was disconnected. Now she'll never come, he had thought. Even in my bad French she knows how desperate I am.

It struck him, coming out of the telephone booth into the veil of synthetic hilarity that hung over Paris, that he would be an absolute mess by the end of his furlough. His face would break out, his tongue would turn brown, his disposition would curdle on all the chocolate milk he would drink between now and then, but he would not give in. If he gave in, she would never come. So long as he hung on to his vow, there was a chance he might be rewarded, that Jacqueline might come.

My god, he thought, automatically picking up the Hershey bar wrapping and the Tootsie Roll band, crunching them into a neat little ball, the way they had taught him in the Army, how many gallons of chocolate milk do you suppose I drank in those next four days? Thirst had been the one motivating factor of his existence. He had fled it all over Paris, up and down miserable streets in the shirtsleeve section, in and out of avenues and boulevards in the Homburg-and-briefcase area. But it never left his heels: there, panting and sweating, it came after him until, dog-tired, blind with despair, he turned into the first doorway that smelled of resinous wine and gasped out, *Avez-vous du lait au chocolat?*

Then suddenly all that miserable, painful last night came over him. She had not come. Probably she had latched on to some officer by then. He knew that no vow would ever make his vision into reality and he had only one thought in mind: to get back at everyone and everything.

He had started to drink with a vengeance. He supposed his stomach was out of condition. He was still weak from his wounds. Sweating with something close to the terror of the front, he went down, a drowning man, drowned in some drink along the way. The MPs had picked him up and, sick as he had been, they had got him ready to go back.

Oh, he thought, sitting up with a jerk, my god, going back to Springfield is like going back to the outfit after that terrible drunk. It's the same kind of useless, silly gesture; meaningless. Jacqueline didn't come. Going back won't make it any better for the kid. Nothing I can do is going to change what is.

He turned and looked at his wife. You goddam Kraut, he wanted to shout at her, what did you go and get me into all this for? Do you think having a kid is going to change what is? Don't you know anyone with any sense would never bring a kid into a world like this?

Chapter Six

THEY could never meet in bars comfortably. You couldn't talk in movies, and drug stores and soda fountains were too public, the park too far out, and a streetcorner too awkward. Finally they arranged for her to stand in front of Walgreen's and he picked her up in the car and they went somewhere and parked.

Eileen never thought of it as meeting him on the sly. The situation was merely one of the conditions of living the kind of life she did, doing the important things in secret.

All her friends were married and settled in houses of their own, with one, two, three children whose demands had by necessity changed their interests so that she, still unmarried but going with the same boy year after year, was a kind of oddity, one of those people friends remember vaguely and speak of inordinately but seldom see. The friends had dropped away, the boy was still there, but getting tired of the same old excuses, her own life constricted to the point where it was pacify her mother in the morning, pacify people on the telephone during the day, and pacify Stan at night. In her real hours, when she could shut herself up inside, she imagined herself suddenly rich and famous, someone people looked up to with envy, a woman with a beautiful face, shining furs, rich jewels, a doting husband.

The pure heroine of her daydreams stood sweetly and demurely looking down at her folded hands as the applause rose in a deafening crescendo around her. Then she stepped forward and the people stood up, clapping and shouting, and there by her side was the man for whom she had waited patiently all these years, Stan, but with a face suddenly transformed to Clark Gable's.

Presently all around her there were notes in the society columns about her activities: *Eileen Ames's first anniversary present from her ever-lovin' spouse was a box of green orchids flown specially from Haiti. Later that evening they were seen polishing the parquet at the Plaza. . . . Who is the secret admirer that Eileen Ames doesn't even know who sends her a single perfect red rose every day? Rumor has it that it's a well-known playboy who has mended his manners in admiration of that rare, old-fashioned virtue, chastity. . . . It's unusual in this day and age to spot real happiness, but it could only be that which made Eileen Ames's face so radiant as she tripped down Fifth Avenue. That gorgeous stole, by the way, was another present from her happy husband. Lucky man. . . . There's only one woman no one ever breathes a breath of scandal about at the tables of all the best bistros. It's lovely Eileen Ames, and she deserves all the compliments that people always couple with her name. . . . The latest in a long line of well-deserved good tidings is that Eileen Ames is infanticipating. . . .*

"But you have to make the break sometime," he said, leaning over and turning the dial on the radio, breaking into her thoughts. She looked at him quickly, but his face was obscured. His hand held a glowing cigarette to his mouth; in the dark she could hardly discern the features of his face. The slow, surflike melody of "Stardust" floated up through the cigarette smoke. In the car, with him, she smoked. In the car, with him, sometimes their Cokes were spiked with whisky. In the car sometimes with him . . .

"Eileen—" He caught her round the shoulders and turned her toward him. His face was checkered with light from the dials of the radio; back of his shoulders the full summer trees beat their limbs together and rasped hoarsely against the hot night. Whenever she thought of him as he was, and not of him as Clark Gable, she had a picture of him hunched back from the steering wheel, the car window rolled down, the night noises melding with the music, the hot, still, smoky air pressing against her moist temples.

Fumbling for her purse, she said, "It's gotten to the point I don't know what to do. Mother's at me in the morning, I'm on the phone in fights with people all day, and at night—"

"I'm at you," he finished, then added bitterly, "At least those nights you can sneak away to see me."

. . . *wonder why I spend the lonely nights,* sang the radio.

She took out her lipstick and compact, carefully holding them down to the little light from the radio. It was time to make up and go home. "You have to give me a little time—"

"You've been saying that for years—*years,* Eileen. First it was let's wait until after the war. Then you just wanted a little time to get re-acquainted. By then Mother was in the hospital and we didn't have any choice, we had to wait. Now—well, now, if you still went on working a little while, you know we could swing it."

"I know," she agreed quickly, painting her mouth. "I'll talk to her, Stan, I'll—"

"Talk to her!"

"I promise. Tomorrow I'll sit down and have a serious talk with her."

. . . *dreaming of a song,* the radio volunteered.

He leaned forward, fumbling at the dial. "I hate that damn song," he said. "They must play it ten times a night. How many times a night do you suppose they play that damn song all over the world every night?"

"I don't know," she said mechanically.

Someone selling cigarettes shrieked through. He pushed a button.

Irene, good night . . . lamented the radio.

Click went the pushbutton.

. . . *haunts my reverie,* sang the heartbroken voice.

"Oh, to hell with it," Stan said. "To hell with everything."

Eileen sat up. She was damp all over. Her hair stuck to her temples, her dress was crushed, she felt as if all her make-up had been ground into her face. They had been two hours in this deserted lane, making love and smoking cigarettes, running the radio, arguing intermittently, trying to hold back from going too far and not always succeeding until the last minute, until it was almost too late. She was tired and she didn't feel like talking any more. Her whole body ached. She had been on the brink of fulfillment not once, but time and again, at the edge, but never fulfilled. Now her nerves were protesting; she felt a singing in all her senses, her muscles in both legs were quivering, she was close to tears.

She had been through enough of these evenings to know that after she got home she was going to have a bad time of it, lying tense and sleepless far into the dawn, then having to get up for work, no matter how awful she felt, listening to her mother ask again and again, "You do love me, don't you, Eileen? You won't leave me, will you? You know I can't get along without you. Oh, Eileen, who would do the shopping?"

She had even begun to look back on the time he had been away, at war— Peaceful, she thought. If he hadn't been away all that time, one of the last to come home, would they have . . .

This was something they never talked about. The nearest they came to admitting their desire was when he was beside himself and she heard his hoarse voice saying, "Sweetheart, please, *please,* I've got to. You don't know where you've got me. Sweetheart, please, just let me up next to you. Just let me do it like that. I've got to, please. Sweetheart . . ." The voice went on and on, a litany of love, pleading, pushing, demanding.

Then she broke away, afraid, and his face, seen vaguely in the dim light of the dashboard, was desperate, like a criminal's. His breath came in harsh spasms, his knuckles strained against the skin as he clutched the steering wheel. Occasionally he got out and walked in back of the car. She could see him leaning against the fender, gasping into the moonlight.

Then she quickly rebuttoned her blouse, smoothed out her skirt, ran a comb through her hair, stared out at the trees groaning and rasping in the darkness, until he came back, leaning against the car door, looking for his cigarettes.

After one of these experiences they smoked in silence until he began to kiss her; they broke apart and ground out the half-finished cylinders in the ashtray and started all over. This love-making was desperate and terrifying, never finished, endlessly a prelude toward some far-distant act in the future which would presumably give them respite, kept in check, she supposed, only by the fact that in the beginning they had believed, or at least he had believed, there was not long to wait.

. . . not a breath of scandal has ever touched . . . happy husband . . . lucky man . . .

She looked up at him. He had opened the car door and was dangling one leg outside, his face turned away from her. Did the desire she felt, that desire so strong that it urged her toward intimacies she hated, hated later—at the moment she only knew her hands were moving over him, her mouth was making words, she wanted him, a cry would escape her lips, and in the heat, the smothering heat, he was saying, *Darling, oh darling*—did that terrible desire make up for what it led to?

"Men go to the bathroom with those!" That was what her mother had actually said. And she—gross, filthy things flowed from her too.

Only a moment before he had been touching her down there, she had been caressing him—oh, it was too shameful, too terrible to think about!

She fought the image, suppressed it, as she fought and suppressed it every time it rose to the surface of her mind.

If I married him, she thought, there'd be a lifetime of that—night after night of giving way.

. . . *lovely, sweet Eileen Ames whose friends call her affectionately "The Saint"* . . .

She could tell by the angle of his body that he was angry. He often was—sometimes because she came so close to letting him get his satisfaction and then suddenly, at the last moment, pulled back; sometimes because he was tired of asking her to let him give her an engagement ring and listening to her excuses; most often because he felt at odds with the world about everything: her, the tiresome responsibilities of his family, the future which seemed to have no shape. Did he dream in private too, those dreams of applause and recognition and fame?

"If you'd been able to go on to college," she said softly, "maybe all this would—"

"Oh, for god's sake, Eileen, you know that doesn't really have anything to do with it," he said angrily. "Your mother—"

"But it would be different," she insisted. "You'd be able to do something you really liked instead of—"

"You mean I might be more acceptable?"

"No, of course not. Only—"

"Only everyone else married someone who—"

"All I meant"—she started over, trying to be patient—"was that you'd have something else to—well—think about, something else to build on."

"The job's all right," he said shortly. "I make decent money. I can support you and still help out at home, if that's what you're worried about. You don't *have* to work. It would just make it easier."

"I just meant that working in a sporting-goods store must be pretty boring after a while."

"I get along, people like me," he argued doggedly.

"Of course they do, but that isn't really something to look forward to year after year, day in and out—"

"What you mean is that it isn't a job with a future?"

She clasped her hands together, trying to seem calm. "I guess so."

"I'm not going to make a fortune, you're right. I'll never be able to buy you mink, but I'll always have the job if I want it, and I can do well at it with the commissions. You'll have a decent place to live and—are you ashamed of me working as a—"

"You know I'm not," she said gently.

"Is your mother?" The sarcasm was coming back.

"No, she—"

"She's only ashamed of the name," he said for her. "She doesn't want her daughter married to a Polack, that's what you mean, isn't it?"

There was nothing Eileen could say. They both knew it was true.

"Maybe she'd like me better if I changed my name?" he suggested. "Something like Vanderbilt or Rockefeller? You think then maybe she'd be glad for me to have you?"

"I'm sure she would," Eileen said, trying a smile, wanting to make a joke of it. But in the columns, what kind of a name was Stankiewicz?

He was fiddling with the radio again.

Good night, Irene, good night, screeched the voice.

"I hate that even more." With an angry jerk, he switched off the machine.

"We'd better be getting back," she said.

"Where were you supposed to be this Tuesday? Movie with a girl friend? Confession? No, that's only Fridays. Library? Taking a nice little walk by yourself looking over the historic sights—old Lincoln's tomb, the capitol, the state—"

"I went over to Carolyn's to talk about the party they're going to give for Lois."

"Does Carolyn know?"

"Of course she knows. If Mama called—"

"And if she calls and asks for you?"

"I went out with Lois or something."

"And who is this Lois that she's so damn trustworthy you can go out any time of the night with her?"

"She's my cousin from New York."

"Oh, of course *that* explains it. What is she, a hundred and two and ugly as sin?"

"No, as a matter of fact she's younger than I am. And I don't know how she looks now, I haven't seen her in a couple of years, but she was very nice-looking when I knew her. Just kind of thin."

He pulled his leg in, slammed the car door, started the car. "But safe?"

"Safe enough." Eileen laughed. "At least if we were both with Ralph. Ralph is very safe."

"Why should Carolyn lie for you anyway?" He let out the clutch slowly, backing. "Why should she care?"

"I don't know," Eileen said. "Maybe she—she feels sorry for me."

Suddenly he stopped the car, turning, looking at her. "She should," he said. "Listen, Eileen—" His voice stopped, and unaccountably he leaned over and planted a small kiss on her cheek. "Take me to that party with you," he said.

"Oh, Stan, I couldn't, I—"

"Take me to that party, Eileen. It'll settle things once and for all."

"Oh, I—"

"For once in your life, make up your mind. Let's have this out once and for all. Either you're going to marry me or you're not. I'm tired of this waiting. I mean it, Eileen, I've come to the end of my patience. Now it's up to you."

SATURDAY

SUNDAY

MONDAY

TUESDAY

BOOK IV   **WEDNESDAY**

THURSDAY

FRIDAY

SATURDAY

Chapter One

I WAS ashamed of Stu then, Carolyn thought, and now I guess I dread his coming back because it was my fault that he went away, but more because of what his going away did to him—sad, Lois had said, crushed.

"Well, I'm grateful," her mother said. "I tell you I could no more drive a car today than I could turn Protestant." Carolyn tried to ignore the obvious inference that driving her mother to the station was nothing to compensate for having driven her brother away. She bit her tongue and told herself that no matter what her mother said or did she would not lose her temper. It's Mama's big day, Carolyn thought, don't spoil it.

"Of course you can't go to Esther's tonight, Lois, now that Stu is coming home," her mother was saying.

"I didn't know he was coming when I told her I would come, and anyway I know you'd much rather be alone with Stu and his wife their first . . ."

But she wouldn't, Carolyn thought. Her mother was dreading the return as much as she was, maybe more. Her mother was glad enough to have the prodigal son returned, repentant, but didn't—or couldn't—see her way clear, Carolyn would have been willing to bet, to meet with open arms and full forgiveness the wanton wife as well. And you? Carolyn asked herself. That he carries no bitterness, she told herself, and then amended, toward me.

"If that train is late, my heart won't be able to stand it." Then her mother went on quickly, accusingly, "Oh, I know what the two of you are thinking, that it's just indigestion, like yesterday. Well, that doctor didn't know what he was talking about, that's all. Prunes never gave anyone indigestion, they're good for you."

"The doctor didn't say it was just the prunes, Mother," Carolyn explained dully. "He said it was the combination—prunes and pickles, bananas and cheese, milk and chocolate, cookies and dates. He said that would make anyone sick."

"He charged for a house visit," Iris said angrily.

"Well, he came to the house," Carolyn said, keeping her voice even with difficulty.

"Doctor Parker never would have done anything like that. He gave us a flat rate for the whole year. He used to send Papa a bill at the beginning of the year, and that took care of all of us, Mama and the children, Papa, Ella, all of us, and he used to throw in most of the medicine too. He did everything. Why, Doctor Parker was a good doctor and he never would have— Don't you think you're driving awfully fast, Carolyn?"

"Mother, if you think you can do it better, if you'd rather—"

"No, no, it isn't that. I'm glad you're driving, but I wish you'd go slower, that's all. We might get arrested or something."

Carolyn slowed the car and looked ahead grimly, not answering.

"You don't have to get mad just because I asked you to drive a little slower," Iris protested. "I'm in bad health, my nerves are all gone, I have to take care of myself and you know how speeding always—"

"I wasn't speeding!"

"Oh, yes you were. I was watching the speedometer. You were going almost forty, and this is a thirty-five-mile zone."

"Well, I'm only going thirty now—"

"You don't have to take that tone, Carolyn. I was only telling you for your own good. I'm sure you don't want to get a ticket, not today, of all days, not when your own brother is coming home."

The prescience of the pattern for the day swept over Carolyn: she would try to curb her temper, her mother would see this was one of the days when she was trying. Like a small child testing, looking for trouble, trying to find the boundaries for its behavior, her mother would go farther and farther until she finally exhausted Carolyn's patience. In spite of her resolve, she would lose her temper. There would be angry words. Her mother would retreat into a hurt silence. Carolyn would find herself feeling guilty. Feeling guilty, she would swallow her irritation and make an effort once more. Her mother would start pressing her again. The whole pattern would start all over.

She's nervous, Carolyn tried to tell herself, that's why she's sitting on the edge of the seat that way, clutching the dashboard as if she were scared out of her wits. That's why she keeps looking at the speedometer.

One crow, sadness; two crows, gladness. Someone is coming back . . . someone you haven't seen in a long time.

Frances might just as well have said, One brother, misfortune; two, more misfortune, Carolyn thought. Don't think like that, she reprimanded herself. Be glad he's coming back. I am, she thought, it's only that I don't see how he'll be able to put up with Mama for any length of time. That's not your problem, she reminded herself. But I don't want him to go away again.

The idea, coming so swiftly and unexpectedly, surprised her. But it was true. What she wanted, she supposed, was Stu, yes, but Stu regenerated, a true brother on whom she might count. Would Stu recognize, too, that it wasn't *all* her fault he had left, that somehow her mother had driven her to saying those things?

Nobody *drove* you to say anything, she thought in disgust. Don't make excuses for yourself. What is, is. Accept the responsibility. Pay for it.

Then it overtook me that I fell down for thirst, I was parched, my throat burned, and I said, "This is the taste of death." The story of Senike, she thought, 2000 B.C., but all the fables, all the parables, belong in the spaceless silence of stilled time. Like the mediums of old, she asked herself, like those ordained ministers of the occult? *Here is Belladonna, the Lady of the Rocks, The lady of situations* . . .

Two brothers, one stayed and one went away, and both failed. My brothers, whom I have never known. I never go to Pete and Peggy's, I can't help it; I mean to, but I just can't. That house . . .

And Stu?

Make him all right, Carolyn thought, make him—

In a ditch, a dark ditch, in France . . .

Ralph came home, Ralph's alive.

Think of the times you and Ralph have been close—the night Sally came, for instance. He even tried to hide his disappointment in having a girl, hanging over the side of the bed, saying in a hushed voice, "Are you—are you all right, darling?" and she had been too tired to answer, merely nodding, while he took her hand and held it firmly in his. *Carolyn:* the way he said her name: someone took your name and made it sound as it had never sounded before.

She thought of Bobbie sick, and how wonderful Ralph had been then. He almost never left Bobbie's side, sitting beside the bed, his eyes fastened on the vaporizer to be sure it worked, his whole energy seemingly concentrated on making the child get well. He loved his children. He loved his son more than anything else in the world.

His monument to his flesh. Afraid his monument might die. Like Wesley.

Carolyn made a sharp swing left, and her mother gasped and gripped the dashboard, emitting a small cry of terror.

"It's all right, Mother," Carolyn heard herself saying impatiently. "I looked in the rear mirror before I made it."

"I didn't say anything, not a word."

"But you made that funny noise, you—"

"I think I see a parking space near the corner," Lois said hastily.

Trying to save the day, Carolyn thought. She slowed the car and crept toward the vacancy. The space opened on either side of a fire hydrant. "I'll let you two out in front. There's no point in all three of us having to walk."

Why, for once, couldn't Dad or Ralph or even Pete have brought her? Carolyn asked herself. But, no, they all had excuses: Pete couldn't take the day off, her father—what had been his excuse, she had forgotten, something as lame as Pete's—and of course there was no point in even asking Ralph. It wasn't *his* family. But he might have offered, she thought, stopping and leaning across her mother to open the door.

Her mother squeezed herself out onto the pavement, then bent back into the car, fretful. "You won't be long, will you, Carolyn?" She looked so worried, her mother. "The train's due any minute."

"As soon as I can park, Mother. I don't know how long that's going to take."

"Well, just try to hurry. *Tell me,* Carolyn," she said in a tight, frightened voice, "do you think he'll recognize me? Right away, I mean? Do you think I've changed, you don't think I've—I've failed, do you? Not like the rest of them, not like Ada and Esther. He won't—"

"Of course not," Carolyn interrupted swiftly, not able to look at her mother.

"It's been such a long time," her mother said wistfully, pulling herself back toward the curb. "I don't want him to think that I'm—I'm old."

So she knows too, Carolyn thought. She tries to hide the knowledge, but deep down she knows. The failing, failing flesh, the tidal ruin of the flesh, time bearing down with its indelible pencil, lining the face, pointing up the defects of the body, the breasts sagging, the skin lusterless, the veins bulging, the skin flaky and splotched with those little dark freckles that signify the days passing, the cold winds blowing, the mouse-gray waters flowing . . . pity . . . yes, a pity beyond telling was hid in the heart of love.

Carolyn glanced quickly down the first side street and was gratified to see a man pulling out. Without looking this time (deliberately, as if to get back at her mother, if only in her own mind), she swung the car, pressing down on the accelerator, grinding forward until she was directly ahead of the open area.

The space was small, and she had to maneuver carefully. In the dead weight of the afternoon everything was such an effort; if only things would go well, if only— Listen, she told herself impatiently, you have to believe to make things work out. You have to work and work and work to carve out a little happiness, a little well-being. It's no good just *wishing*.

She stopped and hung over the steering wheel. What had happened had happened. One way or another, Stu would have left. If it hadn't been what happened that night, it would have been something else. Stu was meant to go.

There was nothing *you* could do about Wesley. Maybe he was meant to die.

Someone honked behind her. She looked out. A cab was trying to get past, and her big Buick was blocking the way. She commenced straining again, working the big car back, then spinning the wheel and inching it forward. Her whole back was damp with effort. When the car was at last snug, she lay back against the plastic seat cover, gasping for breath. Stu is coming home, she thought, my brother is coming back.

The sons must part from the mothers, the children must cut the cord, the door must be left unopened, the latch unraised. *Land of my ancestors, good-by; O Mother, weep no more for me. . . .*

Carolyn opened the car door and got out. She was looking at an advertisement for a soft drink. There was a bright, happy girl looking into the smooth, bright face of a boy. On the table between them there was a bottle of pop.

My god, they were young.

She gazed at the billboard, feeling a funny little quiver inside, a knotting of apprehension. She was on the verge of some discovery, something to do with the dream she had had the night before.

She and Wesley, they were falling in love. Music was playing, they got up and danced. She had had on a formal, the kind of dress she had worn in college to the proms. That's what was all wrong. She didn't wear dresses like that any more—hadn't since the war.

Wesley, she thought, I see us as young, *young;* we're a couple of kids falling in love, our whole lives ahead of us, we're still full of promise and hopes and dreams, all the mistakes still to be made, none of the expectations dead, we still believe in a world we want instead of the one we have.

G

Wesley, her heart cried out, I am that girl in the picture, you're—

She found herself half running down the street, in flight from that brilliant, happy poster. People were pressing against her on all sides, forcing her along. The pavements glittered up at her as if inlaid with tiny pieces of silver. The sun—the sun hitting silver. They had awarded him a Silver Star, posthumously, the little emblem of the spaces that served to illuminate—nothing, she told herself, just a tarnished medal lying in a drawer somewhere, and nothing of Wesley left.

There *is* something left, she answered herself passionately. It's here, inside my head. It's in Ralph's never buying anything German.

And that makes up for everything, that settles the account? Life is worth the single strand of thought inside one person's head and the meaningless gesture of another's boycotting a country's merchandise? That makes Wesley's death meaningful?

Who of you remembers the war? she wanted to shout at the people passing. Who of you pays penance for those dead?

A man was holding the station door open. Vacantly, numbly, she moved forward. The inside of a closed box must be this dark, she thought. Earth, the roof of the coffin; earth, the deposit of the body; earth, the place where lovers lay down on a summer day to press themselves against the cool, sweet grass.

Move him into the sun, *into the sun. . . .*

She passed the shoeshine stand, the pay and free toilets, made her way into the waiting room with its slabs like pews, its occupants like condemned sinners, its atmosphere of penance and excommunication. And where was contrition?

She felt as if she might take her place in line, move slowly and surely toward the confessional. You pray and make penance, something goes out—the guilt, she supposed. *I detest all my sins because I dread the loss of heaven and fear the pains of hell*—and, she thought, because nothing can bring back the dead.

Her mother was standing down toward the end of the waiting room, Lois at her side, wringing her hands and squinting at something, and Lois was bent over, speaking. Carolyn forced her hand up, waved as she advanced toward them, but her mother only shook her head impatiently, kept her lips pursed as she leaned forward to hear what Lois was saying.

"The train late?" she asked, coming up to them.

"Here we rushed that way, driving way over the speed limit and taking corners like that and all, and they won't be here for at least another hour." Two small tears hung on the ends of her mother's lashes. "It's the waiting around that's so awful. You get to thinking."

And that, Carolyn thought, would never do. Then she looked into the face of her cousin, a face devoid of its silvery smile, and she asked silently, You, too, Lois? You know too? Are you the sister I never had? Come down to the station to reclaim a brother and find a sister, is that the final irony of this reunion, of the life in that house where we all hid ourselves from one another behind the tourist signs and the big pots of ivy, we who never knew one another, and never even tried, because we were afraid, we didn't want any new ties, the old ones were so painful that we had used up all our belief.

Lois, Carolyn wanted to cry out to her, can we never go back to those summer afternoons when we still thought the world would not destroy us, when we believed in a world not of destruction but fruition? Tell me, Lois, do you even believe in going back?

Chapter Two

IN *ten* minutes they would be in Springfield. Ethel was so nervous that she had insisted they get their bags and wait in the vestibule. It was crazy, jiggling and bouncing like this, but somehow he understood. He was nervous himself. Half of it was dread and half something else, excitement maybe, a little expectation even. Anyway, his stomach was giving him trouble; he felt as if he had eaten something that had been out of the refrigerator too long.

He knew that he would have felt different if he had been up front in the Pullman, letting the porter brush him off, giving the guy fifty cents without thinking about it, he and Ethel ready to get off with good decent luggage instead of these battered suitcases, looking like millionaires instead of charity cases. What I want to know, Stu said to himself, is, who decides who is going to make it and who isn't.

Ethel nudged nearer, pushing up against him, as if in all that heat she were trying to warm herself. Wants to warm herself at my fire, he thought, that's a good one, I'm ice right through.

Ice . . . snow . . . Scott. Went to the South Pole and got lost or something—and knew that he would never make it back, so he just said good-by and walked out into the snow. Why did he have to walk out? Must be some reason, Stu thought, I mean the others were still in that tent, why did he have to make the big sacrifice? To rack up points, he decided.

No, it wasn't Scott who sacrificed himself. It was one of the others. Oats, Otis, something like that. Sick, and he was holding the rest of the party back. Walked off into a blizzard, hoping to save the others by his sacrifice. Oats—Otis, whatever the hell his name was—made the sacrifice, and Scott got the credit.

Now he remembered: none of them had been saved. Scott had frozen to death too. So even old Oats's sacrifice had been useless. Like most sacrifices, he thought. People hang themselves upside down on crosses or walk out into the snow, all for nothing.

And the other one, some other guy at the South Pole, also a Limey, he was saved. Shackleton, that was it. Boat got stuck in the ice and the ice just crushed it, kaput, and there they all were floating around on a goddam ice floe in the middle of nowhere. Some way to spend the winter.

Pretty soon the ice starts cracking up and they're jumping around on ice floes right and left and then they see it's no good, no matter how spry they are, they can't go on playing hopscotch like that, so Shackleton decides they got to take these tiny little boats that were left from the big boat and get somewhere. He thinks maybe they can make this island, some island with a strange name for that part of the world, not Penguin, like you'd expect—no, Elephant Island, that was it, and so they start off, and, god, what a trip.

But they make it. And then they get there and they see they can't stay, so Shackleton and some of the others go off again on this incredible trip in an open boat and, my god, they finally get to some whaling station or other after seventy or eighty days, and then they try to get back to Elephant Island to rescue the others, and, christ, they have to make about five or six different trips because they can't get through the ice, it's too thick, but on the last try they make it.

What I want to know, Stu repeated to himself, who decides who gets saved and who doesn't.

The train swayed violently and he was thrown against the wall. He turned and looked at his wife. Her face was puckered with anxiety but she looked back at him with expressionless blank blue eyes. She had had her hair done just before they left, and it didn't look quite so dyed, but the make-up—the mascara hung in beads, like black soot, from her lashes; she had drawn her eyebrows on in a look of perpetual surprise, so that she seemed forever asking, *Who, me? You mean me?* to a world that had never been interested enough to ask her a question in the first place; the mouth was riven into the face in red, a big blank glob of paint driven through the flesh, and her skin was a blank pasty white, liquefied from a tube every morning.

He imagined that embedded right into the pores were years and years of make-up, ground down by hasty washing-ups, and lying, lethal, ready to crush the final flush of youth from whatever cells still functioned. Did anything on Ethel really function? he asked himself, looking into those still, fearful eyes.

Then he thought, Yes, there is something functioning. Oh god, he thought, a child.

For God's sake look after our people: those were the last words written in Scott's diary. The details were beginning to come back now. Oates, with an e. *I am going outside and may be some time.* He never came back. Oates's sacrifice didn't save the three that were left. It came too late. Scott was the last to die. The other two were inside their sleeping bags, but Scott had gotten up. He lay, his coat open, his arm flung across his friends, waiting to be found in that frozen frieze of friendship eight months later.

Those who are about to die salute you, Stu thought. Where did that come from? All the acts of valor were mixed up, you couldn't remember who had done what, who said what where.

"I wish you wouldn't stare like that," Ethel said peevishly. "It makes me nervous. If you got something to say, say it. Otherwise—"

"Otherwise what?"

"Otherwise— I don't know. Just don't stare."

"Tell me something," he said in a low voice so that the man in front of him, the woman in back of her, couldn't hear.

"Yeah?"

"Tell me, what were you thinking just then?"

She looked at him suspiciously. "What do you mean, what was I thinking? What do you think I was thinking? I was thinking I wish we'd get there, just like anybody else would think." A look of perplexity crossed the painted mask of her face. Her mouth curved down in a pout, for a brief flash of time the eyes took on an expression: she was upset. "Why, what was you thinking?"

"I was thinking about some guy who walked out in the snow and died," he said, feeling that in that one small sentence he had cut himself off from her forever, had proven once and for all that there was a distance so great between them that it would never be bridged, not even, he thought with a twinge of remorse, by the linking of the flesh which he had brought into being and which she was feeding and nuturing inside. And my sacrifice? he asked himself.

Your coming home? Is that what you call *your* sacrifice?

She was talking. He heard sounds and he saw that the mouth was mobile, but he hadn't the courage to listen. His heart had sunk into a new but now familiar beat: he was coming home, coming back, going to face them all.

Why? You had to know, he believed, what you were doing to make it meaningful, and he didn't know now. How could a sacrifice be anything if it was just a gesture of instinct—like Ethel, he thought, acting out of instinct instead of any intelligence. Like most people.

The train had stopped. He was starting to turn around to get the big suitcase when he felt her fingers on his arm. Instinctively—always instinct, he thought—he jerked away.

"You didn't hear one word I said," she complained. "You wasn't even listening."

"Oh, can it," he replied impatiently. "We're here. Come on."

The suitcase was heavy, it pulled at his arm with painful insistence. Nevertheless, as if punishing himself for his harshness to her, he picked it up, even though the man in front of him was still standing stationary, patiently waiting for the conductor to get the door open.

Good god, she had started to cry.

He put down the suitcase and turned about. There were two black lines of misery coursing down her plaster-like cheeks. "Your mascara is running, Ethel," he said, trying to sound sympathetic. "You look so nice, you don't want to spoil your face, do you? I'm sorry if I was abrupt. You know how—"

"You don't care a thing—"

"Please," he said, hearing his voice rise. "Listen, it's hard enough—"

"I said I'd come back with you if you promised to act—"

"All right, all right, I promise, I promise, only for chrissake—"

With a clang, the conductor released the bolt of the door.

"Move, will you?" a voice sounded in back of him, and, surrendering to complete despair, knowing the whole damn trip was doomed, Stu picked up the heavy suitcase and moved forward. If she was going to cry, let her cry. Ethel crying was just one more thing in a long series of things.

He stepped down on the upper level of the station, turned and took the light suitcase from Ethel, then helped her down. While she rubbed her eyes, he stood under the gray glassed-in roof, looking about in confusion. The platform was crowded with people. Redcaps were running for business. Stu watched the Pullman porters handing down bags, saw people embracing. With all the people and noise, he was baffled, not knowing where to look. Anyway, he had to go back for the other bag. God, there were so many people and it was so hot that he felt licked before he started. Where was his mother?

She probably didn't come, he thought. Why should she?

Ethel came and stood at his side, sniffling into a soiled handkerchief, trying to look valiant and misunderstood. "Maybe they're downstairs," he said without any conviction at all. "You wait here. I gotta go back for the other suitcase."

He had left the bag at their seat, and when he got back on the train he had the urge to run the whole length, hide, leave Ethel out there by herself while the train pulled out, and he was free of them all. He pictured Ethel and his mother stuck with each other, and he started to laugh. Then he couldn't stop. He was bent double, the whole of his stomach knotted, but he knew it wasn't just laughter.

When he straightened up, he saw his mother, his sister, and Lois, standing at the top of the station stairs. Ethel was only a few feet away from them, but they hadn't recognized her. Then he realized that, so far as he knew, Lois and Carolyn had never seen her, that his mother had only run into her that once, when Ethel had gone up to her in the market and tried to introduce herself, and his mother had acted so awful.

Stu dragged the bag from under the seat and supported it half by hand, half by knee. Getting down the aisle took a long time because people were standing up and stretching or looking for things they had dropped, or just generally getting in the way. Even when he shoved against them with the suitcase, they weren't in any mood to move. On the narrow metal top step of the car, he stopped, taking a good look at his mother. She was fatter, but he had expected that. He had been expecting to find her hair grayed, her face lined and full of suffering; but the face hadn't changed at all, she had hardly aged a bit. She stood, balancing on those silly high-heeled shoes she always wore, peering anxiously up and down the platform, her face a schoolgirl parody of middle age. She would never really grow old, he supposed. You had to suffer to grow old, and, while his mother thought she suffered, she never allowed the suffering to take hold. She chose from the past only that which served her, and the suffering couldn't serve except as an example of how she had triumphed; it was the triumphs she remembered, not the failures. She would never grow old—or wise.

She saw him. Suddenly her old-young face broke into a quivering smile, she clutched Carolyn's arm, she let herself rise on her spiked heels, and she seemed, for a moment, to hang on the air in her exultation. Her voice, piercing as a scream of grief, sprang out over the suitcases and raced down the platform.

"Stuuu," she screamed, "Stuuuu." Then she fell back down inside her shoes and stood squatly on the ground, gaining momentum; the next second she had leaped away from Carolyn and was running toward him as fast as her fat formless little legs would carry her.

In her haste and excitement she sprinted right past Ethel, not even giving her a glance, but shoving, using her elbows, the way he always remembered she used her elbows at sales and in streetcars, jabbing viciously to right and left to clear a path, and now she jabbed—almost unconsciously—as she sped toward him, giving Ethel a good one as she went by; the next instant she was at the bottom of the platform, looking up at him with a flushed, radiant face.

"You've come home, come home, the way I always knew you would" —and before he could answer she hoisted herself up the first step, grabbing hold of the handrails of the car, boosting herself the final two steps, then throwing herself on him with all the weight of sorrowing, suffering, vindicated mother love; he felt her hands clutching at his neck in the grasp of final, irrevocable justification; her hot, happy breath was tickling his neck, her moist mouth came down on his chin and he smelled chocolates and raisins and tasted in his mouth the nervous bile of his own anxiety. "Hold me," she panted into his shoulder, gripping him with all her might, her little voice a squeak. "Kiss me. Oh, kiss your mother, honey."

He was using one arm to hold the suitcase and trying to manipulate the other to put around her, but she was holding him with a grip like death, her arms encircling him like a metal band. "Mom," he said, "if you'll just let go—"

Before he could finish, she released him, the tears starting. Nothing but tears, that's all I get today, he thought.

"You don't even want to kiss your own mother, your own mother you haven't seen in twelve years—"

"Eleven and a half."

"—come back after *twelve* years and you won't even kiss your own mother."

"Listen, could we just get off this train? It's going to start and we'll still be standing here arguing. Could you just get down and let me get this suitcase off and—"

She let go of him, crushed, miserable, crying. She heaved against the side of the train and wept, her hands knotted against her mouth. "All this time I've been waiting and praying and hoping—"

He sprang past her down the three steps, pulled the suitcase down, knowing that this was the fatal moment of his life, the one time when he had to put aside all his own feelings and convictions, or everything would be lost, not only for him but also for his son. He turned and lifted her bodily off the train, holding her against him as if she were someone wounded, a helpless woman he had to carry to help. For all her weight she seemed light as she lay, wounded and weeping, on his shoulder.

Now he did not mind her crying. For the first time in his life it did not rub his nerves so raw that he wanted to shut her up any way he could, driven to the old violence of feeling he could kill her without a qualm. For the first time in his life he felt he was in absolute control of himself. She's like me, he thought. I suffer and I don't know any way to say it. We're alike. I never saw that before.

He put her down, and his arms went around her, his mouth was against her hair, and he was holding her, the way a man in love holds the woman he cares for, his body reaching out to speak to her. "Mama," he heard himself say in a strange, hoarse voice, as if he were actually crying out *I love you,* "Mama, I've missed you."

"My boy, my boy," she said softly, not moving, letting him hold her, seeming to understand that he had seen at last that she loved him, but more important that he had also come to the recognition that he loved her, and had fought against it, and run away from it, and kept the knowledge from himself for all those long years because he was afraid of this love, as he was afraid of any of the claims of love, the responsibility to provide and protect for those one loved. He had never wanted any responsibility, he had never wanted another human being to hold any claim over him, all his life he had fought against involvement because involvement meant loss of freedom, involvement meant you had to take sides, you were responsible for the people you loved; only the strong could take that, and he had never felt himself strong at all, not in any way, least of all to be responsible to the ties of love, those strongest of all ties, he who had always been carried, never a carrier.

I came home, I came back, to start over, that's why I came back, he thought. To begin again at thirty-four.

He could forgive her, and in forgiving he was free of so much of the past, of so much of his guilt, of so much of the rancor and hatred for the acts that had been committed by both of them. He could look on her as another person—stubborn, difficult, given to nervous prostrations and exasperating tantrums—but with other mitigating qualities as well, love and sacrifice and hard work and a bottomless well of hope for her children, those children who were forever disappointing her. No wonder she had turned into a—no more labels, he thought to himself. Just let her be what she is and love her for that and forget what you can and forgive what you can, but try to love her for what there is to love in her. If you can do that, you might even be able to get along with her.

He wanted to laugh at the notion, it was so absurd. But at that moment anything seemed possible.

Then he was laughing. He released her, standing back, holding her back with his arms, looking down on her. "You look great. I thought you'd be old and gray, but you're just as young as ever, younger. You look better. A little fatter, maybe, but then we'll put you on a diet and pass you off as—who knows, some silly age."

Smiling through her tears, a look of disbelief on her face, his mother stared back at him.

"Well, where's that sister of mine, the one who started all the trouble in the first place?" He let go of her and turned, waving toward Carolyn.

Ethel was still standing over their big suitcase, but she looked as if she couldn't believe her eyes. Stu read the look on her face clearly: *You've gone and lost your mind, that's what you've done.*

He went across to her and leaned down, kissed her on the cheek. It was cold and hard underneath his lips. How long had it been since he had kissed her the way he had kissed his mother a moment before? God alone knew. And was she too suffering down deep so that no one could see? Were they all suffering and no one seeing?

"Ethel," he said, trying to find a language common to them both. "Listen, honey, I've been a son of a bitch and I know it. I'm not just saying it this time, I know it, but try—" He could not finish. He took her arm and she felt as limp and unresisting as his mother had when he lifted her down from the train.

"This is Ethel, Mama," he said and tried to stop smiling, but the smile was there, fastened to his face, he couldn't do anything about it. Why was he so goddam happy? All he wanted to do was smile—and drink chocolate milk, he thought suddenly. I'll drink chocolate milk the whole time I'm home. That'll be a kind of sign, to show them I've changed. No liquor until they see I've changed.

God, he thought, you never have sense to give up until you're dead, do you? Not even then, he thought. Scott was still trying to bring back a little warmth of life long after the two friends were frozen far beyond it.

Chapter Three

YOU see a sign, even in your own mind, it mean something, Ella thought, feeling her way upstairs to her room. She was so tired from all the things that had happened that afternoon she just had to lie down, rest a little, so she could get her strength back, so she was fit to fight with the dinner.

It was to be extra special, young Mister Stu come home this way, with his wife; but even if they was all going to celebrate, that didn't mean them boarders wouldn't still come in starved, come in and eat everything put on the table, you go and put out a piece of meat and it gone before you turn your back to get the potatoes to go with it.

Lydia, Lydia Timble, Ella wanted to call out to the heavens, can you see? Can you see the time of love here, in this house, come back to this house after all this time? You see Iris, you see how she so happy, she run around like those chickens we used to keep? You remember those chickens, Ella called out sternly, as if accusing Lydia of having forgotten, those chickens out back and the eggs we used to fetch every morning? You recollect how my eggs was most always bigger than yours? she demanded. You remember I had the brown? The brown eggs always was better.

You remember the time I say, It funny, but everybody look in such strange places for love, and you say, *No, it's not strange. People almost never love what they already have, they're always looking in other places.*

You see, Lydia, you see love come back, the sign is here?

Ella's fingers ran in the braille of the blind along the walls and furniture, so that her feet went, light as down, soft as a little chicken, soft and slight and light, in the hall; she made no sound, blind old Ella working her way toward her room.

Lydia, she called out to the vast stretches of the universe, does Clara come talk to you 'bout how you kill her chicken? Does she come talk to you 'bout who took her money? Do you know now?

That the past, Ella told herself resolutely, this the present. Young Mister Stu home. Lois, she home. The house full of love.

Young Mister Stu, he came in and she couldn't see him, but she could feel right away that it was all right, there was this feeling in the air, and he came over and he put his arms around her, young Mister Stu put his arms around her same as Lois had, same as if she was white, and he held her close and Ella knew what she had been waiting for all these years. It was to have them both back, those two come home. Come home to stay. Stay with us, Ella prayed, we need you. Don't go away no more. This where you belong, this your home, don't go way no more. We need new hands to hold on to in this house.

Hands, they seemed to Ella always in her mind—perhaps because her own hands fulfilled so much of the necessary life she had to follow, hands that had her own life in the touch. And other hands—Organdy's hands, Organdy's long slender hands pressed together in prayer, in penance; the hands of that preacher, them black-topped, white-palmed hands, raised that summer night years and years before. *O Death, where is thy sting? O Grave, where is thy victory?* And the horse, he talked about the horse, that horse that came for Organdy, that came for Clara, that came for Frank Timble, that came for *her,* for Lydia Timble. The pale horse.

Soon he come for me, riding down, coming fast, his sword raised, riding down on me and I won't even see him, an old blind woman like me, good for nothing but remembering the past. It's here, she thought, tapping her breast, I hold it here, the past, but what good is that?

Love, her heart cried out, why you so hard to hang on to? Love, why you take so long to come and why you go so fast?

I have loved you, saith the Lord. Yet ye say, Wherein hast thou loved us? Was not Esau Jacob's brother? saith the Lord; yet I loved Jacob. . . .

I never figure it out, Ella thought. All this love and hate. How can You make two brothers and love one and hate the other? You love Jacob, she thought, but You hate Esau, was that fair? How could Esau help it he was born bad? He never had no say, Esau. Like being born black, I never had no say.

Ella's hands touched molding. She paused, holding on to the wood, thinking that she would give anything, the rest of her days here in Iris's house, just to know that Lydia Timble did know the time of love was back. Ella prayed, closing her milky old eyes, seeing inside her head a picture of Lydia Timble when she was young and beautiful, those little hands and feet so swift and soft, like small, sweet birds, and Ella looked at her, thinking, She got a husband and I don't. She got children and I don't. But she's gone now, Ella thought, and the children are almost the same as mine.

The big difference was in that word *almost.*

Voices drifted from behind a closed door, strange, soft, half-strangled voices, not voices she knew, not any of the boarders talking or that new voice of the past few days, Lois's voice; not voices from the radio, which she knew too; no, these were strange voices; they caught at her and made her stop, asking herself, Who that talking, who that making all that noise?

A man talking low to a woman and the woman not answering much, a small murmur as the man talked and the woman just answering in a single syllable, a hum Ella couldn't catch. Who those people? she asked herself, and then, with a start, she heard low and clear the man say, "Couldn't we just try?" and she thought, It young Mister Stu talking, talking to his wife, that girl that don't say nothing when she come in and I couldn't see her and if she don't talk, how I know what she like?

Ella crept down the hall quietly, her ears straining to make out that girl's voice. No girl, she told herself, that voice go with a woman. Ella didn't know whether the door was open or whether the voices might be coming from the open transom above the door. The only safe way to find out was to stop halfway down the hall and listen.

She crept, fingers running along the cracks of the wall, testing out a bump in the wallpaper, feeling for the break where wood started, knowing just where she could stand and listen.

The voices were a little louder now, seemed heavier, as if they hung on the hot air waiting to be caught and clasped to her. In a blur of words, sounds clutching one another, nothing distinct, she paused listening. No, the door was not open.

She moved to the hinges of the door, letting her fingers run down the crevice. There was no space. Then it must be the transom open an inch or two, the way Iris kept all the transoms open so that if an argument, a loud, bad argument, started, she could hear and put a stop to it.

The woman had started to speak, and Ella crept forward and stopped directly under the transom, stood alert, listening. ". . . it's a new feeling," the woman said in the voice of one confessing. "I know I was always ready and all before but—"

"You said only the other day you felt like it all the time," the man protested. "And now you say you don't want to, you—"

"I know I said that, but that was before—before—"

"Before what?"

"Before I saw it wasn't going to make no difference, things was just going to go on the same old way. I wisht now I *had* got some pills and—"

"Don't talk that way, Ethel. I'm trying to tell you, I'm trying to explain. Maybe things can be different, but you've got to try too."

"I've tried all I can. I can't change myself. I saw how your mother looked at me. As if I was dirt, *dirt*—well, I may not have got myself a college education like some people and I may not have the best, oh—" and the voice stopped for a moment. Ella hung on to the bitter, sad, lost words, thinking, A woman who don't know where she's been, a woman who don't know where she's going, who don't know where she wants to go, a girl with a lost, lost voice. Stu, he had a voice like that too, only different. His was bitter, bitter about where he had been, sounded as if he was going to be bitter about where he was going. But he knew all about destinations and how you got delivered to them. Then the woman's voice picked up again. "Oh, I know I got faults, but—don't, Stu, please. Don't, I don't want to."

There was no sound, only the late-afternoon stillness hanging in the air, a stillness Ella could feel, a stillness that felt soft and warm to her bones, as if she were going to be wrapped in velvet, as if she were hugging warm air to her and being softly and gently warmed until she was almost smothered by the soft, still air.

"Honey," she heard the woman's voice call out in coarse, passionate exclamation. "Honey—"

"Ethel," he said.

"Don't stop," the woman begged. "Don't talk, not now, honey, please. Don't talk, just keep—"

"Ethel," Ella heard young Mister Stu say again, and then the voices died, Ella heard the sound of bodies moving through the afternoon stillness, bodies that were falling the next instant upon the badly-sprung bed of Iris's boarding house, Room Six, and Ella knew its every detail, from the broken springs in the mattress down near the bottom of the bed (where Iris said they didn't count) to the little splintered pieces of wood in the drawers of the dresser (which Iris said didn't matter, they could be covered with paper).

The sound of love, bodies making the sounds of love, even in the midst of all the bitterness of those voices. And why not? What was there to hold in the world that was meaningful save a man and woman come together and love one another and say, It all right, just for now, we together?

She had never been brought to bed for love.

But there were other kinds of love, weren't there? Love of a house, like Iris had for this big, aching old house; love of a child, the kind Lydia had for Organdy, the baby, and the kind Ada had for her daughter, had had for her mother; the kind of love she herself had had for Lydia Timble, for Frank Timble. There was the love of the land, which maybe they all had, some stronger than others; and love of money, that Esther had; and love of life, like Frances had; or love of God, maybe that was really what Organdy died of, her heart broke over a God she loved and couldn't understand, or who didn't understand her; love—oh, love of so many things, but all of it love, wasn't it?

But this kind, this love, was this the final meaning of love?

He put himself inside her, Ella thought, he invade her, he make his body go into hers. She take him; and that different from anything else people do. Everybody kiss, everybody clasp, but bodies inside each other, that different, that a kind of love I never know, I never feel. And it ain't the same as the others.

All the other kinds of love, they extinguish. The house and money and children go; the God hardens His heart; the land belongs to no one and knows no one; the master turns his back on the servant and the servant plays the role of Esau: Why did You make me black? Why did You make me blind? Why have I come old and black and blind and lonely only to live in a house full of trouble—and only a few days of love, but the darkness always waiting at the end?

It's all Esther's fault, Ella thought. Things was never the same after old Clara died. Ada, she hate her sister 'cause she think her sister take her money. And Organdy, she go do that terrible thing, and their Mama, she just seal herself up, she don't say nothing.

But *I* know, Ella thought. Their Mama, she think Esther take that money. Then why she never do anything about it? Ella asked herself. But she knew the answer. Lydia Timble's pride was stronger than her convictions. The girls had to be loyal; they had to respect one another, even if they didn't love one another: that what their mother wanted, and she gave her whole life to that, and what happened in the end?

She die knowing they don't love one another, they don't respect one another, that one of them stole off the others, another go away all alone and kill herself.

They kill their Mama, Ella thought. All of them, each and every one of them. Frances leave her husband. Ada say those terrible things the night of *her* birthday, and Iris—she never made up to her Mama for all the others. Lydia never had—Ella marveled—one girl she could hang on to. There never was a boy, and not one of them girls was good enough for her. That's what broke her heart.

The bedsprings gave up a cry of release. Life, the springs sang, *life.*

And what have I known but death? Ella asked herself.

I know the feeling of life, she answered herself silently, the feeling run through this house these past hours. That's something to hang on to: to believe in life and not death. But if I believe in life I have to have love, and where is my love to hang on to?

Inside, she answered herself. I have kept it there, inside, all these years. It's still there. Inside. *Let not your heart be troubled:* your Father's house has many mansions. . . .

Chapter Four

SOMEONE was knocking.

"Yes?" Lois said. "Just a minute, I have to get my robe."

She had managed to get in and out of the bathroom without too long a wait; wrapped in one of Iris's big towels, she had carried her things hastily down the hall, stripped down, and done the final drying in her room. She didn't want to hold down the one tub any longer than necessary.

"It's me," Stu said, and Lois breathed a sigh of relief. She had been afraid it might be Iris wanting to "talk." About Ethel, of course. But talk as much as she might, Iris could not change what was. The Ethels of the world, she thought, will be going on long after we're all gone. And the Carolyns? The Stus? She herself? Riddles too big to answer.

"Hold it a minute, Stu, I'm just about decent."

"Take your time," he said as she opened the door and stepped back to let him in.

He was obviously embarrassed. First he stared at her and then he looked away, careful to keep his eyes focused on the far wall. "I didn't know—I can come back later if—"

"It's all right," Lois said. "It's a bathrobe, but I'm fully covered."

"It'll only take a minute," he said uneasily, staring over her head. Not moving. Then he made up his mind; he came in.

She closed the door and looked around for her cigarettes; then she remembered—they were half hidden in the top drawer, a small concession to Iris. As she went over to get them, she brushed against him and he drew back, startled, and said, "Oh, excuse me," and she didn't know what to say to make him feel more comfortable. Why should he be so upset about her being in a bathrobe?

It was the fact, she supposed, that he knew she had nothing on underneath. Bathrobes were for bed, and bed was not something that polite, nice people thought about. Dear, wonderful, lovable Stu, she would have liked to put her arms around him and hug him, but he would have hated that. He hated, she knew, any demonstration of affection.

No, he had taken her hand on the stair. Whenever she thought about him at all, she thought in straight declarative sentences; then she always had to put in the modifiers and the qualifications. He was always more complicated than she thought.

Now he stood in the middle of the room, staring at the wall, and Lois stood for a moment looking at him. She knew his mood immediately; the expression around the eyes and the set of the mouth were dead giveaways. When he was like this, it was better not to talk. He was embarrassed and annoyed and somehow humble, if you could ever say Stu was humble—but she knew better than to help him out. No matter how long his silence lasted, no matter how uneasy his hesitations made her, she wouldn't give an inch. Not because she didn't want to help, but because helping only made him worse, as if he hated the notion that people pitied him. As she supposed she did.

No one ought ever to pity Stu. Sympathy, yes; compassion, perhaps, but maybe that was too close to pity too; but feeling sorry for him, never —he was so much stronger, in the long run, than the rest of them. Than even he knew. It was his never turning away from anything, his making himself look at a thing and see it for what it was and accept it and take it into him, a part of knowledge that he would never, never, under any circumstances, try to hide from.

"Stu," she said impulsively.

He did not look at her but shook his head. "Yeah?" he said gruffly.

"Did you know—did you—" But she couldn't ask him about Eileen.

Eileen had her rights, too. If Eileen wanted her to know, she would tell her. "Nothing," she said. "Just a thought, and then—I don't know, I lost it." Even if he wouldn't look at her, she could maybe make him smile. "I mean," she said, "I knew you were coming all along." His head jerked up, surprised. "The first night I was home Frances told me. She saw it in the cards. Only she didn't know it was you. Just some strange man. When she said strange, she meant someone she didn't know, but you and I always know what 'strange' means." Her tone was light, the joke on the edge of truth, so close that if he caught the full implications, it should make him terribly amused. He always loved irony more than anything else. "In this family," she said, "strange always means us."

His face was still, and then—yes—he was smiling. "The losers," he said.

She remembered how he had talked about a bunch he ran around with, and some crazy friend of his who couldn't keep a woman because he was so short. Every time he had a woman he would feel compelled to show her off to Stu, and every time he did that he would look up at Stu and just give up. Stu never wanted his woman, he had said to Lois, laughing, it was just that both of them saw how preposterous it was—and for the only time she could remember, Stu had mentioned Ethel. "You see," he had said, "there was Shorty with this good-looking dame and he was so short and dumpy and ugly and all, and here I am, tall and—oh, I don't know—not *too* bad-looking, and what have I got? Ethel," he said. "So when we look at each other, Shorty and me, we see how preposterous the whole thing is, and I don't want the dame, and now Shorty doesn't want her either, we're both losers, and we get to laughing, and you know if there's one thing women hate, it's being laughed at."

The cruelty of the humor had struck her to the heart. How could he laugh about what had made him suffer most? I suppose, she thought now, looking at his face, he has to—that look, it was the kind you saw so often on people in New York, on the faces of those people who got on buses, sat by themselves, and commenced to talk in a high, hysterical voice about the terrible things that had happened to them, how the city was crushing them and no one cared, the injustices and outrages that went on against them and there was no one to whom they could turn for help, while all about the bus people sat as if turned to stone, reading newspapers, gazing out the windows, silently contemplating their own problems. Lois thought of the people who sat next to her at the luncheon counters, poring over the want ads, and when she looked down at their feet their shoes were so old and broken that they told the history of a whole lifetime; no one would ever hire anyone who wore shoes like that, except for the menial and manual jobs.

She glanced down at Stu's shoes. But she had known all along.

A whole panorama of all the jumbled, tangled mess of the city, its poor, its refuse, its defeat and hopelessness, came back to her; she thought of the ailanthus and she wanted to cry out, Don't, Stu, don't let them beat you.

"I came to ask a favor," he said, letting his face register exasperation with himself. "About tonight— I know you're going out to Esther's and—"

"Well, let's just say she asked. That still doesn't mean she'll let me in."

"Well, that's what I came to ask you, that's the favor, not to go out there, to stay with us." He turned, looking out the window, onto an Illinois lawn, Illinois oaks, and the tall, trembling beech at the corner of the garden, which glistened for an instant in the sun like silver. He hadn't looked directly at her the whole time, just that blank, distended expression that meant he was cutting himself off from everyone. "The thing is, I don't know whether I can get through it tonight or not, not by myself. A family dinner," he said, and Lois caught her breath at the tone of his voice. "In that kitchen."

"Stu," she said, and this time he turned, he still wasn't looking at her, but at least he was facing her. "I'd be glad to do anything I can to help, you know that. It's not just that I'm fond of you—I *am*," she said, seeing the expression that crossed his face. "But it's not just that. It's because I think I understand—a little, anyway. I lived here and I know —well, how things were, but more than that. My mother," Lois said, talking rapidly, remembering their pact—never to speak of anything serious, don't talk about Ethel, and I won't talk about your mother; don't ever talk about anything serious—and knowing that she was going to break that pact, that she *had* to. "I think it must be a little like my trying to find my mother. I can't believe she's really gone, that I'll never know her, that she's—she's dead. And in a way"—he was looking at her at last, but in the one brief glance they had when their eyes met, she knew now that it was she who couldn't face him— "I've always felt that about your mother too, that—well—you'd never really known her, that something had happened a long way back to make her go away, and you could never bring her all the way back to where you wanted her."

She said all in a rush before he could stop her, "I just wanted to tell you that—that—well, I think you're being awfully good, coming back this way, the way you were at the station, all of it, facing up to them. With Ethel," she said, and she knew that when she said "Ethel" she *had* to look at him.

"With Ethel," he repeated, and, though she could hardly believe her eyes, he was smiling. For a little moment he laughed. "With Ethel," he said again, and then stopped laughing and looked away. "Lois," he said, and it was hard to make out the words, but her name came through clear and distinct, "I had to come back. Ethel is going to have a baby."

There was nothing she could say. How could she say, But Stu, what are you going to do? She couldn't.

"The thing is," he said, sitting on the bed, looking down at his shoes, "I don't know. I probably won't tell them, not tonight, I mean, but—but you never know what Ethel's going to say. I thought, down at the station—I don't know, I thought I could work it all right, but I don't know whether I can keep it up, whether I've got that kind of patience. I've never exactly been known for my patience. And you don't know how I am when I get going, when I really get carried away. You don't have any idea at all. It can be pretty bad," he said slowly, looking at her so that she could see he meant what he was saying.

She thought of that one time he drank too much up at her place and the low, mean tone that came into his voice, a vehemence that frightened her. *Everyone knows Esther's nothing but a crook,* he had said, *but what really bothers them is that she beat them all to the punch. She was smarter than the rest of them, she got the money.* Oh Stu, she had protested, but he wouldn't listen. *You take Ada, she's even worse because she doesn't care about the idea of stealing, it isn't that she thinks it's wrong; what she hates is that she's the one who didn't think of it, that Esther was smarter than she was, that's what bothers her. Esther's money—where she got it and who she's going to leave it to—that's all any of them care about. That damn money has poisoned the whole family.* No, it hasn't, Stu, she had said, trying to explain. The money is only an excuse for all the other things everyone is really afraid to talk about. *Like what?* he had asked suspiciously. Like maybe a kind of meanness. I mean—and she had faltered, wondering how to put it—something that was passed along, or that grew with the family, was one of the family traits, not in the old sense, but in the real sense, the thing that the family thrived on, a kind of narrowness, a—a selfishness, she had said. I think that's it—the terrible self-centered selfishness of most of us. *I don't care what you call it,* he said violently. *I hate them all*—and he had risen, looking around the room as if he were going to start smashing the place, and she held her breath as he said, *Every goddam one of them.* Then he went out, and she hadn't called him for a long time. She didn't want to see him like that, that part of him that could hate so intensely.

She didn't hate like that. She wasn't even sure she would know how. But Stu, he knew.

Stu, she wanted to cry out, don't tell me. I know a little, but not all. I don't want to know all.

He got up off the bed. "So, if you wouldn't mind," he said, "I'd appreciate it if you'd—well—call up Esther and postpone going tonight."

"Of course I will, I'd be glad to."

"How's come"—and he managed another small smile—"you don't mind doing so many things?" He was trying to be light, the way she had been a few minutes before, and she smiled back at him, feeling cold and frightened. "You got the family martyr complex?" he asked.

"It looks like it, doesn't it? I come with such good credentials."

"If they're going to affect you that way, pack your bag and get out right now."

Lois paused. "I might even stay," she said at last.

"Stay?"

"I've been thinking about it. That's one of the reasons I came back, to make up my mind. I feel I owe them something, especially your mother, for all she did for me, taking me in that way and all. You know, to kind of pay her back. I think—I just have this feeling—she'd like someone in the house."

"She sure would, someone new to yell at and bully and nag and make miserable. Dad's no fun any more, she's worn him out long ago, and Ella doesn't really pay any attention to her. Listen, Lois," he said urgently, "I don't want you to stay. *I* wouldn't even consider staying, and I'm more equipped to get along with her than you are. You'd let her walk all over you because she knows how to use your own good instincts —there it is," he said bitterly. "Always the instincts, never the intelligence, but in this case it would be some intelligence maybe," he said, as if admitting something he didn't want to. "You'd *think* she deserved a lot more leeway than she does."

"But—"

"Lois, I love her—in my own way, I do," he insisted. "But I know that she can be death, too. She's just like a poison for which there's no antidote—you know the one I mean, those poisons that attack the central nervous system. Well, that's what she does: attacks the central nervous system and paralyzes any will you've got. The living death," he said, "like Dad."

"Don't, Stu. I don't like to hear you talk like that because—"

"Because it's too true and you're just like the rest of the family, you want to pretend that kind of thing doesn't exist—no, I didn't mean it like that, Lois," he said quickly. "What I really mean is—hell, maybe you're like me, you've been looking all your life for a family. The one we had was never any real family and—well, *I* couldn't even pretend. But you want to. Maybe that was what was the matter." He gave her a searching look. "You've been out to the house, haven't you? To Grandmother Timble's house, and that's what—"

"I haven't been able to get away, Stu. I thought maybe I'd sneak out there on my way to Esther's."

"Well, don't tell Mother you're going."

"I won't. I suppose I have the same feeling you do—that she wouldn't want me to go. But she does try, Stu, in her own way she tries all she can."

"I know it. I try to tell myself—what difference does it make what I tell myself? Maybe the rest of you are right, it's better to pretend; better to get in the game and sacrifice yourself for them, whether they appreciate it or not. Who knows what's right and what's wrong?"

Before she could answer, he interrupted himself. "I don't believe it makes any difference one way or the other. *Nothing makes any difference.*"

"Maybe it doesn't. Maybe there isn't any difference, not outside, Stu, but inside, maybe there's a difference inside."

"Maybe," he said.

"But you must have felt something pretty much the same, Stu, to come back." She saw she had gone too far. "I'll call Esther," she said quickly, "and see if it's okay to change nights."

"Thanks," he said abruptly and started for the door. She had expected something more. Gratitude, was that it? Why should he be grateful? He doesn't owe me anything, Lois thought. But I owe him something. Why? she wondered. I don't know, maybe because I feel sorry for him. It's as if he were doing penance for a whole lot of people. For all of them. Her, too.

And because in a way she supposed she loved him like the family she did not have and he had accused her of wanting. He might have been her brother. The eyes.

Chapter Five

I'M GOING to keep my own name. It'll look better in print. Stankiewicz is—too long, too long and too foreign.

EILEEN AMES ON THE SPOT!
*America's newest sweetheart answers questions
on her life and loves*

A nice picture of me in my new house (to get out of that room, that awful room, she thought, to have a place all my own), my own beautiful new house; I am leaning up against a bookcase, lots of books, important-looking books, and I am wearing a simple little dress with dart pleats, a small narrow belt, and pearls, real pearls around my neck. One simple strand. A dog maybe at my feet, and I'm looking down, pensive and slightly forlorn, as if the weight of the world, the wisdom of those books, was on my head. But sympathetic. *Sweet and sympathetic,* the caption will read, *Eileen Ames in her new home* SPRINGFIELD, *the house she named after her home town.*

Photoplay with a color picture on the cover, or *Silver Screen* with the middle spread; maybe both. . . .

IN ORDER *to find out the truth about America's newest sweetheart— the girl who has suddenly rescued virtue from the doldrums and put old-fashioned values back in circulation—I drove my little sports car at twilight one day last month to the mountain retreat of Eileen Ames. Eileen, who loves people and whom people love, has been forced to find a haven from all her fans. When she lived on fashionable Sunset Strip, she never had a moment's peace from the wildly screaming, incessantly shouting flocks of fans who stormed her electric gates, trampled her imported oleanders, and made a mess of the miniature Versailles gardens of her estate. The only way to have a normal home life, which Eileen wants for her husband and herself, was to take to the mountains, but she is still occasionally bothered by a persistent fan who* WOULD *climb the highest mountain to get an Ames croquet mallet personally autographed.*

THE HANDSOME *house, Spanish style, reputedly cost $400,000, and its salmon (Eileen's favorite color) swimming pool and adjoining soda fountain (Eileen doesn't drink) in cerise are the talk of Cinemaland. The pool is the biggest in Hollywood and the ice-cream parlor has 58* *flavors, all especially flown in by Howard Johnson, with a full-time soda jerk to serve guests! The day that I arrived Eileen was dressed in a simple little frock (salmon, needless to say) and served me Howard Johnson's Eileen Ames Special: salmon-colored ice cream topped with whipped cream.*

EILEEN IS *very proud of her new house, and before we settled down by the pool she insisted on showing me around. The house is a living dream. Its huge multiplaned structure is so precariously perched that only Lloyds of London will insure it on a special quarter-to-quarter basis. The living room is glassed in on three sides (only the bathroom off the left is closed in), and the step-down "living" area hangs three hundred feet over a chasm. The interior is of course in Eileen's favorite color, and the fixtures for the whole house were baked to order in the world-famous pottery plants of Monterrey.*

EILEEN'S ADORED *mother, Mrs. Ada Ames, has her own apartment at the rear, and Eileen introduced her mother first thing.* "Some people," *Mrs. Ames hastily explained,* "think it's funny that I don't live in the house. But Eileen and Stan want their privacy and so do I. I just love my own quarters, and Eileen has had them done in *my* favorite color. It's kind of a periwinkle blue, only a little lighter. I understand the color, which was especially mixed for me, is becoming very popular. They are calling it Timble blue—my maiden name was Timble, you know."

EILEEN EXPLAINED *that Stan, probably the most envied husband in America, wasn't home. He was attending to business back East. He and Eileen have invested in a string of sporting-goods stores which keep him away from home a good deal of the time.* "I try to keep my daughter from getting too lonely," *Mrs. Ames explained with winning diffidence.*

EILEEN IS *beautiful in a striking way. She has dark hair which she wears in a simple chignon in the back, and her pretty dark eyes need little make-up. But her most outstanding feature is her mouth, which manages to combine the sweetness of sincerity with the insouciance of a childish pout. Her lips were painted a subdued salmon, and her only jewelry was a decorous string of pearls. She looked much prettier than her pictures, which tend to lose the impact of her natural charm, which is more an essence, an esprit, if I may use the French word, than something which can be photographed.*

WE WENT OUT *to the pool and Eileen herself insisted on mixing us the Eileen Ames Special. Then she sat down, broodingly touching her lips with her free hand.* "I'm not much good at 'confessions,' " *she said.* "I get so embarrassed. I don't like to talk about myself."

EILEEN'S EYES *made a Cook's tour of her beautiful estate, lingering on the drop from the front window.* "Some people say that I'll move when we have children"—*she looked down, blushing*—"but I can't imagine ever leaving this." *She glanced around quickly; then her eyes finally came to rest on my pencil. She spread her hands out and studied the unpainted nails, and I could tell her mind was going a mile a minute. She is no slouch intellectually, this girl. She has brains as well as beauty. Suddenly she seemed to pull herself together with great effort.* "I guess we might as well get at it," *she said.*

Q. HOW DOES IT FEEL TO BE AMERICA'S FAVORITE SWEETHEART?

A. I'm very serious about the responsibility I have to keep faith with my fans. When all this business first started, I was scared—naturally—but I made a vow to myself, one I hope I'll never break. I will never do anything to spoil the image the public has of me.

Q. ARE YOU AFRAID ALL THIS ADULATION WILL SPOIL YOUR MARRIAGE?

A. No, Stan and I have a very deep understanding. We both agree that if at any time we seem to be drawing apart, I will retire from the public limelight and devote myself strictly to my home. I wouldn't hesitate to sacrifice my career for my marriage; that comes first—as it should with every woman.

Q. THEN YOU DO WANT CHILDREN?

A. Oh, yes. I'd like to have a big family, four or five. I want to grow up with my children. I believe that parents should have their children young.

Q. THERE SEEMS TO BE SOME DISPUTE ABOUT HOW OLD YOU ARE. I WONDER IF YOU WOULD JUST SET US STRAIGHT FOR THE RECORD.

A. Oh, I—

Q. YOU'D RATHER NOT SAY?

A. What woman would? (*Looking down demurely.*)

Q. IT'S BEEN HINTED, THOUGH, THAT YOU'RE NOT AS YOUNG AS THE PUBLIC HAS BEEN LED TO BELIEVE. IS THERE ANY TRUTH IN THAT?

A. Some ugly stories always start about anyone who's famous. I don't blame these stories for getting started. I'd just like to say that I want to be accepted for myself, not for what age I'm supposed to be, or what I've done, or—

Q. WHAT EXACTLY HAVE YOU DONE? IS IT TRUE YOU'VE BEEN SIGNED FOR THE LEAD IN "ST. URSULA AND THE 20,000 MARTYRED VIRGINS"?

A. Let's just say we're negotiating.

Q. BUT YOU'D TAKE THE PART?

A. If I felt it was right. I want to be known as an actress—a *serious* actress—as well as just a celebrity. I've been studying very hard, you know. And, of course, the religious ideas would have to be right. I wouldn't consider appearing in anything that wasn't deeply serious.

Q. HOW MUCH FAN MAIL DO YOU GET?

A. About five thousand letters a week. My mother and I answer every letter personally, in longhand. I never learned to type. It seems too unladylike somehow. Oh, I have nothing against girls who type, you understand, but I just can't imagine myself doing it. Anyway, Mama and I feel that if all those nice people can take the time to write, we can make the time to answer. I autograph pictures every Thursday and I make radio and television appearances for any worthy cause. Of course I never take *money* for those appearances. I donate my services. I don't want anything personally for myself. I hope you'll emphasize that. Stan and I have these sporting-goods stores—we feel it is so important for young people of today to have wholesome pleasures, to devote themselves to the good, worthwhile things in life and to keep their bodies fit; we have a little slogan we use with our merchandise, "A fit body is always the beginning of a fit mind," and we try to get teenagers to go back to the good old-fashioned pastimes, like croquet and badminton and things like that. Stan says golf is all right, for men anyway, but for teenagers we try to emphasize the more family sports. A family that plays together prays together.

Q. WHAT ARE YOUR GLAMOUR SECRETS?

A. Oh, I don't think of myself as glamorous. I don't want to be like that. I want to be—well, I think girls should be neat and wash their hair once a week and act like ladies and dress in feminine clothes. No slacks or shorts; you don't need those for croquet, you know, and a good wide skirt will work for badminton. One thing I'm particularly against is blue jeans. I think they're so bad for posture. Girls in blue jeans always slump.

Q. OH, I SEE THERE'S A DELIVERY MAN COMING. I'LL HAVE TO WAIT WITH MY NEXT QUESTION.

THE BIG BOX *was tied with an enormous white bow into which two dozen red roses had been worked. Inside was a gorgeous mutation mink. Eileen couldn't resist the temptation to try it on. I was particularly struck by the fact that she looked, in spite of her heavenly new coat, just like the girl next door. Perhaps this is the secret of her appeal.*

SHE PUT HER *hands in her pockets and pirouetted for my approval. Then she let out a little squeal of surprise.* "Oh, there's something in this pocket," *she said, extracting a little box. It was a diamond ring!* "My favorite cut, a marquise," *Eileen exclaimed, passing me the card. It was from her husband and said,* In celebration of selling our millionth croquet set.

To CELEBRATE, *Eileen asked for another ice cream. I said I would pass up the opportunity; I had to watch my calories.*

Q. DO YOUR FANS BOTHER YOU MUCH UP HERE?

A. Well, it's better now. But when we go away we're always surrounded by people. Most of them just want to touch me, but a lot of them ask me for souvenirs, and I've taken to carrying these little cards around. They have inspirational sayings on them, with my name at the bottom, and the name of our stores, of course. And then I sign them, if I have the time. Most people are nice and polite, but when I make a personal appearance sometimes things get out of hand. Riots. People screaming and pushing, tearing my clothes, trying to touch me, you know. They mean well. They're all so sweet and dear that I don't mind a bit.

Q. WHAT ARE THE MOST IMPORTANT THINGS IN YOUR LIFE?

A. I love animals, and children, and my mother . . .

. . . my mother, my mother who is downstairs and waiting for me to come down, and Stan who is at the shop waiting for me to call, to say that I've talked to her, that it's all right, she knows he's coming to the party.

My vision, Eileen thought, my lovely lovely vision. It's spoiled. The way everything is always spoiled.

Not to leave this house, like Mama, to stay inside, safe; to be able to stay in this room, read my magazines, dream my dreams, just to be left alone, all alone.

Not even Mama. No one. Maybe Mama, she thought, maybe Mama and me. The two of us against *him.*

Down in the basement walking around, pushing the cartons around, all those cartons with the broken bottles in them, his private place. Like this room is my private place. He lives his life down there, down in the cellar with his broken bottles and his surplus army cot. No one can spoil his daydreams down there. What does he dream, Daddy, down in the basement?

I dream all the time. About the mice. Those poor little mice. The little orchestra of mice, all dressed up in tiny white uniforms, each playing a tiny little instrument. So cute, those little mice in their military costumes, playing their little horns and drums and trumpets, all marching about, following the baton, saying the Declaration of Independence, pledging allegiance to the flag, playing martial tunes.

There is a high fence around the park where they're performing, and a lot of old men dozing on benches, sitting in the sun, half listening to the music, and the mice march up and down rattling their drums, blowing their bugles, making little military tattoos.

The Trainer: an old man who sometimes looks like Stan, sometimes looks like my father, sometimes has a face I can't recognize: he stands at one side of his truck and watches the mice, beaming approval. The box from which he has taken the mice is at the side of the truck, its wire top lying on the ground.

In her dream she went up to the man and asked him about the mice. Wasn't he afraid someone might hurt them, step on them, for instance, or those dogs—the ones leaping and barking at the fence—wasn't he afraid that the dogs might get at them? No, he said, watching his mice proudly, and Eileen looked quickly at the fence, frowning while the pack of dogs leaped up, trying to get in.

"I think you ought to put them back in their box," she always said, but he only shook his head and answered, No, they are all right; and then in her dream, at just that instant, the dogs leaped over the fence and ran down on the mice. They were on them before either Eileen or the trainer could move.

Chomp, chomp, like the sound of breaking bottles, like the sound of the radio being turned from station to station, like the sound of someone crushing a package of cigarettes, chomp, chomp: the mice were all eaten. Their little uniforms and their little instruments—the drums and horns, the clarinets and all, even the flag—disappeared into the dogs' mouths. Oh, it was awful, too awful, and it was too late. There was nothing she could do.

The trainer stood as one paralyzed, tears running down his cheeks. His life was gone, devoured in one moment, he was powerless with grief.

"You can—maybe you can train some more?"

He put his head into his hands and sobbed as if his heart would break. It took seven years, he said, to train *each* mouse and now he was old, he was an old, old man, and he would never have an orchestra of mice again.

Then, slowly, he took his hands away, wiped his eyes on the back of one, and bent down to put the lid back on the box and put the box in the truck. Without looking at her, he walked around to the front and got in. Just as he started away he put his head out the window and said, "It was bound to happen. I should have known. You can't keep anything. I should have remembered that." Then he drove off, leaving Eileen with the dogs dancing around her feet.

If only she could warn the trainer sooner—the next time she started the dream, for instance, if she could get him to put the mice back in the box—she could save them. But she knew that she would never be able to stop the progression of her dream. It was all her fault that the mice were eaten, went on being eaten, she could not stop what was.

People will never know about my dream or about my father in the basement or about those nights in the car. They will look at me, pretty, sweet Eileen Ames, and they will say, "She's a sweetheart, America's sweetheart. . . ."

Q. WHY DO YOU ALWAYS SEEM SO SERIOUS?

A. I guess I just see things in a funny kind of way. I don't have the kind of personality that jokes and kids around. If I seem serious, maybe I am.

My own name, I will keep my own name. Eileen Ames.

I'm not ashamed of his name. It's only—only that, well, nobody would remember it, a long, funny foreign name like that. Lots of people change their names, don't they? You have a long, funny name, impossible to spell, there's nothing wrong with simplifying it so people can remember it.

You're thirty-one years old and you won't even go downstairs and tell your own mother you want to bring the man you're supposed to marry to a family party.

Mama, Mama, why can't you understand? Why can't you be the way I think of you?

Why can't Stan see that I can't go away and leave her in this house with *him*—my father down cellar drinking, my mother shut up in this house, and at night the white mice inside my head.

If he understood, really understood, he wouldn't have insisted on going to Lois's party—a mink coat, a marquise diamond, two dozen red roses. . . . Lois, Eileen thought. Maybe Lois would help. Maybe she could get Lois to call her mother up and say, "Look, Aunt Ada, I was just thinking. Almost everyone at the party is married, and so they'll all come in couples, so I thought maybe there was someone Eileen could bring, so she wouldn't feel left out." Her mother couldn't say no to Lois, it was Lois's party. And if Lois called her mother up, then *she* would have to suggest inviting Stan; Eileen would not have to ask her at all.

Lois would help, she *had* to help.

Stu: In the beginning I had an idea he might help. I thought—I don't know—he ran away, he's in New York, he had to get out of that house, get out of Springfield, he should understand.

For a long time Eileen hadn't been able to bring herself to do anything definite; then, at last, with the war on and all, she knew something might happen to him, she had to get in touch before—before anything happened. Ethel's mother, she thought one day, Ethel's mother will know where Ethel is, and Ethel will know where Stu is. It had taken more than a month to get the courage to call. Surprisingly, Ethel's mother had been *nice*.

Eileen didn't know what she had expected—anger, bitterness, maybe even being hung up on—but Ethel's mother had listened quietly while Eileen stammered out her apologies. She was sorry to bother her, she knew how she must feel, after all these years and no one in the family getting in touch, but the truth was, Eileen confessed, and she said she didn't know how to explain but that she'd been sorry, the truth was, that she was worried about Stu and wanted to get in touch. I want to know about him, Eileen said, but I wouldn't want to—well—write him direct. But I thought maybe I could write to Ethel and tell her how sorry I am that— I was just maybe wondering if—if you would give me her address, I could write her. . . .

Eileen had written her first letter to Ethel that evening, explaining that after all these years it must seem funny to hear from someone in the family, but that she thought Ethel might understand, they were maybe a little alike. Ethel had answered—not to the house; she had sent her letters through Stan—and then, after Lois went on out to New York, to check, Eileen had written Lois and told her that she knew where Stu was but that she couldn't say how she knew and would Lois go look for herself and tell her what she thought. Lois's answer had been guarded, but Eileen knew the truth anyway by that time. Stu couldn't help her. But she had begun to think she had a friend in Ethel, a girl she had never even met. Yet year after year, sometimes months passing between letters, the two kept up a thin strand of communication, as if both were inside hostile army quarters and could get in touch only perilously, yet convinced of the ultimate need to hold onto the idea that peace might eventually be restored, the two camps be free to converse and mingle again.

And now Stu was back home, and Ethel was with him. Was it possible that after all this time she was going to have a *real* friend?

Someone I could be close to without being afraid, Eileen thought. A real friend all my own.

I don't want to run away, even with Stan, Eileen thought. I want to have a home and friends and children and all the things other people have. I want to be happy, she thought, what's so wrong with that? Why won't Mama realize and let me get married the way other people get married, in church, with a big wedding, and a party afterward where everyone smiles and stands around and says how lovely the wedding was and how nice the bride's dress looked and weren't the bride and groom a lovely couple. I'm only asking, she thought in desperation, for the same chance everyone else gets, to lead a normal life.

Why is that asking too much?

Chapter Six

DON'T waste your energy on outrage, Carolyn told herself, flinging an arm over her head, listening to Ralph grunt, struggle with the bedclothes, cough, clear his throat, mumble something, and settle, sighing, down on the springs. So there's no satisfaction, not even a little one; so you try to pretend—what was it that damn article she had picked up in the beauty parlor said? *Better pretense than offense; what you pretend you may actually come to feel.* So there's a small circle of hysteria inside, be grateful it's small.

It's the desolation, Carolyn thought, that's what's so hard to reconcile, the sense of bereavement—sweated, spent, and no joy to pay for it.

The act of love, that article had said with firmness, might bless or curse a woman's life. Then there had been a nice little chart of what to expect—the encouraging information that most honeymoons were hopeless failures; the five years following, an unrelieved strain, a constant battle for adjustment, each partner struggling to keep the other from knowing the total failure of most of the matings (a curse or a blessing, Carolyn thought, someone had the nerve to write that and then the unmitigated gall to go on and present the whole terrifying spectrum of what was ahead); then came five years of some kind of pleasure, or at least some kind of adjustment, passive acceptance if not enthusiastic participation.

I could write them an article, Carolyn thought, fighting back an ache of longing to switch on the light and find a cigarette. What that article doesn't say is that after the ten years, then what?

Resignation, isolation, bleakness.

"What is it?" Ralph demanded, disgruntled. "Can't you get comfortable?"

"I'm all right," she said sharply. "I just can't figure out what to do with my feet. They're always so hot." Even in winter she couldn't sleep with her feet covered. Under the blankets they felt—suffocated. Outside they felt frozen. She was always thrusting her feet outside the covers, then jerking them back under. In and out, all night long.

"Well, try to settle down, will you—honey?" The first was a cry of exasperation, the last a plea for reconciliation. "Go ahead, shift. What I can't stand is that sort of sneaking around."

"I can't help it if I'm restless. All the books, all the magazine articles you read, say you get this let-down feeling afterwards, *post coitum triste,* that's what they call it, it's perfectly natural. Two people grind away at one another and then they—"

"Carolyn!"

"I'm only repeating what—"

"Do you think you're being funny?"

For a moment she wondered how he could ask such a question. *There is often an hour, after the act itself, when both parties retreat into the bitterness of utter isolation. . . .* "Would you mind if I turned on the light? Had a cigarette?"

What could he say? she wondered. He grunted; that was the answer.

Groping, Carolyn found the knob of the night light. The tumbled sheet leaped into illumination, his white, naked body covered with the golden down, the hairs on his arms and legs harshly dark by contrast, the hair under the arm that cushioned his head coiled in sweaty ringlets. The aftermath of love, she thought, knowing her own hair must be disheveled, little jewels of sweat gleaming on her shoulders.

I hate being seen, she thought, taking the cigarettes from the bed table. I hate making love in the daylight. It's an unnecessary exposure, a violation of privacy. In the beginning he even used to want to take baths with me—the terrible male need to reassure himself, the endless panorama of the outstretched hands, demanding some sign of love. Look at me, let me look at you, love me, let me love you, over and over, until you wanted to scream.

Leave me alone, she wanted to shout at him, just leave me alone for a little while. Stop following me around trying to force me to tell you how much I love you, clutching me in the kitchen, saying, Tell me you love me, show me you love me, trying to force the reassurances I don't want to give, *can't* give.

Statistics, that article in the beauty shop had said, and Ralph would have loved that, he would have been crazy about the graphs and charts, showed that men committed crimes of passion in the bedroom, women in the kitchen.

"You want one too?" she asked.

His eyes, closed against the light, opened. He stared at her. "Okay, I guess I might as well."

She handed him the pack, waited while he took one, then bent close to him with her cigarette, waiting while he got a light. *Better pretense than offense . . .*

Silent, they smoked. But it was not of her husband she was thinking, but of her brother. For that brief moment alone with him at Sans Souci, she had tried to tell him how sorry she was about the fight that had sent him away. Faltering, stumbling over her words, embarrassed but determined, she had seen in mid-sentence that the one thing that had preoccupied and frightened her about his return—the fact that she was responsible for his having gone away in the first place—hardly concerned him at all. He had put the whole thing out of his mind. He had never blamed her at all—never even, incredible as it seemed, thought about it.

"Ralph?" she said tentatively.

"Hummm."

"I wish we could do something about Stu. He's—"

"I'm sorry I got mad that way, about your staying over at Erwin's Sunday. It's just—I don't know—we never seem to get together any more, I hardly ever see you, and when you're out like that I always . . ." He took a drag on his cigarette, the smoke rose shroudlike around him, while Carolyn thought crazily,

> *Who will make his shroud?*
> *"I," said the beetle,*
> *"With my thread and needle,*
> *I'll make his shroud."*

H

". . . about the drinking, I mean—only sometimes—" His voice stopped. "Forgive me?" he said, leaning over, using his free hand to clutch at her; it was *his* aftermath of love, forgiveness. A shower of black ashes fell on the sheet over her breasts while she tried to suppress the blind instinct to pull away from him.

"Listen, Ralph," she said frantically, "there's something I've got to talk to you about—about Stu, to help—" His eyes so close, the cigarette perilously near her. "Look out, you're going to burn me." And he moved away, she felt the panic recede, the shrill siren of warning die down, a little moment of quiet fill her head, and heard her voice, once more calm and seemingly affectionate, go on. "He's out of a job. That's why he came back, I think, because—and you know, about the letters, about mother opening the letters, I was the one—"

"He need money?"

She shook her head. "It's a job, Ralph. He's got to have a job." She thought of what Stu had told her that moment when they were alone. *Ethel's going to have a baby and*—Stu, Ethel, and a baby. Carolyn took a quick drag on her cigarette.

"You want me to take him on, that it?"

"I just thought there might be a place, you know, where—"

God, he was angry. She knew that look. "Of course, if there isn't," she went on hastily, "I wouldn't want you to make a place, just because he's my brother. You know that. Only I thought if there was a place, you could just—you know—he's had a lot of bad luck, Ralph."

"It's not good policy, Carolyn. You take on one of your family, everyone knows he's not the same as the next man. The supervisors, they can't bawl him out like anyone else, everyone goes easy on him, it's bad for morale," he ended stubbornly.

Don't say anything, Carolyn cautioned herself. Give him a chance to think it over. Let him answer himself.

"It isn't that I don't think he'd try, nothing like that. It's just that it's bad policy," he repeated. "Those things never work. You didn't say I would give him a job, did you? You didn't make a definite commitment, did you?"

"Oh no, of course not," Carolyn said quickly. "You know I wouldn't do that. I just thought I'd see if there was anything open."

"Well"—so relieved, Carolyn thought—"so long as you didn't say anything definite, well, I guess you can just pretend—you know—that you sort of forgot to mention it." He had the decency to sound apologetic at least.

"I couldn't do that, Ralph. No, I'd rather tell him that it's company policy. That seems fairer. I'm sure he'll understand. A rule and all, you couldn't break a company rule."

"It isn't a written rule," Ralph explained. "It's just one of those things everyone in business recognizes, that you don't create a job for—"

"But I don't want you to do that. All I said was that if there *was* a job, then I wish you'd consider Stu. Just as if he were anyone else. It seems sort of unfair to me that just because he is in the family he can't even be considered, but—"

"The thing is, there isn't a job." Her husband sounded as if he had found his way out.

"But even if there was something, you couldn't—you wouldn't—consider him, that's what you meant, wasn't it?"

"But since there isn't—"

"But if there were?"

"Well, I suppose we could *consider* him, if that's what you want. Only wouldn't it be worse to consider him and then have to turn him down?"

"Yes, of course, since he's *my* brother."

"If he were my own brother, I—"

"But you don't have a brother. Anyway, what I can't understand is, I mean, it's *your* father's business and he took *you* in—"

"It's not the same, not the same at all, and you know it."

"No, of course not, he's *my* brother, it's *my* family." She took a quick puff on her cigarette. "It's perfectly all right for *your* father to take you in, but it isn't all right for you to take *my* brother in. It's not the same kind of thing at all. Of course it isn't. *You* went to Princeton, *you* had all the advantages. What do *you* know what it's like growing up poor?" she asked him, her eyes blazing, jabbing the air with her cigarette, her voice getting shrill and harsh. "Really poor, so you wear other people's cast-off clothes, so you never have any money for the essentials, let alone the extravagances." She sat up, clutching the sheet to her, shaking with anger. "Princeton and maids and your mother, your beautiful elegant bitch of a mother—"

"Now just a minute, Carolyn—"

"I don't care," Carolyn insisted passionately. "She's never liked me, not from the start. No matter what I did, it was wrong. Even naming Sally after her couldn't please her. Sitting there," Carolyn said, half in tears, half in outrage, "in her real pearls, with her securities in the bank, and James, *James,*" Carolyn repeated, giving Ralph's father's name the same faintly condescending, faintly worshiping tone Ralph's mother used, "to take care of her, judging everyone, as if she were god almighty herself. I hate her, I tell you, with all her smug—"

Ralph, his face dark with rage, leaned over and grabbed her shoulder. He's going to hit me, Carolyn thought. It's the only way he knows how to stop me. "Go ahead," she challenged him breathlessly, waiting, staring at him, putting out her chin as if to defy him. "Go ahead, hit me, the way you usually do."

A little nerve trembled at the corner of his mouth. He bit his lips, the teeth bared as they came down on the tender flesh. The arm which held her, tight, painfully tight, grasped harder, the fingers sinking deep into her flesh, and for that second she waited, almost wanting it, as if the sheer force of his hand striking her across the face would release the tension inside, that terrible tight knot of unfulfilled desire, her whole body beginning to tremble, thinking, he's weak, weak, *"Weak"*—until the word was out of her mouth, and he flinched, drew back his arm, and then jerked up, let his arm fall back, he was in control, he would not strike her.

"Carolyn, Carolyn," he said, throwing himself on her and pleading, "I promised, the last time, I promised I wouldn't. Never again. Remember?"

How does he think I can forget? she wondered.

His head crushed against her breasts, the sheet seeming a merciful protection against his bare flesh; she was ashamed she lived in the same house with him, shared the same bed with him, humiliated that all the things she held against him now were the things that had originally tied her to him—the money, the Princeton background, the cool poise of his mother that stood in such contrast to the feverish complaints of her own mother; she had married him to escape, only to be caught in a worse trap.

So rudely forc'd . . .

He would want to make love again, she thought, listening to his heartbeats pressed up against her own sheet-covered breast, feeling the shudder of his body straining toward hers. These scenes—particularly the ones where he came to violence—seemed to arouse some primitive chord of lust in him so that he had no sooner struck her than he rushed forward to beg forgiveness, his whole body abeat with desire, a running rhythm of what was stirring him to a feat of love he never attempted when he was simply satisfying his instincts. The violence lifted him up. He would ravish her with something close to the first animal mating, his body an instrument of punishment beating down on her, one enormous blow of blood and flesh after another, a rain of fists in the form of his whole body, his voice going on and on, words spilling out, without coherence or sense, until in a great upward drive, like a piston straining at the last possible effort, like a great machine pounding over a recalcitrant country-side, driving as men drive in war, his body came smashing down on her, and she would lie defeated, not even knowing if she had fought her own battle of desire or not, only knowing she lay vanquished, an enemy crushed.

I can get up and go downstairs, she thought, make up the couch in the study, retreat into silence; or I can wait him out, let his desire work itself to such a pitch that the price of capitulation is a job for Stu. For once, she thought, get something out of all this.

"Carolyn," he said softly, slowly, and she knew that sound, that dry catch in his voice, was ready for the way he lifted his head and looked at her beseechingly. "What's the matter with us? What makes us act this way?"

Dare I tell the truth? Carolyn wondered. I dare—but won't. It wouldn't do any good, it wouldn't get Stu his job—and Ralph, how could he ever understand? The only thing that ever happened to Ralph that meant anything to him was stealing a chicken on some windswept plain in France.

The only thing that happened to me that mattered was that he was the one to come home. I have kept someone else in my heart all this time, she thought, someone not even seen, a ghost hanging onto my heart, claiming it, haunting it, crying out inside me with all the love I have denied you. The dead lover. Living in her heart.

I still shut my eyes and pretend the arms around me are those arms, she thought, the tears spilling over, so that Ralph jerked up, held her away from him a moment, misunderstanding, thinking perhaps she was weeping over them, over him, crying out, "Don't, please don't, Carolyn," while she shook her head, angrily brushed the tears away with one hand, clinging to the sheet with the other, and heard herself explaining, "I don't know, I try to tell myself we were never poor, never really poverty-stricken, we just didn't have much money. I don't want to have that on me, you never get rid of that. The smell of cabbage," she said fiercely, "and other people's old hand-me-down clothes."

"Honey, please don't." He was holding her, stroking her hair, his lips brushing against her forehead, while all the while she could feel him stiffening with the heat of desire, knew that in a moment the soft sympathy of those hands would turn to the hard, harsh demand of passion.

Now, she thought. "No matter what I say, you'll never be able to understand."

"But I try, Carolyn. I want to."

"If you wanted to, if you really wanted to, you'd understand. But you don't. You couldn't and still—and still—act the way you do about my family. You'd want to help them because they're a part of me. What hurts them hurts me. Can't you see? I identify with them, especially Stu, *I* know what he's going through, how he feels, and I just can't stand it, Ralph."

She threw her arms around his neck and buried her face against his cheek so that he could feel the tears falling. "You failed me," she cried, as if her heart would break, and she felt for a moment as if it might, because she had spoken the real truth—for the wrong reason, but the truth nevertheless; he *had* failed her, and in the next instant her grief was genuine and she heard herself confessing, "It's that I hold against you, that you've failed me. Again and again."

He was bending her back, and his mouth came down on hers, his body, throbbing with its hardness, covered hers, and he said, clutching her with burning hands, "Why can't we ever get close? Why are we always fighting? Carolyn, can't you ever come to me without wanting something? Do I always have to give something in return for this? Carolyn, just once can't there be nothing between us. Nothing. I want us to be close, just this once. Can't you be close to me just this once? Carolyn, just let me leave the light on. Just this once," he said, his voice ending in a roar, and he crashed down on her, clutching her as if the world were coming apart, saying over and over as he beat out his passion against her, "Can't you love me . . . Carolyn . . . oh, Carolyn . . ." while she lay under him, open and defenseless; she shut her eyes and tried to blot out the thought, He can destroy me like this, he can kill me like this.

But she knew she was wrong. She had forgotten the most important thing, the one thing that would make it all meaningful for her: after he had expended that terrible drive of strength, he would fall down, broken, on her body, the slain warrior on the field of white. She would rise to fight in the morning. His strength came solely in these dark hours, and then only for a little while.

SATURDAY

SUNDAY

MONDAY

TUESDAY

WEDNESDAY

BOOK V   **THURSDAY**

FRIDAY

SATURDAY

Chapter One

"Lois! Lois!"

"I'm coming," she called down. "I must have lost track of time."

"It's the telephone," Iris shouted. "Some *man.*"

Neal. He had tried to get hold of her in New York. He had figured out where she had gone. Now he was on the phone, saying, I made a mistake. Lois—*love*—come back.

Iris was holding the phone in her outstretched hand, as if it might harm her. "A man," she whispered significantly and handed over the receiver, standing, with arms folded, watching Lois avidly.

"Hello," Lois said carefully.

"Miss Greer?"

It took her a minute to swallow the disappointment, to make her voice come out normally. "Yes?" Why didn't Iris go away? "Just a minute." She put her hand over the mouthpiece. "Aunt Iris—" she began.

"I'm just on my way to the kitchen," Iris said hastily.

"Yes?" Lois began again.

"This is a friend of Eileen's, of your cousin Eileen. My name's Walt Stankiewicz. Maybe she told you something about me?"

"Yes, she did mention—"

"The thing is, Eileen—well, I just talked to Eileen, and she said she wanted to call you, only I asked her if maybe—if maybe I could get ahold of you first. I wanted—could you give me a little time for a talk, in private?" he said.

"Well, yes, I suppose so, I—"

"The thing is, I was wondering—this afternoon, maybe? I know it's not much notice, but I can get off early, I could pick you up and—"

"I'm going downtown myself," Lois said. "I was just on my way out."

"Well, that would be swell, if I could meet you down here, then."

"I've been away a couple of years, Eileen probably told you—I don't know my way around too well any more, but how about meeting in front of the capitol? That's not hard to find."

"Anything you say."

"Would twenty minutes, half an hour, be too soon?"

"No, that's good. Twenty minutes, say, in front of the capitol."

"How'll I know you?"

"I'll be driving. A Pontiac. Black. I'll—"

"I've got a blue suit on. I'm tall and I've got dark hair and—" How in the name of heaven did you describe yourself?

"I'll spot you, don't worry."

He had hung up, but she still held the phone, looking at it as if it might now speak with Neal's voice. But of course the things you wanted to happen never happened, except in your mind.

"The last thing in the world I'd want you to think is that I'm prying, honey," Iris began from the doorway as Lois replaced the receiver. "But—well—you know I— Is it someone you know well?"

She's been listening all this time, Lois thought. Keeping tabs on us, keeping tabs on everyone, monitoring our morals, Lois thought, saving us from ourselves. She's always done it, she always will.

"It wasn't that I was listening or anything," Iris insisted. "I had to come in here for— I couldn't help hearing," she protested.

Lois bent over to place a small kiss on her aunt's cheek. Iris had taken her in, Iris had raised her, she must remember the Iris who wrapped her sandwiches for school, saying, *Lois, you eat them both, every bit of them, you're so thin.* "I'll be back sometime tomorrow. Don't worry about any meals for me; I don't know quite when I'll make it."

"Oh, I'll call you at Esther's, don't worry," Iris said immediately. "I want to be sure you get out there all right, and I'd be calling anyway, as a matter of course, to see that Esther's all right. She's out there all alone, I worry about burglars so. I'll know when you're coming back."

"But I've got a couple of errands—"

"Don't trouble yourself," Iris persisted. "We'll work it out, Esther and I. You just go ahead and have a good time. And Lois—"

"Yes?"

"There isn't any—any message you maybe want to leave, in case that man calls back?"

"It wasn't anyone in particular," Lois said carefully. "An old school friend who heard I was in town—heard it from Erwin, just called to say hello."

"Oh." Iris breathed a sigh of relief. "Well, that's nice—that people still remember you enough to ring up and all. He ask you out?"

"He's married. He just wanted to say hello."

"But I thought you were going to meet him. I thought you said—"

"Just to hear the news, just for a minute on my way out to Esther's."

"Even if you did go to school with him, you know you can't be too careful."

"No, you can't."

Neal would never have called, she ought to have known that.

Consign him to the past, she thought, forget him, let him go, like your father, out in California with his new wife. She thought of that summer, before the new wife, when her father was still in Winnetka, and she had gone to visit him, hopefully, turning her back on the reality of what he was, imagining him as she wanted him to be, refusing to recognize the blunt, egoistic, self-centered man who had charged her fifty dollars for a summer of tennis lessons because she had lost the match at the end, that man who retreated behind a newspaper because the newspaper was a wall against the world, the man who walked with his feet turned out, two firm, flat pointers to the paths he could not decide to take, the one toward affection and extension, the other toward withdrawal and rejection, and the last time she had seen him he was still walking that way, his feet a little less firm, but the important thing was that his eyes were staring straight ahead, up the walk to where he went to work. He had made his choice.

A little girl without a mother, she thought, stopping on the curb and glancing down the street for a tram, a little girl who wanted a father.

That summer so long ago, when, trembling with hope, she went up on the train with all Iris's admonitions inside, locked in safely as if their practice would insure her father's love—to wash her pants every night, not to pick her nose, to say thank you when someone gave her something, to keep quiet when adults were talking, not to ask for anything but, if anything was offered, to take the smallest or least expensive, no matter what she wanted, and above all, as Iris had told her again and again, *to keep out of the way*—sitting silently pressed against the train window, the little purse with the five dollars Iris had given her ("Men forget about how even little girls need money sometimes; here, honey, you take this and don't say anything about it, so you'll have something for your own"), staring with dry eyes at the fields rushing by, her heart pounding, her stomach quivering; she had not even been able to eat the sandwich Iris had wrapped up for her, she was so excited, feeling as if she might actually be ill, she had wanted so much to please him.

Hour after hour the train joggled along and she sat staring out the window. When the train pulled into the big smoky, sooty station at Chicago and the porter—whom Iris had given a dollar to look after her, and he had stared back at Iris as if she had insulted him, and maybe, Lois thought now, Iris had, but she had been doing the best she could, a dollar was still a dollar to Iris, who had gone through the depression, inflation meant nothing to her—that porter had come up and told her to wait in the vestibule, he would see she got off. He did, and that was all. Once she stepped down from the rusted steps and stood in the middle of the concrete passageway she was on her own, so frightened that she actually felt the breakfast of hours before surging up in her throat and she gagged and stood, tears blinding her eyes, clutching to her one hope, *Oh, he will come and meet me, he said he would, oh, he's got to be here,* and started to follow everyone else toward the exit, sure in her soul that he would not be there, that she was all alone in Chicago with Iris's five dollars and no way to know what to do.

He was behind the rope. He had a suit on she did not recognize, and he was wearing his good summer hat, the one he was always so careful to hold by his fingertips so that there wouldn't be prints on the gray brim. He had the hat on, he always wore it whenever he could so that he wouldn't forget and put his hands on it, and she had thought, coming through the doors, That means he won't kiss me. Not if he's got his hat on. It might just accidentally get knocked off or something. No, he won't, and she had been surprised to find that she was relieved. She had been dreading the moment of decision all the way up from Springfield to Chicago, whether she should kiss him on the cheek or on the mouth, and now she could just shake his hand.

Somehow that seemed better. She had this secret feeling that he blamed her for what had happened to her mother. Lois had been the one who had wanted to take the tennis lessons, and if she hadn't wanted to take them her mother never would have gone out to the country club that way and met that man, and if she had never met that man she . . . Shaking hands was infinitely preferable, Lois decided.

They went toward each other warily, not even smiling, and she put out her hand and he took it and said, "You have a good trip down?" and she nodded and he looked around and said, "Where's your bag?"

"The man on the train has it."

"What man on the train?"

"Uncle Stewart gave it to some man on the train."

"Haven't you got a tag or anything?"

She shook her head.

"Well, how the hell am I supposed to find a bag I've never even seen if they didn't give you a tag or anything?" he asked impatiently, in that old voice she recognized at once, the one she knew was really his.

She thought for a moment and then said, "I know what it looks like. I guess if we go where the bags are, I could find it."

That seemed to satisfy him, and they started off. Then he stopped in the middle of the station, looking down at her. "How long did Iris tell you you were going to visit? Did she explain I gotta go to Detroit, so it's only two weeks instead of a month?" Lois nodded, and he seemed to be reassured now, his tone was hearty and full of good spirits. "We're going to have a swell time," he said enthusiastically. "I'm going to take you to the zoo and the museum and the amusement park and all kinds of swell places. I know lots of places you'll like," he said proudly, walking so fast that she had to run to keep up. "You're going to like Chicago, it's a swell city. I live in Chicago now. Did Iris tell you that?"

Iris hadn't, but Lois knew better than to say so.

He had known lots of places, yes, but they had not been the kind that brought a child to wide-eyed wonder. The places they went were houses of other people, older people who as a rule didn't have children, and they went on Saturday and Sunday afternoons, early, and the adults sat around drinking and laughing, talking and droning on and on in their happy, relaxed voices, while she sat in the kitchen and drank Coca-Cola or wandered about the back yard trying to think of some way to amuse herself but *keeping out of the way*.

Once he took her to a movie and once they went out to dinner together, to a big restaurant where he told her she could have anything she wanted, but reminded her it was Friday and she ought to be eating fish, her mother had been a Catholic, she didn't want to forget that. "Iris, she makes you go to church, doesn't she?" he asked, and Lois nodded. She did what Iris had admonished her, letting her eyes run down not the list of entrées but the price column, and when she found the cheapest thing on the menu, which was indeed fish, she said she'd have that, and he seemed pleased, and said, hell, why didn't she have dessert too. She had watermelon, which was so difficult to eat that she had to give up in the middle; she was ashamed of the mess she was making on the tablecloth. She supposed she had once known the name of the restaurant, but it had long since left her mind, and now, as she stood with her cigarette, staring down the street, waiting for the streetcar, she thought that she had never liked watermelon since and that of everything that had happened to her that year the worst were those afternoons sitting in some strange kitchen hearing the hum of voices from the living room and staring at the refrigerator trying to think of how she could make herself even more inconspicuous. The adults, on their way for re-fills, passing her, always looked surprised and upset, as if they had for-gotten there was such a thing as a child in the kitchen.

Perhaps they had.

She saw the big restaurant, done all in brown, a heavy dark place full of the past and of the expensive bills presented to sated men who could afford them, their big hands going confidently to well-padded pockets, their large cigars resting on the ashtrays in front of them, in front of the crumpled napkins, as they went to pay the bill. Cigar smoke and her father's taciturn face across the plate, his heavy figure pushed up against the table: she always thought of him as he leaned forward to pick up his silverware before he used it, examined it, wiped it off, set it down firmly on the table, looked at her approvingly, and then swayed slightly forward toward her over his steak, one finger up to his nose, rubbing it softly, his meditating mouth remarking, "This is the best place in town. Everybody who's anybody eats here."

Was it that scene, always in her mind, the picture she always carried of her father, and by extension her picture of all men, which had prompted her to be so smarty-smarty with Neal the first time she met him, playing the cool, witty, lighthearted sophisticate, saying to him, when he asked her what she wanted to do, "I want to be like Sarah Bern-hardt in Saint Petersburg and have a red carpet rolled over the snow and men in place of horses to draw my carriage through the streets while the people cheer and call my name"—all the time knowing it was wrong, but once she had started, how could she stop, seeing the disgust and dis-belief on Neal's face, but he only looked at her and said, with a slight twist to the corners of his mouth, "Well, that sounds like a pretty modest request to me"?

There was no way to retreat, no way she could raise the white flag. She had tried to pass herself off as something she was not and, once committed, how could she turn back? Going on with one bright, brittle, and not-so-clever remark after another, trying desperately to capture his attention, which was straying further and further every moment, but they were in a corner at the party and he couldn't very well just walk away and leave her, although she had the feeling he might even do that if she kept on, but she had kept right on, unable to stop herself. "You know what people said of Bernhardt? 'She is unique and no one can take her place.' I want that on my tombstone."

"Put it in your will," he said, "and leave enough to pay for it, and who's to stop you?" And then he had said, "Will you excuse me for a minute, I want to see someone over there"—and he was gone, that big, raw-boned, beautiful man who had come into the party and it was as if the whole room had fallen in on her.

Frances would have some occult explanation. The harmonies of the universe. Astrological chemistry. Something. But the truth was that he looked like the picture in her head she had carried around for years, the blurred portrait of that face bent over the tennis rackets, the face of the man her mother had run away with, looking so confident and serene as he said, "Don't worry about losing. I only wanted you to try for practice. So you won't get nervous when you have a real match you want to win. For the experience," he had said, straightening up and smiling, patting her on the head.

It was only now she recognized that the man had been blond, Neal dark. Something about the face, though, she told herself, throwing down her cigarette.

A streetcar was coming. She opened her purse, fished out a quarter, climbed on, waited for her change, sat down next to a colored woman.

Neal, she thought, staring into that dark, perplexed face next to her, I was in love with you from the beginning. I thought of you all the time, weeks went by from that first night and I never saw you, you probably had forgotten I even existed, but I used to invent scenes with the two of us, I used to try to plan how it might be if you did care, I knew that I could never learn to love anyone, I had to fall in love at the first moment, that was the only way I could believe that it was something more than just *learning* to love, and maybe that was why you didn't trust me, because you didn't think anyone could ever fall in love from the first moment, you thought I just wanted to be in love, and—and because, she thought, because you didn't think I could ever understand the Jewishness, that because I wasn't Jewish I was a world away. Is that what you thought, Neal?

He suffered, Lois thought, he really suffered.

All right, he suffered; all right, all of them have suffered; all right, I know all about the quota systems in schools and the restrictions in real estate and country clubs and all the rest; all right, I know about Auschwitz and Belsen and Buchenwald, all the crematoriums, the genocide practiced not just by Germans but by centuries of cultures and peoples. But I didn't want to love Neal for those reasons. I wanted to love him for himself. Not because he was Jewish; that didn't matter.

And if he were colored? she asked herself, looking at the woman next to her. How far does love go?

I don't know, she thought; sometimes I think I don't even know where it begins.

She thought of the night she and Neal came out of her brownstone, his arm went around her, they started down the street. He was humming, pleased about something. He looked down and laughed. *I have a surprise for you, I'm blowing us to the ballet.*

Oh Neal, she had cried, how wonderful. Those tickets are so expensive.

He held my hand all through the second act, she thought. Afterward we went to the Tavern on the Green and danced. It was a real celebration, and I didn't know the reason until the end, later, lying in bed.

This is our sixth anniversary, he said. Six months today.

I'm a lucky girl, I said, you should waste so much time.

Just so long as you know it, he said, starting to dress.

But what she had known that night, the possibility of which led inexorably to the East Eighties, she had not told him.

She put her hands up to her head, feeling a faintness. Don't think about it, stop it, she told herself.

With a jangle of bells the streetcar reached the corner of the capitol. Lois descended, stared out at the familiar scene. She had lost something in leaving Springfield—perhaps her attachment to it. It was New York she loved now, with its canyons of concrete which tried to pass themselves off as streets; with its astringent parks where dogs couldn't run free and people who could afford the expensive hour on a horse were admonished never to gallop because policemen patrolling the park gave you tickets if you were cantering above the speed limit for horses, whatever that was; you got tickets for everything nowadays in New York, but it didn't matter. Like all the other inconveniences, she supposed the law originally had been formulated to make someone comfortable, even some eccentric who hated to see dogs unleashed or horses running free before the wind.

A car pulled alongside and she was conscious that it was black and, looking closely at the hood (for she had never mastered the game of adolescence, identifying cars, had never been good at any games, not even the game of love), saw that it was a Pontiac. She stopped and turned.

In the white blind heat of four o'clock she stood on the corner of Second and Monroe and stared into the car. The face that stared back at her might have come out of one of those photos printed in the books that were published just after the war. The face of the captive countries. You knew it anywhere.

Those unforgettable eyes, those dark, slanted eyes that held a world of sorrow and suffering and hadn't been defeated by it. Not quite defeated. The eyes of the Jews. The Slavs. The eyes of those sent to the concentration camps for one reason or another. The gypsies. Those who were to take their part in the final solution. My love has come from far away . . . my love has come from captive places . . . my love wears bands about his arm . . . my love has numbers woven round his wrist . . . my love is branded with a six-pointed star . . . my love has been to a far, far place . . .

The dark, dark eyes of the lost races.

Clutching her purse, she stood in the middle of the sidewalk, staring into the car. Those strange sad eyes . . . Stu . . . Neal . . .

It had these big, beautiful white flowers that hung down. . . . Mama and I were walking to the tennis court that day, the day she met that man. She ran away with him. Then came back. She ran away with him again and went to Denver and killed herself. We were walking to the tennis court that day, the day she was talking about the tree, the day she met that man.

The death card in your house . . . a great loss . . . a dark man has failed you . . .

"Lois, are you Lois?"

. . . *the most beautiful thing I saw every spring was that tree in your grandmother's front yard* . . .

. . . a terrible loss . . . in your house . . . death in your house . . .

"You're Lois, aren't you?"

. . . *the whole front yard was white. We used to go out and throw great handfuls of white flowers at each other, your Aunt Frances and I.* Aunt Frances, her mother and Aunt Frances, running across the yard, her grandmother's yard, long ago, throwing white blossoms at each other. Long, long ago when the tree was still standing, her grandmother was alive, her mother was alive, and her aunt was so young that she had thrown flowers.

Mama, she wanted to call out, standing with one hand holding her purse, the other on the handle of the black Pontiac. Mama, why didn't you leave a note—why didn't you tell me why you did it, so all my life I wouldn't wonder? Couldn't you have just told me what made you do it?

Neal, her heart cried out, I never understood, did I?

Mama, Neal, her heart cried out, and then the sidewalk rushed up at her, the capitol seemed to spin and topple, was going to fall down on her. She felt the purse drop from her hand, she was clutching at the car door, and then with a great wave of darkness she felt herself going down, sinking in a darkness that she could not hold back, her mouth was making words, words that made no sound, and she heard herself trying to call out, the next moment her legs gave way and she was sinking, she could feel her whole body relax and give way, plunging into space, falling . . .

Chapter Two

. . . INTO that feral dream of death, that dark dream of death, the recurrent theme of her worst hours, when she hugged death to her—not death itself, but the moment of dying, when she imagined herself plunging in an airplane, falling from a ship, slipping under dark waters; when she heard the screech of tires, felt the impact of car against car, when the prowler seized her by the throat, hands closed round her and the breath caught, strangled, in her windpipe; the moment of falling on the knife, struck by the bullet, felled by the club—all the patterns of her nightmares, all the fears she fought back that came to accuse her in her dreams or to accost her walking down crowded streets or sitting in the subterranean subway: that feral dream of death.

She was falling, falling, sucked through space, tumbling over and over through the bright, white air, and when she stopped? The hard earth would break her.

Plunging down, seeing mountain slopes on either side of her, sheer precipices of stone, a few scraggly firs rooted in rock; pointing to the clear clean sky, she tried desperately to clutch at the foliage, break her fall; but she plunged straight on, down, down, through the bright white air, seeing below her the crest of rock she would hit, a tangle of big boulders and small, sharp stones, and not one free, soft spot which might cushion her fall.

She was going at last to be destroyed, bones broken on rock; dying, she thought, plummeting down through that final gasp of space, knowing what it's like to fall . . . falling through space . . . falling . . . to the hard earth below.

Someone was holding her. There were strong arms around her and against her ear she heard someone saying, "Are you all right? Can you stand now?" She leaned in toward that strong, steady flesh and felt the arms circle her, the voice droning on, asking her something, the words didn't matter, it was the arms, the strong, reassuring arms that mattered. Someone was holding her at last, at last someone had put his arms around her and was holding her.

She opened her eyes.

"Are you all right?" he asked anxiously. He held her propped up against the car, both its doors open, the engine still running. People had collected around the automobile and were staring at them with curiosity. My god, Lois thought, I must have fainted.

The black car, the man inside, the moment when he leaned forward over the wheel and she said something and then—falling. He must have braked the car, rushed around in time to catch her. She seemed to recall saying something, or perhaps she had simply fallen. She could not remember.

He lifted her gently, helping her into the seat, reassuring her with a monotonous murmur of words. He closed the car door on her side, tried to clear away the crowd, made his way around the front of the car, got in his side, slamming the door. Then he reached over and released the emergency brake, waiting a moment for the people to disperse, finally honking for them to get out of the way. The car inched forward slowly, and the crowd moved back grudgingly.

Lois closed her eyes. "I'm terribly sorry. I don't know what was the matter with me. In the middle of the busiest intersection in town—did I fall?"

"You sort of sank. Are you sure you're all right? You don't want to see a doctor or anything?"

"No, I think I'm going to be all right. Just a little wobbly."

He had stopped the car and was looking at her critically. Those dark eyes seemed fastened to her face. Neal, she thought: that same intensity, that same look, withdrawn, wondering.

I never knew what intensity was until I was pregnant, she thought. I seemed to feel everything threefold, as if I had been given some strong drug and saw the world in brilliant flashes of essence, one bright image after another pounding at my head with the weight of a blow, the sound of a terrible explosion, even the smallest things—shadows on the sidewalk, the shock of a color exploded inside my eyes, as if I were looking directly into the heart of the sun, as if I were in the core of an explosion; music moved me as if someone had taken me by the shoulders and was shaking me.

I knew almost right away, she thought, but I didn't want to believe. Quinine and gin, scalding baths and Ex-Lax, none of it any good, and all the time my senses were running away with me, I was sick with sensation.

Neal, she thought, as if he might actually be able to hear her. Do you still go to our Armenian restaurant, take someone else to talk to the woman that ran it who was always shouting to the chef back in the kitchen and he never answered her? We used to say he didn't exist at all, she just made him up to give the place tone, standing by our booth screaming, "Two mussels and two kebabs," and then stamping out back and winding up the old-fashioned phonograph, talking over her shoulder, and not so much as an answer from the kitchen. We used to say she slipped out and fixed the food herself.

There were noises, though, Lois thought, noises out back while she was up front with us, so someone must have been back there, the silent chef stuffing the mussels. And what happened to him?

I always had to drink a lot of wine, she thought. I could never make love unless I was half drunk, and sometimes not even then. Terrible when you got halfway through and had been working and working and suddenly knew no matter how you tried or what he did you weren't going to make it. Too much of the time, she thought. Why can't I make love without the alcohol?

I always liked the *look* of love better than love itself. What pleased me was being able to share with someone, to feel connected in some way. I'm always wondering if *he* knew anything about love, but how about me, did I?

"You know—" he said, and she opened her eyes. He was smiling. "If you have to faint, make it dramatic, I always say. Like right in front of the capitol." The car sat motionless, next to the curb, people occasionally stopping to give them a second glance.

"It wasn't intentional. I couldn't have been half so original on my own. I only say and do the dramatic inside my head—except once in a long while when things get beyond me, when I don't expect them." Going up to the Eighties alone, would that qualify as dramatic? Probably, she told herself, but Mama, she was the one with a real sense of drama.

She thought of that tall, beautiful woman with the white streak slashing one side of her dark hair, her mouth moving sweetly over her words. "A room up high—away from all the noise—I'm not feeling well." Was that what her mother had said, standing at the hotel desk, staring at the desk clerk?

Her mother had put her on a train to go down to Iris's. Had she known then that she was never going to see her again, or was it something that had happened in Denver, was that what had prompted her toward the twelfth floor that late summer afternoon?

And while her mother stood at the sill of the hotel, she herself might have been standing at the upstairs window of Iris's house, staring down at her uncle bending over his tomatoes tenderly, one of his hands holding a stalk gently, the other carefully nipping unwanted buds. He pruned back the blossoms, leaving the strength for a few instead of dissipating it amongst the many. Uncle Stewart's tomatoes weighed half a pound on the average; they had fattened under his love. A man working out his warmth behind the garage, picking over the tomato plants— one of the first laws of life: love only that which can reciprocate.

"You sure you're all right? I'll take you home," the man next to her said, starting the car.

"No," Lois said, "I don't want to go home. I think I'd like a drink, something good and strong. Brandy," she said.

What had driven her mother to death? Walking behind the bellboy, past the men loungers—they must have looked at her hard, a handsome lone woman—until the elevator swallowed her up, the doors slid closed, the hum of machinery, a catch as the car stopped, and lightly, firmly her mother's feet fell on the thick carpet as she followed the bellhop down the hall.

Key in lock, door swinging open: a room like every other hotel room in the world, built around a bed; was there pain in her mother's heart looking at that bed, that symbol of all love, there in the center of that lonely, sterile room, as a bed on which she had made love stood in the midst of her lonely, sterile life? Did she see symbols then or did she only hear the sound of the window opening? That was the first thing bellhops did, open a window, wasn't it? How long had her mother been in that room before she herself went to the window and looked out, condemning love—was it love she condemned, was that what had brought her to her fall?

"I know a nice place, not too far from here. Cool, too." He pressed down on the accelerator. She opened her eyes. The profile was somehow better than the full face: stronger, more appealing, even more com-

plicated. A very complicated face, she decided. Not intellectual, but
knowing.

He glanced over at her swiftly, glanced back at the road, then jerked
his head back and looked at her again, as if he too were seeing her for
the first time. Then he swung the car abruptly into the outer lane. They
had barely missed a boy on a bicycle.

He had made her think, with that swift, appraising look, of Stu on
the stairs, of Erwin on the campus pressing the hundred-dollar bill into
her hand, of Neal bent across the little booth in the Armenian restaurant,
taking her hand and saying, "You know I like you an awful lot, don't
you? More than anyone I've—" But he never finished the sentence.

Neal never finished anything.

The car had stopped; they were in front of a white roadhouse. B A R
was painted in big black letters over the front door. There were dusty
rose bushes climbing the wall at one side, but the grass was burned down
to the roots.

"You wait until I get around and can help you out. You look awfully
wobbly to me."

She was still shaky getting out, and he held on to her carefully as
she stumbled up the path. I can't fall, she told herself, he's holding me.

The bar was nice, cool, with the air-conditioner going, filled with
bright patches of sunlight from the main windows, smelling clean, merci-
fully free from the odor of malt that these places usually had.

"You sit here," he said, "and I'll get you a brandy. It's the slow time
of the afternoon. The bartender's probably off and the guy who owns
the place is out back. He buys a lot of equipment from me," he said,
and then added, "sporting stuff. I work for a sporting-goods place."

In Denver far away, where her mother had gone to meet that man,
the tennis coach, there had been something about a sporting-goods
store too. She had forgotten.

What's the matter with me? she thought, putting her hands up to
support her head. I've got to pull myself together.

He was putting a brandy in front of her, looking down at her worriedly. "You're sure you don't want me to—"

She shook her head. Alcohol always helps, she thought. Alcohol fills
you up with illusions, alcohol makes you feel strong. Able to love.
"Listen," she said, gripping the edge of the table, "I don't know what
you want from me, but I can tell you right now I don't think I'll be any
help. I came here—back to Springfield—half sick myself."

His eyes were expressionless, looking at her from across the table, from over the rim of his glass, and she said, taking up her brandy, "Forget it, I only—"

"Don't, please, don't— Lois." He said her name tentatively, as if experimenting with it. And then he smiled; he had liked the sound.

There was so much to the sound of a name, that overpowering urge when you loved someone to repeat his name, bringing it up every chance you had, so that you could put your lips around the word, caress the sound, like a magic portent of love itself, the obsessive need to name the one you loved, perhaps an old carry-over from the belief in magic, that saying a name put the person whose name you uttered in your power. She remembered how she was always trying to bring the conversation around to the name she loved, the magic name, Neal. . . .

She thought of the way Neal used her name, how harsh his voice was when it fell on her name.

". . . Eileen trusts you," he was finishing. She had not been listening; inside her head a name was ringing and she saw that radiant flesh, that beautiful white, velvet flesh, and she was saying to herself silently, over and over, Oh, we have done a terrible thing, we have had a terrible loss.

"Eileen trusts you," he repeated, leaning across the table. "You know that, don't you?"

As if he could see right inside me, she thought; as if he saw my mother poised on the window ledge, crouched in that instant before leaping, as if he knows; looking down into my eyes and there is my father who failed me, his face turned up coldly, one hand at his nose gently massaging it, lightly stroking the nose back and forth. "I'm getting married again and moving out to California so naturally—" and he sees the frightened face that is mine at the brownstone door, my face looking at the doctor, the door opens—

My child in *that* sink—

Neal never loved me, Daddy never loved me, Mama—

Let them cut it out of me.

Three-thirty-eight in the afternoon.

In the sink in the Eighties.

The child I will never have now.

"Drink your brandy," he said. "Go on, I'm going to get you another. You look terrible. No, don't argue, just drink, and if you don't feel any better, I'm going to call a doctor." He waited. "Go on," he said authoritatively. "Drink."

"That's what I always used to do when—" And her head dropped down on her breast, she felt the whole room tilting toward her, and the next thing she knew he had knelt down beside her, he had his hands, his strong, reassuring hands, on her arms.

"What is it?" he asked urgently. "What's the matter?"

"I don't know," she said truthfully. "I just feel—feel, so empty."

Her head had begun to clear, the room was in focus again. He was still kneeling beside her, those lovely eyes looking at her. Perhaps he *does* see, she thought. With eyes like that anything is possible, anything at all.

"What do you see?" she asked.

It took him a time to answer. "A nice person," he said at last. "Someone who's going to be all right." He stood up, taking his brandy off the table, holding it up, but not drinking, looking down at her, and she had a strange feeling he didn't want to touch her, he was afraid of her. Like Erwin.

I tried to tell Erwin. In the kitchen, drunk, she thought; in the kitchen, bursting into tears, wanting Erwin to make it all right.

"I'm not a nice person at all," I said. "And the truth is—" "I won't buy that," Erwin had said, and she was not sure, even now, whether he had managed to interrupt her before she had told the truth or whether she had told it and he had pretended not to hear. But one thing she knew very well: he didn't *want* to know.

"Do you think she'll have the courage to get out?" he asked.

For a moment Lois couldn't identify the *she*. Then she thought, Eileen, of course, that was why he called, he wanted to talk about Eileen. "I don't know," she said, and for a fact she didn't.

"Eileen wants you to talk to her mother. She wants you to ask her mother if she can bring me to the party, she wants you to—"

"But Aunt Ada wouldn't listen to me," Lois interrupted.

"It's what I said," he admitted. "But the truth is—" He fiddled with his glass, looking out the window. The expression on his face reminded Lois of Stu, Stu not able to look at her, concentrating on an invisible point outside. "The truth is Eileen can't do it herself—can't talk to her mother, she wants someone else to do it, and I can't do it, her mother wouldn't listen to me, so—" He leaned over the table, half pleading, half demanding. "Don't you understand? Don't you know—know how she is? Doesn't she write you?" He waited for Lois to answer, but she couldn't. "Doesn't she tell you," he demanded, "about how we meet? About how she has to sneak out to meet me? Meet me on streetcorners because her mother doesn't think I'm good enough for her? Doesn't Eileen tell *you* what's going on?"

Lois caught her breath. What he was really asking was something else, something she couldn't define, as if he were counting on her being able to understand without his having to put it all into words. "I want you to give me an answer that's honest, Lois. Will you do that?" And she nodded. "You don't think there's any hope at all, do you?"

"That doesn't sound like a question to me; it sounds more like an answer."

"And that's *your* answer?"

"I guess it is. I've got to go," she said. "If I don't go now, I'll never get out to my grandmother's house."

"I'll drive you."

"No, you don't have to," she began, and miraculously her voice came out as cool and remote as she wanted it. It was even faintly antagonistic; she had managed not to convey one whit of the closeness she felt toward him.

"I can't let you go wandering around when you've just—"

"I don't even know where this address is any more," she said, and it was impatient, the voice saying that, when all the time she was longing to reach across the table, take his hand, say, I'm sorry, I'm so sorry things have gone badly.

What did people say in a situation where pain and pity were confused with sympathy and understanding—let's get a bottle of wine and go out with a blanket in the sun and love each other and forget everything for just one afternoon of our lives?

What's the matter with you anyway? she thought, finishing the last of her brandy. First you break down in front of Erwin that way, and now you're about to do the same thing with a perfect stranger. Pull yourself together. *Stop it.*

Courage is— What had been her definition that terrible afternoon? Even that was forgotten.

One day even the pain will be gone, she thought, buried and forgotten, and I will think about that whole afternoon as something that happened to me a long time ago and in another place.

His voice had changed. "Well, I *am* going to drive you," he was saying, and she was smiling, thinking, And that, my dear, settles that.

"I've got the address here." She opened her handbag and took out a piece of paper. "I'm not quite sure where it is, it's been such a long time since I've been out there, but I'm sure I'll know the house when I see it." She handed him the paper. "Do you know where it is?"

A funny look crossed his face. "But it's—it's the colored section."

"The colored section?"

Haven't I known all along it would be something like this? she asked herself. Haven't I known something terrible had happened to the house. Terrible? What is terrible about that? she demanded of herself. Why shouldn't colored people live in that house? she demanded of herself again, looking at the strained face across the table from her, searching the eyes for an answer, any answer. He thinks it's "terrible" too, she thought, and how can he think that when he's what he is—the undependable Hunkies and Polacks and Slavs, wasn't that the stereotype people had? Drunkards, brutes, wife-beaters, she could almost hear her Aunt Frances rendering judgment; "But, honey, you know, a very low type."

Walk into Erwin's well-groomed house, stare at the Stamos, no, they do not allow Jews here, and outraged; and now he says, It's in the colored section and—

She stood up, ashamed and angry. "Well, why shouldn't colored people live there?" she demanded. "Haven't they got a right to live in a decent place too?" And part of her anger was the knowledge that at the first instant she had felt the same way he had, that it was wrong for colored people to be living in her grandmother's house.

The brandy seemed to be burning its way through her stomach, there was a ringing in her ears. Through the persistent buzzing inside her head, she heard his voice, ". . . don't know what you think . . . I don't care . . . you ought to know I wouldn't . . . you're shaking all over . . ."

And then he had his hands on her again, he was holding her up, and the room went back to its rightful order.

"I know I'm shaking," she said between clenched teeth. "I'm shaking because I'm angry with myself. My first reaction was exactly the same as yours, and that's what made me mad, because I'm not one iota better than all the others, the ones who seem so— I'm sorry, it's not you, it's me. I hate myself when—"

"Sit down," he commanded, and the arms seemed to be forcing her down. She sank slowly into her seat, looking up at him, waiting. "I'm going to pay the bill and then I'm going to take you home. You can't be—"

"I don't want to go back. I'm supposed to spend the night with my aunt, with another one of my aunts. I've got aunts all over Springfield, the women in our family are ubiquitous. They even go on from the grave." It was a choice between tears or laughter, and she chose the latter. "Do you want to know how they carried on after my grandmother died? Well, it was bad enough the first few months, the weather was warm enough, then, and that was a godsend, because when winter finally set in they really went out of their minds. 'Iris, Iris'—screaming into the telephone—'she's out there under that cold ground. I just can't stand it, thinking of her out there under that cold ground, and the radio says the temperature's going to drop again.' And do you know what my Aunt Iris said, and she was serious, she was perfectly serious. She said, 'I've been thinking maybe we ought to move her to a mausoleum, they're warmer. But then I thought, Supposing we put her in a mausoleum and there was a tornado or a cyclone or something, and it blew away. We wouldn't know where the body was then, would we?' That's what she said, and so they all decided she was better off freezing in the cold earth of Springfield than having her warm bones scattered around Kansas and parts of Canada and god knew where. They were always perfectly sure that part of her would end up in Kansas. To this day I can hear them saying *Kansas* with that special shrill, as if Kansas were the end of the earth. For a time I even thought of Kansas as a place, like purgatory, you went when the winds, the bad winds, got you."

He was staring at her, and while she watched him there suddenly came to her a whole intuition—that she was going to fall in love with him, had started already, and she didn't want to, but it was like Neal, she couldn't help herself, it was all in the eyes, she was lost because of a look.

"Come on," he said, taking her arm, helping her up and starting, his arm guiding her, across the room. They stood at the bar, waiting while change was made, then walked out in silence. His hand on her arm gave off a language of its own, as if the fingers might say what the tongue could not. The eyes, she thought, the language of the eyes; and touch, the speech of touch: salvation, that was really what you were looking for, she thought, someone to save you.

Lost by one, saved by another: that was what the heart, the foolish heart, believed. That was its undoing, its special form of madness: the belief that one love would rescue it after another had just finished destroying it.

He had started the car, they were moving.

She turned to him. "Haven't you ever got fed up—with Aunt Ada, with Eileen? Haven't you ever just wanted to give it all up?"

"I suppose so," he said slowly. "But then—"

She waited.

After a moment he said, "When I wanted to get out, when I was fed up, I couldn't. You see I was away a long time. Overseas. And then when I got back my mother was in the hospital, and the last couple of years I kept thinking— I guess I knew that if it wasn't me it wouldn't ever be anybody. And then, to be perfectly honest, there was—you know how people are," he ended lamely. "I kept thinking that next week, next month, she'd—she'd give in, and then maybe something would happen, take it out of our hands."

My god, Lois thought with a start, sitting up straighter, he means they've never—never done it. It's not possible, she thought, staring at him. It's absolutely impossible that in all this time—but no, it was true, he was blushing. "My god," she said.

"I know," he said, shrugging his shoulders. "But sometimes things just get out of focus. And then after a while, you can't just leave someone. You can't walk out. You're tied. Look, I think I'd better stop at this gas station and ask directions."

He stopped the car and got out, walked quickly across the pavement. I don't believe it, she said to herself.

But it was true. He hadn't been lying. Aloud she said to herself, "How is it possible?"

If he had gone on, constantly being denied, how had it been possible for Eileen, if she really loved him, to keep on denying, in the face of that loyalty? I could never have done it, she thought. I never would have wanted to.

But now she could understand very well why Eileen sat in her room writing those letters, cutting out all those sordid stories from cheap magazines, dwelling on the impossible, no, not the impossible, the inevitable, which Eileen could never face.

"It's right near here, a couple of streets up and over." He took out a cigarette, silently handed the pack across to her. "You still feel up to this?" And when she nodded, he shook his head.

He hadn't gone around to his side of the car. Her window was lowered, and he leaned on the sill, smoking, watching her. She kept her eyes focused on the handbag in her lap. His face was close to hers, so close that if he had leaned forward a little his lips would have been touching her cheek.

Finally he threw the half-finished cigarette down, walked around the front of the car, and climbed in. "So?" she said.

"So there we are."

"Yes, there we are."

He turned toward her, his eyes on her mouth. "Not there, here," he said. "Right here, the two of us." He turned the key in the ignition, started the car, but they had gone no more than a block when he pulled the car over to the curb, shut off the motor, and in the next instant she was back in those strong, sure arms, but this time his mouth was on hers, the way it should be.

Chapter Three

WE LOAN YOU UP TO ONE MILLION DOLLARS IN STRICTEST CONFIDENCE
No collateral, no questions asked
EVERYTHING BY MAIL
We rush you any amount needed. Strictest confidence. No letters to friends, family, employer, government. No witnesses. No cosigners. No embarrassing investigations. No interest. No specific time to pay.
Make one small convenient yearly payment. Name your own price. As little as a dollar a year. No liens on your insurance. We also take care of taxes, medical costs, insurance premiums, sickness, car repairs, medicines. Remember, it is to our benefit to keep you alive.

That was the ad he was looking for, one that promised you everything and asked nothing in repayment. And god knew, Pete thought, that would be only the start of solving his problem. Still, money was a real beginning. With enough of it, maybe you could even pay someone else to worry. Who would be dumb enough to take on his mother, with her everlasting bellyaching about the universe and how it didn't understand her; grabbing you all the time and looking at you with this look that says, Love me, love me? Or his father, looking up from his chair with the same silent supplication? Didn't his father—didn't his mother —know, Pete wondered, that you can't ask for love?

Naw, of course not. People never knew when they were stepping out of line. He hadn't known himself when he had hinted to Morris that he needed a raise—though he should have; if there was one thing in the world that people hated to be nailed on, it was the business of money. And, after all, Morris didn't decide on the raises. That was the big cheese himself, upstairs. But couldn't you just maybe put in a good word for me? Pete had heard himself saying. You get here on time and keep your wife off the phone, and then maybe we'll talk turkey, Morris had said.

He didn't know any better than to hound Morris about money, but he sure as hell knew better than to hang around that little number at the package counter—she was a pretty package herself all right—and what the hell had got into him to ask her out to lunch?

To hell with it, he thought rebelliously. I got as much right as the next to have a little dough in my pocket to spend the way I want. So I spend it on tuna and a milkshake, whose business is that? Peggy spends every cent I make. Even when the money was coming in good, she saw that it went out fast enough.

Nevertheless, he regretted the money he had spent with such a lavish gesture, but then how lavish could you get picking up a check for ninety-five cents and saying, The sandwich is on me? To make a real impression you gotta spend big money—flowers and jewelry, things like that. But he knew damn good and well he had no business hanging over the marble-topped table at Walgreen's drooling over an eighteen-year-old girl with lavender lipstick. But, god, what knockers she had!

He thought of Peggy's breasts, limp and flattened by five little mouths that sucked the life right out of them, hanging like dried, dead grapes on a vine. Hell, who wanted to put his hands on those?

This girl in packages, Carol Wilson, she had swell bazooms. And she knew how to make the best of a good thing. You didn't find her running around in those grisly old dresses Peggy wore. No siree, Carol Wilson wore good tight sweaters and long beads that kind of hung over her boobies, dangling there, sending out a radioactive warning: touch and you'll be burned. He felt a little vibration of pleasure, just thinking of those glass beads trembling on the edge of her bust, bouncing up and down, sending out their message in the fluorescent overhead lights of Walgreen's, while Carol Wilson leaned forward and gazed at him wonderingly, her eyes all innocent and yearning, her teats wobbling inside her sweater, while she said, "I think Morris should recommend you for a raise. Everybody knows you're the only real gentleman in shirts and ties."

Did she know about him? I mean, he thought, that I'm married and all? Sure, he told himself, she must. Everybody knows, Peggy calling up that way half a dozen times a day. You couldn't hide something like Peg and five kids. So, I mean, he thought, if she *knows*, that must mean . . .

Christ, he thought, I gotta be careful. I'm getting ideas already. Just give her a little feel, he thought, that's not asking too much. Touch but don't taste. Not more than a couple of hand runs over those—

A lady was wending her way through the sale on shirt seconds, her arms hugging her sides as if she were afraid that if she touched the merchandise, even inadvertently, someone would accuse her of shop-lifting. A comparative shopper maybe? Pete asked himself. Naw, some-one looking for *soiled* seconds. She would paw every single sample on the tables and then, if she couldn't find one that looked really moldy, she would just shove them all aside and leave, looking haughty.

She won't buy, he thought in despair, but I gotta pretend she will, just the way she's gotta pretend she's got all the cash she needs right inside her purse, the only reason she's down the basement looking at seconds is she's economy-minded.

We all gotta pretend, he thought, as he forced himself from behind the counter and went out to meet her. "Were you looking for something in particular?" he asked, staring at the small beads that clung to her upper lip. It was perspiration, he saw a second later, colored by her powder, but she looked as if her skin were peeling away. Don't look at her too close, he warned himself, or she'll think there's something funny about you, you're a sex maniac or something, and start looking around for the manager, and the last thing he needed now was some goofy woman screaming at Morris that he was crowding her up against the counters and trying to get a free feel.

Looking out over her hennaed head, he thought to himself, Who'd want to feel you, lady? and then, having unburdened himself, at least silently, he forced himself to look back at her. Purple lipstick: sticky-looking purple lipstick. Carol Wilson's lips . . .

"I was thinking maybe I'd pick up some shirts for my husband," the woman said, shifting uneasily from one foot to the other. "Seconds, you know—we're going on vacation and I always say there's no sense in sending your good stuff to some laundry that you don't know."

"What size?" Pete heard himself asking her abruptly. Irrationally, he hated her. It had come over him the moment she said vacation. Where would he ever get enough money to go on a vacation? No, just hang around the house and get talked into vacuuming and helping with the laundry, stuff like that. What kind of holiday was that for a man who had to scrimp fifty weeks of the year and couldn't even buy a nice young girl who worked with him a sandwich and a milkshake? It's not like I was spreading my money around the Waldorf, he thought bitterly.

"I'll just look if you don't mind." A smile, falling right off her purple lipstick, so false it made you sick. "I gotta brother-in-law might use a couple too. Don't pay me no mind. You go right on with what you was doing."

He felt an urge to tell her he had been mentally mauling Miss Carol Wilson, package department, upstairs and in back, you want to go see for yourself. Instead he nodded curtly and turned to see his fantasy of a moment before descending the stairway in the flesh. From where he stood, or at least by moving a little closer, he could look right up her legs. He moved.

She had no stockings on. It was summer and most of the girls went without, but what gave him a little shiver of excitement was seeing that the leg make-up ended above the knee. Her thighs were white, milk-white, with tiny down running up the inside. When she moved, her summer dress swung around her legs and her thighs rubbed up against each other and then moved free, a flash of white with the pale pink pants cutting them off at the crotch. They were a little fat maybe, but then he liked them fleshy. Peggy was worn right down to the bone. Whenever he threw himself on top of her, he was impaled on bone. Christ, making love to her was like falling on spikes, he thought, and lost the last sight of Miss Wilson's thighs. She had reached the bottom of the stairs.

She threw him a smile, a sweet comradely smile, while her eyes traveled from table to table, her hands clasped themselves in anguish. It was Morris, then, she was looking for. Business, he tried to reassure himself. Morris wouldn't be chasing such a young girl. Why not? Morris's wife was the kind anyone would run from, there was a bitch, one you had to watch out for, a trouble-maker, Morris's wife. But Morris was the basement manager, he made a lot more money—and he didn't have five kids to worry about. Just some cat or other that his wife owned. What if Morris was stuck on Carol Wilson?

The idea of Morris, horrible, bald, paunchy Morris, putting his arms around her behind the water cooler and letting her have it through his trousers, letting her get a good feel of what she could have if she wanted it, the way he knew a lot of men did with the salesgirls, he had heard them talking in the can, Morris rubbing up against Carol Wilson, sickened him.

He went across the floor and stood beside her, trying to act business-like and efficient should horny, bald old Morris maybe be watching, and he said in a low tone, "You looking for the old goat? He's gone out"— Pete decided to be funny—"he's gone out to adjust his two-way stretch."

Carol Wilson giggled.

Feeling encouraged, Pete moved around to the other side of her so that he blocked off her view of the downstairs, of that awful redhaired harpy hanging over the shirts, blocked off everything save himself and his suddenly palpitating chest and perspiring face. "Carol—" he said hoarsely.

"Oh, Mr. Goldmeyer," she shrilled, pushing past Pete, "I been looking everywhere for you. Mr. Gordon wants to see you upstairs, right away. Somebody made a mistake on those shirts. They're not seconds at all, they're our firsts. And we been selling the firsts as seconds and the seconds as firsts, and customers are complaining and Mr. Gordon says . . ." Her shrill little voice carried over the room; out of the corner of his eye Pete saw the dyed head of the customer jerk up unbelievingly, and then the whole body went rigid and she started scrambling around the table, picking up shirts right and left.

To hell with her, Pete thought, concentrating on what was really important, Morris's reaction to the girl in front of him. Morris didn't look real interested, more just annoyed, but then Morris was good at covering up. You never knew what he thought, massaging his big stomach and staring out into the hemispheres as if he were tuned in on short wave to the dictates of the universe.

Still, it seemed to Pete, Morris hung back unnecessarily far behind when Carol Wilson went up the stairs. That bastard is looking up her dress, Pete thought in outrage. A man his age, he ought to be tarred and feathered. I got a good notion to tell his wife, call her up—no, write her an anonymous letter. *Did you know your little lovey-dovey Morris has got a*—you didn't say "popsie" to people like Morris's wife, he supposed—*a mistress,* he thought triumphantly.

She'd come down here, Morris's wife would, shouting and screaming, carrying on for everyone to hear, and then Morris would get fired and he would take Morris's place, with a good substantial raise, and he could maybe afford to send Peggy and the kids off on vacation, while he stayed in town, and Carol Wilson and he . . .

All you got when you were poor, he thought sourly, was daydreams. The rich think they got all the problems—the rich think they got a monopoly on everything—but they don't know nothing about how it is to dream your life away, that's a special prerogative of the poor.

Henna-hair was standing at the cash register, holding up a stack of shirts a mile high. Let her buy them, he thought, nobody said anything to me. What do I care if there's a loss, it's no skin off my back. From the belligerent look on the woman's face, however, Pete knew that he ought

1

to kick up a fuss, that her sense of satisfaction would be ruined if he didn't make a stink. "You know these shirts are—" he began, letting her have her day.

"The price is marked right on them," she began bellicosely, and he suddenly didn't care anyway, he was too tired to give her the satisfaction of thinking she had put one over on him. He shrugged his shoulders. "I couldn't care less," he said and started wrapping them up. "It's no skin off my back."

But there was a current in the air, something sharp and indefinable, but definitely there. He looked up, alerted. The woman was leaning across the counter indignantly, staring at him as if he had tried some hanky-panky with her, and before he had a chance to ask her what had got her gall bladder in such a state, she was screeching at the top of her lungs, "Manager! Manager!"

"What is it? What's the matter?" Pete demanded. The horrible pitch of her voice, a voice that sent splinters right through his spleen, that reminded him of his Aunt Esther, of his mother, was worse than an alarm. She sounded as if she were trying to alert the whole country to some national catastrophe.

"You pink," she shrieked at him. "You no-good, low-down commie. I gotta small business, I know what robbers you people are, rob me blind my help does and no way to stop it. Manager! *Isn't there a manager in this store?*" she yelled at the top of her lungs.

Morris was scrambling down the stairs, his fat legs working just like the bad pistons in Pete's car. "Coming, coming," he kept saying excitedly, as that terrible piercing siren voice rang in steady alarm.

The woman nearly embraced Morris as he came up to her. She threw herself at him with a vengeance that almost knocked him over, and she was talking and explaining, gesturing and shaking her hands in Morris's face before he had a chance to ask her what was the matter. Pete could only stare. What *was* the matter?

". . . was going to let me take these shirts, he knew they was firsts, he heard you talking to that girl, I don't care, he says, It's no skin off my back, I couldn't care less. That's the way they all feel, these dirty rabble-rousers. . . ."

Holy Christ, Pete said to himself, she's nuts, absolutely, utterly, completely crazy. Morris was trying to calm her. He had put out one of his stubby hands and was trying to propel her toward the stairway. "I'm not going without my shirts," she screamed and turned back on Pete in an assault that made him draw back. "You wrap them up, you lousy, good-for-nothing . . . I know my rights . . ."

"But—" Pete began.

"Wrap them up," Morris said abruptly.

Pete wrapped them. The woman handed him a twenty-dollar bill and waited, tapping her foot, while he counted out the change. "I want to see the store president," she said, her voice a little calmer now. "I run a business of my own, I know what kind of problems he got, I'm sorry for him. I'm going to tell him what kind of pinko employees he's got—you wait and see," she said to Pete, "and you too"—turning to Morris. "If you had any gumption at all, you'd have fired him right then and there, but—"

"Just a minute," Morris interposed.

"Don't you just-a-minute me, you take me to see the president, and right this minute." This time it was she who snatched Morris by the arm and pushed him forward ". . . cheats and crooks, don't care about a man who is running an honest business, trying to make a living . . ." The shirts were clutched to her bosom, Morris was hanging at the end of one of her strong arms, she dragged him up the stairs, angrily hoisting herself from step to step, dragging Morris after her, going on and on.

Pete went out back where the packing cases were and sat down. It was hot, it was dark, it was smelly. He needed a smoke, but he had run out at lunch (smoking one right after the other, staring at Miss Wilson's knobbies) and he couldn't see his way clear to buy a pack, spending money right and left the way he had been. He just sat, staring at a pile of boxes marked F R A G I L E . They reminded him of the basement at home, at Sans Souci—his own house was never home to him, just a place to hang his hat and to mate, produce children; it was the big brick house on the far side of town he thought of as home. The basement, he thought, that big black place Stu and I were always trying to sneak down to when we were kids, so we could play, hiding behind all those boxes.

My goose is cooked, he told himself.

Two hours ago I was sitting in Walgreen's with a thousand ideas, seeing Carol Wilson in all kinds of fine places doing all kinds of great things, undressing her right there at the table while she told me I was the only real gentleman in shirts and ties, and now, two hours later, I'm going to.get fired and I'll never see her again. Of everything—losing his job, having to face Peggy and his mother, not having any money in the bank, not having any real experience to help him get another job—

the worst thing, the one and only thing that had come to roost in his heart and make it break down over the prospect of the hopeless future, was the fact that everything was going to be over with Carol Wilson.

Someone was calling his name. "Ashwell?" he heard the voice ask querulously. It wasn't exactly a shout, but it was louder than usual. Someone was standing in the other room, looking around, saying in a little higher tone than normal, "Ashwell?"—and he knew damn good and well who it was. The store manager, the big cheese. Not that jerk Morris, who only looked after the basement, but the big boss, Gordon, who was responsible for the whole kit and caboodle.

I could just walk out, never come back, Pete told himself. But he knew he couldn't. If he walked out, he would lose his two weeks' pay. They fire, they got to pay for the privilege. I could send Frank around for it, he thought. Naw, he told himself, I couldn't do that to Frank.

He walked out and there was the big boss himself and he was flushed in the face and flustered, that awful red-haired woman trailing right alongside him—to make sure he does his duty, Pete thought—and when he came up to them, the woman burst out, "You're going to get what you deserve, this man is going to—"

Pete looked at both of them. "Just hand me the envelope and get it over with," he said wearily. "I gotta wife and five kids, you don't need to tell me what this has cost me."

"You'll have to go up to the office and—" Gordon began stiffly, but Pete didn't wait to listen to him. He was already at the bottom of the stairs. Not more than fifteen minutes before, he had stood in almost this exact spot, looking at the white thighs, dreaming his dreams. White thighs, he told himself, what about unemployment insurance, how many weeks will that last, how far will that go? We could maybe go on relief, he thought. How did you go on relief? He didn't know but he was willing to bet that he couldn't qualify. They would look into his background and they would say, You can't collect relief when your mother has a big house like that. Go live with her. And then there would be his mother to face: *Lost your job? Oh no*—recriminations, tears, prayers, heart attacks, the whole works.

If I had any decent insurance, he thought, I could commit suicide. But the only insurance he held was a five-hundred-dollar burial that he got wholesale working here, and it was probably canceled the minute he was fired. I'm not even worth anything dead, he thought. That's some consolation. Not worth anything alive, not worth a damn dead.

When he got to the top of the stairs the rest of the employees were standing around in frightened groups; they stared at him curiously, as if he were some kind of freak. He walked on, trying to look haughty and above it all, that kind of Humphrey Bogart business that meant, Here's a man not to tamper with—Casablanca, a picture like that. He lost the girl, though, Pete thought, coming up to the cashier's window.

"You gotta sign this," she said nervously and then pushed a paper out to him. He scratched his name on the line marked with a big X, and she handed him an envelope—sealed, he thought. I wouldn't put it past those guys to try to put one over on me, try to get rid of me without the two weeks' pay. He opened the envelope and checked, thinking, the unemployed can't afford to be proud.

Then, experiencing for the first time a deep sense of embarrassment and shame, the humiliation and cowardice of those who have just been fired and have to face the people they used to work with, knowing at last the final dregs of self-disgust, he turned and stared around the store. There was a big cold knot inside his chest and it got bigger and colder when he looked at Carol Wilson behind the packing desk and she looked away quickly. She was ashamed of him, ashamed that she had let him buy her a lunch. He had been fired, and nobody got fired, even the people who deserved it; there was something shameful about a man who couldn't hold down a job when he was a "gentleman."

Surely one of them would come over and say, Gee, Pete, I'm sorry, something like that, but as he looked around, his eyes traveling from counter to counter, he saw that they were all avoiding looking at him, that none of them would jeopardize their jobs to give him that small grain of comfort. It would be a big gesture for them and small solace for him: why not let it go?

He walked quickly toward the door, avoiding looking at Miss Crimm behind gloves, who was staring at him not with sympathy but with horror. He thought of all the times he had comforted Taylor about her drunken husband and bum of a son, and he stood at the door thinking, Taylor will come up at least, but she did not come.

He turned for one last surveillance of the place he had worked for the past four and a half years and he saw that Taylor was hiding behind hosiery. He could just barely make out her face through the legs of beige stockings that hung like long, limp condoms off the display rack. She must have seen him looking at her, because she ducked, and he knew she was crouching behind the counter, down where all those little flat boxes of hose were kept, waiting for him to go on and get out.

Go on and get out, he told himself, and he walked rapidly now, pushing open the door and feeling the heat hit him after the air-conditioning inside. The cold, hard knot in his chest expanded, and for a moment he thought he was going to be sick.

I need a drink, he thought, fingering the change in his pocket. No, there was just enough to cover the garage—he had been late again that morning and had to pull into the first available place.

Carolyn, he thought suddenly. I can go out there and get a drink, tell her what's happened. Maybe she could help. They had never been close, not the way some brothers and sisters were, but she was his sister.

You can't just give up, he thought, that was what his father had done. For the first time he held some pity for his father. If his father had ever felt like this, just knocked out of the game, as if the wind had been driven right out of him and he had to be carried out to recuperate, lie there and think, I've got to get back in there and fight, and know it was all just words, he wasn't going to go back, he didn't have the strength, if his father had felt like this, then Pete was pretty sure there was reason to pity him. Pity all us failures, he thought, not for our weaknesses— god, not for that—but for the fact that we still feel.

He paid the garage attendant and stood back, surveying the buildings around him. He would have to find another job and find it fast—how much money was in the account? He didn't know for sure, but it was around twenty dollars, he thought. With the two weeks' severance pay, they could squeak by for a while, and he knew that in dire circumstances his mother would come through, with sound and fury, but she would come through, but still he had to get going. He and Peggy didn't have any Sans Souci to fall back on the way his mother had when his father gave out.

He had to have some help.

Carolyn was the only one who could give it to him. He would have to go out there and just pray she was in and alone and that she would— would, well, maybe just speak to Ralph.

He felt better. He had a plan. You just kind of jolt along, not knowing where you're going or what you're going to do, things got out of control, but the minute you had a plan, any plan, your life took shape, you could see some sense, you got this idea that maybe things might work out all right after all. So long as you had a plan.

Chapter Four

"WHAT's the matter? What's happened?" The words burst out of Carolyn before she had a chance to think. Pete had given her such a start, standing white as death, still as stone, on the front stoop when she opened the door.

"It's kind of a long story," he said.

"You all right? Peg all right? The children all right? You look— You'd better get in out of that sun."

He followed her into the living room, not saying anything. He looked desperately tired and unhappy, opening a china box, looking into it furtively. "The cigarettes are over there," Carolyn said.

Whenever he came—which was seldom enough, but even then seemed too often—he never had any cigarettes. When I'm not looking, she thought, he'll stuff his pockets. Why should I begrudge him a few cigarettes? He's my brother. Aloud, she said, "You want a drink?"

"Sure, that would be fine. Yes, sure, if you're going to have one," he mumbled.

"Scotch? Bourbon? Martini? Manhattan?"

"Whatever you're having."

Is he going to try to borrow money? she asked herself.

Then she thought she knew what was the matter. "My god," she said, holding up the bottle of gin. "Is Peggy—"

He shook his head.

She heard herself give a little gasp of relief. Her mother all over again. "I'm having a martini," she said, "but you can have anything you want."

"That's okay, a martini'd be fine."

"I just have to go for the ice. I don't know why we can't have a refrigerator in here, but Ralph— Sit down, make yourself at home, I won't be a minute."

Her brother was staring at the open book on the couch, as if the open book were gross and obscene. He probably had never heard of Euripides. Why should he? Carolyn asked herself in annoyance. Euripides isn't the answer to everything.

Maybe he isn't the answer to anything, she thought.

To me he is. But Pete would think—oh, I don't know, just that it was odd, reading about people who had been dead a couple of thousand

251

years, not understanding why anyone would want to read about old dead Greeks.

Carolyn put the ice cubes into the silver bucket, a wedding present that was beginning to flake. It wasn't even real silver, she thought, trying to remember who had given it to her. Like everyone else in the family, she thought, you scratch the surface a little and you find the base metal.

Why does he always have to look so beaten down? she wondered as she came back into the living room. She tried to keep from the annoyance and exasperation his look of defeat always sent through her. He could have taken night courses or something, couldn't he? Other men got into jams and had to marry girls, then went on and made something of themselves—Shakespeare, for instance. He left his wife his second-best bed. I'll bet she was furious. None of those books ever said who got the good one. An interesting academic problem: Who got Shakespeare's best bed? Might be a whole new insight into the plays, the sonnets. The Dark Lady got the best bed, something like that. Wonderful title for a book, she thought, measuring out the vermouth.

"The first of the day," she said brightly, hollowly, taking a glass across the room and holding it out to him. He's your brother, she told herself. What's the matter with you, anyway?

"I guess I shouldn't have come here," he began apologetically, "but I just—"

"Why shouldn't you come? You're my brother, aren't you?"

"Yeah," he said, sipping his drink. He didn't sip his drink like other people, taking a little and savoring it, rolling it around on his tongue; Pete went right on sipping and sipping until the glass was halfway empty. She found herself fascinated, watching him go right on letting the liquor run into his mouth steadily, and then she understood: he didn't really know how to drink—not martinis anyway. Probably all he and Peg could afford was a beer now and then. Why am I always so damn superior? she asked herself. Supposing I were on that kind of beer budget, would I sit around reading *The Trojan Women* and thinking about Shakespeare's beds? You bet your life I wouldn't.

But I wouldn't sit that way either. I'd take night courses or get out of town and start over, do something.

Don't be so sure, she admonished herself.

"Listen, Carolyn," he said, leaning forward, holding his drink on his knee, balancing it with one hand and staring at it as if he were terrified he might upset it. "I just lost my job."

"Oh, no, oh, Pete, I'm so sorry, I—"

"Yeah, but the thing is—well, I—"

"You need some money?"

"No, not yet anyway, not now. But I— I don't know how to tell Mom, how to break the news to Peg. It's a tough break, it really is, it wasn't really my fault." And Carolyn wondered whether it was her imagination or whether his voice had really taken on their mother's thin, self-pitying whine. "This nutty woman came in and for some reason or other she got real excited and started shouting for the manager and saying he should fire me, and then the next thing I knew there I was out on the street, canned."

He stared at her with bleak, empty eyes, waiting. "You want me to call?" she asked, and he nodded absently, still staring at her, waiting, waiting for something else. What? Carolyn asked herself, knowing the answer already. He wanted her to ask Ralph about a job. I can't, she thought. I've just asked about Stu; I can't expect Ralph to take on Pete too.

Give, she seemed to be shouting inside herself, the good know how to give. "It wasn't such a good job anyway," she heard herself saying rapidly, the words pouring out. "You can get a better one, a much better one, I know you can. Only it does seem a rotten thing to do, to fire you right when you were probably getting ready to go on your vacation and—"

"Go on our vacation?" he asked in a high, hysterical voice. "What do you mean, go on our vacation? We haven't got any money to go on a vacation. We can't even pay the bills we have. We—" He got up, upsetting his drink, staring down at the rug with a stricken face. "Oh god, I'm sorry, I just wasn't looking. Have you got a rag or something I can wipe it up with?"

Carolyn stood up, looking with amazement at that stain on the carpet. It was the first time anything had marred the perfection of that room. She picked up a towel from the bar and ran over, bending down to mop up the drink. She knew she was making too much fuss for such a small spot, but she couldn't help herself. God, what if the architect saw it? He would go out of his mind. When he put the place together, he never thought of people who spilled drinks or let their cigarettes burn the table. He never thought of people at all, that architect, all he cared about was space, not the people that had to fill it.

"Liquor doesn't stain," Carolyn said, more to reassure herself than him. "Don't worry about it. It'll probably dry right away and nobody will ever know the difference."

Down on his hands and knees, trying to mop up the spot with his crumpled handkerchief, he made no answer.

"Pete," she said, standing up and looking down at the dandruff on his frayed collar, the cheap suit which was going to pieces, speckled with its little shower of dandruff, "please don't worry, let it alone, it'll be all right."

He looked up, searching her face, looking at her with those pale, expressionless, blank eyes. "Sometimes I just feel like I can't do anything right."

"Don't be silly. It'll be all right. Look, it's drying already. Nobody'll ever know."

"It looks darker to me, it looks—"

"Don't be silly. It'll be fine. Forget it. Here, let me make you another."

"No, don't bother, really, I don't want you to go to any trouble."

"It's no trouble. Come on, forget it, I'll make you another." She stood at the bar, her back to him, not wanting to see that face, not able to bear the patient, cowlike resignation, the expectant knowledge of rejection that crept into every tone, like Daddy, always like Daddy, defeated, done for, the two of them so alike. They would go out the back door, in twilight, the bats swirling over the back of the garage, the sky streaked with black smudges, a child's drawing really, big black streaks across the violet sky, and Daddy went down the walk carrying the sack for the frogs, Pete tagging after him, his sneakers making a funny squish-squish noise on the cement path; they got into the car, and the engine was like a song on the summer night, a fine, steady humming as Daddy warmed up the motor. They had seemed so close, going out to get the frogs, and she, who had never been close to her father, had envied them the drive out to the lake when they would be alone together and could talk

"Pete," she said, "I've always meant to ask you, but you know we haven't been, well, real close and—"

"No," he agreed in a muffled voice, "we haven't."

"But I've often wondered, I couldn't help it. What did you and Daddy talk about, all those times you went out to Lake Springfield frogging?"

"Oh, just things," he said uneasily. "You know, the usual, about how to catch the frogs, things like that."

"That was all? I always thought—oh, I don't know, that you must have said something important, something I would have liked to know,

that—that somehow I would have been—oh, I don't know—closer to
Dad if I had gone too."

"I wish you had," Pete said. "I hated those damn trips."

"You hated them? But why? I should have thought—"

"He was always—oh, I don't know, Carolyn—he always carried on
so, talking about how sorry he was he didn't have a job, like other
fathers, you know, and stuff like that, embarrassing stuff. I hated it.
I didn't want him talking like that, my own father, he shouldn't talk like
that, he should have more pride."

"Pride," Carolyn said softly. "Tell me," she said, stopping, thinking .
of her mother saying, Tell me, what do you think of . . . "Tell me, does
it bother you I live in this house? Don't answer," she said quickly. "It
was a stupid question. Ask a stupid question, you deserve a stupid
answer. I had no business asking. I'm sorry." She walked over, holding
his drink in her hand. "If it's any consolation to you, it hasn't been all
that wonderful."

"Yeah, the rich have all the problems of the poor, only they have to
worry about money too."

I deserved that, Carolyn thought, but she was still upset—not angry,
but upset. "I don't think it has much to do with money. I think it has
more to do with—with what's inside." God, that sounded superior.
"What I mean is that I'm not more sensitive or intelligent than anybody
else, it's just that—I don't know—that I don't know how to get outside
myself. I'm always inside, and inside we see how small we are." She was
still holding his drink, she realized. Silently she handed it to him. She
felt that, if she could make him see, they might still make a bond, the
bond of people who tell things they shouldn't to each other, the bond of
sharing secrets.

People don't want to share, she thought, and certainly not their
secrets.

The maid was bringing the children in. It was time for them to go
upstairs and bathe, change, get ready for their supper and bed. She saw
them passing through the hall, and Sally looked back at her, the child's
eyes curious and hopeful. Impulsively, Carolyn raised her hand. "Come
on in, honey," she said. "Your Uncle Pete's here"—while all the time
she knew that she was only using the child as a way of not having to face
Pete alone.

Sally hung back for a moment, staring at Pete. The child saw him so
seldom that she forgot him in between visits. To call him Uncle Pete
was silly, Carolyn realized, only a convention. Sally was looking at him

with the bold crudity of a child, so that Carolyn, turning, looking at him
anew, felt that she saw her brother with her child's eyes, a tired, badly
dressed man, the kind who had not bought her a present, the kind of man
not to be remembered.

Sally crossed the room carefully, but Bobbie stayed in the doorway.
"Uncle Pete?" the little girl said, and it was more a question than a statement of recognition.

"Hi," Pete said self-consciously. "I'll bet you don't remember me, do
you?"

"Do you know what's black and white and red all over?" Sally asked.

"A newspaper," Pete said immediately, and it was all wrong, he never
should have done that, Carolyn knew. He had spoiled Sally's fun. He
didn't know how to pretend.

"I know another one," her little girl went on doggedly. "When is a
door not a door?"

Carolyn started to interrupt her brother, she was just about to say,
"That's an awfully hard one, honey," and perhaps she had actually
said, "That's——" when she heard him say in the matter-of-fact voice of
the tired and depleted who have a handful of children hanging off them,
asking the same questions year after year, pestering and prying, Pete
never able to get away from the childish repetitions and whining, the
sing-song questions and parrot-like parading of all the stages of the
four-, five-, six-, seven-year-olds, so that in the end he saw not one
child, but only the endless tedium of all children—her brother answered,
"When it's ajar."

Sally flung one contemptuous look of anger at Carolyn, then turned
and marched out of the room without another word. Carolyn couldn't
blame her. "You know how children are," she said helplessly.

"Yeah, sure."

"I know they just . . ." Carolyn began and ended, not able to
define what she meant. The effort of so much explanation defeated her.

But her brother did it for her. "I guess I shouldn't have said it, that it
was ajar. You know, they like you to ask them."

In her gratitude, Carolyn got up and went to the bar. "You want another?" she asked, beginning to mix, not able to look at him. I've
always wanted to ask you something else," she said rapidly. "Are you
sorry that you—that——" no, that question about Peggy she could never
ask—"that you couldn't go to war?" she ended, carrying the cocktail
shaker over to pour him a new drink.

He looked at her in surprise, holding onto his glass carefully. "I haven't thought about it in years." Then a look of comprehension spread over that face that was so much like her father's. "You think maybe that has something to do with why—with why I never get ahead anywhere? That they think maybe I was a slacker, that they don't believe that story about asthma? That they think I cleaned up during the war, working that way and all?" He looked at her eagerly. "You know, I'll bet that is it. I'll bet that all this time—" He drank down his martini, finished it just like that. "But what can I do? I couldn't help it I had asthma. You know that. It runs in Dad's family. It wasn't my fault I couldn't fight. I don't know, Carolyn," he said, looking at her pleadingly. "It seems sometimes that so many things aren't my fault."

She looked away. It was coming now, he was going to ask her to speak to Ralph.

"But you know—Ralph, he's always kind of understood, he's never held it against me, even if he had to go. He hasn't, has he, Carolyn?"

Carolyn shook her head.

"Ralph is the only one . . ." His voice trailed off. He was staring down at the spot on the rug. And she knew at that moment that, much as he wanted to, he wasn't, after all, going to ask. He wasn't capable of asking.

"Pete," she said.

He looked at her and she knew that he understood she had been going to say no and that was what had stopped him, that he couldn't stand one more person saying no to him, not this day or maybe for a long time to come, perhaps never again; he had heard no too often. "Pete, would you like me to talk to Ralph? To see if maybe there is some place he knows where he could—well—work you in?"

For a moment he couldn't answer. Then his face brightened, he looked at her as if he couldn't believe his ears. "Gee, that would be awfully white of you, Carolyn," he said, "but I don't want to ask favors, just because I'm your brother and all."

"It's all right, I'll ask him."

"You don't have to do that," he said, making his last attempt at self-respect and not sounding convincing.

Yes, I do, Carolyn told herself silently. Somebody has to help you. You can't help yourself. And if we do not honor our debts, even to ourselves, what do we honor?

". . . but if you think Ralph would think I was stepping out of line, I wouldn't want you to . . ."

"It's all right, Pete," she said, getting up, tired and ashamed. Even if we honor our debts, but do it for the wrong reason, what have we gained? she asked herself. "I can't promise anything, but I'll do what I can."

He was twirling his glass hopefully, and Carolyn automatically started to make him another drink. She didn't want one herself. She felt as if she didn't care whether she ever had another drink in her life. The alcohol was just one more way of deluding herself. But Pete—give him a little liquor, she thought, get him a job, let him cache a few cigarettes, that wasn't much for the blood bond between brother and sister, was it? Those old Greeks, she thought, they asked a lot more.

Chapter Five

"THAT'S it," Lois said, keeping to her side of the car. It was the first sentence that had been spoken between them since—since the incident.

Stan stopped the car, and she stared out. Strange, the way everything around Springfield had been cut back, uprooted, torn out. Once, a long, long time ago, there must have been a big, bright plain here, long grass blowing in the wind, great groves of trees, big bunches of green against the golden grass, and then the restless ones had started moving West, trappers and hunters from the Carolinas and Virginia, streaming across the Alleghenies; the plains were stripped, the trees cut down, houses went up, small squat houses, with one room, the windows covered with oil paper, and then a new, big wave started, and the houses clustered, pretty soon there was a town, and then a county seat, and finally the state capital. The more people you had, the fewer trees you kept. It must be proportional, Lois thought. Look at New York, hardly any trees at all, only on the streets where the rich lived and in the parks, where you couldn't let your dog run free and you better not gallop the high-cost rented horses.

"Lois," he said.

She didn't turn, kept her eyes on the denuded lawn in front of her. It wasn't what she had expected at all. The house was the same, but it looked so strange without the big tree in front. I always think of it with the tree, she tried to reassure herself, but the house will be the same.

"Lois," he repeated.

"Yes."

"Don't call Eileen's mother."

Turning, she gave him a puzzled look. "Don't call Aunt Ada?"

"I don't want you to. It wouldn't be right. I don't want—I don't want to go. I can't face Eileen now, not after—"

Did he think that because he kissed her he had to give up everything that had gone before? Did he think that because he had spoken her name that way— "Don't be ridiculous," she said, deliberately keeping her voice light and distant. "Are you crazy?"

"Maybe." He was angry. "For the first time in years I feel like being crazy. A girl comes into your life for a couple of hours and you make up your mind she's never going out of your life again. Isn't that just too crazy for words? Particularly when the girl—"

And then he had a hand fastened to her arm, he was pulling her toward him, and those lips were on hers again, and she only thought, Yes, he's right, we're both crazy.

Mama went out to the country club, she was never the same again. One person reshaped her life. Was that what brought her to the sill of that strange hotel window—that she fell in love with the wrong person?

My father didn't want me and my lover didn't love me enough and now I've come back to sit in front of my grandmother's house and kiss the man my cousin wants to marry.

She pushed him away and fumbled with her purse, then opened the car door and got out. With her back to him, she said, "I want to go on alone. I'd rather you didn't wait."

"And if I do?"

She turned and looked at him. "You'd fail me."

"It wouldn't be anything new," he said, "you know, to fail."

"I suppose not," Lois said, "but it would be a nice change. To have people *not* fail, to find someone who would be—if not a success, at least competent. To know *well* people. That's what I'm looking for, the well people who don't *always* fail."

She caught a flash of his face as he turned and started to work with the ignition. It had a kind of outraged determination. The motor started, the car caught, she closed the door. "But come to the party," she began, while he worked with the wheel. "Stan—"

The big black car moved away; a second later it was speeding down the street, while she looked after it, saying, Go, and be gone, I don't want to be in love with you, I don't want to be in love with anyone.

A silent summer afternoon, insects drowsing in the few remaining trees along the block, clouds like birds winging across the sky, a yellow arrow of sunlight on the far pavement, pointing nowhere, her mother's tree gone, not even a root visible.

What is destroyed stays destroyed; what is dead remains dead.

But the house remains, she thought. The house I have come back to see and am afraid to face.

What's the matter with you? she asked herself. You don't have to worry. You're going to marry royalty. Didn't Frances tell you so?

The cards never lie. Stu came home. A dark man has failed you . . . death in your house . . .

In my father's house there are many mansions . . . in my father's house there are many rooms . . . and at the end, instead of shade and green grass and a place to rest, the blind wall.

You must never believe that, she told herself.

But I do believe it. That's the trouble.

She started up the walk, her heart beating tempo to her heels, tap tap, taptaptap, tap tap, taptaptaptap. Gray porch the same, paint peeling, the big rusted screws where the swing used to hang; three doors, the frames outlining the glass windows shedding splinters of wood, big blisters of paint at the edges. Three doors, why would anyone want three doors to get into a house? One of those mysteries, like why the rooms were all so small and the ceilings so high that you felt as if you were in a long, narrow box standing on its side. Dark rooms with big pieces of old-fashioned furniture. The only bathroom downstairs, an addition years after the place had been built. Was there still a pump in the kitchen?

She stood uncertainly on the porch, looking out to where the rock garden had been, with its bent holders, empty of flowers or greenery, to the old patch where her grandmother had raised the white iris. Nothing but an expanse of brown, beaten-down ground. There was a shed just beyond which had not been there before, an old rusty lawnmower leaning against its side, the door wedged open, overalls hanging on a nail.

Out behind the house the streetcar where the "girls" played had once stood, tumbling in on itself, and beyond that, the old stable. The streetcar had been hauled away, but was the stable still standing, the walls leaning in at crazy angles, the upper story ready to cave in? And the chicken coops, falling apart, had someone had the sense to take them away? The streetcar, the stable, the catalpa, the chicken coops, the magnolia, the parlor with her grandfather's portrait, that grandfather who was dead before she was even born, the Eastern palms, the big bed upstairs where the "girls" had all been born: these were with her as she raised her hand and rapped on the door, thinking, It is a kind of pilgrimage I have come to make, and when the front door opens, what will I find? The same old odor of camphor from the front parlor, seeping under the closed door, the shades still pulled because Grandma was afraid the rug would fade, and the piano nobody played still there, upright, out of tune, so monstrously ugly it was the first thing you saw, the last thing you remembered, about the room?

No, only the room, the physical room, would be there. The furniture was gone, the piano, the palms, even the plaster saint with its missing hand and fervent smirk, would be gone, impossible as it seemed, sent— like everything anyone in the family didn't know what to do with—to the Salvation Army.

"Who is it? Who is it down there?" a voice screeched, and Lois looked up, startled, and saw a head wrapped in an old red kerchief stuck out one of the upstairs windows. The window in her grandmother's old room. "What is it? What do you want?" the voice insisted.

It was an unanswerable question; how could she shout up to that head that she had come home on a pilgrimage, that she had come back to find the part of herself that was lost, and that she needed, she absolutely must have, to go on?

"What do you want?" the voice shouted insistently.

"My grandmother used to live here," Lois shouted back. "Could I just talk to you for a minute?"

"I don't know nothing about it. Come back when my husband's home. He is the one who know about that kind of thing."

"But I don't want anything," Lois insisted, desperate, thinking, She doesn't believe me, probably she thinks I'm trying to sell her something. "I just want—"

The window slammed shut and Lois stood, looking up, the dizziness on her again. I can't make her let me in, she thought, there's no law that says that those who owned a life here in the past have a right to come back and try to reclaim it.

She sat down, trembling, on the steps and stared out over the bleak front yard. I used to come here—I used to come here, she wanted to shout up at the window; it's the place that's meant most to me in my life, and now you won't let me in.

What do you want? that woman had shouted at her. Why didn't I shout back, I want love?

That is the kind of truth you're not permitted to say, she told herself.

Mama loved, didn't she? Lois's heart cried out to her. How can that be a sin? She paid, didn't she? she cried out to the universe all around her, which here looked stripped, bare, vengeful, a world which would hunt out its offenders and punish them without mercy, without mitigation, without understanding.

How can you expect me to believe? she asked, standing up, seeing before her the rough path going out to the sidewalk, the denuded yard, the smooth earth where once the catalpa had bloomed. How can you expect me to believe in a world which destroys those I love, which punishes those I care about, which deceives the things my heart holds dearest?

Suddenly a singing seemed to burst from the bare earth around her.

From all along the street the sound of insects rose to sky, a steady, siren-like song. It was the locusts; they had suddenly come to life, started to send out their song.

Filled with wonder, she stood still, listening, remembering that as a child someone had told her that the locusts came every seventeen years, that they buried themselves and hibernated in those other lost years. Come every seventeen years to claim their just due, rising out of their long sleep to run over the fields, to eat back the leaves, to lie in dead swarms all over the city.

Once every seventeen years come the locusts to claim their just due. There was a line for Neal. Write it down, seal it up, send it to New York, break down his wall for one moment. Would his wall ever be broken, even for a moment?

Neal, Neal, she thought, oh Neal, forgive me, her heart cried out to the singing; I can never undo what has been done.

But even in the midst of the bitter desolation that the locusts brought, they sent up a song. She must remember that. It was very important to remember that. Without remembering that, life became a defeat, a retreat from event to event, like some long, nightmarish journey back across a barren countryside, lost, irretrievably lost, paying the final penalty, surrendering to the enemy, the slain warrior fastened to the chariot, and the wheels of the chariot spinning faster and faster, Achilles raising his golden arm and striking the backs of the sweating horses with his rawhide whip, the chariot speeding faster and faster over the yellow sand, dizzy with speed, the face of the fallen warrior mutilated and bloody as it hit the rocks and stones, the horses galloping faster and faster, until the third circle is made, the triumph is ended, death is the victor.

But it is Hector we love, not Achilles.

Our enemy is also love.

She turned and looked at the house. I have found what I came back to find, I have finished my pilgrimage, she said to it silently. I do not have to go inside to know the full measure of my return.

We live not with the past as it was but as we see it. Grant O God, she thought, turning and going down the path, that I may remember my duty to others but that I remember also that I can never give to others until I have given to myself that which is lawfully mine, that I strike the bitter balance between self-indulgence and self-abnegation.

Grant O God the inner grace which is the self. Give me back my sense of self.

Chapter Six

STU heard them as he was coming down the steps. Without thinking, he stopped to listen.

"Well, I don't care," his mother was saying. "I wish she'd waited to go out to Esther's until *after* the party." There was a pause. "Lois is a lovely girl, Dad, you know I've always said that, but I have to think about my own—I mean," she went on hastily and Stu could tell she was flustered, "if Stu were to make up a little to Esther, she might leave him the money. He *needs* it," his mother said as if that settled the question.

"Who put all this chocolate milk in the icebox?" his father answered.

"What chocolate milk?"

"There are five quarts of chocolate milk—"

"Of course the fairest thing would be if she divided it up, but Esther's never been what you might call fair. Go on, take it out, I told those boarders not to put anything in my icebox without telling me, I don't care if it does go sour, it will teach them a lesson."

"I can't do it," his father said after a moment.

"Well, I can," his mother said. Stu could hear her at the sink washing her hands. "Go call Esther, I want to know if Lois got out there all right. She's had plenty of time to get crosstown. It's not that I begrudge

Lois the money. I mean, she's had a hard time, I always say that for her, but she doesn't need it— I mean, she's got that good job, she doesn't need it the way Stu does."

Stu couldn't listen any more. Putting his feet down heavily so that they both knew he was on the stairs, he went down, hearing his father say, "But it sounds so snoopy—"

"Say, Mom," he interrupted, trying to sound cheerful.

"Down here, Stu, in the kitchen."

He came down the last four steps, determined to do his best, knowing that he had already done it, down at the station. "I'm thirsty," he said, trying for heartiness. "I went out and got some milk a little while ago. Hope it isn't crowding you." He went to the refrigerator and opened the door, extracting a bottle, flipped off the wax top, and tipped it up, drinking.

"Don't you want a glass?" his mother asked. She was looking at him with alarm. "Right out of the bottle—it isn't *nice*," she said.

Lots of things aren't, he wanted to say—like figuring out how to get Esther's money for me. Aloud, he answered, "It tastes better right out of the bottle." He raised the bottle and drank, looking at her over the rim.

"All that sticky stuff isn't good for your health. You want to watch your health, Stu, that's the most important thing you have."

"I thought your eyes were," he said. "That's what you always used to say, that your eyes were the most important thing you had, that you only got one pair of eyes."

"Well, they are important," she admitted. "I mean, you only do have one set and all, but they sort of come under general health. Tell me," she said earnestly, leaning toward him, "tell me, Stu, are you glad to be back?"

"Of course I'm glad to be back," he said, lowering the bottle, trying to hold off his irritation. "You know I'm glad to be back," he said emphatically as he saw the distress building up inside her.

"You've been gone so long," she said, sinking down at the table, her hands automatically picking up a meat-loaf mixture in a bowl and starting to knead it. "So many things," she said. "You never even saw your grandmother, at the last. Those people at the funeral parlor, they did wonders with her, everyone said she looked just like a duchess. They had a little flower in her hands, a little pink rose, and they changed it every day. I just wish you could have seen her. She looked so aristocratic. Don't drink so much of that stuff," she begged. "It'll make your face break out, and you want to look nice for the party."

"My face is thirty-four years old," he said angrily. "It can take care of itself. Why can't you— I don't want a party, Lois doesn't want a party, Ethel doesn't want a party. What are you giving a party for?"

"But it's all planned," she protested. "And anyway, I mean—" She let the meat-loaf mixture drop. She bit her lip. She looked away. "If you'd just be nice to Esther—"

"Get that idea out of your head," he said. "She's not going to leave me her money, and even—"

"But she's got to leave it to someone, Stu," his mother protested. "It wouldn't hurt you to—to make up to her a little."

Wearily, he put the bottle of chocolate milk down. "And even if I were nice to her—'made up' to her—she wouldn't leave it to me."

His mother's face was incredulous. "Why do you say that? She *might.*"

He shook his head.

"But that's why," his mother went on persistently, "it's so important that I have the party, so she has a chance to get to know you, so—"

He couldn't stop himself. "I don't want her damn money," he said furiously.

Puzzled and hurt, his mother stared back at him. "What do you mean, you don't want her money?"

"She stole it."

"Why, Stu, whatever makes you say a thing like that!"

"Because it's true, goddam it, and you know it. I don't want her goddam stolen money that she swiped from the rest of the family. Let Lois have it. She at least deserves it."

His mother winced. "Why should Lois have it— I mean, all by herself —when—"

"Because it would be fun for her to have it."

"Fun for her—"

"What I mean is," he said, trying to hold back his exasperation, "she'd do something decent with it, throw it away on a gesture or blow it in Europe or give it away—"

"Esther's hard-earned money!"

He had to laugh.

"I never said she took it," his mother said defensively. "You were the one who said that."

"Don't you think she took it?"

"Well—no, of course not. She's my own sister. I mean, my own sister—if you'd just be nice to her," his mother said wistfully. "I want to have a real celebration, with everyone home. I let Peggy charge a new dress for the party." Then her face brightened. "Ethel can charge one too. That would make— What is it? What's the matter?"

"I wouldn't buy her anything, not now," he said.

"Why not? Why shouldn't Ethel have a new dress for the party? You want her to look nice, don't you? I want everyone to see what a nice wife you've got."

"Mama," he said slowly, "if she buys anything now, she won't get any use out of it. She's going to have a baby."

His mother's hands reached up to grasp her throat, she seemed to be suffocating. "You came home because of that, you didn't come home because you wanted to, you came home because you *had* to—"

"Iris—" his father began.

"You keep out of this," she cried to her husband. "What's it got to do with you? You're just like he is—all you want is a roof over your head, food in your mouth, you don't care how hard I have to work to put them there. When have you ever thought of me? When have any of you thought of me? Who's ever thought of me at all?" she demanded.

"God," Stu answered her. "That everlasting God you're always calling on and driving us all to believe in. Doesn't that everlasting God of yours take care of you, or has He failed you too?" Struggling for control, feeling a terrible thirst growing on him, the uncontrollable kind he had felt in Paris, he went to the table and started to pick up the bottle of chocolate milk.

"Don't, don't," his mother pleaded. "Your face will be a mess."

"I tell you," he said, losing control, "it's *my* face. I'm old enough to know what I want to do with it. And I'm not going to any party. I don't want to go to any party. Can't you get that through your thick head?"

"You don't have a brain in *your* head," she wailed. "If you had a brain in your head, you'd make up to Esther, you'd—"

"Stop talking about my sucking up to that goddam Esther."

"Stu!"

"Once and for all, can't you understand that I don't want her goddam money?"

"It's not that. That's not why you don't want me to have the party. It's because you're ashamed, ashamed of—" His mother stopped.

He was calm. He felt as if he could go through anything now; the truth was going to come out at last. "Ashamed of what?"

"Nothing," she said, not looking at him.

"Ashamed of Ethel, is that what you were going to say?"

She didn't answer.

"Well, at last," he said, and he had to smile. "At long last, I finally made you tell the truth."

"I'm the one who always tells the truth," his mother said dramatically, pointing her finger at her breast. "When I said you came back because you had to, not because you wanted to, *that* was the truth."

Stu put the bottle of chocolate milk back down on the table. "Everything you say is true, in a way, but it isn't *the* truth. Can't you understand, can't you ever understand, how people act? Won't you at least try to listen? I came back, yes, because Ethel is going to have a baby. And yes, it's true, I'm broke, I don't have a job. But I didn't come back to sponge off you—or to get Esther to leave me her money. I don't want something I didn't make for myself. Oh, I know you don't believe that, but that is *the* truth. No matter how little it is, I want it to be my own. The kid is my own," he said bitterly. "Something I thought I could share with you. I wanted to make it up to you for what had happened—the way I walked out and never wrote or anything—and I wanted the kid to know his family." He looked at her. He shook his head. "The kid doesn't mean anything to you, does he? It's just one more mouth to feed, that's the way you look at it, that's the way you've always looked at everything, children or grandchildren, or husbands, or anything, just one more mouth to feed."

"Son," his father said.

Stu looked at his father. Didn't his father know, after all these years?

"I hope you're satisfied," his mother said in righteous anger. "I hope you think you've got the last word in now."

"There's no such thing as the last word," Stu said. "Go ahead, have your party," he said after a momentary pause, "but we won't be here for it."

"No, no," his mother screamed, rising. "Don't leave me again." And she ran toward him, she threw herself on him, her fingers digging into his arm, her mouth vainly trying to reach his. "I won't say a word, not a single word. I won't mention one word about money, I promise. Only don't leave me." She shook her head, as if trying to clear it. "We can work out something," she said in the voice he recognized as the one she used with the boarders when they were behind on their bills. "I'll make over some of the work to you, you can handle part of the business, that'll entitle you to a percentage—"

"Mother, I want a job of my own, a place of my own, I'm only here on a visit. Ethel and I can't live with—"

"We'll talk about it later," she said, fighting down involuntary sobs that seemed almost to choke her. "You have your little visit and then we'll talk about it later. A grandchild," his mother said, and her face looked drawn and unhappy. "I've got another grandchild on the way." She was still standing next to him, but he saw that her attention had left him. She was biting her lip, puzzling something out. "Lois," she said. Then she turned and started out. At the door she stopped and looked at him. "She's got more sense than I gave her credit for," his mother said, and Stu was shocked at the tone of her voice—she thought Lois had gone out there to make a play for the money.

SATURDAY

SUNDAY

MONDAY

TUESDAY

WEDNESDAY

THURSDAY

BOOK VI   **FRIDAY**

SATURDAY

Chapter One

RALPH swung the car easily into the small gravel incline that linked the street and Sans Souci. At the right of the drive was an enormous tangle of green—indefinable brush, half-grown trees, the spiky leaves of rhododendron—down to the left a street of small random houses in small yards with sparse plantings. The big old pre-Civil War house looked out of place jutting up among all those bungalows with cheap siding and metal awnings. But it was still protected by a large yard, all that was left of the hundreds of acres the Ashwells had once owned. There were no gardens and the lawn was unkempt, with wild weed patches at the back corners of the lot, but the trees were lovely, great green shields against the sky. Lois was standing by the big oak, gazing off toward the colony of cheap cottages that trailed the big house like pilot fish following a shark. Long after Sans Souci was torn down and forgotten, those hideous little houses would be dividing and multiplying.

Carolyn leaned across the front seat of the car and put her hand on the horn. Ralph gave her a startled look, then put his foot on the brake and the car slithered slowly under the protective shade of the garage. Lois had started to wave.

"You take the kids in, will you, Ralph?" Carolyn asked. "I want to stop for a minute and talk to Lois. And will you give Mom a hand until I get there—you know how she is when there's a party." Not answering, he pulled the emergency brake. But she knew he would try, no matter how difficult and irritating her mother was. She had let him make love with the light on. Did he feel that now she thought she had the right to ask anything of him she pleased? She didn't want him to feel that way. What did she want? For him to be strong. If he were strong, she thought, everything would be different. She leaned over quickly as he opened the car door. When he turned she said so low that the children couldn't hear, "You know sometimes—" And then the thought was lost; she didn't know what she had been about to say.

"Sometimes what?"

Instead of answering, she gave him a quick kiss. For a moment, with her cheek next to his, feeling his quick, soft intake of breath as her lips brushed his cheek, she had the sensation he knew what she meant better than she did. If they had been alone, she would have—

"Come on, Daddy," Bobbie said from the back seat, and his father turned to help him out, held the door while the two children scrambled to his side. He held out one hand to Bobbie, then paused and held out the other to Sally. Holding a child by each hand, he went up toward the house.

She did love him, she wanted to love him, but . . .

He was going to give Stu a job, she ought to be appreciative of that. I've got to get Stu aside, Carolyn thought, and let him know he can count on a job with Ralph. Pete will just have to wait. I can't ask everything at once. She would give him a little money to tide him over.

I'll bet he still hasn't told mother or Peggy about losing his job, she thought. He's waiting for me to do that. Well, do it, she told herself, and stop dwelling on everyone's inadequacies. You have enough of your own.

"Well," Carolyn said as she came up beside Lois, "how's old Esther? I've been dying for the details."

"We— I went out, and—she didn't let me in, Carolyn."

"Didn't let you in?"

"I got out there—a little late—I got held up on the way," Lois said in a funny way. "Anyway I got there and I banged and yelled and went around trying to see in the windows, but she never came to the door. I finally just gave up."

"It's just the limit. I'll bet mother was fit to be tied."

"Yes, she was mad, but—" Lois broke off. "I don't know, not as mad as I thought she would be. Almost like she was—relieved." Lois shook her head. "What I can't understand is why Esther would ask me out and then not let me in. She made such a great thing about my coming and then, when I got out there, it was as if nobody was home. But she must have been inside. She knew I was coming. She just wouldn't open the door."

"Esther," Carolyn said, "is just— Esther." Inside her head she had composed the whole tableau: Lois banging on the doors, ringing the bell, pounding and ringing and calling out, while the house remained silent, shut up, not a shade moving, but behind one of those windows, watching, Esther. Carolyn could picture Esther saying to herself, *There was no reason for Lois to go to New York, Springfield is a very historic place. If Springfield was good enough for Lincoln, it ought to be good enough for Lois. That girl doesn't know when she's well off.*

"She's bats," Carolyn said, shaking her head. "She ought to be committed."

There was something the matter with Lois. She wasn't herself at all. She was like someone who had suddenly been awakened from a deep sleep and couldn't concentrate. She wasn't really listening. She didn't even seem *interested*. What was bothering her, anyway?

"Something the matter?" Carolyn asked at last. "Mother in one of her moods?"

Lois shook her head and Carolyn waited, but that was all she got. If it wasn't the family, what was it? Something in New York, Carolyn decided. None of my business. She reached up and tore a leaf from the big dappled oak. When she shredded it between her fingers, a faint milky substance stained her fingertips. At that moment, holding the leaf, staring up through the spangle of leaves at the bright blue sky overhead, conscious of the dark green grass underfoot, she suddenly felt reassured, as if things had an order, a meaning, in the universe, it was all only a question of seeing the schematization. Maybe it was just the summer day, the heartbreaking summer day.

"I ought to get back," Lois said, motioning her head toward the house. The sun caught her hair and glistened through the short dark curls. She reminded Carolyn of a Chagall— "The Artist and His Model" —Lois's face had that same self-condemned beauty.

"Things are pretty much under control, but I still have to set up the table. It's buffet but your mother wants it to have a pattern. The cooking's almost done. Ella just has to finish peeling the potatoes for the potato salad."

"They're making potato salad *now?*"

"Your mother wanted German potato salad—you know, the kind you have to make hot at the last minute."

"She would."

"Aries," Lois said.

"Mother and her parties."

"Frances and her salt dips."

"Esther and her money."

"What do you suppose they'll say about us? I mean, your children when they're grown up. And mine—if I ever have any."

"Oh, you'll get married one of these days, before you—"

"No," Lois said, and she was serious, "I don't think so. Every one of the men I meet that I think I could marry—insurmountable obstacles," she said in a glittery voice. "Like loving someone who doesn't love you," she said brightly, brittlely, "or falling in love with someone you have no business falling in love with. I never make very good choices."

If Lois had someone like Ralph, how would she have treated him? Better—much better—than I do, Carolyn thought. Lois might even have made him happy. But people like Ralph never fell in love with girls like Lois; they made the mistake of wanting what they shouldn't have.

We all do, Carolyn thought.

Dead in France.

"I didn't mean to embarrass you," Lois said.

"You didn't." But it was true, she was embarrassed. She was grateful when she saw Pete's old car turn into the gravel drive. "I've got some pearls for Peg," she explained, and knew she was fleeing. The expression on Lois's face was frightening.

Are you whole, are you intact? That was the question she had asked earlier. Now she knew that what she really should have been wondering was, How bad is it?

"You know how you're always talking about a basic black," Peggy had said on the phone earlier. "Well, I went out and bought one—charged it, actually, to Mother Ashwell, she said I should, for the party—and I don't know, Carolyn, it looks sort of depressing, like I'm in mourning or something. What do you think I should put with it, to make it look a little better?"

"Just pearls, a strand of pearls and plain pearl earrings," Carolyn said. "The simpler the better. Of course I haven't seen the dress, but it really doesn't matter. You can't go wrong sticking to pearls."

"I haven't got any," Peggy said bitterly. "The closest I ever came to having pearls was that day out at the old house—Grandmother Timble's house—when I *saw* them upstairs in her old jewelry box. But then— well, you know, even if someone hadn't taken them, I wouldn't have gotten them anyway."

"I'll bring mine," Carolyn promised and she had kept her word, though at the last minute she had had to run back in the house and get them.

Mother and her parties. Esther and her money. Frances and her salt dips. I wonder what they'll say about us, Lois had said. Carolyn and her drinking. Stu and his awful wife. Pete and those kids. And Lois, what would they say about Lois? It was too early to predict. Lois still didn't have a label that fit.

Peggy had gotten out of the car, and Carolyn had a moment to take in the dress. It was black, but it wasn't really basic. There was a bow in front, near the bust, and a matching one in back, at the waistline. The dress made Peggy look as if even the thin flesh that hung on her bones had given up and was slipping down, discouraged, to drop to earth and rest, but her face was radiant as Carolyn held out the pearls.

"The house is an absolute mess," Peggy said breathlessly. "I haven't even bothered to make the beds, but I took a nap—a nap, Carolyn! I haven't had a nap in years, and I spent a whole half-hour in the tub and no matter who screamed or hollered or wanted in, I didn't answer. I just lay there and relaxed. It was wonderful. I didn't know how wonderful a long bath could make you feel. And the kids," she said, looking around. "Let them pull and push, let them scream and holler, I don't care. I'm going to have a good time," she said earnestly.

How can she have a good time here? Carolyn wondered.

Pete was trying to do something with the children, but they were only at the edge of control. Peggy, walking up to the house beside her, seemed oblivious to the scrapping and arguing. When the two of them reached the back door, Peggy paused and pushed at her hair. She ran her tongue over her lips and moistened them. She pulled and patted at her dress. Then, for just a brief instant, she put her hand up to each cheek and pinched so that a flush of color burst out. She was trying to make herself pretty, something Carolyn had never seen her do.

Inside, the kitchen smelled of Virginia ham. Her mother was kneeling in front of the big ham, basting. Carolyn watched her mother start to break off a little sliver of meat, then draw back her hand, look at it as if it were a disobedient child. Her mother sighed, took the dipper and basted the top again, then scooped juices from the bottom of the pan and anointed the sides.

"Mama's recipe," her mother said happily. "Mama's old recipe, you can't beat it. I searched all yesterday, rummaging around my drawers, going through the pantry, running around looking for the recipe until I was a nervous wreck. And then you know what? Ella came in and she said, 'What's the matter?' and I told her and she said, 'No worry, I got it right here, in my head.' We had to send Dad out for the pineapple juice. The orange juice we had, but I had forgotten all about the pineapple juice. Maybe that was what made it so special."

"Where's Ralph?"

"He took the children on up front—to get them out of the way. He *offered* to help but—I love that dress," her mother said to Peggy. "It just does something for you. You can always tell when you put money into a thing. Peggy paid twenty-five dollars for that dress," she said to

Carolyn. "But I told her to get something she really wanted, never mind the cost—so long as you don't go over twenty-five, I said. Isn't that right, Peggy? Didn't I tell you to get exactly what you wanted?"

"You like it, Mother Ashwell? You really like it?"

"It looks *very* expensive." Iris paused. "Don't you think so, Carolyn?"

"French Room," Carolyn said, trying to be helpful.

A look of doubt passed over Peggy's face. "That's the real good place, isn't it?" she asked.

Carolyn could have bitten off her tongue. She turned to Ella at the sink, while Peggy went quickly out the door. On her way, Carolyn wondered, to the bathroom to see how she really looks? There was a little mound of potatoes almost to the top of Ella's head, and Ella's quick hands were lifting up potato after potato, running a knife around each until there was a perfect little curlicue of skin to drop in the sink; then Ella ran water over the naked white body, cleansed it, dropped it into its bath of ice-cold water. At the last minute, after the potatoes were boiled, she would dress them with minced bacon, onions, celery, and dill pickle and a hot sweet-and-sour sauce of sugar, vinegar, and spices.

"You need a hand, Ella?" Carolyn asked.

"I near done," she said over her shoulder, not breaking the rhythm of her peeling. Her black hand held up the bald white potato; with a small splash it fell into the waiting pan.

"And then after that," Iris said, "after that, Ella, I want you to check that we have enough celery. I don't think we fixed enough celery."

"I just wish I had someone like Ella around to help, Mama. You don't realize how lucky you are. She takes you for granted, Ella, that's Mama's trouble."

Ella's shoulders shrugged, but there was a small smile on her face. She went on peeling. Then Carolyn wasn't even sure it was a half-smile she had seen. The face, over the potatoes, was expressionless.

"Well, if there's nothing I can do—" Carolyn said, and her mother waved her out, pushing the oven door closed with her hip. "Too many cooks," she said, panting. "Oh, I swear, it must be a hundred and ten in here. I hate the heat. It just makes me sick all over."

She passed her father in the family parlor. He was sitting near the window, reading, and as she came through he looked up, nodded, and then turned back to his reading. Her father's defense against her mother was withdrawal—and Ralph's against her? Ralph's good, she told herself. He tries. When he tried so desperately and she tried so desperately and nothing came of it, those were the worst times, far worse than the ones when they quarreled and fought and flew at each other. But divorce was no solution. There were the children. She loved them—she did, more than she was willing to admit to herself. If there had been anyone else—

But there would never be anyone else.

How could you know a thing like that?

You couldn't know it, but you could feel it.

Stu was standing in the front parlor, looking out the window. When she came in, he turned quickly. "Oh," he said, "I thought it was someone else—Pete's wife. Every time I've turned around the past five minutes, there she is, and I can't remember her name. What the hell is her name anyway, Carolyn?"

"Peggy," Carolyn said.

"She's a funny girl. I mean, she just sort of pops up at you. Nice, though," he went on, as if he was trying to convince himself. "I mean," he said, "she probably means well, probably wants to show that she's friendly. Doesn't she know this isn't a friendly family?"

"She's got a new dress, she wants to have a good time. She hasn't had many good times lately." Quickly, before he had a chance to interrupt, she said what was really on her mind. "I'm glad you're back, Stu, I really am. I don't think you'll ever know how happy I was to see you. And—well—I know how things stand, I mean," she plunged on in confusion, "coming back here, with Ethel—you know—what I mean is, I hope you're going to stay. We all want you to stay. You know what Ralph told me? He said he was sure you could be a big help to him if you stayed. Down at the plant. I mean, he could trust you and all. He *needs* help down there."

She hadn't said it right at all.

"That's awfully nice of you, Carolyn—awfully nice of *Ralph*. But I couldn't take a job with Ralph. I couldn't work some place where I'm not like everyone else. I don't want special treatment. And if I worked down there, I'd get it. Because I'm one of the family. But you tell Ralph I'm real grateful and all, it's just I couldn't consider it."

If Stu didn't want the job, then Pete—

"I've got to go up and see what's holding Ethel up. You know, she's a little— It's hard for her to come down and face everybody."

"Does Mama know?" Carolyn asked, while he nodded. "How did she take it, Stu? Was she real surprised?"

"She has the same reaction as everyone else. She wonders how I'm going to make out." As if he could read her thoughts, he said quickly, "I didn't mean you, you know that, don't you, Carolyn?"

"Yes," she said, but she didn't for a minute believe him. She watched him move swiftly over the polished teakwood floor. He was going up the stairs, ascending toward the high curved ceiling. She stood staring up, looking at the beehive pattern of that plastered ceiling, seeing it so clearly that it went right into her mind, stretched over it like a net, repeating the pattern, hexagon after hexagon, until Carolyn's whole mind was suddenly filled with a sense of schematization, the world as a well-ordered place.

Cells, that was what the vaulted ceiling brought to mind, the smallest organized unit of which all things were composed—plants, animals, man—the basic unit. The cells went on splitting and multiplying, withering and dying, day and night, year in and year out, the body wearing out, replenishing itself, the mind not even conscious of the action, unmindful that life and death were operating side by side, living and dying going on at the same time, in the same body, without the organism's even knowing it.

The cells were dying and splitting right now, even at the instant while she was standing here; part of her was dying, part being reborn.

Was that what God was like? Going on continuously without giving any outward sign? For a split second she had a vision of her own death, as if her heart had stopped pumping—a vision of her own life, as if she had been granted a reprieve, death had been held off; so that she had been issued two lives, one in which she had made her mistakes and another, afterward, in which she might be allowed to profit from them.

It was as if something inside her had called out, It's not too late. You're not dead, you still have your whole life ahead.

Live . . . *live* . . .

Ralph, she thought, and turned, stumbling back toward the kitchen. If she could only find Ralph, if—

"Oh, here she is, here's Esther now," Carolyn heard her mother proclaim with a cry of joy. "That makes everybody. Now Ada," she was saying as Carolyn came into the kitchen and saw Ada at the sink, her back angry and straight as a ramrod, "Ada, you promised, no trouble"—and Ada let the tap water run faster while she held up a long, cool, slightly green stalk of celery and stripped away the fiber, as if deliberately and carefully removing the membrane from a living organ. It seemed to Carolyn that everything Ada touched turned to anger; her hands transmitted a peculiar violence to every task she took up. The long cords of celery crackled as Ada stripped them away. With one snap she yanked them loose, threw them down in the sink; in the sink they lay in attitudes of outrage, long green wisps of mutilated rage.

"Ada," her mother repeated with emphasis.

"I hear you."

"No trouble, you promised."

Ada looked up. Her eyes were dark and shining. "We let all that be a long time ago," she said, "the night—"

"Yes, I know," her mother interrupted. It was obvious her mother didn't trust Ada. "You say you promise," her mother insisted.

"Iris," Ada said, "I'm nearly sixty years old. I don't need to promise anything."

"There you go, talking like that again. You will start trouble, you know you will, talking like that. Not tonight," her mother pleaded. "Not with Lois here. Not with Stu and his wife home. Please, Ada, promise."

Ada turned with a jerk and gave a sharp pull at her knife. One thin long fiber of celery peeled away and spun into the air for a moment, like a vapor passing before her, then disappeared into the sink.

For a moment Carolyn watched while her mother stood looking at Ada helplessly. In that pause she turned to the back door—no one save the boarders ever used the front one, the back door to the kitchen was the family door to Sans Souci; the front one the boarders' entrance to the Green Lawn Boarding House—and there stood Esther. She looked around hurriedly, her eyes resting for an imperceptible moment on Ada at the sink, then flitting nervously around the room.

"I'm just furious with you, Esther Timble, that's what I am, plain furious," Iris said, rushing over to her sister.

Esther looked up, surprised, her eyes widening. "What is it? Am I late? Isn't this the time you told me—five o'clock? Isn't that what you said, 'Don't come any earlier because I have to fix the food for the boarders,' weren't those your exact words?" Esther asked, clutching a brown handbag closer to her, hugging it to her chest, looking at Iris as if it were Iris's fault she might be late and had missed something. Then she said suddenly, excitedly, "It was for dinner, wasn't it? You did ask me for dinner, didn't you? It wasn't for lunch, was it?"

"No, it wasn't lunch," Iris answered in exasperation. "You know very well it wasn't for lunch. I never had anyone to lunch in my life, not with all the work I have to do in the morning; and you know very well what

I'm talking about. You let Lois come all that way out there and then you wouldn't let her in, that's what."

"She didn't come," Esther said with certainty. "She was probably off with that man you told me about, Iris. If I were you, I'd have a good talk with her. She's staying in your house, she could give it a bad name. Everybody knows what happens to a place like yours if it gets its name in the paper. Ruined, ruined," she said, shaking her head. "You ought to give her a good talking to. Running around with a married man!"

"What on earth are you talking about, Esther? I never said Lois was running around with a married man. Not while she's in my house. I can't vouch for what she's doing in New York, but in my house—"

"I don't like that, Lois having a man and your trying to hide it," Esther said, short of breath, running her words together. "I don't like it one bit, and I'm going to say so to your face. A *married* man, Iris, you said so yourself, you—"

"I didn't say that. All I said was that some strange man called up and she said he was an old friend from school and he was married and she said she was going to—"

"I'll have a good talk with her, you can count on me, Iris," Esther said. "I've been meaning to anyway. You know, about the alcohol and all. I know Carolyn drinks," she said, turning toward Carolyn, shaking her head again.

"You have to drink a little if you belong to the country-club set," her mother said. "It's expected."

"Lois drinks, and I know she smokes, and now she's carrying on with a married man. I know she doesn't have a mother of her own, but—" Esther paused, inhaling deeply, getting in a big supply of breath so that she could finish without interruption, stumbling right and left over her thoughts, leaving a trail of overturned ideas and upset syllogisms along the way. "I've been meaning to talk to you about that. I've been thinking. You know, Iris, I have that big house out there, I live there all by myself, and all that furniture, I'm well provided for, I need someone to keep me company, someone who can help, and I was just thinking, maybe Lois would like to— She didn't come. I was there all the time, and the only people who came were the police."

"The police?" Iris said in alarm.

"About the car. Someone was trying to steal my car. I heard them. Trying to get in the garage. Someone wanted my good new car."

"It's not new," Ada said from the sink.

"What do you mean, not new?"

"It's *at least* four years old."

"I'm not talking about the *age,*" Esther said with dignity. "I'm talking about condition. It's practically a brand-new car, just the way it came from the factory. And the insurance wouldn't cover; those companies, they never give you anywhere near what your things are worth. I've taken very good care of my car," Esther proclaimed. "I don't want to lose a brand-new car and get money for a no-good, half-baked old one."

"I don't think anyone was trying to steal your car at all," Ada said calmly, letting the water run over a long stalk of celery, keeping her eyes on her work. "It was Lois trying to get in, that's what. You try to make out it was—"

"I ought to know who was trying to get in the house and who was trying to steal my car," Esther said heatedly.

"Well," Iris interrupted, trying to pacify both of them, "maybe someone was trying to take your car. But Lois was out there too, and you wouldn't let her in."

"She didn't come," Esther insisted. "I was there the whole time, and I certainly would have known if someone rang my doorbell."

Iris cast her a look that plainly showed she didn't believe her; then her face took on an aspect of guile. "Well," she said, "I just don't understand it. Lois says—well, never mind. Come on in and see Stu, Esther, he's been dying to see you."

"How's he working out, Iris? What kind of work is he in now? There in New York?"

"Carolyn," her mother said quickly, "why don't you take Esther on in? I'm sure she wants to see Stu and— Take her on in," her mother said urgently.

Her mother was evading the issue, as she always evaded issues she didn't want to face, but Carolyn had a kind of admiration for the bald bluntness of her mother's tactics. It seemed to Carolyn anyone could see through them, but her mother forced people to go along with her *pretending*.

Of course Esther stole the money, Carolyn thought. That's why she doesn't want anyone out at her house. That's why she wouldn't let Lois in at the last minute. Afraid. There must be something out there she's afraid someone will find. The earrings? she asked herself. No, something more.

God, she thought, what a way to live.

Was it true, then, that the sins vested their own payment? Was what she had seen in the beehive ceiling, that schematization of the world, the world as a well-ordered place, perhaps, after all, right? No, it was something she wanted to believe, not something that was necessarily—logically—true.

She had hold of Esther's arm. Her aunt moved along reluctantly; there was something bothering her. Carolyn supposed it was the scene in the kitchen; then Esther reached over and grabbed Carolyn conspiratorially. "I want to tell you something," she said. "I want you to know what your mother did. Your mother," Esther said indignantly, "tried to get me to pay Stu's bills—yes, she did too," Esther insisted. "I think he— I think your brother—put her up to it. I do, Carolyn, as God is my witness, I think he egged her on. Come back from New York City with a wife on his hands and no way to support her—your mother isn't putting anything over on me—and he probably said to your mother, 'Go ahead, call Esther up, she doesn't have anybody to leave her money to,' and you know how soft your mother is—"

"Aunt Esther," Carolyn said sharply, fighting down an impulse to take hold of her and shake her.

"—my own sister, bold as brass, right on the telephone, trying to talk me into taking your brother on—'someone good with the heavy work'—don't think she fools me, not for one minute. I know what she's got in mind. She wants me to look after Stu. She's got her hands full with—"

"Stu wouldn't even consider such a thing. He—"

"Wouldn't even consider such a thing? Why, he's *dying* to get his hands on my money. Let me tell you something." And Esther gripped her arm harder. "You just listen to me. I'm not leaving my money to just anyone, I'm leaving it to the one who deserves it."

"Listen"—Carolyn could feel herself trembling all over—"we don't want your money—"

"Hah, that's a good one. You don't want my money. Well, maybe *you* don't, you caught yourself a·rich husband, but let me tell you a thing or two about that brother of yours—"

"Don't, Aunt Esther, please—"

"Your brother is trying to get something for nothing. You all are."

Esther stood in front of Carolyn, twisting her gnarled hands around the brown bag. She was suffering, she was angry, she was in full righteousness. Trying to control herself, Carolyn said quietly, "I've got to go back and help mother."

"Run away from what you don't want to hear. I suppose your mother is to blame. She brought you up the way she did—and your father,"

Esther said. "Yes, your father. Irresponsible, the both of them. It shows, it shows."

"Irresponsible?" Carolyn heard herself saying in a high, angry voice. "You don't even know the meaning of the word. My mother's worked for every single thing she's ever had, and none of it has come easy. But you—you want to know what we all think of you?" Carolyn demanded, her eyes blazing. "You want to know what everyone really thinks— that you took the money, you stole Aunt Clara's money. Do you think that's better than working hard for it? Do you think Mama's worse than you are because she worked for her money and you stole it, is that what you think?" And before Esther could answer, she leaned over and took her aunt's arm. "You're nothing but a mean, selfish, dirty, self-centered old woman."

Chapter Two

JUST like Mrs. Polaski and the beer: you know what you ought to be doing, but you won't do it. Go over and help, one side of Stu commanded himself, she's your mother. To hell with her, another side of him said, let her shift for herself. You try to help, what does she do? She yells.

It'll be the same with Ethel, he thought, picturing his wife running after their little boy, screaming, "Stop it, stop it this minute, I've had enough. I can't take any more, I tell you. Stop it before I give you something good to cry about."

And the youngster, not understanding, giggling and running, would plunge on until he tripped, went sprawling and the hysterical mother rushing after him, a big monster suspended over him, shrieking, "Now you're going to get it. I told you you were and you are." Whack! A child's shrill cry and Ethel, at the end of her rope, collapsing in a chair, weeping, saying, "I just couldn't help it. I just can't control myself sometimes."

It would be a repeat of a hundred scenes in the past, his mother half out of her mind with fatigue shouting at him, slapping Pete, screaming at Carolyn.

"You feeling better?" he asked over his shoulder, unwilling to turn around and face the figure in back of him. It was the question he always seemed to be asking her. His wife was sick, she was fretful because she thought she was beginning to "show," and she was mad at him because right before the party they had had a scene. He had gone upstairs to get her, knowing it was going to be a struggle, she didn't want to go down, not that he blamed her, but the point was she *had* to put in an appearance. She was sitting on the bed, tweezing her eyebrows, her face in one of the few expressions of concentration he had ever seen on it as it watched itself in the mirror and drew with small sharp pincers the hairs from their roots. He went over to her. He wanted to put his arms around her and comfort her, but she moved away from him. For the past few days she had shut off her desire and centered her feelings in a self-contemplative glow as if her eyes were focused inside and she were smiling to herself, murmuring over and over, "Yes, dear, I see you. Yes, honey, go on growing. Mama's here. Everything's all right. Just make yourself into a big, strong baby for Mother."

"I don't feel so good," she said. "I think I'll—"

"Now, listen, Ethel, don't start that. I know what you've got in your head. You think you're not going to go down at all, don't you? You think you're going to make one excuse and then another until the whole thing is over." He had to try to be sympathetic. She was going to have his child (*Preggy, preggy,* a voice called out inside him, *hung up*), going to have his child, he repeated savagely to himself, and she was sick and scared and whatever else happened to women when their bodies started feeding the young inside. Try, he told himself, goddam it, *try.*

She went on fussing with her eyebrows. "Cut that out!" Her face got its set, stubborn look. He was in for it now. He would have a hard time bringing her round. He knew that getting too close made her nervous. Stay close enough to reassure her, he told himself, but not too close, not so close she gets nervous. "Ethel, you mustn't feel Mother is against you. She isn't looking for faults in *you*. She—all of them—they all want to like you. And your dress, it looks fine, it's all your imagination that you think it's—it's too tight. Honey, once you get down you won't be nervous. I swear it. I'll be there, I'll look after you."

She glared up at him. "Oh, I know those words," she said bitterly. "All you ever do is try to act big, but when it comes down to it—" Tears had started to roll down her flaky cheeks, big round white buttons, they seemed to Stu, moving so slowly that they seemed almost sewn to her pasty face. Ugly, ugly, a voice called out inside him, and he tried to hush it by saying, Sick, sick.

"I promise—" he began.

"Promise," she broke in, sitting up, glaring at him, chewing her lip in anger. "Promise what? You don't know nothing about what a promise means. All you know is talk, talk, talk. Come on home, you say, it'll be different. Try, just try, you say, and I am trying." She wept. "God alone knows how I'm trying and what does it all mean? Just that you put your hands all over me, that you're at me day and night, and me in a condition."

. "All right, I'll leave you alone. Does that satisfy you? Does that make you feel better? I promise—"

"I know what your promises mean."

"What do you want from me? What is it? Just tell me and I'll try to do it. Can't you see I don't want things to be the way they were either, can't you just try too? What do I have to try to make you start over?"

"Leave me alone"—she wept— "I'm so tired. I'm so sick," she wailed. "And all you ever do is—"

Oh, he thought, I wish they could make a little movie of this. Oh, all those lovely Technicolor films and the man is standing on some balcony looking out over tall buildings, twirling a glass in his hand, looking so damn sophisticated, saying, "Come on out here, honey, and look at the stars," and this pale, thin little shadow comes up behind him, and it's this girl, all dressed in some thin, wispy dress, a soft, creamy girl looking at him like he was John D. Rockefeller, and he should be, he'd need all that money to keep a place like that going, but in the movie he's only some schoolteacher or sociologist or something, an ordinary person, at least what Hollywood thinks is ordinary, and this girl she gazes up at him, and says, "Harold," and there is music and the camera turning itself inside out and a big wail of sirens, fire engines and police cars rushing through the night, and you know damn well what that means . . .

Make a movie of me, he had thought, going down the hall. Start with this house, this crummy old house, and inside the house there is my worn-out mother and my beaten-down father and my sister who's frantic to get out, and my brother who's already loused up his life by the time he's seventeen, and all these beaten-down boarders—the misfits, the derelicts, the failures, the botched-up and broken-down, one example of mishap and misery after another, wouldn't that make a beaut of a background?

So you take me and focus your story on me, he thought, pausing and staring down at the teakwood floors his mother worshiped, and you show me going off into the wide world to make my fortune, and instead of ending up with a penthouse and a white, creamy girl on a balcony, you bring me right back to where I began and show me with my wife upstairs, and what are we doing?

I'll tell you: we're yelling and hating and wondering how in the name of god we ever got stuck with each other, but there we are, stuck, and no damn way to get out.

I should have stayed in the Army, he thought. They retire you out of that. I'll be working all my life, if I'm lucky enough to get a job, keep it, working until the day I drop dead, if I'm lucky. In the Army at least they give you three squares a day and a bed. A living allowance, too, if you got a family. A place.

Where is my place? Stu asked the broad, gleaming boards of wood under his feet.

He hated these floors. It was because his mother set such store by them, as if she cared more about them than she did about him, about Carolyn or Pete. Perhaps she did, he thought now. The floors at least couldn't hurt her.

Could he get into the Army now, find some place to work out a little security? No, too old. The Army, like everything else, wanted men who were young—young and pliable, Stu thought, so they can turn you into the mold they want, not what you want.

I couldn't go into the Army again anyway, he thought. Couldn't kill any more. At least I don't think I could. Walking over those fields, looking at those blackened corpses, and that smell.

With me still.

Always will be.

I gotta get a job, Stu thought, a job that pays. I gotta find a decent place to live. I gotta start thinking of the future. Last week, this time, walking down the street, I had nothing more on my mind than maybe going to a movie, drinking some beer with Mrs. Polaski, getting out of seeing Ethel for the evening, and now I'm a man with responsibilities. Do you get any points for that?

If only, he thought, it weren't Ethel. If it were someone I could make a real new beginning with—in another town, get a job, find a little house, just the two of us waiting for our child, and me starting, really starting, all over.

Come off it, he said silently and sharply to himself. Forget an hour ago, pay attention to the present. "You all right?" he repeated to his wife standing in back of him. "You want some help?" he asked his mother, who stood across the table from him, spooning out the potato salad.

"Why don't you just stand here? So you'll be on hand, so you can give me a hand if I need it."

He turned. People were crowded up against one another; he was directly in front of Pete's wife. Peggy, he told himself.

He knew he ought to say something to the wife, but she made him jittery, looking at him like that, expectantly, as if she were waiting for him to say something. What was it she wanted him to say, for crissake?

Tremulously a smile broke over her face. "How are you, Stu?" she asked softly.

"Good, okay, fine," he said abruptly. "The same as ever"—and he pushed past her and went toward the hall. He just didn't feel like making small talk, and certainly not with her.

He was in the good parlor, near the hall. He would go out and have a cigarette, maybe even a drink. Erwin was the kind who would bring a bottle to show what a good guy he was. Smart cooky, Erwin. Too smart. Stu didn't like him. Still, he thought, you like him enough to drink any liquor he might have out in his car.

She came abreast of him, that thin girl in that ugly black dress, fingering the pearls at her throat, looking up at him with wide, hopeful eyes. What the hell was it with her, looking at him that way? Go away, he wanted to shout at her. Why was she looking at him like that? Then in that great wide wound of a face she was trying to smile with—it was enough to make you sick—the mouth opened. "What are you thinking about?" she asked timidly.

"Snow," he said abruptly.

"Snow?" she asked in a small, hurt voice.

That awful female hanging-on-ness, that awful female feeling of smothering you. Snow. Shackelton. Scott. In all this heat, all this animal heat of family, the cubs rubbing up against one another, the cubs nosing about for their mothers, the cubs poking and pawing one another, crowding in, what he'd like was a little snow.

"It's hot. It makes you think of snow. You smoke?" he asked. If they were smoking, they wouldn't have to talk. He held up the pack and looked at it. "You want one?"

Pete's wife nodded. Reaching out for the cigarette, she was all funny and awkward; and just the way he knew she would, she dropped the cigarette, her fingers grasped at his, the cigarette fell between them like a great elongated snowdrop.

He bent over and started to retrieve it just as she knelt down. Their hands touched, and she started, her whole body gave a convulsive jerk.

"You're Pete's wife, Peggy—it is Peggy, isn't it?" he asked as he put the cigarette in her hand and tried to get out his matches.

He couldn't look at her face. He gazed absently around the room while she went on, "I'll bet you do all kinds of interesting things in New York. We never do anything interesting in Springfield. There isn't anything interesting to do. I guess maybe that's why you went away." She stopped in confusion. "Because," she said, faltering, "you wanted to do all kinds of other things."

"Yeah, I guess you could put it that way."

"I've wanted to get away so many times. I—listen, Stu, I—"

Now she really frightened him. She was clutching him, looking up at him as if he were supposed to take her in his arms and comfort her. He had to get away from her. "I gotta find my wife," he said abruptly.

She was still standing there, staring up at him. He didn't know what to do. He couldn't just go away and leave her, not when she was looking at him like that. "My wife's sick," he explained, trying to think of some way to get through to her. "She's going to have a baby, she's not feeling too well."

"A baby?"

What the hell was the matter with her anyway? She'd had five herself, hadn't she?

"Hey, Ethel," he called into the next room. "Ethel!"

Goddam these women, he thought. "Over here, Ethel. *Will you come over here?*"

Miraculously, Ethel was moving. She left the line, holding her half-filled plate, and started toward them. God, she looked terrible. If she just doesn't open that mouth, he thought, I can stand it. If she just doesn't open her mouth and make one of those terrible little statements like I been dying to meet you, leaning forward and putting her hand on her stomach and saying, Have you heard the news? We're enlarging.

"My wife," Stu said, turning to Peggy. "I don't believe you've met."

"You'll have to excuse as how I was late," Ethel said. "But"—giggling—"but I suppose Stu told you."

Pete's wife stood dumbly, staring into Ethel's face.

"Oh, I thought as how he would have told you. I mean, you're the one with all the kids, aren't you? Well, we're having one of our own," Ethel's painted face said, smiling.

"You're going to have a baby? You and Stu are going to have a baby?"

"It's all confirmed. One of those little rabbits, you know. They take them and put your wee-wee in them and they turn some color or other. At least I think that's how it happens, and then they know. I had a very positive reaction," Ethel said proudly. "The druggist said they told him it was one of the most positive reactions they'd ever had."

"Peggy," his mother called. "Peggy, where are you? The children need some help. You have to cut their meat for them. Peggy—"

Stu caught one look at her; the face was twisted all out of shape. "All right, *all right*," he heard her say. "I'm coming. Just give me a minute, Mother Ashwell."

"Grandma, Grandma," a small voice screeched, frantic, fearful, urgent, "I have to go to the toity. Grandma, Grandma—"

He looked at his wife. She was smiling, probably thinking, just like a kid. . . .

She hadn't wanted to get rid of the kid. Didn't that make a difference? What did make a difference?

The three men who walked up and took him with them. The one man who walked off in the snow by himself. The man who went back to get his comrades, far south, in the snow, at that island with the strange name. Yes, there were things that did make a difference. And you? he asked himself, would you have stopped for a wounded man? Would you have gone back for other men when you had finally saved yourself? Would you have walked out in the snow?

If I were God, Stu thought, I wouldn't trust you one minute.

He doesn't, Stu thought.

He let you live, didn't He?

You get any points for that?

Chapter Three

FRANCES had been acting funny from the first moment she had popped, early, into Lois's room upstairs. "I've made up my mind," Frances said from the doorway, "I'm getting out of here first thing. I might even go back with you. That would be fun, wouldn't it, going back to New York together? And then I'm off to Europe. In First Class you don't have to worry about Dun and Bradstreet. Anyone in there is bound to be in the chips, and it's confined, First Class is, you're sure to run into at least one widower on the loose. I'm going to Europe," Frances had said decisively, "and if I don't connect going over, I'll just sign up and come back. You go back and forth across the Atlantic four or five times First Class, you're bound to turn up at least a medium-sized tycoon. Springfield," she said, "Springfield, Illinois, where are there any magnates round here? You wouldn't—you don't happen to have anything in your suitcase, do you? I mean, something in the way of kicks? I'm dying for a drink if the truth were known. I don't think I can get through this evening without a little something to grease the wheels."

She had drunk in Lois's room; she had been drinking, Lois knew, at Erwin's car. It was Frances, as a matter of fact, who had come up to whisper to her later downstairs, "I know where there's some of that divine nectar," propelling Lois out with her to the car. Frances had just been pouring a drink in the paper cup when someone had come up behind Lois and put his arm around her.

She would have known that touch anywhere. "Erwin," she said, turning, pleased, smiling. "I was hoping I'd get a chance to talk to you alone."

She and Erwin had turned and looked at Frances, waiting for her to finish her drink and go back in the house. But Frances was taking her time, leaning back against the car door, the late-afternoon sunlight catching the color of her necklace and reflecting it in the hood of the car so that it seemed there was a little row of bright blue beads along the rim of the door. "This is just like the old days," Frances said. "Like the river, when I was young. My god, the times we used to have"— and she sighed. "There was this boy from across the lake, a very exciting type—"

"Damn it anyway, Mother," Erwin had exploded, "Lois and I want to talk."

290

"Well, why didn't you just say so?" Frances asked in a hurt voice. "There's no need to get mad." She finished her drink, put the cup back in the car, and remarked, "I'll know mine by the color of the lipstick," and then, with an air of injured dignity, made her way up the walk back to the house.

"You all right, you all over—over that business the other night?" Erwin asked her. The light was still quite clear, it was late afternoon light, pale pinkness, the hot flush summer afternoons held.

"I'm sorry I broke down that way," Lois said, looking down into her paper cup. So he was going to admit what had happened after all.

"It's all right, we all do once in a while, but—well—you want to be careful. Some people—well, you know . . ."

"Yes, I know."

They were silent, standing there, the soft glow of early evening touching them—part sunlight, part liquor—both of them silent and absorbed, but close. She felt very close to him.

"You know," he said at last, "you've always been my favorite cousin."

"Cousins can never be close, really close. Not after a certain age, anyway. It's too bad."

"If you weren't living in New York—"

"No, it isn't just that. It's that when people grow up and marry, they grow away from one another. If they stay too close, they take away something that belongs to the wife—or husband, if I had one," she said. "We're better off the way we are."

"Yeah, I guess so," he said, but he didn't sound very convincing. But it was true nevertheless. If they had been close, really close the way they were when they crouched under the blanketed card table in the basement and talked about "hit," she would have been able to tell him about—about everything.

"Do you know what I've been going through?" Stan had asked her on the telephone. Yes, I know, she had thought, I know, I know.

But she had not answered him, that boy her cousin loved.

"We have to get all this straightened out before I talk to her," he had said. "You're avoiding me."

"Yes."

"Why? Don't you see—"

"I'm afraid of the moment when all my resolutions break down," she said into the receiver, that black impersonal instrument that carried the important communication of so much of life, wanting to add, I'm afraid of the end of love, I remember the white-hot light overhead and counting all the way to nineteen. What she had said at last was, "Help me to help myself. I want to be good, I want to do the right thing."

"I want love," he had said hoarsely, while she held the receiver and thought, Don't we all, oh don't we all?

Is he going to come? she asked herself. Oh, make him come. And then an instant later, No, don't let him come.

Eileen had called her the day before and asked if everything was all right; her mother, Eileen had said, hadn't mentioned anything about *his* coming to the party and she was worried. "It's all right, isn't it? she had asked anxiously over the phone. I haven't heard from him, but— he's coming, isn't he?"

How could you say to Eileen, I don't know whether he's coming or not, and if he comes it won't be because of you. You see, when we got together, out in the car, you see, Eileen, he started to drive me out to the old house, grandmother's house, and what happened was this, Eileen . . .

"I hope so," Lois had said. "But—but, well there are some difficulties. Your mother, you know . . ." And she had left it, ambiguously, at that.

Startled, Lois turned quickly. Someone was touching her, someone she didn't know. For a moment she was afraid it might be Eileen, Eileen asking the same question.

"I'll take care of anyone who needs anything," her Uncle Stewart said. "You go eat. You haven't eaten anything."

"I'm not hungry." And it was the truth.

"You should eat," he said earnestly. Like all the family, he thought food was the answer to any problem.

"I'll just cut a couple more pieces of ham," she said, "and then you can take over."

Lois stared out the window into the bright, fierce sunlight that beat down on the front lawn. So there we are. Yes, there we are. No, not there, here.

Not here, not now, not anywhere really. The knife slipped through the ham effortlessly; knives in this house were always keenly honed—and the meat overdone.

Be here. Come. I want you to come. No, don't. Don't come. It's not right.

"Honey, are you all right?" Iris asked anxiously. "You're acting so strange."

In her head he had just been taking her in his arms, his mouth was meeting with hers, he held her in his arms, his strong arms.

Erwin lost by two cars. What did Eileen lose by? she asked herself. *Where is he?* Eileen would ask, and she would have to give some kind of answer.

"Aren't you hungry, honey?" Iris asked worriedly. "You haven't taken anything. You haven't eaten a thing. Get a plate, take a little of everything, it's good, it really is."

Stan, Stan, Lois repeated to herself silently, picking up one of the plates, trying to smile at Iris, while all the time the golden A gleamed up at her. The good Ashwell plates Iris loved so much. The golden A. No longer scarlet, our sins are golden now, paid for in cool currency. Five hundred dollars he had charged and assured her she was getting a bargain. Neal, she thought. Neal . . . "I was just waiting for the others to finish, Auntie," she said.

She pressed her eyelids closed. Don't come, she thought, I remember how love ends: in the Eighties.

"You eat well now, you hear? You need some meat on your bones, you're still way too thin, Lois." Her aunt was clutching her arm. "Promise me," Iris pleaded, "Promise me right now that if you ever marry" —she said *ever marry* as if there was a strong doubt—"you'll be married here. In this house. You know I've got my heart *set* on a wedding here."

"I promise," Lois said, moving back. Then suddenly she saw Eileen was coming toward her, trying to be inconspicuous, keeping in back of most of the people, out of sight. She's coming to talk to me, Lois thought, I'm trapped behind this table, I can't get away, and she knows it.

"Lois," Eileen said. "Lois," she repeated, putting out a hand timidly. "I've been wanting to talk to you."

Lois could feel her smile fading, retreating slowly from the center of her face to the mouth, crouching down at the corners, waiting for what was to come.

"Where is he? Do you know where he is?" Eileen asked urgently.

Lois shook her head.

"But you—but when you talked to him, didn't he say anything? Didn't he ask you—didn't he tell you that he wanted to ask you if he could come? Isn't that what he talked to you about?"

"Yes, that's pretty much what we talked about."

"Then where is he?"

"I don't think he's coming," Lois said slowly, looking down at the floor.

"What is it? You've got to tell me, I've got to know. He—he won't talk to me"—and a terrible look of pain swept over Eileen's face. "You know," Eileen said in a half-whisper. "How do you know? *Answer me, how do you know?*"

"Eileen—"

"What did he say to you?" Eileen demanded. "Just tell me what he said to you. Why can't you tell me what he said? Can't you see how I—"

"He told me—" Lois began, stopped, her voice breaking off. "He told me," she began again, "that he didn't think he would come."

"But why not? That's why he went to see you, so he could come. Why should he decide he didn't want to come?"

"You'd better ask him. I don't think—"

"It's something to do with you," Eileen said slowly. "Isn't it?"

Lois looked at her. "Yes," she said. "I guess it is."

"Hey, Lois," Erwin yelled, "we've been saving a place for you. Here, over here."

"I don't give a damn who you leave your money to!"

It was Stu's voice, that same voice that had said, in her apartment, *I hate them all, I tell you, every goddam one of them.* He was standing over Esther, his face set, his mouth a thin, tight line, hands clenched in front of him, Esther staring back at him as if he had lost his mind.

"I want that understood once and for all, you hear?" he said, and his voice carried all over the room. "I don't give a good goddam about your money. Leave it where you want, but leave me out. I'm not going to trail after you to get your money, no matter what you and Mother think. I'm—"

"Stu, Stu." His mother was in action at last. "Stu—"

"I mean it," he said savagely. "The two of you think you can pressure me—"

"I don't want you out at my house," Esther said shrilly. "It was your mother's idea. Your mother is the one who wanted you to come out. I never wanted you, not from the beginning. All I said was—"

"All you said was, maybe I could come out and give you a hand with a couple of things. You think I'm so dumb I don't know what that means? I'll do it because you think I'll think I'm getting in good with you and then maybe you'll leave me the money. So I come out and do some things for you, you get them done free, you don't have to pay me, you—"

"Stu!"

"Stay out of this, Mother. I want it settled once and for all."

"He's hopeless, just hopeless," Iris said to anybody who would listen to her. "He's his own worst enemy."

"If you wait long enough, people give themselves away," Esther said. "Lois, not coming that way after she was invited, after she postponed coming when *I* wanted her; Carolyn, talking like that to me out in the hall; now you. You're not getting any further ahead on my list, you three, acting *that* way."

"I don't want to be on your goddam list, I tell you"—and Lois was really alarmed now. Why couldn't Esther keep quiet?

But Esther was saying, "I've thought it all out, I'm not *just* dividing my money, I'm giving it to the one who deserves it."

"Don't you mean the one who should have had it in the first place?"

"No trouble, please, Ada, you promised."

"That's all she's ever done all her life, make trouble," Esther said. "She wanted Papa to love her best, and of course he loved Frances best, but Ada blamed me, you know she did, Iris, you can't deny that—"

"Please," Iris begged, *"please."*

"—she killed Mama, you can't deny that either, Iris, no matter how you stand up for her. She killed Mama, you know she did. If she hadn't said those awful things, made that scene, the night of Mama's birthday party, Mama never would have had her stroke, Mama would be with us today."

"I won't listen, I won't," Iris cried, putting her hands to her ears.

"I'm going to sue her, that's what I'm going to do, take her to court to make her stop spreading all those lies about me."

"She took the money," Ada said. "She stole the money from Aunt Clara. She was with Aunt Clara at the end. She stole Aunt Clara's money, you all know it, all of you, all these years you've let her get away with it. Took the money, took it—"

"I invested my money, I was smart, I—"

"Took the man, the only man I ever cared about, stole John from me—stole everything I've ever wanted." Ada was rising in her chair, she grasped the handles of the wicker chair, and all about her people were staring at her in disbelief. "I've never forgiven you, never. I don't care if the others let you get away with it, I never will. Never. You took that money. You know you did. Thief! Thief!"

Ada was standing in the midst of Iris's room, and to Lois her eyes seemed sightless, as if covered by a thick membrane; her ears stopped up, as if she couldn't hear the cries on all sides of her; Ada was listening inside, her senses numb, feeling nothing save perhaps the steady beating of her heart pounding the life through her, and the little song her heart made was, Gone, gone, *gone* . . . the man who could have loved me, the money that could have saved me, the daughter I have clung to. Going or gone, all of it. Everything.

Ada's mouth made a little movement— *"Gone,"* she said, and sank down, her lips trembling, the tic in her cheek working. "Gone, all of it gone."

"Not to be tolerated, you hear!" Esther had her brown handbag clutched close to her. "I won't tolerate it, I tell you, years and years, the same thing. Everytime I come out she goes at me, because she's jealous. My money—" And Esther's voice stopped; there was a little lilt, the word *money* hung in the air among them, and they all stared at her, she was crazy to talk about money when Ada was the way she was; Esther pulled herself tall, a gesture Lois remembered her grandmother always used when she was angry, that little proud woman seeming to push herself right through the crown of her head, growing before Lois's very eyes; but this was Esther, a little untidy woman in blue growing into majesty before their very eyes, proud and regal in her anger and determination, proud holder of her own esteem (*I could write a check for a hundred thousand dollars and never feel it*); Esther stood in front of Ada, Ada staring out, sightless, murmuring, "Gone, gone," not even looking up, her lips moving, her hands moving, the tic in her cheek moving up and down.

"Now, listen," Frances began, rising. "Listen," Frances commanded, looking at Ada, looking at Esther. "I mean it. *Listen!*"

That colorless face lifted itself, the tic in the cheek moving up and down. "What? What's the matter with *you?*" Ada asked. "A divorced woman, *divorced,*" Ada said, and the eyes had begun to come to life, there was a small spark of venom in back of each, a little flicker of light had worked its way through and shone, resplendent, from the tarnished depth, come into its own at last.

"Let's not start that," Frances said, pulling her mouth together in a thin tight line.

Ada stood up. "Never," she announced, "never coming back here again. Years and years, you have let her get away with it—years and years. Not one of you has cared," Ada said. "I never want to see any of you again. Never."

Esther stood in front of her.

"Get out of my way," Ada said.

Esther did not move.

"Get out of my way," Ada repeated.

"I'm not in your way."

"Move."

"You move."

Ada gave Esther a shove, and Esther, caught off balance, surprised, lurched against the chair, threw out a hand, caught hold of Ada.

"Don't touch me!" Ada cried, moving back. "Don't ever touch me!"

Esther's small soiled hand lay on Ada's arm, the fingers sinking into Ada's flesh, while Ada trembled, tried to pull away, but the hand lay there, still, heavy, attached. Ada brought her own long blue-veined hand up, shook Esther loose, and with a vicious slash, as if her hand were a knife, brought it down straight across Esther's wrist. There was a funny sound, an odd, sickening sound. Ada looked down.

Esther's hand hung limp, dangling down at the end of her arm, wounded and stricken, sick as a fallen bird; there were tears of pain gathering in Esther's eyes. She held out her hand and looked at it; the tears began to move slowly down her cheeks, she bit her lips, she looked at her sister with big gray eyes filled with pain. "Broken my wrist."

Ada looked at her, her face working in on itself, all the lines and bones suddenly seeming to collapse, the face a ruin of planes and shadows, and unbelievable as it seemed to Lois, Ada threw her arms around Esther, she hung on Esther's shoulders, crying out, trying to bring up a veil of tears, she who never wept, as she never smiled, but the tears were not there, only agonizing cries fell from Ada's lips, and in the air the sound of despair, the cries of caring.

At that moment the telephone rang. They all looked around.

"Somebody . . ." Iris began.

Somebody was always Stewart. Even he seemed to know that. He got up and left the room. From the hallway came sharp, insistent shrieks; then they stopped, Stewart must have picked up the receiver. Stiffening, Eileen and Lois looked at each other. They both knew.

Without looking at Eileen, Lois went past all the people crowded around Esther, round the buffet, out into the good parlor, and past the parlor into the hall. "It's for you," her uncle said in surprise. "I was just about to call you." He handed her the phone without waiting for an answer and started back down the hall.

"Yes?" she said into the receiver.

"You mad?"

"No, *why* should I be?"

"Because I didn't come."

She was silent.

"I want to come over and see you. After everyone's gone. That all right?"

"No, not tonight. I've had as much as I can stand tonight, I can't take another thing, not tonight."

"Listen, Lois—"

"I can't listen to anything, Stan. I've heard too much already. I don't want to talk to anyone. I just want—"

"What is it? What's happened?"

"I can't talk now. I'll see you tomorrow—if I can. I'll call *you*," she said, and before he could argue she hung up.

The eyes glittered. Like her mother's, Lois thought.

"He called *you*"—throwing out a hand, a hand like her mother's. "It was *you* he called."

I'm sorry, Eileen, Lois thought.

But what good is being sorry?

That's what my mother always used to say, I'm sorry. And what good did it ever do her? Just to say you're sorry, that never does anybody any good. Being sorry is nothing.

> *Knowing You to move in mysterious ways*
> *Knowing You to move in strange and mysterious ways*
> *I have turned O Lord in fear and trembling*
> *And never quite believing, never quite not believing*
> *I have sinned and am sorry*
> *I have believed in the blind blank wall*
> *And am sorry*
> *But being sorry is never enough.*

And so, stay silent.

Chapter Four

ONE day she will be dead, Eileen thought, looking at her mother, and Papa will be dead, and Aunt Esther—all of them—dead. Even Lois. But not for a long time, not for what will seem forever and ever, and all that time, all those years and years that I am waiting, I will be the one who is alone. All alone.

Alone. Ethel has a husband, Eileen thought. Ethel's going to have a baby. She thought of Ethel taking her aside and saying, "Do I show?" while Eileen stared at her in astonishment. "I'm"—Ethel's hot hand had pressed against her cold one—"gonna be a mother." She's just like all the others, Eileen thought. She'll have her husband and her baby and what will she care about me? What did she care anyway? she asked herself. I was just someone to write letters to. What does anyone ever care? Stan used to—

Mama never forgave Aunt Esther, Mama never stopped hating her. All these years Mama has carried that around with her, and that's the way it will be with me. I will never forgive Lois, never as long as I live.

You will be punished. No matter how long it takes, you will be punished.

Mama waited all these years, but she got what she was waiting for. Mama, Eileen's heart cried out to her, how could you? How *could* you?

He could buy her a ring. They would get married just as soon as they could find an apartment, just as soon as they could get some furniture together. She didn't care what her mother would say, what his family would say.

We've been going together for years, she thought desperately, and now out of a clear blue sky he just stops calling, he won't answer me when I call him, he calls Lois—*Lois.*

He had promised nothing would ever come between them. All these years letting him touch her, letting him— Years and years nothing had ever separated them, nothing, and as soon as Lois—

Clutching her hands together in silent prayer, she had watched the door, waiting, all these past hours, while all the time Lois knew. He had called her. He had called *Lois.*

Eileen turned and looked at her mother. She was standing by the window, her head lowered, her eyes on her hands, her face closed to all but her own thoughts. Anyone looking at her would have thought she was daydreaming, but Eileen knew she was seeing in her mind the whole scene, reliving every moment, nursing her grievances, trying to reassure herself she had a right to revenge, that after all these years it was only just she be vindicated, that Esther, gone now to the hospital, had got only what she deserved.

Mama, Eileen cried out to her silently, Papa heard you say that about the other man.

Her mother looked up, as if she had heard Eileen's silent voice.

Eileen took a tentative step toward her mother. "Mama," she said, "let's go home"—and she felt as if she were sentencing herself to her own punishment: to go into that house permanently, to come out only to mount the bus and ride to work, finish her hours in another office, tied to a telephone, forced to listen to insults and anger, day after day, year after year, released only temporarily to return to that house she hated and feared, her father down cellar, her mother trailing her through the house saying, "You think I was right, don't you, Eileen? I was right, about Esther, you think I was right, don't you?" Year after year with the telephone ringing all day down at the office and never ringing at home at night, she would never see him again, never. Lois—

Mama broke Esther's wrist. Mama said that terrible thing about the other man. Papa—

Lois and Stan.

He had called *her.*

Lois and Stan.

Took the man, the only man I ever cared about, stole him from me . . .

Lois, Lois and Stan—

"Mama," Eileen cried out, "let's go home."

"Home?" her mother asked, as if the word had no meaning for her. "Mama, she used to say we all have to pay for our sins. Is a broken wrist payment for having taken the money?"

"Mama—"

"We will never really know," her mother said. "That's the worst part. We can never really be sure. Maybe," she said at last, "we can't be sure of anything." She took a step toward Eileen, one hand outstretched in supplication. "You believe she did it, don't you?" her mother cried out. "You believe she took the money, don't you?"—while Eileen stood motionless, wondering whether she even *cared.*

Chapter Five

KEEP OFF THE GRASS.

STAY IN THE LEFT LANE EXCEPT WHEN PASSING.

PAY YOUR BILLS ON TIME AND AVOID PENALTIES.

THE PARLOR LOUNGE IS RESERVED FOR THOSE WHO HAVE PAID FIRST CLASS FARE.

SMOKING POSITIVELY PROHIBITED IN THE LOBBY.

Signs, this way, that, everywhere you turned, a life fenced off by other people's idiosyncrasies.

THIS BEACH IS RESTRICTED TO RESIDENTS ONLY.

MEMBERS ONLY ARE PRIVILEGED TO PARK IN THE LOT.

BICYCLES ROLLER SKATES DOGS NOT PERMITTED PAST THIS POINT.

And always, at the end, the big billboard in his brain

MONEY MAKE MONEY

Aw, to hell with it. What good did thinking about it do? You can't manufacture money with your mind, Pete thought, pulling Frank along. And sure as God made little—little children, as sure as God made children and man made money, his goose was cooked. God, why did that have to happen to Esther in his mother's house? Never leave them any of her money now. She would blame them. Even if it wasn't their fault, even if they had all done all they could, getting her to the hospital, and staying to see she was all right. But he knew Esther wouldn't think anything had been offered at all. Pete bet that right this minute Esther was in that hospital grousing about them all. Everyone knew how peculiar she was.

Peculiar, that was a hot one. Cracked, that was more like it. Nutty as a fruit cake. Marbles in her head. Bats in the belfry. The windows wide open upstairs and the wind whistling through.

"I can't keep up," Peggy complained. "Not and—"

He slowed, not listening. She was in back of him, the children woven in between them like stitches in an irregular pattern. They only had four hands between them, and with five children it was hard to keep track. Frank was always dragging one along beside him. Pete looked down. Yes, he had hold of Blake, pulling Blake as firmly as his own father was pulling him, the three of them joined together by a relentless bridge of flesh.

Five kids to bring up, Pete thought with a sinking heart, and no job. Still, Carolyn had promised. But Ralph hadn't said anything yet. Carolyn had talked to him, hadn't she? God, she *had* to. Still, with this family, he thought with a sinking heart, you never *knew*.

The whole family was bats, that's what. His Aunt Esther, screaming and hollering to take her to a general practitioner, what did she want to go down and have all those expensive X-rays taken for; that stupid Ada, imagine going and walloping someone right in front of everyone—broke her goddam wrist, he thought in amazement, she hit so hard she broke the bone—and the kids right there, looking at the whole thing. It was criminal, that's what it was, someone ought to take action against her; even if she was his own aunt, he'd testify against her.

He looked down at his oldest son, and Frank stared back at him with dark, antagonistic eyes. Every time anyone looked at him, looked at him closely, Frank went on guard, as if he were expecting to be misused. He's got the same goddam blood, Pete thought.

Imagine hitting your own sister so hard you busted her wrist. He shook his head. It was simply beyond him.

Why couldn't they all just get together once and have a decent time, drink a little beer, tell some jokes, horse around a bit, eat, go home—*in peace?* But no, that was asking too much. Never go through that door, he thought, thinking of the back kitchen door which he and Peggy automatically always used, without knowing, without being absolutely sure I'm heading for trouble.

There was a babble of voices all about him, the children arguing and at one another, as usual. He supposed they had been going on like that all the time, but he had learned the trick of shutting himself off from the racket around him and going inside, where he stayed, still, with his own thoughts. Carol Wilson, he thought, and stared out at the tumbled weeds in back of the garage.

Funny thing about a woman—about money. When you didn't have a woman, when you were short on cash, you could think of nothing else, pursued night and day by worries about money, wondering how in the name of heaven bills would ever be paid, how the salary could be stretched, where in the future there was a breather from debts and obligations.

And someone like Carol Wilson, a full, voluptuous woman with deep-cut dresses and flashing white thighs . . . That was the sum of his life: endless dreams to delude himself; the reality was right in front of him, the sagging garage, the ravaged patch beyond where his father had once

grown the tomatoes, a streaked sign: PRIVATE PROPERTY, DO NOT PARK
HERE.

Always a sign: even on the tombstone. R. I. P. *Died in the service of
his country* (not me, not me, I had asthma, *asthma*). *Beloved of* . . .

No more tomatoes. His father hadn't grown them in years, and yet Pete
seemed for an instant to see his father, late in the afternoon, moving
among the plants. His father always went out in the early morning and in
the late afternoon on his round of inspection. In the morning he was
watering and pruning; in the afternoon he was looking for bugs. He would
walk slowly and solemnly through the rows of plants, bending down,
using his deft fingers to pinch off bugs. He carried, in the twilight, a little
can of kerosene and dropped offenders down to drown. Nothing en-
ergized his father more than an attack of insects on his new leaves. His
father nearly went wild with anger when he saw a leaf that had been
ravaged, his hands holding it up in shock and disgust as he saw the little
chewed section, the sky showing clear and blue through the green. *Bugs,*
his father would say with such violence he made Pete wince.

Then, one year, his father just didn't bother to put in plants. He never
said anything about why he didn't, he just didn't, and it wasn't, Pete
thought now with surprise, until almost the middle of summer that anyone had thought to comment. They had all noticed, he supposed, but they
just hadn't gotten around to asking. His mother had finally looked up
once and said, "Say, Dad, you didn't put your tomatoes in this year, did
you?" and his father had just looked up, calmly, matter-of-factly, and
said, "No," and that had been the end of that.

How's come after all those years he had stopped? Pete wondered.

Too much trouble, Pete decided. We could never use all those
tomatoes anyway. Mom was always having to can them. She was probably glad he quit. Like those damn frogs. Everything Dad did just turned
into trouble for someone else. That's what they'll write on his tombstone:
I was always trouble for someone else.

And on mine? he asked himself. *He told himself there was always
someone worse off than himself.*

Must be, Pete thought. But, logically, carried to the final conclusion,
who would be the world's most worst-off person? He tried to refine it:
strip it down to the most terrible picture he could conceive. Crippled, of
course, and blind; deaf and dumb. And black, yes, black—although perhaps this wouldn't have any significance if the person didn't *know,* and
how could he know if he were blind and deaf and dumb? There was the
problem, he decided, getting into the car.

Well, he would have to *go* blind, Pete decided, so that in the course of life the one last remaining prop would be removed. Before, this person, the world's most worst-off person, had at least seen: couldn't move (crippled), couldn't hear or speak (deaf and dumb), black (living in the South, Pete decided), and then starting to go blind. An orphan, abandoned on some doorstep, brought up in some cold, cheerless institution.

No, Pete decided, worse than being an orphan would be being born into this family. But if this guy was deaf he wouldn't be able to hear all that crap that went on. And, god, to make it really awful, to be so bad off nobody else was worse, one of the conditions would have to be hearing all the guff his mother gave out, witnessing all those crappy scenes with the rest of the old biddies, being forced hour after hour to answer questions like, *Tell me, what do you think God really thinks about— about suicide?* Biting her lips and looking down at the ground, really perplexed. She was thinking of her sister Organdy of course. Another loony one.

Whole family full of them. One myself, he decided bleakly.

The motor was warming up, but he could hardly hear it over the children's voices. They had zeroed in on him again. My brood, he thought, and then (looking at Peggy), My brood mare.

She over the curse yet? he asked himself. Should be. And it's one of the safe days. We could have a little relaxation, he decided. And, god knows, we deserve it, after this night.

He leaned across and gave her a light kiss on the cheek, and she glanced up, startled, and threw him a suspicious look. She knows what's up, he thought. Now, what's the matter, why doesn't she want to? It's a good safe time, right after she has the curse that way, you get four or five days, no worry at all. Why doesn't she want to?

She looks pretty good in that dress. Nothing like Carol Wilson, he thought with a sigh of resignation, but the Carol Wilsons of the world were not for him. He could have counted on that in advance, like everything else. No matter what he wanted, he always knew it was going to cost more than he could afford.

They could put that on my tombstone, he thought.

He eased the clutch out and began backing down the drive. God, the number of times his mother had jammed her car against the bank in back. So, he asked himself, what do you care? It's her car, let her wear it out. It's her life, let her ruin it: *You've ruined your life, ruined it,* there was a phrase for you. She must have screamed it at him a million times when she first heard about Peggy getting knocked up.

Trouble was, it was true.

He had absolutely no feeling of wanting to go to bed now, and that showed you how deep the whole business went, because—hell—driving a car, that always increased his desire. He looked through the windshield sullenly, watching the lights of the other cars spin by, thinking, Frank was the start of it all. Not that it's Frank's fault, but . . .

I'm thinking just the way she does, Pete thought. Peggy holds it against him, I've got to be careful I don't—he went and broke that radio set right off. Two ninety-eight just plain wasted. And then she—looking sideways quickly at his wife—went and carried on something awful. The waste, the waste, that's what *she* always screams when she gets going.

A family of screamers, his mother, Peggy, all of them. Even the children screaming. "Cut out that screaming," he shouted at them, feeling the rage rise in him. "I want a little peace and quiet for a change."

For a moment the car quieted down. He could feel the kids holding themselves in, but from past experience he knew this wouldn't last. They would be at it worse than ever in five minutes.

He let his imagination soar in the unhoped-for silence that settled about him, giving it free reign in the splendor of sudden silence.

A fancy hotel with a big bed, one of those oversized beds you saw advertised in the papers, and she had on that swell dress he liked, the tight green one with the low bodice, she wore it to work, he suspected, when she had a heavy date later, and when she bent over to write out the sales slips you could see the top of her big breasts, pushed up, the bra she was wearing must be pulled real tight, because her breasts were pushed up, two pinkish apples whose tops showed, god, he wanted to lean over and put his teeth against them. Carol Wilson would be wearing that dress and he would . . .

"Cut it out, just keep quiet, will you?" he demanded, for the girls, Mary and Sue, had started one of their fits of giggling, and if there was one thing that really bugged him it was that terrible shrill sound their voices made when they started teasing each other. He could stand bickering and quarreling, even the whining which really drove Peggy up the wall (she would stand in the middle of a room, her hands pressed against the sides of her head, screaming at the top of her lungs, "If you don't stop that whining, I'll go right out of my mind"), but he absolutely could not take the sound of that childish giggling.

His daydream was ruined. It was a kind of nightdream, he corrected himself, looking out into the darkness. My nightdreams, he thought. If Peggy knew what went on in those dreams, he told himself, boy, would I

be in for it. If she knew, for a matter of fact, how I kind of imagine it's
Carol Wilson when I'm doing it with her, boy, would she—but all the
same it was hard making believe. I mean, he thought, you run your
hands over her, over Carol Wilson, that is, it wouldn't be the same at all.
She was made, really stacked, whereas Peggy—

To hell with it, he thought, down there it's all the same, isn't it?

I don't know, he thought. I'll bet it isn't. I'll bet it's different down
there too. Carol Wilson— He sucked in his breath, trying to obliterate
the image in his mind. No good getting himself excited, Peggy wasn't
going to.

Why not? he wondered. She should feel like it. And anyway, I mean,
he thought, she should do it anyway, whether she feels like it or not, it's
been five, six days now since I've had it. It isn't good for a man to go
that long. No wonder I start thinking of other women, no wonder I want
to mess around. If your wife won't let you do it, why shouldn't you look
around? That was fair, wasn't it?

You have a right to expect—

He left the thought unfinished as he made the turn into his own driveway. They had left the light on over the front porch, and the house
looked nice; with the small light illuminating it, all the peeling paint and
the cracking window frames didn't show up. It would be a nice house,
too, if it were fixed up, if there were only, say, two people living in it.
Lots of room, lots of privacy, lots of— If I came home with Carol
Wilson, to a house like this, just the two of us, we wouldn't even go in
the house, he thought. We'd do it right in the car, in the garage.

It was an exciting thought, but he knew it didn't do any good to dwell
on it. The kids—it was out of the question. Instead they would both go
in and start getting the kids ready for bed; by the time the five had gone
to the bathroom, changed their clothes, brushed their teeth, got drinks of
water, done whatever else they were always doing, Peggy would be
tired and cross and really impatient and the desire would be drained
right out of him, all that waiting, and they would just get in bed and lie
there, staring up at the ceiling, hearing the fan going on the dresser, the
insects at the window, they had at least been able to get screens last year,
just lying there trying, he knew, to work up the energy to do what ought
to be a lot of fun, the pleasure gone out of the only free thing they could
do that might be a little fun, lying there, staring up at the ceiling, and he
always had to ask her, that took something out of the whole act too;
leaning over and saying, for instance, You feel like it tonight? and she
would let go with one of those martyrish little sighs, just like the sound

his mother used to make when she started collecting the laundry or getting supper, as if, well, I have to do it (sigh, sigh) so I might as well get at it (sigh, sigh); Peggy would emit one of those little martyred sounds and say, Okay, or All right, or something equally romantic, and then she would just sort of flop over and throw her arms around him and make with that flat I-guess-I-have-to-go-through-it love-making, her kisses as stale as her breath, her body as flat and unresponsive as her caresses, she never liked to do anything different, she always wanted to do it the same old way, not one goddam new innovation in years, just pressed up against him, handling him like he was a hot dog or something, no gentleness or tenderness or passion or anything, pulling him over on top of her and just grinding away under him as if she were doing the dishes or mopping the floor or any of her other little chores around the house, until *pffft* off he came in spite of himself; then what did she do? She pushed off, leaned over, took a tissue, wiped herself off, just as if she were going at one of the children's noses, sighed again (oh, it was a family of sighers all right), turned over, and in a minute she was breathing steadily and sleepily into her pillow and a second later snoring.

That goddam snoring.

Everyone else was out of the car; he was still leaning over the steering wheel. He hadn't even turned out the car lights. Brutally, relentlessly, remorselessly, he was going over the painful details of their cohabitation. They came in on him with all the clarity of their infinite repetitions; he could imagine how the night ahead would be because it would be a repeat of a hundred—no, a thousand, he thought—nights of the past, those short, sweaty sessions on soiled and sewn sheets, his lust and desire emptied out of him into the cold container of his wife, she counterfeiting scarcely at all even the outward symbols of response. She cared so little that she didn't even bother make-believing, just lay there under him in resignation, *getting through it.*

Even in the beginning, he thought in cold and honest self-appraisal, even when we were out in her grandfather's barn, even that first time, messing around in the hay, when we just sort of got carried away, and I pulled up her dress, and she was all moist and warm (she's cold and dry now, he thought), all moist and warm and furry, he had nearly gone off before he could get down between her legs, even then there had been a feeling of disappointment. It was that look in her eyes, her eyes all wide and dilated, looking up at him, and her mouth stretched out under his, almost, he thought, with a twinge of intuition, as if her mouth were like her—

Twisted and hurt, that's the way her mouth looked. I knew I'd come too fast, it hadn't been any good for her, but I couldn't help myself. And then later when we took more time at it, I don't think she much enjoyed it anyway.

Why not?

Scared of getting pregnant maybe, and then getting pregnant, and maybe all the time now she's so scared about making a mistake again, she can't relax and enjoy it.

Well, what the hell, he asked himself angrily, why can't she at least relax and enjoy it on the days like this, the safe days? That would give her some times during the month when she wouldn't have to freeze up.

Why can't I have a wife that feels a little passion once in a while? Why can't I have a wife who's interested in experimenting once in a while? Is that too much to ask, just a wife who gives me a little lift in bed every once in a while?

"What are you waiting for, Pete?"

"I don't know," he said abruptly. "Just sitting here thinking. Just sitting here having a little peace and quiet."

"But you've got the keys. We can't get in until you unlock the front door."

"Okay, okay, I'm coming."

He opened the car door and climbed out. The garage was a mess, kids' toys all over everywhere, some of the lawn stuff pushed up against the back. A mess, he thought, a goddam mess, and I don't even feel like making the effort to clean it up. What's the use? he thought. A couple of days, it'll be back the same way. With kids that's all there ever is, a constant process of cleaning up, everything getting messed up again, cleaning and messing, cleaning and messing. It's driving me out of my mind, just the way it's maybe driven Peggy out of hers, always knowing that nothing's ever going to be straightened up. I want a little order and neatness in my life.

And money, a voice inside cried out. How about a little money?

He went up the walk, jingling the keys. They would put the kids to bed, they would put themselves to bed. She would lean over and take him into her indifferent arms and press her indifferent mouth against him and run her indifferent hands over his flesh, and in indifference he would go through the motions of love. What was their life? And he remembered his earlier image: to sweat in bed on soiled, sewn sheets.

Leaning up against the side of the house, waiting for him to unlock the door, her eyes closed, her face still, Peggy looked dead in the white light.

He stared at her. My wife, he thought, looking at that still face which seemed to him to be growing older every minute, the lines and wrinkles enlarging, the skin getting flabbier and flabbier. She looked terrible. A moment of fright passed over him. Supposing she were sick, supposing something happened to her and he was left to look after the house and the kids as well as have his job? Carol Wilson would never take on five kids, five screaming, messing kids. "You all right?" he asked anxiously, leaning over her.

She opened her eyes, staring up at him. She looked just terrible. "I guess so," she said, sighing (always sighing, he thought). "It's just— just that it's been a terrible evening. I don't know—for once I thought maybe I might have a good time. A new dress, and all," she said, her voice dying away on the words *and all,* those two little words seeming to express all the disappointment she could not put into words.

What did she mean *and all?* What the hell did she expect from one of those crazy parties of his mother's? That she would have a good time?

He bent over her, examining her sharply. The face, how old and tired it looked under the porch light. And the eyes— Pete looked away quickly. It was like looking down on a rainy day and seeing those little streaked specks of oil, two small drops, black and iridescent, ugly.

"Well," he said uneasily, fiddling with his key, "maybe we can get out sometime—next month maybe. Go out to dinner, you know. So you can wear your new dress again."

"Oh, Pete, how can you?" Her voice was as bitter as the line of her mouth. "We can't afford to just go out. With the money for a baby-sitter and all—it doesn't matter anyway," she said. "I mean, just eating dinner out, that doesn't change anything."

He turned around, a little frightened. In her voice he had surprised genuine despair, not the whining, nagging complaints he was used to, but defeat, total and real, as if she had surrendered any hope of a reprieve and were reconciled to—to things too awful to put into words.

"Aw, baby—" he began.

"It doesn't matter," she said wearily. "Let's just open the door and get the kids to bed. I'm so tired I could drop right on the spot and never get up again."

The door swung open. The children crowded up against him, pushed past him, but she still leaned against the side of the house, her eyes

L

closed, her hands hanging limply from her arms, dead weights. "It's open," he said at last.

"You go on in. I just want to stand here a minute. Just," she said, opening her eyes and seeming to apologize, "to breathe a little in, as you'd say, *peace and quiet.*"

"Well, okay, Peg, if that's the way you feel. Sure, you just stand there for a while. I'll tell the kids to get started."

There was no answer. She had closed her eyes again and she was so still that it was hard to tell whether she was actually breathing or not. Got to, Pete told himself a little anxiously. She can't just keel over like that, die standing up against a wall. That's not how people die. What's the matter with you, anyway? he asked himself. She's not sick. Why should she die?

She looked dead, though.

He went into the house and stood in the middle of the living room, glad to be away from her. There were kids all over, and the place was a mess. Then he remembered that Peggy had just let the house go, even the beds were unmade; she had taken a nap—a nap—that afternoon. She must have been looking forward to the party, really looking forward to it. It's because she had a new dress, he told himself, she hasn't had a new dress in ages, hasn't had anything new in I can't remember when.

But he wasn't sure that was all of it. There seemed to him something more must be involved, to upset her that much. What? he asked himself and sat down to consider the problem.

But his mind remained blank. He couldn't for the life of him figure anything she might have had to look forward to. She couldn't stand his mother for any length of time. The rest of the family, well, she could take or leave. She liked Carolyn, he knew, but she never felt at ease with her. Carolyn had too much money, too many new clothes. And what could she care about Lois? They had nothing at all in common. Who else was there? Eileen—but I mean, he thought, who'd raise any temperature over her? Erwin and Helen—no, it was not one of those people. He simply for the life of him couldn't figure it out; it must be having the new dress for Stu's and Ethel's coming home. Just a new dress, and then everything was spoiled with Ada and Esther carrying on like that.

Upstairs there was terrible confusion. Pipes were throwing up water. Someone was running the tub, someone else the sink. The toilet flushed, there was the pounding of feet from room to room, doors slammed, drawers opened and shut with minor explosions, arguments broke out, voices were raised in anger and fatigue. "Settle down up there," he shouted.

Of course it did not one bit of good, screaming at them that way. It didn't even do any good to go up and try to bring them to some kind of order. With five he genuinely doubted if there was anything that would make any noticeable difference. Maybe money—always money—a vast estate where the children could just lose themselves, and he could find a number of hiding places, maybe that might make a difference.

That's what they'll put on my tombstone, he decided: *He looked for any number of hiding places.*

And never found one.

Looking for a hiding place, always on the run, keep off the grass, stay in the corridor, the straight white corridor . . .

Using his wife as a hiding place, her body the place he hid from himself, sinking down to oblivion in the satisfaction of the senses, not even a real satisfaction sometimes, more a stupefaction: hiding in the stupefaction of the senses, that was the only escape.

Does she know I'm hiding when I come to her? he wondered.

He got up and went across the room swiftly. She was still leaning against the house, still as a statue, white as death. Scary. "Peggy," he called out softly.

"Huh?"

"Listen, Peg, I just wanted to—" But how could you ask your wife a question like, Is it any good at all in bed with me? Do you feel you're hiding, you're safe, when you're with me?

He stood in the doorway, staring at her; he wanted to try to make up something to her, her not having a good time tonight, for instance, his being so—so inadequate. But what could he ever do to make everything up to her, all those countless nights she had lain back, tired out, beyond caring, worn out with work and crushed by the demands of the children, and still ahead of her she had to hide him, care for him, what could he ever do or say to make up for all those terrible, trembling nights? Just some sign, he thought, some gesture, that will show I understand, I care.

"You want a beer out here," he asked, "a nice cold beer? There's one in the icebox."

Then he told his lie, the little lie meant to ease his conscience, to bring his soul's salvation, thinking that it was a gesture, a sign to her of his good intentions, a sign to show her he was ashamed and wanted to do penance, a sign, no matter how small, that had some meaning, because if you made the gesture and the other person knew about it, and saw you cared, then that made up for what you *hadn't* done, didn't it, that rectified the past, didn't it?

He gave his sign. *"You* take the beer," he said, and then he told his lie. "I don't want it."

She opened her eyes. She stared straight at him, straight into him, seeming to see right into the center of him. "I don't want it," she said coldly, looking at him with eyes full of unforgiveness. "What good will *one* beer do me?" she asked, looking straight into the heart of him.

He stood still, stricken, speechless. If you can't do good even when you're trying, what hope is there?

Chapter Six

A feast is made for laughter, and wine maketh merry: but money answereth all things.

All the wisdom in the world you could find in one book, Ella thought. It was true: money did answer all things; money meant more than wisdom or love or loyalty or blood.

Ella thought of the night Lydia had died, how she had saved herself by submerging her arms in hot, soapy water, how she alone had washed and dried all the dishes, the one time in her life Iris had been too preoccupied to carry on—at least about her good plates.

Ada did that to her own sister, all because of money, Ella thought. . . . *if the thief be found, let him pay double.*

But who could say for sure Esther was the thief? I could, Ella thought. I know, not by my eyes, not by anything I see, but down deep in my heart. She took the money and when she took it she put a curse on the whole family.

When is that curse over? Ella asked herself.

When none of them care no more, she answered herself, when that money no longer matter.

But it seemed to Ella an infinity lay ahead before one or the other of them wouldn't stop in the midst of daytime chores or lie awake far into the night asking the poisoned question: Who gets the money when Esther is gone?

Someone handed Ella a pot, and gratefully she began to dry. If she couldn't keep busy, Iris would make her go to bed.

It would have been better, she considered, if that old woman, old Aunt Clara, had never come. But she had come, and Lydia had let her *stay*. Knowing about the money, Ella thought, coveting the money, that money that cause the quarrel that kill her, that money that keep Ada and Esther apart all these years, that money that now was starting to poison the children. She thought of the moment Esther had been taken to the hospital, how Ada had given that one cry, "Gone," knowing the money was lost not only to her, but also to Eileen, watching while Iris said, "Stu, Stu'll drive you," knowing Iris wanted the money for hers. Ella thought of Frances nervously breaking in, saying, "Erwin—let Erwin drive you, he's such a good driver," while Esther had taken her time, seeming in the silence to be weighing, judging, saying at last, "I'm going with Erwin. He's got good sense. Let Erwin drive me."

And Lois, she never spoke up once, Ella thought.

The pot was dry. She put it down, waiting.

"You go to bed, Ella," Iris said. "You're just standing there, staring into space. You're dead tired. You've been on your feet all day, and you know your feet—now you just hurry along and go to bed, leave the rest to us."

Sent to bed—that was what she had been afraid of all along, being sent to bed before she had had a chance to talk to Lois.

All my life I been with women you can't go against, she thought, feeling trapped and helpless, and don't look like at this late date things gonna change. I don't want that girl go back to New York without a talking to. It up to You, Lord.

But before, presumably, the Lord could intervene, Lois said in her ccol, self-contained way, "I'll go up with her, Auntie, see she's all right. You won't miss me for a minute, will you? There's something I forgot upstairs. I won't be long."

A hand, cool as that voice, fell on Ella's hot, feverish one. The fingers were long and slender, blunted like a man's, the nails short, without polish. Small hands, they run in the family, Ella thought, not hands like that. That come from her Daddy. Oh, that wicked, wicked man, Ella thought, moving forward, leaning on Lois, thinking, I got a seeing-eye child; that wicked man, he never care for nobody but hisself.

Ella smelled whisky straight off. Like her sense of touch, her sense of smell had been distended until it stretched taut as a sensitized instrument of recording, the least vibration setting up a response all out of proportion to the mechanism on which it played. Like life, Ella thought, things all out of proportion in importance to what their effect be. Who else think a *little statement* make such a big difference? But you take "One of the family, *really!*" and play it against "I just wish I had some- one like Ella around to help, you don't realize how lucky you are," and there was a big difference. God had given her her sign at last. He knew she was one of the family. Frances, long ago, that night her Mama die, she might not know. Lydia, she say, "Why, she's one of the family." Frances, her favorite, she say in that mean voice, "One of the family! Oh, Mama, *really!*" Frances might not know, but Carolyn knew. The young knew, and it was the young who needed her now, it was the young who were her family now, not Frances, not Ada or Esther, not even Iris. Carolyn and Stu and Lois, they were her family now. Much as she wanted to, she couldn't care about the others, but she could care about Carolyn, about Stu, and mostly about Lois.

A seeing-eye child, she had thought, but it was not true; the true seeing-eye was the second sight, a gift in one way, a curse in another. Get with the right hand and give with the left—the law of life, if you were lucky. Some seemed always to be getting, some always to be giving.

Second sight ran in Ella's family. Her mother had it. The day Ella's Grandma Lil dropped dead, early that morning, a morning like any other, Ella's mother had said to her, staring out past her head at Granny Lil in her rocker on the porch, where she was put in the morning and stayed all day, even eating out there, rocking gently back and forth until it was dark, staying on, sightless, but she said she was counting the stars, Granny Lil who was so old she needed bedpans and so proud that she held off all day long, rocking and mumbling, the smallest of the children around her, her hands wandering over their heads as if she were sorting apples, the way she had in the old days, the hand pausing here and there, the face frowning, as if she suspected she had found a marred one, fearful about its effect on the rest—Old Granny Lil had loved Ella as her mother had never loved her, so that her mother's words that long ago bright May morning struck terror to Ella's heart, as if one of the swords of sunlight had come down and pierced her heart— "You know," Ella's mother had said, "sometimes you know. They got that look. No mis- takin' that look. Some people, they can smell death, it hang over a man like the smell of sweat. Death coming down here today."

Ella's mother had the gift, Granny Lil had it, now Ella thought she must have it too—not so strong, weakened as it was passed on, but still something, a kind of special sight, a special way of seeing inside.

To look for her Mama, to find out why her Mama did that terrible thing. She come home for help.

And the second sight said to Ella, Don't let her stay, tell her to go away. If she stay, she ruin her whole life. Make her go. Tell her: Go away.

Ella stopped, turning sharply. Why did she feel that now, when only a day or so before she had wanted Lois to stay?

Ella grasped Lois's arm. They had stopped. "Honey," Ella began, and one hand went up. Ella was going to touch that face. Then she knew she couldn't. For one thing she was afraid; for another, she already knew —in her heart. "Honey, you come talk to old Ella," she said.

"I—" Then the voice died, a little as if a big puff of wind had hit a nest of dried leaves, your back was turned and you thought there was going to be a big storm; then the next instant the wind had died, vanished off the face of the earth, and when you turned there was a stillness, but all the leaves lay trembling, quivering for a moment before they fell still, so that even though you couldn't see the wind, you knew it had been there: that was the way Lois's voice sounded.

"You tell me," Ella urged. "You come tell this old woman, she love you."

From down the hall the bathroom plumbing went into operation. They heard water rushing into the toilet, the whir of water running through the pipes. Far down the hall someone snored.

Ella pushed open the door to her room and advanced toward the bed. The room was sparsely furnished. What, after all, had Ella to take up space? The clock Frank Timble had given her, that hadn't worked for years, what space did a little clock take up? There were some clothes, but what did she need with pictures or books or anything save an old rocking chair? The only book she cared about was engraved on her mind.

Instinctively, once she came abreast of the bed, she made for her rocking chair, settled herself in it, and began at once to rock back and forth. Like Granny Lil, she thought, come at the end to wait out death, rocking back and forth, easing the spirit in the rhythms of the past, those memories hanging by threads in the fabric of the mind. Oh, I have heard death in the silences, in the long night of silences; moved, I have, through silences that are sound, those voiceless cries the old know. Us the silences devour.

If Lois sat down, that would be a sign, that would mean Lois was ready to tell. She rocked. She waited. After a pause Ella heard the bed-springs sing out, the cry different from the one that day with young Stu, this sound more a sob than a shout, oh, the sound of love, the cry of love—pay attention, she told herself.

She rocked. Waiting.

"I guess," Lois began after a while, "you must wonder why I came back, I mean after I'd stayed away so long, two years—"

"I figure you come back," Ella said, rocking, "to look for something. That why most of us go back any place. If we happy, we glad to keep moving; when things go wrong, we think maybe we go back, find out where we done wrong and make amends, then we can go on again."

"I'd like a smoke," Lois said. "I know how you—"

"I never had no feelin' one way or the other. It was your grandmother, she was fixed on the notion. You want to smoke, you go ahead. Leastwise in my room."

"I'll have to go down the hall and get my cigarettes. If you don't mind waiting." Lois must have stood up—the bed gave a cry of release—and Ella bent forward, stopping the rocker.

"But you comin' back?" she asked. "I want you to come back. I want to talk with you."

"I'll come back, I promise."

It was the daughter of her baby Organdy, the daughter come back, and sometimes I don't know, Ella thought, whether I talking to the mama or the daughter. Lydia, Ella called out silently, can't you see fit to help me? To make me say the right thing?

Then, a second later, Ella knew that even if Lydia saw fit, she wouldn't —or couldn't. She had never really, it suddenly came to Ella, said the right thing—not to the girls. If she had said the right things, Ella thought, wouldn't they all be different? Wouldn't Ada have left her husband a long time ago, the way she wanted? Wouldn't Lydia have said something straight to Esther's face about the money, and the poison of that missing money wouldn't have been running through the family all these years? Wouldn't she have made Frances behave herself and have helped Iris? Wouldn't she have saved Organdy?

"Ella," Lois said from somewhere across the room, and Ella heard at the same time the sputter of a match. "Ella, what made my mother do it? Do you know, do you have any idea?"

Whish, whooo: she taking the smoke in, Ella thought, then she putting it out.

"The rest, they Timbles, but your mama, she—well, she a stranger," Ella said at last. "She different." She paused, for in Ella's mind, echoing and re-echoing in the small dark chambers back inside her head, a phrase floated up, one she could never, never use to Lois: *I am a stranger and a sojourner with you: give me a burying-place with you.* . . . "She had a lot of lovin' in her, your mother, and your papa, I don't think he had much, and the two of them, they live together and it was like puttin' salt and fire in the same house. You keep the two apart, they do fine. The fire, it heats the food; and the salt, it make it taste. But you put the salt to the fire—what happen then? The fire go out. Your mama, she like a flame, all her life she got that thing like fire, a big flame. Your papa, he like salt. Cold," Ella said, while in her mind she thought: an arrogant, self-indulgent man.

Ella stopped rocking a moment. . . . *Give me a burying-place with you* . . . the flesh, always the flesh, Ella thought, fire and the flesh, and no burying-place among you.

"A fire," she said, hearing her voice like the voice of Granny Lil, old and waiting to die. Death, O death my refuge and my fear; death, my final resting place. "A fire, it can't function without fuel, and after a while your mama, she was dyin' inside. Then she met someone who made her—blaze up again. The only trouble was she thought that wrong, to blaze. Nobody in the family do that. And so she think she done wrong and she go back, she throw the salt on the flame." *And a fire was kindled in their company; the flame burned up the wicked.* She wasn't wicked, Ella's heart cried out, it was him, *him.* "She just ashes, remembering the brightness, trying not to be sorry for what was, but something—I never know what—it make the flame burst up, something the salt hadn't completely covered; all of a sudden she found she on fire again, and then she run away—"

"You mean she went out to Denver?"

Ella nodded, Ella rocked.

"But what made her— If she— Why did she—"

"Your mama had a fine, sharp feeling about doing what was right. More than any of the others. She could see deeper somehow, and whatever she saw out in that faraway city, it must have seemed wrong to her, so she go and—"

"But you said—"

"I said she like fire, and she was, she was. But she didn't understand things the way other people did. She take them too hard. She consume herself. Maybe that it, maybe that it. Honey, I never know neither what made her do it. Only—" Ella paused, and inside she felt that something had moved, some piece of herself had come loose and seemed to be floating, free, about the area of her heart, as if she had dislodged a piece of knowledge she had never known she possessed. "Only you take anythin', I don't care what, and it don't give a little, it in for trouble. In this world what is hard, you bring a hard force against it, a thing harder than it, it gonna break. Honey, you gotta give a little. You got to be flexible. And when, at the end, your mama found maybe she wasn't like fire any more, but more like a stone, fire and stone, only gone hard, the way they say the earth do, first being hot and runny, and then gone cold and hard— I don't know, it the only way I can explain it."

They were silent. Ella could hear the scraping of the package of cigarettes. "You just like her," Ella said at last. "You hard and inflexible. You gonna break. Honey, you gotta give a little." She waited, but Lois, lost in the dark shadows, not even a vague outline to her, but lost completely, said nothing. "You gonna tell old Ella what happen?" she asked at last.

The bedsprings twanged again. Ella could picture Lois rising. Wait, she told herself, the hard things hard to bring out.

"I don't know," Lois began. "Maybe if I could get it out, it would be better. Maybe if I could just talk it out, some of it would go away. But you can't just tell anyone"—and there was a special plea in her voice, as if she were asking Ella to understand that she wanted to tell but that something held her back, Ella wasn't the one, the right one, the one who could heal her. "And now it's all locked up inside and I don't know whether I'll ever be able to get it out or not. I don't know whether anyone will ever give me back the confidence to believe—to believe I can open up and confess. I just don't know, Ella, not any more. That's part of the trouble, I'm all closed up—inside. There's this big hard knot inside and I don't know how to get it loose."

Lois paused, then she seemed to be summoning up strength. "I want to," she said. "Nobody knows how much I want to, but I can't. Not with anybody. I think I've lost the knack of knowing how to love. I gave too easily, I think, I got hurt, and now I'm all closed up, I can't give at all, and it bothers me, bothers me terribly, because that seems to me what's wrong with so many of us, we're all closed up, we can't love, and if we can't love, what can we do? What is life without getting outside yourself, if only for a little while? I came back to get back *inside* myself," she said. "To find out about Mama, a kind of pilgrimage, I suppose, looking in Springfield for the mother who died in Denver, and who was lost to me, to everyone, out in the cemetery all by herself, and I didn't find anything really but myself, the sense of having to have a self, and that's closed me up again—because," she said, pausing, taking a breath, "if you have a sense of self, it's also a sense of sin, the self in sin," Lois said slowly. "You have to go back out into the world, you have to sin, that's the sense of self. You have to go *outside* again. And there you are," she concluded, "words—how I've come to hate them." She stopped. Ella heard her catch her breath. "What's going to happen to me?" she asked, and it was a plea, a begging for direction. "What am I to do with my life?"

"Go away," Ella said, rising in the rocker, frightened, for the voice had sounded with the same notes as the mother's, the lost, lost mother, and it was the same question Organdy might have asked, standing there long ago in the house that was gone too, asking, What's going to happen to me, what's going to become of me? What's going to happen to all of us? Oh, Ella, what's going to happen to us?

She can't stay here, Ella thought. If her mother a stranger, she one too. "Go away," Ella said. "The only way is to go away. *Go thy way for this time; when I have a convenient season, I will call for thee.* The Bible say that, and the Bible know. Honey, I never thought I tell anyone go away, but you, you gotta go away from here, from this house, from this family, from that—" how could she ever say it, but she must, she must— "from that grave."

She forced herself to go on, not to pause over the word. "You find what you lookin' for outside here. You not the same as the others, you *marked,* that's what they used to say down in Kentucky."

Where the grass grows green, down in Kentucky, the land I never seen. Land of Tomorrow, the red people call it, my Granny say, the land I long for all these years, that land I never going to see. Down in Kentucky where the grass grows green. There a blight on this land, on the people too. If the land be marked, how can the people not be so? But she, she can go.

"Lois," Ella said, and even to her own ears her voice rang with conviction, "you go. You get out. Go find something more than just what here. What here not enough for you."

Ella crossed the room quickly, oh so quickly, knowing the exact count of steps, just how far it was to where, in the shadows, that girl must be standing, breaking her heart on sorrows her lips could not tell, and then she had Lois in her arms, her dark old failing arms, and she reached up, blind and near tears, and placed a kiss on Lois's cheek, saying at the same time, "Go, girl, and go with my blessing. I give it to you for your mama. I know she want you to have it. Don't think, Old Ella, she give me her blessing; think, My Mama, she give me the blessing.

"Go, and the blessing be on you. You don't need the guilt when you got that. It was the guilt killed your mama. Go with my blessing, child."

SATURDAY

SUNDAY

MONDAY

TUESDAY

WEDNESDAY

THURSDAY

FRIDAY

BOOK VII   **SATURDAY**

Chapter One

SOUNDS on all sides of him, and darkness: Erwin was dreaming. Faces emerged out of the darkness, distorted, magnified out of all proportion; then they receded, until, blurred and misshapen, they dissolved into a faint fraction of light. At first the dream was hard to define; people moved back and forth too quickly, the darkness obscured what was happening. But though the events and characters were obscure, his feelings of terror were not. It was a nightmare, intense and unrelenting, that he was having.

Suddenly out of the darkness a bone was being shattered, someone screamed. Esther . . . yes, it was Esther, her bones being broken . . . the missing money . . . someone had stumbled onto a clue at last . . . she has pearl earrings in her ear, a voice cried, and money inside, she's had it hidden there all the time . . .

Groggily he jerked his head up. Someone—Esther?—was calling his name. The dream shattered, splinters lodging for a moment in his mind, hanging perilously, swaying, falling away. He was awake. It was not fragments of a dream, but a voice that hung on his conscience. Someone was calling to him. "Uh—huh," he grunted, straining toward awareness. He was still trying to hold on to his vision: someone—Esther—lying on a table, coins coming out of—

"Erwin, oh, please . . ."

He shook his head.

"Erwin, in the hall . . ."

God, it was Helen's voice. Something had happened to Helen. "Where are you?" he shouted, groping in the empty bed.

"Hall— I'm in the hall. I'm so hot. I feel as if I were on fire."

In the hall? What in the world was she doing in the hall? At this time of night? One of those whims they get, he told himself. Flinging off the covers, he sprang from bed.

She was lying sideways on the floor, her nightdress pulled up so that she was almost completely naked, her swollen stomach cradled in her arms. "I'm so hot, Erwin," she said, looking up at him with eyes he did not recognize.

Her legs hunched up in a spasm, she gave a gasp, and he bent down, hearing his own voice murmuring words of encouragement as he tried to lift her, and she pushed against him, fighting him off, straining against him as if he were an enemy. "No, no," she begged. "Let me lie here. I'm so much cooler."

"You have to get up, Helen. You can't lie here."

"Why not?"

Her voice was petulant, childish, but it seemed to him that even in her stubbornness there remained some part of the cool, commanding logic that was her particular stanchion in life. Why, indeed, couldn't she? Why would she be any better in bed than on the floor?—and it would take such an effort to move her. After all, it was summer, there wasn't much danger of her catching cold. "All right," he said after a moment. "You wait here. I'll call Mother."

"I don't want your mother," she said sharply. "I want the doctor." Her speech came quickly but with effort. When she said *doctor* she tore the word in two, breaking it off in pain. "Doctor," she repeated, twisting about, her whole face screwed up in pain, looking mangled in the moonlight. That mouth—where had he seen it? Or one like it, somewhere, where?

"Don't worry," he said, bending over and patting her hand. "I'll get both of them."

There was no answer. She had turned away from him, hugging her belly, whimpering, her head turning back and forth restlessly. "Hot," she cried. "It's so hot. I'm burning up."

When he switched on the light in the living room, the room sprang out at him as if it were ready to grab him by the throat. For a moment he had the sensation he had been seized, but a second later he saw that what had frightened him was that everything looked as if it were grotesquely distorted, one of those carnival houses where the mirrors enlarge and magnify, contort and change so that the images thrown back are of a world seen in a madman's mind, or the mind of an abstract painter.

Helen would have the doctor's number filed in her little black push-button telephone book. She was very methodical about keeping all the numbers and addresses up to date. While he was trying to find the number under D (wouldn't it have been sensible to file the man's name under Doctor?), he dialed his mother. The phone kept ringing, Erwin went down all the Ds, then tried M, for Medical: no doctor was listed.

Why the hell couldn't his mother answer her phone? It must have rung twenty times. Cursing, he finished the Ms. Helen must have filed that blasted doctor's number under his own name. For the life of him Erwin couldn't remember it, although he'd heard her mention it dozens of times.

"Hello," his mother said sleepily. "Who is it? If it's the wrong number—"

"Mom," he said impatiently, "what the hell is the name of Helen's doctor?"

"What's the matter? Is something the matter with Helen?"

"Of course there's something the matter with Helen. Why else would I be calling you this time of night?"

"You don't have to get so mad."

"Look, just tell me the name of her doctor, get dressed and get over here, will you? I'm sorry," he said a second later, "but I'm worried sick. She looks awful."

"I'll come right away. I won't even do a real job on my face. Expect me in half an hour, honey"—and she hung up before he could ask her the name of the doctor again.

"Goddam it," Erwin said into the silent phone. He got up and padded down the hall. Helen was quiet, lying with one hand flung over her forehead, the tears streaming silently down her face.

"Is it that bad?" Erwin asked, kneeling beside her.

She shook her head, but he couldn't tell whether that meant yes or no. "Helen," he said, afraid that maybe she wouldn't understand him, that she was past comprehension. "Helen," he repeated, enunciating her name very clearly. "Listen, what's the name of the doctor?"

"Barlow, it's under B in the book," she said slowly. "Under B and under O, Obstetrician."

"Okay, honey, you just take it easy. I'll get him right away."

I need a drink, he thought. God, what if she lost the baby, right there, on the floor, before anyone got here? What would he do? You had to cut the cord or something. There must be a first-aid book around somewhere. All those books Helen collected, she must have something useful somewhere.

"Doctor Barlow?" he shouted into the telephone, and a sleepy voice cleared its throat preparatory to speaking, but Erwin couldn't wait. "Doctor Barlow, this is Erwin Mueller, my wife—my wife Helen—she's going to have a baby, the end of October, the first part of November—only something's the matter. Can you come over, right away, she's—"

"Is she bleeding?" the sleepy voice asked.

"I don't know. Wait a minute, I'll see." He ran to the door. "Helen, are you bleeding?" he shouted down the hall. He waited, wondering if she would answer.

"No, I don't think so," she said at last.

He ran back, fumbling with the phone. "She says no, she doesn't think so, but she's in awful pain, take my word for it, can you come right over?"

"All right. Keep her quiet. I'll be over as soon as I can."

Erwin ran back down the hall. "He's coming right away, Helen. Don't worry, don't worry one bit, you just be quiet." He looked down at her. "You don't want the doctor to see you like that, do you?" he asked anxiously. "Come on, let's get you back to bed, cover you up."

"I can't move."

"Sure you can. I'll help you. It isn't far, just a little way," he said encouragingly. "Let me carry you."

She shook her head. "Let me be. I'm so hot."

"But you—you're all exposed."

"Just give me a minute, just let me rest a little, then I'll get up."

Erwin tried to think of something he could do to help. He could get himself a drink, steady his nerves. God, he was shot—all that company in the house late, the hours they kept, that party at Iris's, and the last straw, that business with Ada and Esther. Now this.

He went back and poured himself a double Scotch and drank it neat. He ought to have had better sense; it almost made him sick. He went into the kitchen and opened the refrigerator, ready to begin the battle with the ice trays. They always stuck.

God, right here in this kitchen, Lois standing right over there, leaning against the sink, he had been taking out the ice, just like now, and she stood there saying through clenched teeth, If you must know the truth, I've just come out of an abortion. . . .

For the first time, earlier that evening, out at Iris's, he had felt really close to her. He remembered the talk they had had by the car, he thought of how like her old self she had looked in the warm afternoon light, he recalled the way she had turned to him on the way back to the house and said, "You know, it's funny, I can't think of you as married, as going to be a father. I always see you bent over the cereal box taking out the coupons and looking at the pictures and saying you already had Joe DiMaggio, couldn't that crazy old company print anybody else's picture. I always see you the way you were when I was eight or nine and you were twelve or thirteen and we didn't know what the world was really about and I was so crazy about you that I followed you everywhere."

She had paused. He would remember that pause all his life, the way she had stared up at him, so serious, so determined, and there had been a warning in him that something special was about to happen to him. "I think I must have loved you then more than I could love anybody else in my life, maybe more than I'll ever love anyone else. Isn't it a shame we have to grow up and lose that wonderful uncomplicated, uncritical kind of love? I don't think I'll ever feel it again."

Like an omen: I can't think of you as married, as going to be a father. A sign, his mother would say, a bad sign. You shouldn't ever talk about anything you don't want to happen. Maybe there was something in all this occult stuff after all.

And then later, when he had insisted he be the one to drive Esther to the hospital, there had been something about the look Lois had given him—

He put two cubes in his glass, hastily closed the icebox door, and fled from the kitchen. What a way to think. I mean, he thought, we let Mother do that card business and all because it's funny, it's just a game really, nobody takes it *seriously*.

I'm not such a hot Catholic, he thought, but I believe in God. That's the principal thing, isn't it? I miss church once in a while and I forget it's Friday now and then, but those aren't big sins, nothing you have to worry about really. I make confession at least twice a year, at Christmas and Easter, the times that count, and well, I mean, Helen—

Helen was Catholic, that was one of the things, he supposed, that had—well—kind of made marrying her easier. There wasn't the religious problem. She was liberal enough, but her old man—

It was beyond Erwin how anyone in this day and age could take religion that seriously. You know, he thought, looking at his glass, you're just easy about it; you don't ask your friends and they don't ask you. You go along, making your money and letting them make theirs. The chancers, they get ahead; the chickens, they just make out. But nobody—well, cheats. You can operate, he thought, like Chet, but you don't cheat. I didn't cheat in that game. Those queens and tens came naturally, but I played it for all it was worth, I sized up the situation, that's what makes the difference in the long run, how you look things over.

He was a little surprised to find he had finished his drink. Gotta watch it, he thought. Don't want the doctor to think I've been drinking. Don't want him to think I'm letting my wife down.

That damn dog, he thought irrelevantly, fetched for *her*. How's come she can do all the things I can't? How's come she knows about people like Stamos and takes all those strange little magazines and makes such a fuss over people nobody ever heard of? How's come she sneers at *Time* and *Life* and the *Reader's Digest:* what's the matter with *Time* and *Life* and the *Reader's Digest?* How's come she gets the *Manchester Guardian* sent to her, how can you read something like that, a newspaper practically printed on toilet paper? She got it at Smith, he decided.

There had been a time, he reflected uneasily, when he had been a little like that too. But, christ, it was a stage, I mean you didn't *stay* with it. It was all right for France and all but when you were in Springfield, hell, things were a lot different. He had never even considered bringing Denise back. That showed he had his head where it should be.

He had to get Helen back in bed. He didn't want the doctor—or his mother—to see her stretched out like that, her nightgown pulled way up so that she was all exposed. It wasn't decent.

He put the bottle back, started to carry his glass out to the kitchen. On second thought he put it in the cupboard next to the Scotch. Just in case.

He stood for a moment, reflective and uneasy. It was something about seeing his wife with her nightgown all hiked up that way. Reminded him of Denise. That damn Denise, she never even wore a nightgown. I mean, he thought, it was war and all, there were shortages, but it was kind of like she wouldn't have anyway. Sure he had done a lot of things in France he wouldn't have in Springfield, but now he was a married man with a *position.*

The hall was empty. Instantly relieved, he knew she had made it back to bed by herself. Good girl, he thought. He ought to have realized Helen would have better sense than to let the doctor see her like that. Everyone knew she had good sense, but more—taste. Hell, the Junior League hardly ever made a move without consulting her—and she was Catholic too, that really showed how far up she was. Everybody knew how the Junior League felt about Catholics.

There was no light on in the bedroom, but the moonlight was strong. Helen's face, in a slash of white, looked like one of those old-fashioned realistic sculptures she was always mocking. Her eyes were closed, her arms flung out across the top of the pillow.

"You feeling better? You're better now, aren't you, Helen?"

Without opening her eyes, without answering, she shook her head.

There wasn't anything he could do, anything he could say. For a moment he stood in the doorway, staring at her still lips. Only they weren't still, they were moving, she was saying something to herself. With a start, he realized she must be praying.

The lips moved steadily and surely, the way people's did when they were repeating a prayer. *O my God I am most heartily sorry for having offended Thee. . . . Our Father who art in Heaven, hallowed be thy Name. . . . Hail Mary full of grace. . . .* She's in a bad way, he told himself, frightened, embarrassed, not wanting to see her weakness exposed this way. Why, people only prayed when they thought they were going to die.

Unnerved, he retreated back toward the hall, his eyes still on those softly moving lips. How could she remember that many prayers? She was just going on and on. Must be saying the Hail Mary and the Our Father over and over. Like doing the rosary, you did—how many Our Fathers? How many Hail Marys? He couldn't remember; anyway they had it set up so you didn't have to count, you just felt your way along. When you came to a big bead, you changed over. Did you make the Act of Contrition on the Rosary? Christ, he couldn't remember.

He was back at the cabinet. Sweating, he poured himself a little drink. Maybe he ought to be praying. *Our Father who art in Heaven, hallowed be Thy name. . . .* But he couldn't remember any more. The words had deserted him. He tried the Hail Mary. But that wouldn't come either. Try the Ten Commandments, he thought. Honor thy father and mother. Don't take the Lord's name in vain. Don't commit adultery. Don't murder. How many was that? Four. He'd never get six more. There was one, wasn't there, about not bowing down before false idols, something like that. It would count. He had five. Half of them, and he couldn't for the life of him remember the rest.

If Helen was losing the baby, he ought to call the priest. Somebody had to baptize it or bless it, do something about its soul. Otherwise it wouldn't be saved. He didn't think it would be damned, not burn, that is, but unless it was baptized it seemed to him that he remembered it would have to wander. Some place where little unbaptized souls spent all eternity. Limbo.

But supposing he called the priest and the priest came and brought all his stuff and it was a false alarm? How would that look? But supposing she lost the baby and he hadn't called the priest? Her father would be furious. Oh god, he thought, why did this have to go and happen?

He heard a car coming down the street. A moment later he saw the headlights outside. Since it hadn't turned into the drive, he knew it must be his mother. She never parked in the drive because she couldn't back very well. Nobody in the family could.

His mother would know what to do about the priest. If the baby was lost and there was no priest, he could always say that his mother, who had a lot of experience in these kinds of things, hadn't thought he should call. Might frighten her anyway, he told himself, thinking of Helen. She would get scared seeing a priest. No, he would not call. He would just take the chance.

"I got here as fast as I could," Frances announced from the doorway. "Where is she?"

"In the bedroom. I wish—you'd take a look at her. She looks so—so pale. See if you think she's really bad. See if you think I should call the—"

Frances brushed past him. "The fifth is a critical month," she said. "All the uneven numbers are the ones you have to watch. Three, five, seven, they have special significance."

The dog was barking. He must have heard the car. "That damn dog," Erwin said. "He'll wake up the whole neighborhood. We've had enough complaints as it is."

Frances went quickly down the hall, into the bedroom, and over to Helen's side. She leaned over and peered down. "What's the matter, honey?" Frances said. "Don't you feel well?"

For a moment Erwin thought he was going to laugh. Helen lay there looking up, she couldn't even speak, her lips were still moving, making those prayers, and his mother comes in and looks down at her and says, "What's the matter, honey? Don't you feel well?" If he had been lying there, he knew he would have risen up and swatted her.

Someone was pounding on the door, and he turned and ran down the hall, thinking that with the doctor and his mother there he could relax a little, let them take charge. The dog was hysterical now, barking and screaming, running back and forth, jumping along the fence. If that damn howling kept up, everyone in the neighborhood would be on the phone. People might even call the police. That was all he needed at a time like this.

The doctor had his black bag and he was also carrying, incongruously, a paper bag. They went together silently through the hall, and when they got to the room Helen began to cry, real sobs of pain and fright. His mother fell back, as if someone had turned on her and denounced her. There wasn't much room between the bed and the window, and when the doctor went brusquely and professionally toward the bed he pushed Frances aside impatiently. She just stood there, squeezed up against the wall, staring at Helen aghast. It occurred to Erwin that his mother had never seen Helen cry before and that she was more shocked by that than she was by the idea that Helen might be losing the baby.

"You can wait in the hall," the doctor said over his shoulder, already opening his bag and scrabbling about for something. "I'll let you know if I need you." But Frances still stood staring at Helen, her face shocked and disapproving. "Wait in the hall, please," the doctor repeated more sternly, and finally Frances backed away, clucking her tongue, shaking her head, kneading her hands together.

"I'll get you a drink," Erwin said to her. "You look as if you could use one."

"She's sick," Frances said wonderingly. "She cried. Did you see her? The minute she saw him she started crying."

While he was pouring them both drinks she said, "I can't understand it. Estrella did her horoscope only a couple of days ago, and she didn't say anything about anything going wrong. I just can't understand it."

"Oh, Mother, for god's sake, don't start that now, can't you—"

"She didn't say anything about any trouble at all. She said it was going to be—"

"I tell you, I don't want to hear anything more about that nutty woman. I'm—"

But Frances wasn't listening to him. "You don't know what it's like," she was saying. "You don't have an inkling of what women have to go through. No man does. Oh, when I had you—oh terrible, terrible," she mumbled, looking down at her drink. "Waking up in the dark all strapped down that way, and squawking I was going to die, and they just left me alone in that room all by myself and Mama had never told me anything about what it was really like, and I thought I was going to die, I started screaming, and this awful nurse came in and she had the nerve, the unadulterated nerve, to tell me I was just having labor pains, it was nothing, it was going to get *worse*. I was never so mad in my whole life."

The doctor, looking upset and frowning at them, was in the doorway. Erwin tried to think of something to do with his drink, decided he couldn't do anything with it, considered asking the doctor if he wanted one, then thought, No, they can't drink when they're on duty, can they? and was still trying to make up his mind when Dr. Barlow said, "She's started to dilate. I'll need some medications. One of you can find a drug store and get them made up and bring them back. I think we can save the child, but—but it's going to be touch and go."

Erwin put down the drink, picked it up, finished it, then started down the hall for his clothes. Helen lay on her side. She was cradling her stomach in her arms again and she lay weeping softly, saying, "It's hot,

I'm so hot, oh can't somebody do something," and he didn't know what
he could do, so he just took his clothes and went into the bathroom and
started to get dressed. He had forgotten his shorts, so he just put his
pants on over his pajama bottoms. He realized he was a little tight—or
maybe just nervous—because when he tried to button his shirt he was
trembling so badly that he could hardly fasten the front.

But at least the dog had stopped barking. That was something.

Chapter Two

IT WAS curious how jubilant he felt, especially when he considered the
past few hours: Ada and Esther tangling that way and the sinking certainty he was out of the running for the money. They all were. Esther
would never forgive any of them.

Helen is going to lose the baby, he told himself. How can you keep on
worrying about Esther's money? Probably, he decided, because the
money was as good as gone and it was still even-steven about the baby.
He was right to worry about the more critical thing.

Erwin sat hunched over the wheel of the car, envisioning the scene of
his triumph in his mind: he came back with the medicine, the baby was
saved, Esther appreciated his driving her to the hospital and left him
her money, he came down a long street, riding in some kind of open car,
there were crowds on each side of him, people waved flags, he stood up
and held his arms over his head in a kind of boxer's salute, and the
people screamed and hollered and someone started the singing. *For he's
a jolly good fellow, for he's a jolly good fellow . . .*

All the boredom and monotony of the past days suddenly evaporated;
he was a man with a mission, on his way to get the medicine that would
save the life of his child. Helen would get well, he would sell some cars
in the next few weeks, rack up all those commissions, he and Helen
could take off for Paris the end of August. Hadn't one of those travel
books said September was an ideal month to go, with the schoolteachers
and college kids back in school? Cool then, too. Everything was going
to be all right, he had a feeling about it.

He drove rapidly, making for the center of town. No use hanging around here hunting, go right in to Capital and Ninth, bound to be a drug store open around there.

Nice night, really: lots of moonlight, stars all over the place, nobody around: peaceful. Surprised, he spotted a Walgreen sign up ahead, gave the car an abrupt swing and pulled in, gazing into the well-illuminated interior. A man in a white smock was leaning against the candy counter, reading a magazine. Around, illuminated by the powerful glare of fluorescence, bright stacks of merchandise emphasized the frail passage of flesh through the material world.

Erwin went in, trying to look properly worried, the way the husband of a wife who had started to dilate should. He gave the druggist the prescription, then fidgeted around the counters while the man went out back. It suddenly occurred to him he had never seen so much stuff for human misery and frailty before—pills, powders, plasters, tablets, drops, lozenges, inhalers, deodorants, sanitary napkins, dandruff removers, an endless pyramid of bottles and jars, packages and pillboxes stacked in ziggurats before him.

Maybe he should buy Helen some perfume. Evening in Paris. That was a good brand, wasn't it, and anyway it would remind her of the Europe trip, give her an incentive to get well.

"How much you want for the Evening in Paris?" he shouted toward the back.

"Two-fifty the set, the toilet water and powder."

Erwin looked at it. Might as well, couldn't go far off at that price, would show her he had been thinking of her. Maybe he should have called a priest. "You gonna be much longer?" he asked.

"Ten, fifteen minutes."

"I'll be back. But hurry, can you?" he added as he started out.

Standing on the quiet corner, the red neon light from the drug store showering over his clothes with an eerie, infra-red glow, he looked down the side street. The best bars were always on sidestreets. Sure enough, a green shamrock glittered at him from down the block. Ten minutes: time for two drinks, that wouldn't do any damage, the others had pretty near worn off already. Nobody could say anything about his having a drink to steady his nerves while the medicine was being fixed, he wasn't taking time out from helping, not if he had to wait anyway. Besides, he hadn't had to drive all the way into town, finding a Walgreen's open out here this way.

There were a couple of middle-aged men in back, talking loud, not really arguing, but challenging each other, something about Korea, who was responsible for Korea. "Nobody's ever responsible for a war," one said. "They just happen."

"The hell they do," his buddy said. "Nothing ever happens. Somebody's got to start it."

The bartender came down the corridor behind the bar slowly. "What's yours?"

"Two double Scotches. Straight. I'm in a hurry," Erwin explained. For the first time he was conscious of the actual time. There was a big clock over the bottles behind the bar: ten to one, it said. That surprised him, he had thought it was much later, three, four, say—surprised and comforted him, because if it was only ten to one there was a lot of time left to help Helen, not the way, for instance, there would be if it were three or four. That seemed to him another sign everything was going to be all right, and he drank his first Scotch with a sense of relief.

Since it was only ten to one, he might call Lois, she could come crosstown. She'd be a lot more help than his mother. She could stay in the guest room maybe, stay for a couple of days, help out until Helen got on her feet. She owed him a favor—hadn't he slipped her a hundred once, back when she needed it? He carried his second drink back to the telephone booth. He had only two quarters and three pennies in change.

"Hey, a nickel," he called out. "For the phone." The bartender leaned across the bar and handed him some change wordlessly; Erwin gave him a quarter. "And, hey, while you're at it, make me another, will you?"

"Green Lawn," a voice said slowly and sleepily.

"Uncle Stewart? This is Erwin. Is Lois there? I know it's late but—"

"Erwin?" his uncle asked, as if he were trying to think who Erwin might be.

Impatiently Erwin said, "You know, Frances's—"

"Oh yes, Erwin. How are you?"

"I'm fine," Erwin said, exasperated, "but is Lois—"

"Everything all right out there? You all right out at your house?"

"Well, as a matter of fact—"

"Nothing the matter out there, is there?"

"Helen has just had—"

"You want to talk to Lois?"

"Yes, just let me talk to Lois."

"I'll have to go wake her. You just hang on."

Erwin got his new drink, paid his bill, lighted a cigarette, and waited. It seemed to him forever before he heard Lois on the other end of the line. "Lois? This is Erwin. I'm in a drug store out here. Something's happened to Helen. I thought maybe you'd shum—" He had meant to say *come* and something had happened to his tongue. He felt betrayed. He'd only had two drinks, hadn't he? "Mother's out at the house," he started again, enunciating very clearly, "only, well, I'd feel better if you'd come out, maybe—"

She interrupted. He concentrated hard on following what she was saying, but she seemed to speak in such circles, saying everything round about. "We don't know how bad it is," he said at last, interrupting her, thinking that, no matter what she was saying, he had answered with a safe thing.

"I'll be over as soon as I can get a cab. Maybe you'd better give me the address. Iris is in bed and I don't want to wake her up after all she's been through."

He told her, working his tongue very carefully, too conscious of the fact he was having trouble with the numbers. He had to start all over and then, when he finally got through, she asked him to repeat it.

"All right, I'll be there just as soon as I can," she said. "Only don't you think you ought to get in touch with a doctor?"

"Doctor?" he asked stupidly. What was the matter with her anyway? He had told her he was in a drug store, hadn't he? Or had he? "I'm in a drug store," he said, thinking this was practically the truth, there was no sense in saying he was *near* it, "getting a prescription now."

"Oh, all right. I'll hurry as fast as I can, and—and I'm sorry, Erwin, I really am."

Ten minutes had gone by; the bartender was obviously closing. Erwin tossed down his last drink, picked up the glass of water on the bar and drank half of that, started out. God, he had forgotten to leave a tip. This whole thing with Helen had really thrown him. He went back and put one of his quarters on the bar, the bartender watching with that same look of aloof detachment, and then he considered a moment and added a dime from his other change. Bastard, he thought, thirty-five cents for putting three drinks on the bar. I wish I made a percentage like that. These guys, they look at you like you were dirt while they're waiting to take your money.

Righteous with anger, he went out, holding his head high. It seemed to him there was a whole conspiracy to rob him of money—Ada hitting Esther, Esther mad because none of them would keep her instead of carting her off to a hospital, that bartender, the doctor back at the house would charge him a pretty penny, Helen had spent all that money on clothes so that they *had* to go to Paris—thinking of Paris reminded him of the lousy deal he'd had on the car contest; he went into the drug store cursing quietly under his breath.

There was a little neatly wrapped package sitting on the counter, the piles of merchandise on either side dwarfing its real significance. "I was beginning to wonder if—" the druggist began.

"How much?" Erwin cut him off.

"Seven twenty-five."

"*Seven* twenty-five? What'd you put in there, gold?" Then, remembering his name was on the prescription, the druggist would know who he was, he tried to sound as if he were joking. "Well, gold or whatever you got in there, I hope it does the job."

The man looked at him coldly, collecting the outstretched ten-dollar bill. Bastard, Erwin thought, you've got your hand out quick enough too. They all do, he told himself bitterly. It's nothing but take, take, take. What're they going to do when I can't give, give, give any more?

"Seven-fifty, eight, nine, ten," the man counted into his hand.

Erwin looked at the change. He kept a quarter, handed the rest back, picked up the box with the Evening in Paris cologne and powder. "What the hell," he said. "It's only money."

"You want it wrapped?"

"Naw, I'll take it the way yis." His tongue had failed him again. Abruptly, angrily, he turned and stalked out. Take it easy, he told himself, take it easy, don't get so excited, there's nothing you can do, those guys (thinking of the drug-store man, the bartender) can charge you what they like, they've got you over a barrel. How the hell can you know how much medicine really costs? How the hell can you figure out what a shot's really worth? To hell with them, he thought.

He had trouble getting the key in the lock, and his foot kept slipping off the gas pedal. His vision seemed blurred around the edges.

Christ, he thought suddenly, clutching the wheel, I suppose I should have called her father. He'll be furious if anything happens. I can always do it when I get back, he comforted himself, I can say I was out getting medicine.

He admired and respected Helen's father, but it was hard to like him. Overbearing, that was the word, at least he thought that was what you called successful braggarts. If he hadn't had all that money, people would have just called him a boaster and a bully (he tried to walk all over everybody, but if anybody--anybody with more money, that is—ever stood up to him he backed down fast enough), but as it was they went on and on about how he was rough on the outside but he had a heart of gold, what a regular old diamond-in-the-rough he was.

The truth is, Erwin thought, peering ahead, looking for his turn-off, that he's just a lucky son of a bitch who knew where to cut corners and not get caught and how to hang around with the right people and make it pay off.

Still there was more to him than his bluster; he had taught himself to know a hell of a lot about cultural things, Helen's father had. Why, he had even hired a teacher to come out from the college and tutor him on painting and literature and stuff like that. That showed you how shrewd he was: Helen's father didn't bother wasting a lot of his own time learning the finer details of that kind of junk, he just paid someone else a measly little salary to teach him important things, the things you had to know to impress people. You had to admire Helen's father, no doubt about it, he was smart. But, god, he could be a pain. He was *always* right.

He's been decent to us, Erwin thought, making the turn at last, helping us with the down payment on the house, and I guess he gives Helen money for clothes, those pictures and all, and when he dies—

He pulled up in front of the house, and the last thing he thought before he exploded in anger was He'll leave us all that money so of course there's no point in alienating him but— And then he heard the dog barking and saw the lights in the houses on both sides of his shining across the street, and there was his mother standing in the front door talking to some man in a bathrobe, who was pointing out back dramatically.

Erwin swung the car into the driveway and saw that the man was Strang, his neighbor on the left, a big blowhard who had made his money in some pretty shaky deals. At least that was what people said, and where there was smoke there was fire.

Strang stood hunched up in his bathrobe, one hand jammed in his pocket, the other waving toward the back yard, his expression truculent. "Listen, Mueller," he said to Erwin before Erwin was more than halfway out of the car, "I'm sorry your wife's sick, but that damn dog's been barking for an hour straight. He's got the whole neighborhood up. You'll have to—"

"Okay, okay," Erwin said abruptly, stomping past him, not even looking at him. *"Okay."*

"It's not that I—"

"I'm not interested in what you think," Erwin said, whirling around at the door. "I don't give a good goddam what you think. Now what do you think of that?"

"Erwin," his mother said, looking at him as if she couldn't believe her ears.

Strang said nothing, staring at him open-mouthed. He and Strang had never liked each other, but they had always made a pretense of being friendly. He's nobody anyway, Erwin told himself, there's no reason why I have to be nice to him. He made his pile in some pretty phony ways, everyone knows that. "Now get the hell off my property," Erwin finished, "and don't come back."

A man's wife was losing his baby, and what did people do? Come and complain about the dog.

The doctor was standing in the dining room. "I've given your wife a sedative," he said. "She's calmer. Now if we can just stop the . . ." His voice trailed off, leaving the unexpressed hanging expressively in the silence that followed.

Erwin came up close to him to hand over the prescription, and as he held out his hand, moving close to Dr. Barlow, the man moved back instinctively, giving Erwin a startled look. It's the liquor, Erwin thought, he's smelled the booze.

His hand remained in the act of holding out the package, though the package itself was gone. He stared down at the outstretched palm, wondering what he could say. "My cousin's coming," he said at last.

But the doctor was going through the door to the hallway, the package tucked under his arm, his short legs working like those of a tired runner. "Can you make some coffee?" he asked. "It's going to be a long night"—and Erwin wondered which of them the doctor had ordered the coffee for. Who does he think he is anyway? Erwin asked himself. It isn't *his* wife. What difference does this all make to him? It's just a case. *I'm* the father. I can take a drink if I want to, to calm my nerves, there's nothing the matter with that, who does he think he is anyway? All those superior-looking bastards looking down their noses at me.

He went to the cabinet and opened the door with a jerk. The Scotch wasn't there. They've hidden it, he thought, outraged. "Listen, Mother," he said in a loud voice, swinging round, trying to steady himself, trying to control the fury that was coursing through him, feeling his breath come in tight spasms of absolute, uncontrollable outrage. *"Did you take that bottle?"*

"Bottle? What bottle?"

"Don't give me that. You know good and well what bottle I mean. The bottle of Scotch that—"

"What's the matter with you, anyway?" Frances asked. "Talking to that man that way, talking to me this way, not even going back to see Helen."

Christ, he had forgotten all about Helen.

But she must be okay, he reassured himself, I mean the doctor didn't say she was worse or anything, so that must mean . . .

He stood uncertainly, looking at his mother. She was biting the nail of her index finger nervously, staring past him out toward the back where the dog was still throwing out a bark now and then, not, thank god, in a steady stream of abuse, but more like the persistent stutter of a sobbing child who is almost ready to drop off into sleep.

She had told the truth about hurrying with her face. The patina of powder stopped at the chin; she had forgotten to do her neck; it shocked Erwin to see how old and furrowed the skin was. Like a chicken, he decided, staring at her. Like that goddam chicken old Aunt Clara used to have, that chicken with the skin disease. Mangy old Hetty, running all over his grandmother's house making one mess after another and getting into all kinds of trouble. He used to be scared to death of it. Mean, that chicken was, real mean. His mother's neck looked just like Hetty's, he decided.

Self-consciously, as if she could read his mind, and he wouldn't have been surprised if she could, his mother turned her head and started tapping her foot at the same time. She was always busy with her hands, picking at herself, fussing with her hair, rubbing her eyes, pinching at her cheeks; her feet could never stay still long either, tapping or swinging or rubbing up against each other. It drove him crazy. Why couldn't she hold still like other people?

Like that chicken, he thought, looking at her with distaste. I don't blame Dad for running off. I don't blame him for not wanting to worry about her. Dad went off and left me to take over, and have you ever shown any gratitude? he asked the withered neck in front of him.

Nobody'll ever remarry a woman with a neck like that, he thought bitterly. I'll have her on my hands for the rest of my life. It's not bad enough we're Catholic, she's got to carry on the way she does, saying that she can't find anything in the Bible about divorce. They didn't even have it then, he remembered her saying in front of Helen's father while he withered right up and died of embarrassment, and Helen's father opened his mouth to give her a good talking to, but his mother just ignored him and went right on. If they didn't have divorce then, how could they make laws against it? she had insisted, looking angry and upset. It's just like that meat business. It's all just a scheme to sell fish, to get rid of something nobody in his right mind would want to eat. You can't fool me, it's a question of economics, she had said, getting that absolutely set look on her face so that you knew no matter what you said it wouldn't make any difference. The whole family owned that look. His mother, Iris, Ada, god, Ada! and dirty, awful old rich Esther.

The broken wrist.

I ought to try to get to the hospital and see Esther. Think of some way to do something she'd be grateful for. Mow her lawn while she's sick. No, I'm not going to mow that damn lawn. But something like that. So she'd see I'm thinking about her, that I care for her more than the rest of them do. Go out there—but how'd I ever get in? he wondered. She won't open the door to anyone. She must have money hidden all over the place. She certainly isn't going to give me a key to get in there and poke around while she's in the hospital.

I'll bet you'd find a fortune behind the boxes and under the crates. Enough to go to Paris and back without thinking about it.

That damn dog had started in again. He was barking his fool head off. "There's someone stopping outside," his mother said, turning and starting on her quick, impatient feet for the door. "Coming, coming," she shouted. "Don't ring the bell," she screamed. "You'll start the dog off again and the neighbors are—"

He couldn't hear the rest for the noise Captain was making. I'll shoot that damn animal one of these days, I swear I will, if he doesn't shut up that barking and get some sense in his head.

"Stop it," he screamed at the back window. "Stop that damn barking, I say."

Then, in a sudden moment of confusion, the doctor was standing in the doorway looking at him as if he'd lost his mind, his mother and Lois were coming across the living room and they were staring at him as if he had disgraced them, and he couldn't stop himself, all the liquor had suddenly gone to his head and he felt sick all over, he didn't care whether Helen made everything a big test or not; he was sick of Helen and her tests, he was getting to the point where he didn't care whether he flunked or not; and he heard himself saying weakly, penitently, the words coming out in a mishmash of self-pity and truncated syllables, "Scuse me.

Helen's pres-sent . . . car . . . I gotta present for Helen. Musta left it in the car. Out in the car. Scuse me. Gotta get Helen's present."

He would bring the present in and everything would be all right. If he only hadn't dropped it someplace; the way things had started going, nothing would have surprised him. He thought of that feeling earlier that everything was going to be golden, how he'd set out like a regular conqueror, full of confidence and jubilation. He must have been off his rocker. He should have kept his eye on the pattern of these past weeks, the dirty way things had of going wrong, remembering the day he lost by two cars, the days when he had made such a fool of himself sweating over that dog, the day Lois made that awful scene in the kitchen, the night—was it only a few hours before?—of Iris's party when Ada and Esther had got into it that way. He thought of Esther screaming at them as they got her out to the car, "You don't care one thing about me, not one of you. You're putting me in a hospital!"

They're not going to beat me, he told himself through clenched teeth. I'm going to get the money yet. Wait and see.

Go out to the hospital and fuss over her, make her feel important, show her I'm the one in the family that cares—she'll buy that, he told himself, wait and see.

Chapter Three

DRUNK, Lois wanted to cry out. He was *drunk,* and it was as if everything she had ever thought and felt about him was suddenly called into question, that he was bent on shattering her last image, determined to pull down her last idol with his own hands, glad to be shattered into his own limited humanity, a mere man reacting as most men would, drowning fear in alcohol, boosting courage with the bottle. She heard on every side of her the soft shuffle of his cardboard armor as it fell from him and he stood in front of her in all his human imperfections.

She wanted to take him and shake him and *make* him behave better, and all the time she only watched with her face getting tighter and tighter; she thought that he must see the word *drunk* written right across her face;

M

or worse, that other word, *coward,* that even as she was fighting to run away from it, trying to retreat from the word that she abhorred above all others, *coward,* there it was, creeping right across the frozen field of her mouth, he would surely see it as he came down the hall looking so proud of himself, so proud of that foolish present—that present Helen would despise, Evening in Paris for Helen!—watching as he came through the archway from the hall and walked unsteadily back toward the bottle of Scotch which Frances had finally found and put, with a bang, on the table, without saying a word, then picked up her purse and gone out the front door, without so much as a good-by, but her shoulders were a whole history of grievances, and both her hands, as she threw them up in disgust, were epistles of all the sacrifices—all of them useless —that mothers made for their children for countless thousands of years and what good did they do, so that Lois could only remember Iris beating her maternal breast and crying, *And they won't even go to Communion.*

None of those cheerful articles back at the magazine she wrote for had had an answer to this; what did that magazine know about the child locked in the prison of mother love, about the mother that fed off her young, of the young who turned their backs on their pleading mothers? What did that eternally, immutably, optimistic magazine know of a world of despair and dying and betrayal, where all love came in the end to rejection or disillusionment and where, in the moment of crisis, people turned their backs on one another and pretended that the call, the critical call at the crucial moment, had not been for them?

He was searching about for a glass.

"Don't," she said. "Please don't. I mean, it's just that—" But her voice faltered and died, lost in the barking of the dog, retreating somewhere out in the dark night among all those houses that had been erected on that mutilated earth. They have cut back the trees and torn out the earth, she thought, to put up this house. He has come, Erwin, to this. She thought of the determination that had been on Erwin's face when he had insisted on taking Esther to the hospital. He had the same look now, clasping the bottle.

Waiting for the final failure, she thought, because we never really believe, we never really have the full faith, we are always waiting for faith to fall. Unarmed in the world, she thought, seeing everything as it is, not as it should be: reality, a voice cried out inside her, the flayed splendor that is reality.

Never turn your back on the truth.

Even your own father . . . "You didn't even try," he always said. That was how her father had felt about everything, that nobody tried the way he did, everyone let him down. And maybe that's how I feel, she thought, that nobody is ever trying hard enough. Neal . . . Erwin . . . and that boy, she asked herself, who put his arms around you in that hot car and held you close . . .

You weren't even trying: her father's legacy to her—to think no one else was ever trying as hard as she. And Eileen, she said to herself. Are you trying for Eileen?

Can I never hold faith long enough not to betray at least one of them among me? she asked herself.

He was pouring two drinks. "No, I don't want one," she said, knowing that she could not keep the harshness, the accusation, from her words.

He didn't answer, just left her glass on the table, picked up his own, and started to drink. "Erwin," she said, "I don't know how to say this, but I've got to." She paused. She caught her breath. "Erwin, please, please don't do this."

"Don't do *what?*"

"Don't let Helen down this way. She's back there, she's back there trying so hard, and you're up here, and it must look—it must look like you're not trying at all."

"Is that what you came all the way out here to tell me?"

"I came out to—to try to help."

"And you think that kind of talk is helping?"

"I meant it to."

"Well, I can tell you one thing, it doesn't."

What can I do? she asked herself helplessly. If Helen loses the baby, she'll need him to be with her. If she keeps it, she'll want him beside her. He can't go to her like this. I won't let him behave like this, Lois thought. I want him to be better, he *has* to be better, I won't have him like this. This isn't Erwin, not my Erwin.

"You've got to behave better," she said angrily, standing up, feeling for a moment as if she were going to knock the glass out of his hand.

The dog was still barking and she went to the window, turning her back on Erwin, unable to bear the stupid, silly expression on his face, the expression of the man who is on the edge of self-indulgent drunkenness, the eyes glazed and the mouth slack, the whole body fiberless.

The white moonlight lay like a coat of fresh paint across the concrete. The dog was running up and down in a frenzy, his head thrown up to the moonlight, the pulse in his strong throat vibrating to the terrible

howls there. He looked like some Greek monster out there in the moonlight, the light glancing off his fangs, that piercing voice wailing skyward.

Neal, she thought.

Erwin. Stan.

Failed Eileen. Failed me. Failed Helen.

Don't fail Erwin, she told herself. You love him so much.

That man in back of her with his hazy stare and his unsteady hand
on the bottle of Scotch—what had he to do with the shining image she
had carried all these years, the boy, growing tall and lovely, whose
shadow she had wanted to fasten to her own so that he could never
leave her?

He was gone, that boy, just as the hills, the birds, the old woman were
gone. This house was here and in it this man, that was reality, she thought,
staring out at the big black shadow in the corner of the yard, a larger
image of the carport from which the shining hood of Erwin's car could
barely be seen, the car, Lois thought, that carried home the Evening in
Paris, the little gift of expiation. Buy flowers and candy when in guilt,
get rid of obloquy with scent and talcum. She turned, a plea once more
on her lips, but the room was empty. She could hear him out in the
kitchen, the water running: taking out the ice cubes, she supposed.

She made her way out to the hall and down toward Helen's bedroom.
The light came under the door, the door was closed. Let him rest a little,
she thought, and then get some coffee down him, get him to wash up.
He would look as if the whole blessed night he had been doing nothing
more than worrying, waiting and worrying, and it was not the truth that
mattered, but what the truth seemed to be.

We all find out the truth soon enough, Lois thought.

The dog had started to quiet down a little. It grows late, she thought,
the dark hour of the night when we are afraid, when the little girls look
for their fathers, look for their fathers somewhere deep down inside,
then turn on hot beds and stare into the sleeping faces of husbands or
lovers beside them, looking for the fathers, thinking, Come and save me,
staring into the dark hours of the night wondering where there is someone of strength left capable of saving even himself. No more a father,
we have grown beyond the fathers, we who have never had any, and are
looking now for a lover, the lover who is going to disappoint us, to fail us,
fail me, Neal, fail me, Erwin, fail me, father that I never knew.

Come and save me, her heart cried out, come and put your arms, your
strong arms, around me, come and take me away.

Never turn your back, Lois told herself, on what you truly see.

No matter how it hurts you. Look at what is real, no matter how ugly, how painful. That one day you may then be permitted a little love for yourself—but only if you earn it.

She went back to the kitchen. He was propped up at the table, his head dropped onto his arms, two pillars of flesh and bone supporting the tired head, the eyes closed, the breath coming regularly. Sleeping. The glass in front of him empty. She supposed he had finished that last drink and sunk down into the merciful oblivion of sleep, thinking, If anything comes up they'll waken me, not seeing it was his duty to be awake and waiting.

She bent over his sleeping form, doing what she had wanted to do all along, shaking it, shaking it with all the outrage she had felt from the first, not only against him for disappointing her, but against all of them, each and every one of them that had failed her, most of all herself, her bottomless disgust and disappointment with herself, standing over him and shaking him until his mouth rattled, his eyes flew open, they seemed to bulge from their sockets, he threw out his arms and flailed at the air. "What? Huh? What is it?"—shouting up at her, and it was terror in his eyes now, not drunkenness, as they stared at each other.

Lois's arms fell to her sides and she said, "Get up and go wash up. Go on, get up. She's going to need you soon."

For a moment he did not answer, merely sat, still shaking a little, looking up at her. "Is she all right? Is she— Lois, she's not—she hasn't lost the baby, has she?" he asked in a small, scared voice.

"No," she said. "She hasn't lost the baby. She's still back there with the doctor. But it's about time you did something—something constructive—even if it's only going to the door and *asking* how she is."

"Yeah, sure," he said, getting up, running his hands through his hair. "Ugh," he said. "My mouth—sure, you're right. I gotta go back and find out how she is. Just must have dropped off, just for a moment, tired, so many people lately, don't get to bed, you know how it is . . ." And he stood up, swaying, going on and on.

". . . good kid, Lois, you are. You're the only one who's always understood. I want you to know I appreciate . . ." on and on while she stared into his face, thinking, The failure, the final failure, but this one was postponed for a long time, for that I ought to be grateful.

It was the doctor who saved her from any more. Helen was all right. He was pretty sure the child was going to be all right. Helen would have to stay in bed for a week or so, have these injections, but the worst of it was over. She was waiting.

As Erwin went down the hall, Lois followed him with her eyes, thinking, Yes, she is waiting, we're all waiting, when do you stop waiting, when do you finally believe once and for all that no one is going to come and save you? When can you face being free of that final dream and that final failure? When do you see the world for what it is?

Tell me, her heart pleaded. I want to know how much farther I have to go.

Chapter Four

"EILEEN, Eileen, open this door!"

Eileen waited, not answering, crouched down in the closet, trying to get the door to swing all the way shut so that she might stay inside in total darkness. But the box was blocking the door. The door would not close all the way; she sat in a whole square of light.

"Eileen—" Her mother must have been out there fifteen or twenty minutes, calling. Eileen waited, not answering; soon her mother would give up and go away; she crouched, the box beside her, and in the box little noises, scratching feet against cardboard, like glass being shaken in a cardboard box.

"Eileen, Eileen—" With raised fist her mother attacked the door, pounding, banging, shouting, then after a moment there was silence outside in the hall; and inside, in the closet, Eileen made no answer, listening to the noises from the box.

"Just for a minute, honey," her mother pleaded. "Just open the door a minute. Please."

A big box with holes in it, to let in air, and from one of the holes a little pink nose protruding: in the whole menacing room, that frightening room with its dark furniture crouched like assailants to spring on her, to claim her, from all the fright of the white light that poured ceaselessly through the windows and aimed at her, malevolently seeking her out, the room, the furniture, the light, the very air itself, in which sinister specks of things were floating, unidentifiable things, but not without their threat—poisonous, poisonous, sang out that warning voice inside—of all the whole wide menacing world which crowded against her, bent on hurting her, and she unable to protect herself, not even able to close the closet door, to shut out the light which was directing all that virulence against her, the only thing that gave her a feeling of reassurance was that small pink nose protruding from the black interior of the box, taking into itself air but not light, that nose seeming to know that light was something to be avoided, that in the wide world outside, from which she had rescued it, there were fences that did not keep out murderers, yards where the trees hid executioners, walks where behind the alcoves of houses assailants lay in wait.

"If you want to keep pets," her mother said desperately from behind the closed, the locked door, "I don't mind. Only your father—I mean, if you want pets, something nice, a dog, a cat, but, Eileen, please, just for my sake, open the door."

She had come into the house carrying the box, walking right past her mother without a word, and her mother had looked up, smiling, her face brightening, and then her eyes had fallen on the box, a frown had started, her mouth dropped open, and by the time Eileen had reached the stairs her mother had risen, a question forming on her face, saying, "Honey, what's in that box? Eileen—"

But already Eileen was halfway up the stairs, running now, seeking the asylum of her room, knowing that she was quicker than her mother, just as her mother had learned to be quicker than her father, running, running, frightened as one pursued, and banging the door shut behind her, turning, one arm clutching the box, the other hastily fumbling with the latch. Then she had been safe, locked in her own room. It was then she had seen, in the yellow sunlight, those terrible little things floating in the air, something she knew had been sent to hurt her.

White, Eileen thought, crouching rigid inside the closet. White: the symbol of purity: the symbol of love. White wedding dress: white gown for those who go into the convent: the bride of Christ: they give you a gold ring, just like you were married. Wed to chastity. Wed to purity. Wed to someone you couldn't see.

"Eileen, open the door. *Please* open the door."

Lovely, sweet Eileen Ames, who . . . she always wears white, winter and summer she wears white . . . sweet, saintly Eileen Ames . . .

"Eileen," her mother shouted, pounding on the door, "open this door, open this door this instant."

. . . periwinkle blue, they call it Timble blue, I was a Timble, you know . . . beautiful, chaste Eileen Ames . . .

Eileen moved closer to the box. There were dangers all about her, the room was filled with peril; like the motes in the air, it was all something strange, something she could not understand, but something she knew she had to fear, to watch out for, to guard against.

Hide, hide, a voice cried out inside her. If you don't hide they will find you, and when they find you . . .

"I love you, Eileen. Can you hear me? I love you. Open this door, please open this door."

The boxes in the basement, was it only broken glass they held? The food in the kitchen, might her mother not have put something in that to make her stay here, to keep her from running away? The soap in the bathroom, the rugs on the floor, the very sheets on which she slept, the air she had to breathe, who knew what was in them?

The trees are rattling against the window, calling out, Beware, oh, beware; the electricity is running through the sockets, silently carrying its messages of danger; the refrigerator has gone on downstairs and hums of peril everywhere, Be careful, oh, be careful. If she could get through to darkness, to the time when the light vanished and took those terrifying specks in the air with it, the voices that were imprisoned under the thick skin of her hands told her, she would be all right, she would be safe. At least for a little while.

But it was such a long time to wait, the veins that carried her blood from her head to her heart and back protested. Until night, until night, be careful until night, you have things to fear until night, until the darkness comes to cover you, the walls of the room warned her.

Can I be sure the darkness does not hide things itself of which I have no idea, she asked herself, as the air has been hiding them all these years and I did not know? Is it not possible that on all sides of me, day and night, there are infinite and unknown dangers that have been waiting to destroy me?

"Eileen, you don't know what it is to love someone and not have that person love you. Eileen, you don't know how all these years I've loved you, the only thing I've had in my life, in my whole entire life, to love was you, and now you— Eileen, if you love me, open this door."

Why should I know what it is to love? Eileen called to her without speaking, for couldn't her mother hear all the things inside her; wasn't it true her mother had known all these years what she was secretly thinking inside? How have I known love, Eileen called to her without voice, when you and Papa never let me know, when you have *kept* me from knowing?

"Eileen, Eileen, it's Mama. Open the door to your Mama. Oh darling, *please.*"

In the hush of silence that fell for a moment after her mother had cried out, Eileen heard a little sound, soft, as if a movement so slight it scarcely carried the weight of its own noise (like my grief, like my fears inside, Eileen thought), and then there was a distinct and clear sound; behind the door someone was moving. "Eileen," her mother pleaded more urgently, "please open the door, please. Baby," she said, "baby—"

Silent, on the floor, seeing the tiny dangerous motes in the air falling down, ready to harm her, Eileen made no answer. If she stayed very still, might they not miss her?

"Eileen," her mother said, "my baby, my little baby. Ei—leen"—that name cried in bewilderment and despair, and no answer, what could she ever say to her mother to make her mother understand, what could she ever say to make her love her the way she wanted to be loved, what could she ever say to span the years and make them all go back, to start again at the beginning, so that she might still have another chance?—it was too late, too late, the destructive drops were already in the air, her mother, Lois, all of them had made those little deadly dots in the air, it was all their evil, all the wickedness of their souls, which they had breathed into the air, and when those terrible thoughts and acts they all did, those other people, came up out of them and got into the air, they went solid and hard, made little specks, which floated about the universe, polluting the unspoiled, raining down on the pure and defiling them, falling on the good until they were spoiled, the whole world was wicked; how could you, who were good, explain that to those who were bad, and the words, you couldn't tell them anyway, you had to feel them, the way she was feeling them now, staring into the clear pure air which every moment was filling with more and more evil, until at last the clear pure air would be choked with evil, there would be nothing left in the world but wrong, the world was ruined, what was the point of speaking, of telling what you saw, when it was already too late?

Her mother threw herself against the door; words came out, a rain of words against the door. *"Love me, oh love me,"* her mother cried, pounding against the door with all her might. *"Open the door and love me, Eileen, my baby, my little baby, oh love me, Mother of God love me. . . ."*

Might not the dots fall on her mother too? If she opened the door and let her mother in, wouldn't the dots fall on her, wouldn't the dots destroy her too?

"All right, I'll let you in," Eileen said slowly, "if you'll help me, if you'll help me sew."

"Sew? What do you mean, *sew?*"

"To make the costumes, the costumes for the little mice."

Chapter Five

RALPH simply couldn't believe his eyes. He stood in the middle of the kitchen, holding the little round red tin of cheese, staring at it incredulously. It said Edelweiss. It must be the brand name, he told himself, trying to stem the terrible tide of anger that was flushing through him. It's just a name, like Camembert or Stilton, Cheddar—they make all those in Wisconsin, don't they? Carolyn wouldn't have . . .

Produced by Edelweiss Dairy Products Co., Kempten, Bavaria, West Germany, he read on the side of the tin. A white-hot flush of anger swept over him, spitting flames raced through him, white-hot tracers sending steel into his brain, every piece hitting a crucial nerve.

He was trembling with pain and shock. The tin lay on the floor. He had neither felt nor heard it fall. Yet there it was in the middle of the floor, a little round spot of red, too bright for blood, light red like wine, like the rosé he had drunk in France after the armistice, the light rosé that put him to sleep so many evenings when he could not trust his mind to rest without numbing it on bottle after bottle of wine, he wandering the dark streets, in and out of bars and cafés. In those days it seemed to take so much to get drunk, so many bottles of wine to dull away the memory of a white battlefront and men lying like dark stumps of trees, rotted now, plowed under to fertilize these fields with the bones of the dead.

Carolyn stood in the doorway. "What is it?" she asked in a frightened voice. "Are you all right? I heard—" Then she was staring down at the floor. "What's the matter, Ralph?"

He could not speak.

"Ralph," she cried in a voice that came to him from a long distance. She had hold of his arm, she was looking into his face, pleading with him dumbly to say something.

"The cheese," he heard himself saying. "I asked you— *I asked you* —never to—*never to*—that wasn't much to ask—*never to*—all I asked you was NEVER to—"

"Darling, please, sit down, what is it, oh please sit down, you look terrible. Oh please—"

He jerked himself free. "Pick it up. Look at it. *Just look at it.*"

Carolyn knelt down and picked up the can. She held it for a moment in her hands, and when at last she looked up at him he saw the consternation on her face. "The maid must have brought it in, Ralph. I'm so sorry. I never thought to look. I've been so upset since last night. Mother's been on the phone half the day about Esther. She's going to be all right, but— I just asked the maid to pick up some things to go with cocktails. I didn't think to look. She must have—"

"Throw it out," he said. "Take it and throw it out, I don't want to see it"—and before she could answer he walked away, leaving her still talking, going on and on. What did he care who had brought it in? Was it too much to ask one little thing of her, too much to expect that she could care enough for him to pay attention to one little thing?

It was too much. Everything was too much for her. With Carolyn everyone else had only eccentricities, *she* had her suffering. She was the best-looking, best-fed, best-dressed, most perfectly maladjusted person he knew, one of those twentieth-century specimens that statistics loved. She would send soaring all the percentages that turned your blood to ice.

He sat down in the chair he never sat in, the brown "man's chair." The cocktail shaker was on the bar. Come in and find her half shot two, three times a week. All right, so one afternoon her brother was here; all right, so he had been fired, they had had a couple of drinks; all right, two brothers she had to deal with—*he* had to deal with; all right, he'd give them both jobs if that would help; all right, so Stu didn't want a job from him, but her other brother had to have one; all right, so her family was at it again, anyone would need a drink after a session with them; but was it too much to ask her to pay attention to one simple little thing? Was that beyond her in her terrible and transcending suffering?

I try to do the best I can. I don't talk about the quarrels, I stand the silences, I let her do whatever she wants. I'm willing to take her whole goddam family into the business. Can't she just read the labels on cans?

She's never seen a dead man, he thought, closing his eyes. She doesn't know what death looks like. She's never had to kill a man or see a man killed. Wesley, he thought . . .

I never even told her the worst of it, how his face was. Half gone and the rest rotted black. The whole side of his head had been blown away. They must have put a pistol right to the back of his head. I told her he had been shot in the back; how could I tell her the whole side of his head was blown out? What does she know about how the inside of a man's head looks?

Why wasn't it me? he asked. Why did it have to be Wesley?

No wonder I don't believe in God. No God would take Wesley and leave me. Look at me, he wanted to cry out to the cocktail shaker, *why leave me?*

"Ralph?"

He opened his eyes. She was standing over him, not looking at him, just standing there, with her head bent, her eyes downcast. On that damn beige carpet his own children couldn't walk on. Why couldn't his kids walk on the rug in their own house?

"Just leave me alone, Carolyn. Please just go away and leave me alone."

"Ralph, I'm sorry—"

"All right, you're sorry. All right, I accept the apology. But could you just go away and leave me alone for a little while? I don't want to talk now. Can you understand that?"

"Of course I do, but—"

"Listen, Carolyn, you're always talking about how people have to be alone, how you have to be alone, how you can't stand to have all the hands in the house reaching out to you all the time. Well, I have to be alone now. Will you just go away and leave me alone?"

Miraculously, she went. In the past, whenever he had to sit in this antiseptic room by himself, he had felt frozen, as if he were encased in ice and permanently estranged from the rest of the world. The truth was, he thought, he had felt that way a long time, not just in this room. Everywhere. Years and years of estrangement. Nothing touched him. He was doing only what was expected, giving to life what it asked, not putting anything meaningful back. Empty, he thought. I felt empty and I found emptiness all around me. In this room, talking to people, going to the office, at parties, even making love to Carolyn.

The room seemed to him at this moment bright and alive. Everything shimmered. Blinded, he looked around. The whole room seemed to be whirling within his eyes, glistening with life. It was as if he could see and feel again, as if his emotions mattered, as if he himself mattered.

Good christ, it was a terrible room. Ugly beyond belief. How had he ever stood it? Those awful heavy green curtains that cut out the light, that shut off the view. That red bar. The chrome.

He stood up, not surprised to find he was still shaking. He stood in the middle of that terrible, trembling room, looking at it like one on fire, scorched by the nerves of sight, burned by the impressions that the brain was feeding to his nerve centers.

It's terrible, awful, he kept repeating to himself. This chair. Those drapes. That glittery chrome. The *red* bar. The whole house has to go, he thought. And first the maid. First of all that overpaid, undergrateful creature who had made their lives a nightmare with her demands and complaints.

We've got to get out of here, he told himself.

I won't stay in this place, he wanted to yell at the top of his lungs.

He crossed the beige carpet, grinding his heels down, trying to make marks. There were small indentations from his shoes but no dirt. As he stood at the foot of the stairs, looking back, he saw the carpet slowly rise, creep back to its beautiful smooth perfection. It has more rights than we do, he thought, looking at that vast expanse of tufted covering, the color of corn. Just you wait, he thought, turning and going up the stairs.

The children would be in their playroom, that horror of a maid reading to them. He knew just what her voice would be like, put-upon and martyrish. Doing the duty she was paid for, not in devotion but in dependence.

He came abreast of the door and stood looking into the pool of pale lamplight. The two children sitting on either side of that frightful woman looked at him in disbelief. He never came up this time of night. Carolyn never came up. No, that was not strictly true. She came up once in a while. Not enough, he told himself. Why doesn't a mother put her children to bed? She should bathe and feed them. She should read to them. She should see to their discipline. She should be a part of their irritations and their excitements. A mother isn't supposed, said Ralph to himself, just to see them at special times. They are her children, not pets she sees at her own convenience.

"That will be all for tonight, Miss Miller," he said, trying to keep his voice under control. "I'm going to read to them myself." The maid looked at him in consternation; the children were wide-eyed. They thought he was going to punish them, Ralph supposed. "I want to read to them," he repeated.

Reluctantly, smoothing her uniform, Miss Miller rose. He was crazy, he was foolish, and—worse—he was disrupting the schedule, but he paid her. Ralph saw it all in the line of her narrow little mouth as she passed him. He picked up the book, staring down at the page of print. "The Red Lobster Inn," he read across the top of the page.

" 'As soon as Pinocchio went to bed he fell asleep and began to dream,' " Ralph read. " 'He dreamed that he was in the midst of a field full of little trees, and these trees were loaded with gold pieces, and every time the wind shook them they went *"Tinkle, tinkle, tinkle!"* ' " Ralph put his arm around his son's shoulder. The little boy moved closer, and Ralph stopped for a moment and looked down at his son.

"I thought I heard your voice," Carolyn said. Her eyes were red, she had been crying. She must still care a little if she can cry, Ralph thought. If I can see so much in that room, let me see more in my wife, he prayed to the universe in which he only faintly believed.

"Mama," Sally said in a high, happy little voice, "Daddy is reading to us."

"He certainly has a book," Carolyn admitted, giving the three a tentative, conciliatory smile.

"Daddy's reading to us," Bobbie said, looking from one to the other. "He's reading about Pinocchio," he said excitedly. "And Pinocchio saw this tree and it had all this gold on it and he— Daddy's reading to us."

Carolyn sat down on the box where the children kept some of their toys. She crossed her legs and the pale lamplight fell on her stockings; in the light they gleamed gold, golden legs, Ralph thought, beautiful golden legs in sheer stockings. "Don't let me interrupt," she said.

"You tell us a story," Sally said. "We can read this old book any time. *You* tell us a story."

"I'm going to tell you a story," Ralph said, closing the book, "but not tonight. I have to have time to think about my story. Tonight we're going downstairs and your mother and I are going to have a cocktail and you're going to have some ice cream with us in the living room and then I'm going to think about the story, and you're going to tell me what you want in the story, and tomorrow I'm going to tell you a story with all the things you want in it."

He stood up and crossed over to his wife, looking down at her beautiful legs. Golden gossamer legs in the lamplight, he thought. He put his arm around Carolyn. "You go down and get the ice cream," he said, "and make us a cocktail. I want to say something to Miss Miller. You take Sally and Bobbie on down with you. I'll be right down."

Miss Miller was in the bathroom, down on her hands and knees, sprinkling scouring powder in the tub. "Miss Miller," he said, standing in the doorway, looking at her resentful back.

She turned. "Mr. Tryson?" she said, making the words respectful, but no more.

"Mrs. Tryson and I are going to move—"

"Going to move, Mr. Tryson?" She really sounds surprised for once in her life, Ralph thought, but when I'm finished she's going to be astounded.

"Yes, we're going to move to another place, and I don't think there'll be as much room there as there is here, Miss Miller, and what I wanted to tell you is that I'm going to write you a check for two weeks' pay and you don't need to come in tomorrow, you don't need to come back any more."

Miss Miller stood up, the can of scouring powder in her hand. "You mean you don't want my services any more, is that what you mean, Mr. Tryson?"

"That's exactly what I mean, Miss Miller."

"You don't have to tell me stories. You can just—"

"I don't have to tell you anything at all, but the truth of the matter is we are going to move and we won't be needing you."

"Not even odd days?"

"Not even odd days."

"I been with Mrs. Tryson four years," Miss Miller said, throwing back her head. "She's never had any reason to complain, so far as I know. She's never said anything to me—"

"No, neither one of us has, because the truth is that you've had us both buffaloed since the day you came, and you know it better than we do, but—"

"Well, I never in all my days heard of—"

"So if you'll just get your things, I'll write you a check and—"

Miss Miller put down the scouring powder with a minor detonation. "I expect you won't be asking me to finish any more of my chores, then, Mr. Tryson, since after all these years you see fit to—"

"Just get your coat, Miss Miller."

Ralph went into the back bedroom and got out his check book. When he started to make out the check, two things struck him: he didn't know Miss Miller's first name and he didn't even know how much they paid her a week. He started down the hall to ask Carolyn and he heard the maid's shrill, febrile voice. ". . . just came in the bathroom, me on my hands and knees scrubbing out the tub, and he—"

"I don't know anything about this, Miss Miller," Carolyn interrupted in a pleading way. "I give you my word of honor I—"

Ralph ran down the stairs. "Carolyn," he said, "please get the ice cream. Take Sally and Bobbie out in the kitchen. Miss Miller, will you get your things?" Miss Miller threw her head into the air, marched past him, and went up the stairs. "Carolyn," he said, looking straight into her startled face, "what is that woman's first name?"

"Miss Miller's? It's Beatrice."

"I don't believe it," he said. "No one would name a woman like that Beatrice. Wasn't that the name of—"

"—the woman Dante fell in love with."

"I knew it was someone famous. How much do we pay her?"

"Thirty a week, and overtime. She's been here twice this week overtime, four hours one night, and four and a half the other. That's—let's see, eight and a half dollars more. Ralph, what's going on?"

"I'll tell you later. Just get the ice cream. I'll take care of the cocktail myself when I get down. I'm going to need one. I'm going to need a couple."

Miss Miller was at the top of the stairs, her coat on, a hat flattened against her head. She was tapping her foot and hanging onto the banister, clutching it as if in need of moral support. "About references—" she began.

"I'll write you a letter which tells exactly what you've done, and I'll be kind enough to leave out the spirit in which it was done," Ralph said. "You can come to my office and get it." He went back to the bedroom and wrote his check. When he looked at it, he hardly recognized the handwriting. I hope they cash it, he thought.

Miss Miller went down the stairs ahead of him. He walked right to the front door and opened it, and the last he saw of her she was stalking the night, as if to capture it and put it in chains, just the way she had held them in chains the last four years.

He went back to the bar and picked up the cocktail shaker. Carolyn had always wanted a refrigerator in this room, she was forever complaining about it. In their next house there wasn't even going to be a bar in the front room. Why the hell couldn't they walk to the kitchen to make drinks, the way most people did? What kind of a living room was it where there was a bar and a rug but where children couldn't come? In their next house they were going to have furniture you could put your feet on and hassocks for Sally and Bobbie, and they were going to live the way people should live.

In their next house they were going to have a huge kitchen where they could make their drinks and talk and putter around. Like France, like those big old farmhouse kitchens in France with the refectory table and a big highboy and copper pots and a huge stove that *always* had something on it. In the next house there was going to be life, there was going to be clutter. And no synthetic leather, he never wanted to see those nylon synthetics again as long as he lived.

He took the cocktail shaker out to the kitchen and put it on the table. The peeling silver ice bucket was on the table, shedding big beads of sweat. "I hate that thing," he said, going to the icebox and getting out a new tray. The children had bowls of ice cream and spoons. Each was standing with a bowl in one hand, a spoon in the other, carefully balancing both. "Go on," he said, "take those in the living room." Sally looked at her mother, and Carolyn shrugged her shoulders. "Go on," Ralph said. "Into the living room with you."

"Your father—"

"Skedaddle."

"I've fired the ogre," he said, struggling with the ice tray under the faucet. "And don't you promise to take her back, no matter how often she calls you on the telephone."

"Ralph—"

"It's all right," he said, turning and holding the tray up in triumph. "Just give me a little time, but everything's going to be all right. Can you kiss me?" he asked.

"Well, I—"

"Come here, come here and— Honey," he said, holding her, "I've just begun to see how much I love you, how much I love all of you. Oh, Carolyn—"

She pushed him away, giving him that look he remembered from the past, the far-distant past, when he had believed that she felt for him all he felt for her, when he had wanted her so much, just as he wanted her at this moment, and he thought, She's stirred too, everything is stirring, we've come alive, oh god, we've come alive again, it isn't all empty, it isn't all dead any more, let me hang on to this.

"Go on, go in with the kids. I'll be in in a minute."

The children were sitting solemnly, self-consciously, on the floor, carefully spooning up their ice cream. Obviously the dispensation he had given them was less a treat than a threat. They were too afraid of spilling something on the rug. When they had finished, and even he could see they hurried, they got up and took their plates silently into the kitchen, then came back, and, like children in a bad movie, went about kissing their parents good night, going up the stairs, without so much as a murmur, glad to get away from such liberty and license. "I'll turn off the light in the hall," Sally said in a subdued voice, and her brother clung to her as if she were his protection against the whole illogical world of adults.

Carolyn and he sat, sipping their drinks, silent, listening as the children went about in the bathroom upstairs, hearing the click of the light switch, straining for the last sounds of the two children getting into bed. There was no mistaking the rattle of the beds and the hushed whispers.

When we stop acting out the routines of our lives, Ralph thought, that is when we truly come alive—even children, even children understand that. Carolyn, he thought, looking across at her, can you understand and forget the past, can you forget and begin again? Can you ever make love to me as if it matters?

"I've always thought if I could tell you some day what it was like to see Wesley"— She looked up at him, startled, distrustful—"lying dead in the snow . . . Carolyn, I lied to you. He wasn't shot in the back. It was in the head. Half his head was shot off, and when I saw him something terrible happened to me, it was as if my own brains had been emptied out in that awful snow, as if *I* had had my hands tied and felt the pistol next to my head, as if—"

"As if there wasn't anything left inside?" she asked, staring at him with such fixed concentration that he wondered if he had the courage to go on, to tell her the whole and complete truth.

"As if there was nothing left inside." He hesitated. "But more than that," he continued, taking a big breath. "I felt that if Wesley had lived, if he had come back, it would have been you—he would have fallen in love with you and you with him and that would have been right. I felt that— I don't know how to say it, how I can say it, it's been inside me all this time and I don't think I wanted to see it, I kept trying not to, I fought back, I pushed it down, but it was there, it was always there: you and Wesley would have loved one another and—and—" He got up, walked across to the window. There was the wide sweep of green curtains. He went to the end of the wall and jerked the cord. The material opened, he was looking out at the night. Across his back yard there were dark shadows against the dark grass and in the sky overhead a multiplicity of stars. "I knew that there wouldn't have been any place for me, and just being alive wasn't enough. There wasn't a place anyway. I was only holding a dead man's place."

He waited, but Carolyn said nothing, and when he turned, she was moving her glass between her hands, like a woman saying her beads, and on her face was an expression of such sorrow and suffering that he cried out, "Don't."

"Don't what?" she asked, looking at him.

"Don't not understand. I want so much for you to understand. You've got to understand."

"But I do, Ralph, I do. I understand better than you'll ever know."

"You understand that you've been living with a man who's been half dead—not half dead," he said to himself angrily, "*dead* all this time. I was dead, I was looking at myself as dead. Because it should have been me."

"But it wasn't"—the flat, prosaic statement of fact: Ralph looked at his wife. He saw that she had not said it to wound him but only to bring him back to what was: *he* was in this room, alive.

"It's taken me a long time to find that out. And now that I have, is it too late, Carolyn? Tell me that, is it too late?"

He blessed her for her next remark because he knew she was telling him the complete truth. "I don't know," she said.

"Would you be—be willing to try again? If I were willing to try, to be someone you could count on, someone who wasn't just going through the motions, someone who was really living, would you try then?"

He waited, but she seemed unable to answer. Then she began to cry. Through her tears, as he crossed the room to comfort her, he heard the snatches of phrases. ". . . I want someone to love . . . I want to be able to have someone I can love . . . I want to be alive . . . I want to believe . . . even if only for a moment . . . even if I know I'm deceiving myself . . . just to have something you believe in for a little while . . . no matter what happens later . . . Ralph, Ralph, help me to believe, if only for a little while. . . ." And then she was in his arms, sobbing against his chest, her sobs picking up the rhythm of his heartbeat, and he held her gently, letting those sobs blend with his heartbeats.

"We're going to get out of this house, Carolyn. We're going to go someplace where we can make a real place to live. We're going to start all over again. I know you think that's crazy, but I mean it. I'm going to take off a week, two weeks, a month, a whole year if I have to, and we're going to find the house we want, the right house, and we're going to make it the way we want it. *We*'re going to take care of the children, make them feel a part of us, and things are going to be different, you've got to believe me, you've just got to trust me. We'll find someone who can come in and help, someone who cares for us, not someone who only works for us for the money, it's going to be a whole new life, I hate this room, I hate this house, it's destroying us, and I won't be destroyed, not now, not with what I feel now, I won't . . . Carolyn, just love me a little, won't you?"

She turned her mouth up to his, and he bent down and kissed her. When his mouth touched hers, she didn't draw back. It was as if her flesh were rushing to his, and he got up and started to turn off the lights, he was going to make love to his wife right on this living-room rug, but before he switched off the last one, she said, "Leave it on, leave the light on, Ralph, the way you want to," and then he lay down beside her, saying, "I'm tired of thinking about death. I want to think about life. I want to make life."

And they lay together and it was as if the trees and the flesh and the very floor beneath them grew with gold.

Chapter Six

HE STOOD on the front porch of the second floor, gazing out at the signs. Downstairs his mother had yet to flick on the switch for the lights, though it was nearly eight; how his mother loved the long summer evenings when she saved electricity! The shadows hid most of the stuff she had stored up here, and the tarpaulins covered the greater part of the ugliness, the raw boards and that crazy life raft left over from the Second World War; still, Stu thought, it wouldn't be home if there wasn't junk all over this porch. No one else ever came out here except him, and he didn't know why he was drawn to it. Something about the height.

A long slope, he'd just glide down. In white moonlight. White snow, white moonlight, all alone on the slopes going down, down in the cool darkness.

He looked out at that last dying moment of twilight when the birds give out soft wounded cries and there is a faint flutter of insects in the air, when the sky is pierced by one small silver plane and one larger bird, dark like a giant shadow against the gray sky, like an omen, a portent of all we do not know.

His hands were on the rails, he was leaning over, looking down. The yard below showed all its shabbiness in the last glow of the evening light, but he was more interested in the angry man battling with an oversized suitcase. It was one of the boarders, the one who had been so enraged at the commotion the night before that he had worked himself to the point of demand: either Stu's mother apologized and did something (what, Stu had asked himself, did that guy want, she cut her throat?) or he would—he would leave. Well his mother's throat was intact, the boarder was leaving, as Stu might have told the man from the beginning.

Stu wondered how in the world anyone who had been exposed to his mother for even a short time could expect her to react rationally in a moment of crisis. That man must be out of his mind, he thought. A borderline case, as his mother would have said, the way she said it about Esther, about Ada. They're my own sisters, but they're borderline cases, I have to be honest, even if they are my own sisters. He thought of the night before, saw his mother running around and screaming, "Her arm's broken, her arm's broken, oh somebody do something."

His mother always went to pieces in a crisis, any crisis, even the milk delivery being late or someone forgetting to set the clocks ahead for daylight saving time. Only in national emergencies, war and floods, famines and fires, did she remain calm. After all, these didn't touch her.

Not like Mrs. Polaski, he thought. Mrs. Polaski stood up to almost any crisis, immediate or peripheral; but when the state of the nation was in peril she went white-eyed with fright. It must be her background, he thought. To her plunder and scavenging and rapine were realities, whereas his mother—his mother would be just as likely to run out and buttonhole some enemy general, grabbing him with those fat little hands of hers, hanging on and screeching into his face, "You've just got to send somebody along. You can't expect me to quarter prominent people—*officers*—when the toilet's stopped up."

Leave it to his mother to get the "best" people.

Whereas Mrs. Polaski would be one of those brown, beaten-down ladies in line for a fast-dwindling ration, one of those defeated before the true tests came. God willing, she was sitting on her front stoop at this very moment, swilling her beer and gazing into the pale twilight, mourning the husband who had wasted his inheritance on the Eighth Avenue harlots.

Faintly he felt that he loved her, that poor broken-down old woman who never really believed in the future but made the best of the present. There was dimension to her.

The man downstairs had dragged his burden to the end of the walk; swearing, he started back toward the house. For a transient he had a lot of stuff. More than I ever accumulated, Stu thought. During all his years of wandering and working and worrying, it had never occurred to him to collect. He discarded his possessions as fast as he got them: the radios that stopped functioning never went to repair shops, they were simply left behind when he moved on; the clothes that wore down were never renewed in those establishments that specialized in giving the poor a gloss of respectability, they were simply thrown out; the money and the work and the time, where had they gone?—simply thrown to the winds, not put into anything that *meant*.

The story of his life was the waste he had left and lost year after year. He remembered that as a child he had always, on his birthday, tried to think through his year, to find in it something that made it worth while, some event or honor that showed that the year had not been wasted. There was nothing now in the past score of years that held any significance; indeed one year was so like another that he could not divide them into this birthday and that birthday; there was just a long stretch of meaningless, uneventful months and weeks that had finally added up to the fact that soon he was going to be thirty-five and there was nothing to show for his life.

Nothing except a half-formed child growing inside Ethel.

Down the hall, in the heat, she lay on the bed, giving life to his child. Even at the end, he thought, I couldn't even have the responsibility or the trust of making the child grow. It was only my seed, but it was Ethel who would nurture it, *make* it.

There rose in his mind an image of his father kneeling down in back of the garage, planting the first tomato seeds. His father would never buy nursery plants. He didn't want anyone else to start his tomatoes for him. His father wanted to start them, transplant them, nurse them in his home-made little glass bell coverings that served as greenhouse, then proudly and defiantly plunge them into the hard just-as-defiant ground. For his father, it had been a battle, Stu supposed.

But if his father had joined the seed in the whole process of maturation, he himself had done no more than plunge his first seed into the ground; someone else would have to see that it grew and came to fruition.

Like most of modern life: the absence of purpose, the sense that there was no self, only a network of instincts at the mercy of any call, a random stimulus sent out without direction or determination (like

Ethel, he thought, instinct without intelligence). Why, thought Stu, should we fear the old idea of death when we have one so much worse now?

Dying on white fields without knowing our assailants. In the cold. In a strange, far-away country. Not even knowing the method of our annihilation: was it mortar or rifle or grenade or indifference? Not that it made any difference. Death is death no matter what form it comes in, steel or germ, despair or meaninglessness.

Because of three nameless men he lived, he was standing on this porch gazing out into the descending darkness.

There rose in front of him, almost as if it came on the air itself, that special scent of August. He remembered it as the childhood smell he associated with the end of summer, a mingling of heavily-boughed trees and strong grass bending under its own weight and skies colliding in the wake of clouds, the kind of night lovers finally came to the act toward which they had been groping all summer. A smell of green, he thought.

The best things had it—trees, leaves, grass, the whole scent of summer, the smell of green, of money. Yes, money had it. Grass, leaves, trees, money, frogs. . . .

His father bending over the old sink in the kitchen—the one that was streaked with rust from the faucet that never quite stopped dripping—his father's sleeves rolled back, and the fine, delicate hands exposed: he was stripping back the skin of a frog, the green skin, it slipped away as easily as the skin was said to have come away from the hands of those at Hiroshima, and as he stood in back of his father he saw the smooth, gleaming white flesh of the frog.

Down at Lake Springfield, flushing out the enemy, the frogs—oh, that our enemy were never more than that. Although he supposed the frogs would have reason to complain. Would the frogs ever rise? No earthly good in going against what you could never in a million years overturn. The Poles (Mrs. Polaski) did, though. And the Greeks—he thought of the Greeks at those places on Eighth Avenue as they danced, their arms held high, their legs straining in the leaps, and that look on their faces—pride, Stu thought, the belief in themselves, that what they did was important, if only to dance. Still, in the end it was man against man. No, man against man and machines. Hardly comparable at all.

Like the Bulge. Hardly comparable at all. The *green* recruits.

When the snow goes, the green gleams through. Like after death. Warmth after cold. The coming of color where there was none before. Like life where there was none before. The child.

My flesh and blood.

Run away to the mountains. Free. Take the child. To the mountains, the clean, cold mountains.

The side that escapes to the mountains is the one that loses the war.

One damn fight after another, one war after another, they just call them by different names.

Why had they taken him, the three men to whom he owed his life?

He gazed out, feeling a quickening of his pulse, the same quickening, perhaps, that the earth felt now with the dying light and the growing night. The light went and night came. For all of us, he thought.

They took him because they couldn't leave him. He felt those three men would have taken him even if he had been German. In spite of the orders on both sides: *No prisoners.* You cannot leave a man in the snow and cold to die. Not those three, they couldn't. He wanted to believe, whether it was true or not, they would have taken any man who had been left behind, regardless of which side he was on.

"I didn't know anyone else ever came out here."

He turned, irritated that his privacy had been interrupted, then unaccountably pleased. It was Lois, and it came to him with that same sudden rush of pleasure that he had experienced the moment he recognized her voice, how much he cared for her. She was the only person he could really talk to.

"Well," he said, "here we are, here we both are, back home."

"Yes," she said, "trapped together"—and she smiled as if only the two of them shared this secret, this joke. He knew he would always remember her as she was at this moment, standing silhouetted in the doorway, looking at him with that smile. He would carry the picture with him always; he would keep it, that image, to love.

"You want a drink?" she asked. "I've got some in my room."

"Gin?"

"No, Scotch."

"That's funny. I thought you never drank anything but gin."

"I usually don't, but you have to have ice with gin—"

"And she even checks on the ice cubes."

"I suppose we'd be safe tonight," Lois said, "but you know I didn't count on a catastrophe when I was packing—although I ought to have. Never a party without a crisis. I thought—I'll get you some Scotch."

"No," he said and surprised himself. He would never have believed a week ago—even last night—that he would be turning down a free drink, that he would be trying to stick to chocolate milk. A week ago, he thought, I was standing in Lois's apartment, looking at all those piled-up books and wondering why she never put them away, and she was saying from the kitchen as she poured the gin and tonic, "I want to see the house, Grandmother Timble's house."

"Well, did you?" he asked. "Did you see the house?"

She nodded, reaching in her pocket and taking out a package of cigarettes, not looking at him. It turned out badly, he thought, just the way I knew it would. Let it go, he thought angrily. Let the advantage go, she's one person you don't have to bother to hurt, you don't want to score on her. He thought of the theater tickets and the drinks and dinners she gave him and the way the two of them had stood on the stairway a week before and he had taken her hand and pressed it. He knew now that his gesture was more than a tribute; it had been an act of love, an acknowledgment of the special quality that bound him to her; and he remembered that he had thought that night that she was waiting for him to give her some kind of quest, but the opposite was true: it was he who had come to her for the quest, and without her knowing it she had given it to him; when she said she was coming back to Springfield she committed him too, though he had not known it at the moment. For this whole week he had thought that it was Ethel's announcement about the child that had sent him back; now he knew that he would have come anyway. And that new knowledge freed him. It allowed him all the leeway in the world. He could say anything he wanted to her because he cared for her, and since he cared for her she had a responsibility to him too. The very act of his caring indebted her. "Who was it?" he asked, catching her eye over the flame of the match she was raising to her cigarette. "Who was it that told you where I was working—that time, that first time, a couple of years back, when you called me up at Bloomingdale's?"

"Eileen," she said without hesitation, staring at him with those wonderful eyes, those eyes that were for him all the sad and sweet and beautiful things he could remember in his life. "She wrote me that's where you were."

"Eileen?"

She nodded, then bent over the match, blowing it out. Tenderly it died on the cool, green summer night.

"But how would Eileen know?"

"I've never had the courage to ask," she said, and the tip of her cigarette glowed pale orange, heavy yellow in the dark. Twilight was over; all around the dark crowded in. The two of us, alone in the dark, he thought. Two people alone, smoking in the dark.

"And has it been all right, coming back?" His voice was low, soft, as if he were saying something intimate and impossible to her, as indeed he was.

They had made a vow once never to talk of anything serious. And here was one vow he knew it was right to break. They had to go on, to go ahead with their relationship; the old one in the past had not been enough. Those things which are to live must continually grow.

She shook her head again. "No," she said slowly. "I'm leaving. As soon as it'll look right. I can't just go, not after I just got here, not after what happened last night, not until Esther's better, and Helen's past the danger point, but I'm going as soon as it's all right.

"I was running away—running away *back* here. I can't explain it myself, Stu, because I don't really—because I can't explain myself. Even to me.

"I want to be serious, to be a serious person—without losing my joy in life. I guess—I think—I've tried to run away from the seriousness be-cause I was afraid of it, because I wanted to keep the joy, and I didn't think I could have both, side by side. Like children dancing in a ceme-tery—it's a private image," she explained quickly. "There's a photograph, of these children *dancing* in a cemetery, dancing in the presence of death. And I think that's why I've remembered the picture all these years, kept it with me, because that's what, fundamentally, I want to be, want to be and understand and accept—dancing in the presence of death.

"And I don't know how," she went on after a pause, "not yet. I thought I could just ignore it, ignore death, by being flip, even talking about my tombstone sometimes, things like that, but that's not joy.

"I'm not even sure I know what joy is, maybe not even death—no, maybe I have an idea about that. But joy—I've got to get away, Stu," she said, "and find out what I really think—deep down—about all these things. Not the words, I think, not those, but the way I really think. My whole creed," she said. She looked at him—with that luminous smile, that smile he loved so much that it made an ache spring up inside. "To leave behind," she said, "the props—the alcohol and the flippancies and the self-deceptions and get to the heart, *the center,* of where I've been and where I'm going, to know something I can hang on to."

"You learn it in war."

"Maybe so, but women—"

"*I* learned it in war," he corrected himself, "from some men who picked me up." He had to stop. He had just seen it himself. "I was hurt—real bad—and these guys, three guys, they just came and picked me up, took me with them, without a word. We had a hell of a night, hiding from the Germans and all, but they didn't leave me, I don't think they ever *considered* running out on me, and when we got back— I don't even know their names," he said.

"But—" And she was genuinely puzzled; he could see in her whole face the effort she was making, the concentration, to understand. "Where is there— I'm sorry, but I just don't see—where is there any *joy* in that?"

"Joy?' Well, maybe that isn't what you'd call it, but I can tell you I was mighty *glad* they didn't leave me."

"It made a difference, it made you understand something?"

"Not until now, but now I think I understand—"

"Maybe that's what I have to go away to find out, what you went away to find out, what you *found* out—but whatever it is, I have to go."

"But if you go away you're going to lose out in the sweepstakes."

"The sweepstakes?"

"For old Esther's dough."

She laughed. "I suppose so."

"You don't give a damn about her money, do you?"

"No," she said, "I don't. It isn't," she explained, "that I wouldn't like the money, or couldn't use it, it's just that—I don't know—I can't really get myself interested enough to make any real effort, to—you know—do anything about it."

"That's a nice way of putting it—*do anything about it.* Don't you mean pander to her? Because that's what they're all doing," he went on savagely, "pandering—sucking after her. Erwin," he said, "especially Erwin."

"Let him have it."

"Yeah," Stu said. "He deserves it." She gave him a funny look. "Birds of a feather," he said.

"He's not that bad."

"Give him a few more years—wait until he's really come into his own. Right now he's just developing his techniques."

"And you—are you—" She didn't finish, but he knew what she meant. Was he going to leave too?

He was staying, he had known it all day and fought to make the knowledge retreat, go away, leave him in peace, and that was why he had come out to this porch, he was always safe, at peace, alone out here, and now even that was shattered. He had come, in this violet twilight and growing dark, to face his own truth. His life was here, in Springfield, in this house he had spent his thirty-four years running away from, with the mother who in his heart lived equally in love and in enmity. He had to make up for the past and eradicate his guilt, and the only way he could do that was by staying.

Here, he thought, with Ethel and the child; here with my brother and his thin, frightened wife; here with Eileen, who kept track of me all the time I was gone, and I didn't even know it; here with my sister, whose face is hard, on guard against us all, against even herself; here with my overworked and overburdened mother, who doesn't know that her children ever loved her and tries to call into question that small corner of love that is still left; here to make up for all I have not done and should have done, to expiate the past, to cleanse myself of my guilt. And, smiling to himself, he said softly, "You knew all along, didn't you—that I'd be staying? And not for the sweepstakes."

She looked at him, her face suddenly happy and radiant.

If Lois were to stay, he thought—but she was going away and he knew it was wrong to try to make her stay. "I wish you—you weren't going," he said, turning sideways and gazing out on the street, the signs, the urns of wandering Jew.

"I'm glad you're not going back to New York. I think it's right—for you."

"But not for you?"

"No, not for me."

"Lois, I—you know I never told you how much I appreciated the way you were so decent to me in New York, how you—"

"It was nothing," she said hastily, interrupting, and he knew she didn't want to talk about it. Okay, he thought, anything you want. You're the one who has all the points. "Look," she said, "there go the lights."

His mother had succumbed to necessity at last; the lights on the signs leaped to illumination; the whole pavement in front of the house was flooded with good strong white light. It looked almost as if there were a light covering of snow. Stu looked down and he asked himself, Who is saved and who succumbs? and he thought, You never know, even at the end. Shackleton was saved, yes, but it's Scott who is famous, who has really lived. In a couple of hundred years no one will remember Shackleton, but some history book or other will still be quoting Scott.

It takes a long time to show how the points really work out.

Just as it had taken a long time to realize the ambivalence of his love for his mother. If it was true that he had swept her up in his arms at the station and felt that he had been reborn, it was equally true that the day before, down in the kitchen, none of that love had been left; he had hated her with all the intensity of the old days. There they were, his two emotions, poles apart, but equal, part of the same thing: he loved and hated her at the same time. That was the truth and probably always would be. But it was also true that in order to hate strongly you had to love fiercely first, and that even in the hatred there was an element of love: it was disappointment and anger and the terrible feeling of being betrayed by your own feelings of love that were part of the whole make-up of hate. Revenge, too, he thought; you want to make someone else suffer for what you have suffered. There is the child, he told himself, I will raise the child in this house in this city; in the summer we will go frogging, and winters I will read, and in the spring we will plant tomatoes together. I will show him about seeds. "Tell me," he said, turning to his cousin, "do you hate them, the way I do sometimes?"

"No," she said slowly, "I don't hate them. I'm sorry for them—" She broke off. "But I can't help still caring. I'm a part of them, and you—and Carolyn. We might," she said, "the three of us, be very close if I were staying." She took a long drag on her cigarette. "But you two can be close," she said. "When I have some money, I'm going away—Europe or something." She laughed. "To give Aunt Fran a little faith, to convince her the cards come out all right. She said I was going to marry royalty, and she's got her heart set on it. Isn't that wonderful?"

While he laughed with her, it seemed to Stu that she really might.

And then she was gone, still laughing. She had ducked quickly and gracefully back through the door, and he could no longer see her in the shadows of the hall. She had brought them both home, and it seemed ironic to him that he should have found something—perhaps the very thing she had come back looking for—and she was going away, as disillusioned as he had been ten, twelve years before when he had walked out the front door without so much as a good-by. Good-by, he thought and looked into the shadows after her, good-by and good luck.

You sentimental bastard, he thought, what the hell do you mean, good-by and good luck, it's like one of those bad films. You still believe in the sirens and fire engines, the penthouses with the fantastic views and the wispy girls looking up adoringly, and then that big spectacular fade-out, is that what you still believe?

Our dreams die hard, he told himself.

RESOLVE, he said clearly inside himself, resolve: that I shall take the family from the cellar of my mind and put it where it belongs, in the attic, with all the other useless, used-up relics from the past—the war, the dead peace, the battlefield of my marriage, my own mutilated ego.

THAT one day I may learn to walk again, but in the meantime at least I have the use of my arms, my arms and my eyes. Let the mouth and mind rest a little.

RESOLVE, he told himself: to try to love them all a little, love them as they are, not as you would wish them to be.

REMEMBER, he told himself, the Loises of the world.

THINK, he told himself, of Lois standing silhouetted in the doorway, smiling.

We came home, the two of us, Lois and I came back to Springfield, and who stays and who doesn't?

Who is saved and who isn't?

You never know, not for a long time, not sometimes, Stu thought, even in your whole life—because wasn't that really the whole object of life, to see how the points worked out, to see who was saved and who wasn't?

Save her, he supplicated the summer night. She's worth saving.

Go for broke, Lois, he said to the summer night.